CHANGES

THE COLLEGIUM CHRONICLES
BOOK THREE

MERCEDES LACKEY

DAW BOOKS, INC.

DONALD A. WOLLHEIM, FOUNDER

375 Hudson Street, New York, NY 10014

ELIZABETH R. WOLLHEIM
SHEILA E. GILBERT
PUBLISHERS

www.dawbooks.com

First Printing, October 2012
1 2 3 4 5 6 7 8 9

DAW TRADEMARK REGISTERED
U.S. PAT. AND TM. OFF. AND FOREIGN COUNTRIES
—MARCA REGISTRADA
HECHO EN U.S.A.

PRINTED IN THE U.S.A.

Dedicated to the memory of
Martin (Marty) Greenberg
and Mark Shepherd.
We'll miss you.

1

Mags shaded his eyes and peered across the uneven ground of the Kirball field at the opposing team huddled up in front of their goal and forced himself to relax. There was no point in getting tense. This was only a game, after all. He had to keep reminding himself of that, even as nervous sweat trickled down the back of his neck, and inside his gloves his palms were moist.

Only a game being played in front of hundreds of people . . .

::*To most of whom you are just a red shape on a white horse. Even with Colin calling the gameplay, they still wouldn't know who you were.*:: The voice in his head was as familiar as his own now, warm and slightly amused.

"Thanks fer makin' a lad feel special, Dallen," he muttered under his breath, knowing the great white horse-shaped smart-aleck beneath him had very keen ears.

::*Don't mention it,*:: came the cheerfully cheeky reply.

Mags was wearing red rather than Herald Trainee Grays because his Kirball team's color was red—although to be strictly accurate, only his padding and helmet were red. But since the Kirball field was deliberately awash with dangerous obstacles, the players wore full-body protection, so very little of his Grays were showing. The same went for the rest of his teammates—unrecognizable in padded helmet in red, metal face-guard in red, neck collar, shoulder pads, upper and lower arm braces, elbow and knee cups, thigh protection, chest and backplate, and armored boots. They looked more prepared for combat than a game.

Not that most people would ever have recognized this as a game field either. Gullies corrugated the field, which also contained a major ravine, little hills with abrupt drop-offs, stone fences as well as rail fences, culverts, bridges, and even a stream that led into the river. There were no big hills, but there were bits of very steep slope, enough to make even the most sure-footed Companion pause. It most closely resembled the obstacle course, or perhaps a steeplechase race-course. But unlike the obstacle course, there was no pattern, no obvious path you were supposed to take around the field. It was, in fact, far more random than nature would have created, a calculated randomness that ensured that there were no "easy" places anywhere except in front of the goals.

At either end were two identical little stone buildings, with ramps up to the tops of them. The ramps had been stone too when the game had first been played; now they were stone and rammed earth, and the squat towers were buried to their ramparts in the rammed earth. After the first four games, the stone ramps had been deemed a bit too narrow and dangerous, and earthen slopes made sure there were no abrupt drop-offs. Flagpoles thrust up from the tops of the towers, flying pennants in the team colors, red for South and green for West, flapping bravely from the tower-tips in a brisk breeze. They needed that breeze today; it was wicked hot. It wasn't only nerves making Mags sweat. The bathing room was going to suffer a stampede.

Beneath him, his Companion, Dallen, was as steady as a statue, which made him feel steadier. It wasn't nerves that bothered him so much as the ever-recurring dread that he would somehow let the team down. He wasn't the only one who felt that way, though, so he was in good company. He knew this because he could sense it. He wasn't just a Mindspeaker who could make himself heard by anyone whether they had the Gift or not; he had just a touch of Empathy too. Enough to be useful most of the time—enough to tell him that his teammates were fighting similar knots in their guts.

The emotional stakes were much, much higher today than they had ever been before. The Kirball game they were playing was part of this concluding day of a week of presentations, tours, and demonstrations put on by all three Collegia for the benefit of the parents and relatives of Trainees and the townsfolk of Haven. Valdemar was bigger than ever, with Trainees coming from farther afield. The Collegia were changing; some people liked the changes, while others were fighting any change at all. The King wanted to show what the results here were, and he didn't want even a hint of elitism or a shadow of secrecy to color peoples' perceptions of the Collegia. He reckoned the best way to nip rumors in the bud would be to throw open the doors for a general look around.

::*Give us a slosh of that water then, would you?*:: Dallen craned his neck around and opened his mouth; Mags obligingly poured most of the water from the half-gallon sized bucket the team runner had just brought them down Dallen's throat. A lot of it sloshed out of Dallen's mouth but enough of it went down to quench his thirst. Mags tossed the empty bucket to the boy, who ran it back to the sidelines to be refilled. Having a team runner was a good idea—especially as the team runners were mostly from the Healers' Collegium. They generally knew when you needed something without needing to be asked, since the ones with Healing Gift also had Empathy.

"Huddle up!" ordered the South team captain, Herald Trainee Gennie. Swathed in her armor and helmet, only her voice betrayed who she was. The whole team converged on her, including the Foot, who moved into the center, standing at the heads of the horses and Companions.

This game wasn't just for Herald Trainees—which was, in part, the point. Each team had been made up of four Herald Trainees, four Riders—who could be anyone with a horse or horses who had tried out for the team and won a place—and four Foot, who could also be anyone, but in practice, tended to be young Guardsmen. In a real fight, Heralds would fight alongside everyone else. In Kirball, Herald Trainees learned how to use their Gifts and skills in partnership with people who had no such advantages.

"We've had the first quarter, and we took it slow, by

agreement between me and the West Captain," Gennie told them. "We wanted the townies and the parents to get a good grounding in Kirball before we went all out. That was why I told you all to play easy and slow. So, now it's time to show the game proper. Gloves are off."

"'Bout time," Pip grumbled. Trainee Pip was certainly the most keen Kirball player on the South team, and may have been in the entire Collegium. He and his Companion were never happier than when they were scrumming.

"Now here's where we need to talk show versus strategy." She grinned at Pip, a flash of teeth showing behind the metal faceguard. "Remember that the point of this whole match is to give the crowd a show. It's a demonstration, and we need to think about how it will all look from out there." She waved her hand at the crowds pressed in along the fences around the Kirball field. A steady murmur of voices came from beyond the bounds. "So don't scrum too long, or they'll get bored. They'll like a bit of football, but they'll like running better."

"West team never lets us scrum much anyway," Halleck pointed out.

"It's those evil little ponies of theirs," said one of the Guard Foot.

Jeffers, son of a wealthy tradesman, gave him a hurt look; he was mounted on his favorite Kirball horse, a scrappy little pony that looked ridiculously small under him.

"Present company excepted, of course," Corwin amended. "Your ponies aren't evil, Jeffers."

"Not evil to you, anyway," Jeffers corrected.

There were three ways to score. The first was to lob a Kirball through the windows or the door of the opposing team's tower. That was one point. The second was to occupy the tower and hold it for a quarter candlemark. That was ten points, and so far no one had ever had the temerity to try it. Sure, you could get in there, but neither horse nor Companion would fit inside, and the enemy Foot were only too eager to mob you and drag you out, ending your occupation. Meanwhile, your own team didn't dare abandon their goal to come to your rescue lest the opposition make goals while they did.

Lobbing balls was a lot faster and easier than an occupation, and your ten points could easily be negated by what they did at your goal while your team held them off while you occupied.

The third was to steal the opponent's flag and get it back to your tower. That was fifty points and pretty much game-ending, because you had to get the flag back to your home base in order to make the score, and it was pretty harrowing to have an entire team bearing down on you while you tried to do that. Foot generally guarded the goal and the flag, although game-winning ploys had, in the games past, been engineered by one of the Foot sneaking close enough to the opposing team's flag to snatch it.

The Foot obviously didn't use mounts, and the Companions were as much a part of the team as the Herald Trainees who rode them, but the Rider units, now—that was where much of the uncertainty in Kirball came from. Mags didn't know horses, didn't understand horses, but obviously they weren't Companions. They could be pressed and harassed in ways the Companions would just shrug off. Many of them didn't like being crowded into the fence around the field, nor the close quarters in a scrum. None of them liked being rammed, although by this point they had become somewhat inured to it.

Not West team's ponies, though. Like North, the West team's Riders were all rich enough to have a mount for each quarter. Unlike North, these were all tough, hardy little mountain ponies, smart and fast, and, if Mags was any judge, as insanely happy to play the game as their owners. They were almost as good as the Companions, in his opinion. Sometimes it seemed to him that all they lacked was Mindspeech. And he wasn't altogether sure some of those ponies didn't have that, as well. The scrum didn't bother them the least bit, they played football with zest, they'd nip in along a fence and scuttle like weasels, and they had no problem with forcing a collision.

What they lacked was sheer size; bigger horses and Companions could ride them down or bowl them over—there were no fouls in Kirball, since it was, at bottom, training for war. The size disadvantage might be the main reason why the other teams hadn't immediately swapped out their mounts for similar ponies.

You couldn't use trained warhorses for this, though; warhorses would be downright dangerous on a Kirball field. They were trained to use hooves and teeth in defense of their riders, and while Kirball was designed to be rough, it wasn't supposed to be lethal.

Mags looked up and down the field, which was entirely surrounded on all four sides by spectators. There were the Trainees from all three Collegia, of course, shoved up tight against the fences in clots of gray, light green, and rusty red. In among them were the Whites of full Heralds—mostly the teachers here, since summer meant that the Heralds were out in the field in force—the sober forest-green of Healers, the scarlet of Bards, and the dark blue of the Guard. But far outnumbering those colors were the colors that were not uniforms. There were parents and siblings of those Trainees of all sorts who could make the journey here, Guards out of uniform, and up on some elevated viewing stands, nobles of all ranks and ages in all their finery as well as those who were not nobles but merely wealthy. Scuttling about and hoping not to be noticed were the pages and squires attached to the Court, who probably should have been at some duty or other, and carefully avoiding anyone's eyes were servants in palace livery other than that of the Guards who were doing the same. Then there were the townsfolk, invited up for this day so that they could see for themselves what the Trainees of the Collegia were about—all craning their necks from behind the rows of Trainees and teachers and nobles and family.

Behind them were the Companions, of every size and shape and age; bonded or not, they were here to see the game.

And mounted up and trotting or striding in and out of the crowd were the players of the other two teams, telling all and sundry how the game was played—and how it should be played.

Glancing at them, Mags felt the nervous sweat start up all over again.

The South Grays were himself, Pip, Gennie the captain, and Halleck. The South Riders were a mix of young nobles and townsfolk who were also taking classes at the Collegia. Jeffers and Meled were two of the latter, Reese and young Lord Wess the former. Their four Foot were all young Guardsmen, though when the teams had been started, two of them had been thought too young to join the Guard proper. Corwin, Danvers, Holly, and Beales. All four were young for the Guard, young enough to be kept here at Haven for a year or two to get in some serious training while living at home before being sent out to a Guard garrison somewhere else. Sixteen was generally the youngest that the Guard would take, and the youngster had to be a very mature sixteen at that. Eighteen was preferred. They were all only sixteen, and the Captain of the Guard here very much approved of Kirball as fine training for them.

They had relief players now, too: two Foot and one Rider. The Herald Trainees, however, had now concluded that while it might be a fine thing to be a Kirball hero, it was also a lot of work, and you had better be at the top of the athletes to play. So the sixteen Grays who were on the four Kirball teams had no relief players.

On the other hand, Kirball had aroused enough interest among the nobles that now all the Riders had four mounts, one for each quarter, presented to them by noble patrons. Jeffers' father had presented him with carte blanche to pick a fourth mount for his birthday. Somewhat to his shock, Jeffers had passed by all the big, handsome high-breds that had been offered him and had chosen a second little cob as like to his scrappy favorite as a twin. The others hadn't had a choice; three nobles had presented them with mounts they deemed suitable. Still, none of those (literally) gift horses had been utterly wrong for the game, and if they were not outstanding, they were certainly good enough for an "easy" quarter.

The first quarter had started off quickly, no matter what Gennie said. There had been nothing "slow" about it. West had nipped in as soon as the game was on; one of their Riders had snatched the ball and made a dash for the goal and got it in. The rest of the quarter had been running up and down the field, over the obstacles, with no one getting a clear advantage until right at the end, when Gennie and Pip had taken clear control of the ball and had traded it back and forth until Halleck got into good position, and he had bunged it in to tie the score.

"Strategy, strategy," said Gennie. "We can't tire out those ponies, but we can make them, their Riders, and maybe even their Trainees lose their tempers and get grumpy. And we can wear out their Foot. So let's leave off trying to goal for this quarter and do that. Pip and I will harass the Foot, make them guard their flag; Mags and Halleck, you and the Riders play some hard football with their Companions and Riders. Don't be afraid to get bruised, but don't knock anyone over, either. Not yet, anyway."

Pip raised an eyebrow. "Isn't that going bit hard for an exhibition? We might upset some parents."

Halleck snorted. "Not as long as there're no broken bones or broken necks. People like to see some danger as long as everyone walks away from it."

Corwin nodded. "Maybe you didn't hear it over the noise, but me old man was shouting at me from sidelines, telling me to break some heads. He don't mean it literally, but he'd have been the first one on his feet shouting hurrah if I'd pulled someone down."

"No broken heads, but no easy quarter of it either," Gennie told them. "If we're given the gift of a goal opportunity, take it, but otherwise, we concentrate on giving them a hard time, and not letting them score on us."

Pip laughed. "Now, wouldn't it be the height of irony if West's captain is telling his team the exact same thing right now?"

The Companions all snorted. Gennie grinned. "That's why we're against West for this exhibition, instead of North or East. Harkon couldn't be more unlike me and still be in Grays. Dean wants a good exhibition game, not a mirror-move chess match."

It was their ball, and Mags had it, and when the whistle blew, signaling the start, he feinted to Pip, then dropped it straight down among the legs of the Riders. He and Dallen stayed to contest it, while Pip and Gennie headed straight for the West goal, momentarily confusing the entire West side, half of whom thought Pip had the ball, and half, seeing Mags drop it, knew it was down among the feet of their mounts.

It took West a moment to sort themselves out, then they were all back into the scrum, leaving their Foot to be harassed by Pip and Gennie.

Now, one of the West's Grays had Fetching Gift. They knew that, of course, and West knew that they knew, and in all the games that had been played before, he had never actually *used* it.

Until now.

They had always assumed that anyone using Fetching Gift would be standing off to one side and concentrating hard to manipulate the ball into the goal, or (more likely) grab the flag from afar, since it was a tricky Gift and required absolute concentration.

So they had assumed. They hadn't counted on the wielder using it for something very small. "Kicking" the ball into the open, for instance; that didn't require any more concentration than hitting it with one of the Kirball sticks. But that was exactly what he did, and the moment he did, one of the other West Grays pounced on it like a cat on a catnip toy.

This was *not* how they had planned things! ::*They have the ball!*:: He "shouted" into the minds of his teammates, together with the projected image of the Gray with the ball, who was even now pelting toward the South goal. Mags and Dallen skittered across the ground to intercept him, the rest a few paces behind.

::*How?*:: Gennie blurted incredulously, then got the image from Dallen exactly as it had happened. Her reply was rude and laden with exasperation at herself for not foreseeing this very thing.

But their Foot were on it, as fiercely determined to prevent a goal as Mags had ever seen them. No matter where the ball went, they were there first, and instead of hitting it back hard, they hit it into the most awkward places they could. The third time they blocked it, one of them managed to shoot it into a tangle of bushes, and at that point it became a scrum again.

It stayed a scrum, right in front of the South goal, until the whistle blew and everyone had to back off, because it was time to start the third quarter and get a change of horses.

"Where did *that* play come from?" Corwin asked, wiping his head and neck down with a towel and accepting water from a runner.

"Fetching Gift," Gennie said, her voice thick with disgust. "Oh, too bloody smart altogether, he's using it to bunt the ball, just a little. He doesn't have to stand off and concentrate on it to do that, he just needs to see it." She took off her helmet, dumped a pail of water over her head, and jammed her helmet back on. "They've been keeping that little play a secret, that's for sure."

"Then we'd better not put the thing in the air," Corwin warned. "He'll bunt it there too."

"Well . . . then we have to keep him from seeing the ball," Jeffers said slowly. "Which means one of us has to mind him."

"That'll be me," Wess volunteered immediately. "This rack of bones is no good in the scrum, and he's tall enough I'm practically sitting on a cliff. I'll mind him for the entire quarter."

Now it was scarcely fair for Wess to call his horse a "rack of bones," but it was one of those "gift horses"— very well bred, rather too well bred for Kirball, and very tall. The gelding was like lightning on straight, even ground, but he couldn't turn the way Jeffers' ponies could, and he got very nervous when his footing was uneven. Oddly enough, he'd take getting rammed and was astonishingly even-tempered about herding or being herded. In fact, his temper was the best thing about him.

"All right; that will leave us a Rider short, so we'll just have to make up for it. By the way, Foot, *damn* fine job on that save." This, in Mags' opinion, was one reason why Gennie was such a terrific captain. "Now remember that if the ball gets in clear sight, it just might start to act unnaturally, so be alert. Expect it to change direction at any point. So, heads up, stay sharp, we'll have to play this quarter by best guess, and go all out in the last. Hup!"

The third quarter was a frantic mess. Wess did manage to keep the Fetching Gray occupied during most of it, but the time or two he broke free and got an eye on the ball, it clearly had a mind behind it. There was no telling where it would go for certain, and all they could do was follow it. And one of those times, the other team scored a goal.

The timing could not have been worse for South; they'd made a series of spectacular saves, but the ball was still in front of their goal. One of West's players managed to scoop the ball into the air, but instead of hitting it toward the goal, he smacked it in the opposite direction. Mags thought he was mad, until he realized that the Fetching Trainee had gotten free of Wess—

He realized that too late. The ball suddenly acted as if someone else had hit it with a paddle in midair— sending it straight for the goal. The Trainees and Riders, who had been in hot pursuit, couldn't reverse fast enough, and just when it looked as if Holly was going to make the save, the ball did a bizarre drop, bounced once, then an invisible hand smacked it into the goal.

The crowd went insane. Mags swore, and he was pretty sure that the rest of his team was turning the air blue with curses as well. Dallen danced under him with frustration.

They were so determined now that it was mere moments from the point where the ball came into play again that they had it in front of West's goal. But try as they might, they could not manage to shake it out of the scrum, and the quarter ended with West still ahead by one.

"This is the point where I should be a good sport and remind you all that this is only a game," Gennie said crossly, as they huddled. "As your captain, I am supposed to keep the greater good in mind."

"Right. Ye've reminded us," Mags managed from between clenched teeth. Now 'ow d'ye really feel?"

"Ballocks to that cant," said Gennie fiercely, her eyes gleaming behind the face-guard. "I know they weren't cheating, but did they *have* to pick the day we're playing in front of half of Haven to pull that trick out?"

"I've got a trick of m'own," Corwin said grimly. "Are there any rules 'bout gettin' help from the side, so long's it's not touchin' the ball?"

There had been some extremely stringent regulations laid down regarding extra players on the field or a spectator using any Gift to interfere with players, ball, or flag. Gennie and the others looked at each other. "Noooo—" Gennie said, slowly. "You know all the rules as well as the rest of us, Corwin, so I assume whatever you have in mind doesn't break anything existing. What are you going to do?"

"Keep 'em busy, but keep half an eye on their goal," Corwin said. "When you see me pop up in front of it, get the ball t'me, anyhow."

Now they all looked at Gennie, who shrugged. "We've got nothing to lose and we *have* to make two goals to win," she pointed out. "Try it, Corwin. Hup!"

So it was football again, with Jeffers *and* Halleck keeping the Fetching Trainee so busy he was never able to put an eye on the ball for as much as a heartbeat. Mags couldn't figure out what Corwin was up to; he seemed to be holding his place in front of their goal, steady as a rock—

When suddenly, he blinked out, just vanished, and when Mags threw a startled glance at the West's goal— there he was!

::Corwin!:: he shouted into everyone's heads, and fast as a snake, Pip had the ball up out of the scrum and in the air, and Gennie hit it as hard as she could in a fast drive to Corwin, while Jeffers and Halleck boxed in the Fetching Trainee and shoved him down a slope.

Corwin leaped into the air and snatched the ball out of it, then tucked it under his arm, put his head down, and charged like a bull for the goal. There were no rules about that, either, although no one in all of the games that had been played so far had ever tried to run the ball to the goal physically. No one could believe that Corwin was doing it. The West's Foot, stunned for an instant, charged for him. They all met in a cloud of dust and a tangle of limbs right at the door of the goal.

The entire South team ran for the West goal. By the time they got there, the pile had sorted itself out, and the referee had gotten there. He really didn't need to make a ruling, though; the ball was clearly just over the threshold. Corwin had made the goal!

But Corwin was still on the ground, groaning and

holding his arm against his body. And three Healers had peeled out of the crowd at a run, with four Healer Trainees and a stretcher behind them.

"Goal for South!" Colin shouted over the field-trumpet. "Foot Corwin down! Substitute for South!"

Corwin's sub, a Blue by the name of Jamson, ran out to join the South Foot. As everyone watched nervously, the Healers huddled over Corwin, who couldn't be seen for all the green-clad bodies. Mags watched, his heart in his throat. How badly was Corwin hurt? Had he cracked his skull? There was an awful lot of stone around those goals.

Finally one of the Healers popped his head up. "Just a broken arm!" he called. The crowd exploded with cheers. They cheered again when two of the Healer Trainees hoisted up the stretcher with Corwin on it and he waved feebly with his good arm. Gennie rode up to him as he was carried off the field, talked with him for a moment or two, then signaled to the referee for a time out as she rode back to join the rest.

As Corwin's porters made their way through a sea of well-wishers, the team gathered around Gennie.

"How in the name of Kernos did he *do* that?" Jeffers demanded.

"Herald Tamlin." Gennie grinned. And as about half of the team, including Mags, looked puzzled, she added, "His Gift is to make you see things that aren't there."

"Wait—what?" Jeffers said, then his eyes widened. "So the Corwin at our goal wasn't really there?"

Gennie nodded. "He's an old friend of Corwin's family. They probably worked this out between them last night." She shrugged. "He was right. There's no rule against it. It wasn't as if he were cloaking Corwin sneaking up on the goal; Corwin's just that good at sneaking. And I can't believe he charged in there like that."

"Me either," Pip said with admiration. He looked down at the substitute. "Think you can play up to that standard, laddy?"

Jamson gulped, but he straightened his back. "I'll give it all I've got, Trainee."

Gennie nodded with approval. "Well said. All right. There's not much time left in the quarter, so do whatever it is you need to do to win this game. Just don't break any skulls. However the game ends, it won't be said that we didn't give them a fight."

If West expected them to be shaken by Corwin's loss, they were quickly disabused of the notion. Play started with a full-on charge headed by South's riders, who were all over the Fetching Trainee. Pip got the ball, and he and Gennie dribbled it up and down the sides of the field, which effectively prevented about half of the West Riders and Companions from closing in on them. Mags and Dallen concentrated on harassing the edges of the action, giving special attention to West's Riders, acting as if they were about to ram, then just brushing by. That rattled the Riders, who kept bracing for collisions that never happened, getting their ponies irritated and in a lather.

And then—

In desperation, the Fetching Trainee broke free. The ball popped straight up into the air.

But Pip was already on it, standing up in his stirrups

as his Companion managed to simultaneously scramble toward the midair ball and keep Pip steady. Pip hit it with a mighty backhanded swing, while the Riders mobbed the Fetcher.

The ball arrowed toward Mags.

Mags saw two things simultaneously, as time seemed to slow to a crawl. He *could* make the same swing and had even odds of getting it to the goal.

But Halleck was in the clear, with a better shot. The odds were in favor of Halleck.

::*Halleck!*:: he shouted, ::*Ball!*:: And he stood in his stirrups and gave the ball a second *whack*, sending it screaming toward Halleck as three of the four West Trainees barreled toward him, grimly, intent on stopping him. They were too late, but they had too much momentum pull up or change direction.

He and Dallen were hit by three Companions with only a moment to prepare. Instead of bracing, Dallen was scrambling backward when they were hit, with Mags clinging to his back like a burr.

Dallen scrabbled and nearly went over sideways; he saved them both with a catlike twist of his body, scrabbled a bit more as dust rose about them in a cloud, and fetched up against one of the drop-offs, which was all that saved them from going over. Meanwhile, the roar of the crowd signaled that Halleck had made the goal and the shrill whistles of the referees signaled the end of the game.

::*Ow,*:: Dallen said, sitting down abruptly. Mags leaped from the saddle. ::*I think I pulled my offside hock.*::

The Companion stood up, gingerly, put a little weight on the hoof, and winced. ::*Definitely. Ow.*::

But a Healer Trainee was already jumping down off the top of the drop-off. He must have jumped onto the field as soon as Dallen felt the first twinge of pain. "Easy on there, old man," the fellow said cheerfully. "Give me a moment."

The Healer wrapped both his hands around the injured leg as Mags fidgeted anxiously. Dallen's sigh of relief was echoed by his Chosen.

"Put a little weight on it, old man." the youngster told him. "See if it will bear being walked on."

Dallen did as he was told. *::Tell him it hurts, but I'll be able to get up to Companions' Stable under my own power. And thank him.::*

Mags did so, adding his own thanks. The Healer waved it off.

"Just stay off it as much as you can for the next two days. I'll come by for another treatment or two barring any emergencies coming up."

Mags never got a chance to thank him a second time; he vanished into the mob that poured over the field to hoist Halleck onto their shoulders.

"I saw what you did, " Gennie told him with a grin, walking up to him with her own Companion trudging beside her. "You could have taken the shot and been the hero of the game, but you didn't."

He shrugged. "Got 'nough just bein' in the game."

Dallen snorted impolitely. *::I'll just get up to the stable then,::* he said with great irony, and turned slightly to limp his way past them.

Mags laughed. "Ye think we'll get i' trouble fer Corwin's lark?"

Gennie shook her head, the action mimicked by her

Companion. "There were no rules against putting an illusion of a player on the field, only against sending in an extra. Remember, these are war games. We'll get faintly praised for thinking of something new, faintly damned for scraping so close to cheating, and they'll make a rule against getting help from off the field that isn't a Healer or a runner. Now we had better go see to our Companions and get cleaned up and changed and out there—" she waved her hand vaguely at the rest of the Collegia. "We need to go be Halleck and Corwin's ever-so-modest teammates."

Mags nearly choked on his laughter, coughing so that Gennie had to pound on his back, and when he had recovered, they followed in Dallen's limping wake.

Mags was scarcely likely to let Dallen limp his way up to the Companion's Stable alone, nor leave him in the hands of the hostlers, no matter how competent they were. He saw to Dallen's comfort himself, of course, making sure he got a good rubdown before he went off himself to a cold-water wash under the pump—anything but a hardship in this blistering heat—and a change into clean Trainee Grays. He stripped as close to bare as he could get and did the job thoroughly. Every bit of him was itchy with drying sweat.

The grounds of the Palace had been cordoned off quite properly, and only those who actually lived within the Palace walls were being allowed to get past the watchful eyes of Guardsmen who knew them all by name. But the rest of the grounds had the atmosphere of a fair. This was aided and abetted by the food and drink tents and the various demonstrations by Trainees of all three Collegia. There was a big official Bardic concert scheduled for the last event of the day, but there were Bardic Trainees scattered all across the grounds, alone or in groups, happily showing off their prowess. The game had been the big event for the Herald Trainees, but quite a few of them were ambling about the lawns with their Companions, making themselves available for questions. And as for the Healers— Healers' Collegium had an open clinic, where anyone could come for treatment; simple cases were treated by the Trainees, more complicated ones by the Healer teachers. And many of the Healer Trainees had little booths set up to teach people about the signs of various illnesses in humans or animals and how to prevent as much disease as possible.

Mags' best friend Bear had one of these booths, demonstrating the use of his standard herb kit. It had been *very* popular all this week; it made sense to people that there were things they could do for themselves, and some parents and relatives of Trainees had come from places where there simply wasn't a Healer nearby. These were the very people who needed Bear's instruction the most.

He had spent all week demonstrating things it didn't take a Gift to do—how to set a bone, treat cuts and other injuries, how to handle common, non-life-threatening ailments, and, most importantly, when to recognize early enough to *do* something about it that what you were facing needed an expert.

One of the full Healers was with him, of course, but in the background. Most people probably wouldn't notice he was there, and if they did, they would probably just be relieved that Bear obviously had Collegium approval. The packs had proven themselves over the winter in Guard stations and in the hands of Heralds on circuit. Now it was time to distribute them more widely, so that every farrier and midwife and priest who cared to could make use of them.

Not that he had the approval of every Healer out there . . . there were those who thought the packs— and this instruction, had they known about it—were an unmitigated disaster in the making. These highly conservative Healers were not unlike the highly conservative Heralds who did not approve of going from the old system of Trainee-plus-Mentor to a Collegium education over a five year period, with a just a year with a Mentor *after* being put into Whites. Never mind that there were not nearly enough Healers to fill the need. And never mind that Healers mostly stayed at their House, requiring the patients to come to them, rather that riding circuit as Heralds did.

Which's pretty hard on th' feller what's far off, Mags reflected. *Ain't like he kin wait, like a judgment can.* Things had to be rather dire before a Healer would leave a House of Healing or his own home village to attend a remotely situated patient—this was on the logical grounds that if he went riding about, no one would know where to find him in an emergency. The unspoken rule was that the patient came to the Healer, not the other way around.

As with so many things in Valdemar, that had been all right before Valdemar got so big that the Healers were stretched as thin or thinner than the Heralds were. And now, well, it did make sense to keep a scarce resource in one place at all times. It made *sense*, but in Mags' view, and Bear's, and evidently that of the Collegium itself, if you were going to put people without a local Healer in the position of "stay put and die, or be moved and suffer," you had better be prepared to offer them an alternative for things that they could handle themselves so long as you showed them how.

Unfortunately, some of those highly conservative Healers were Bear's own family.

He'd fought them once over the packs—they had been using the "scandalous and foolish" invention as the reason to haul him home so he could marry some neighbor girl. Unlike the rest of the male members of his family, Bear did not have a Healing Gift. He was a pure genius with herbs and had the skill of a prize-winning seamstress with knife and needle, but that seemed to matter not at all to Bear's family. Mags suspected that the only reason they had allowed him to attend the Collegium in the first place was with the vague notion that the Collegium might trigger something dormant in him to make him like the rest of them.

Like a Gift's contagious or somethin'. Or like soot, an' it c'n rub off on ye.

When it didn't—and when the Collegium began to foster (with considerable delight) Bear's very real abilities with herbs, surgery, and bonesetting, *their* solution to the "problem" was to bring him back to breed to a willing girl, in the hopes that one of his children would have the Gift that he did not.

Which's stupid an' mean-spirited an' treats him an' thet poor gel like a couple'a prize cows.

Mags approached Bear's booth quietly; it was, on this last day of the "festival" even more popular if that were possible. Like the other booths, it was a half-tent, providing welcome shade for those who came to be instructed and issued a voucher for the kits that would be going out soon with the Guard supplies. Today people were not only listening attentively, they were asking questions. From where he stood, Mags couldn't hear most of them, but the Healer kept nodding slightly with approval and had a slight smile of satisfaction on his face.

No, it was far more than just satisfaction. This was the look of someone who was not just satisfied, but proud of his pupil.

Mags stiffened, suddenly, as he sensed someone who was *not*. Who was, in fact, in a towering rage. He turned slightly, to see a man in Healer's Greens to his right and behind him, whose face was utterly rigid, and every muscle tight. He did not have to lower shields to know why; although he had never actually met one of Bear's family, there was no mistaking the features. The shape of the bones beneath the skin was the same, especially about the cheekbones and chin. The hair was the same chestnut brown, and the man had the same sturdy build, with added muscles that Bear would no doubt acquire with age and work.

Mags did not hesitate. This man was so angry with his young relative that he wasn't even thinking of the damage giving free rein to his temper could cause. The confrontation he was about to start was going to turn into an Incident, one that would cause a great deal of harm, not only to Bear, not only to the Healers, but to all three Collegia.

He half-closed his eyes and concentrated on the Healer overseeing Bear. He didn't know the man, but after all, his Gift was to Mindspeak into *anyone's* head, whether or not they had the Gift themselves. Meanwhile, Dallen would be doing something on his own— possibly alerting the King's Own's Companion, Rolan. He didn't even have to tell Dallen what was going on; they lived in each other's heads so much that unless either of them blocked out the other, what one knew, the other did. Maybe not everyone would care for that sort of closeness and lack of privacy, but Mags liked it, and it certain made things easier at times like this.

::*Sir!*:: he said urgently, and saw the Healer start. ::*'Tis Trainee Mags. One'f Bear's family's here, an' he's about t'make a mighty to-do!*::

The Healer looked about and quickly spotted both Mags and Bear's relative. Mags kept his mind open, and "heard" the man's halting reply.

::*Can . . . you . . . summon . . . discreet . . . help?*::

::*Yessir,*:: he replied immediately. ::*Already on th' way.*::

::*Done, Chosen,*:: he heard Dallen say as soon as he had replied. ::*But it will take them a few moments. If Bear's brother makes a move toward the tent before the 'reception party' gets there—*::

So—it was Bear's older brother. Not good. ::*Got it,*:: Mags said, just as he saw the man's face harden with decision, and the little movement that suggested he was about to stride toward the booth.

He ran up to the man before he had a chance to take that first step and stood directly in his path. "'Scuze me, Healer!" he said, with a combination of deference and authority. "I don' b'lieve ye've got yer badge on."

The man stared at him, taken completely by surprise. "Badge? What—who *are* you?"

"Ye gotta hev a badge, sir," Mags said insistently, without identifying himself, just in case Bear had ever talked about him at home as being a friend. Besides, he was in Grays. That should be identification enough to give him the authority to accost anyone he needed to. "Ye gotta hev a badge. Badge sez who ye are, an' if'n yer fambly, if'n yer teacher. They be clearin' townies out soon. On'y famblies an' teachers kin be 'ere then. Ye gotta hev a badge, sir!"

The man's face darkened. "I don't need some stinking—" he began, and at that point, the "help" arrived.

He found himself engulfed by a crowd of Healers and Guards, four of each. The Healers greeted him heartily, the Guards interposed themselves in such a way that there was no way he could get past them to Bear without forcing his way through, something they were not prepared to allow. His face reddened, but the Healers were all talking loudly, one of them, the largest, flinging an arm around his shoulders. Before he quite realized what they were doing, they had hustled him off toward Healers' Collegium, quite the opposite direction from Bear's booth.

Mags sensed that the confrontation had not been prevented, however. Merely postponed.

He winced inwardly. This was going to be a bad day for poor Bear. No matter what the outcome, Bear always emerged from a clash with his family feeling miserable.

Most likely 'cause he kin never win.

Well, at least he would have had his week of approval before getting hit with the hammer of Family Scorn.

Mags could never figure this sort of thing out. Why couldn't they see? It made no sense to him. And even if they couldn't see, why didn't they just leave him alone? Bear had the approval of the Collegium. Why wasn't that enough for them?

::Possibly because they feel that they know best, and cannot imagine that 'There is no one, true way' actually applies to them,:: Dallen said. ::Remember, Bear is the first of his family to be trained here at the Collegium rather than at home by the elders of his extended clan. They might give lip-service to the Collegia and Healers' Circle, but in their hearts I imagine they think that they have the only answers worth knowing.::

::I'm beginin' t'think ain't so bad bein' a orphant,:: he replied wryly.

::And on that note, you had better go console Lena. She's feeling downcast.::

Mags shook his head, and went looking for his other best friend. He found her, as he had half expected, sitting on the grass of one of the lesser gardens beside the bush that hid the grave of her pet rabbit. She had a lute with her and was playing it softly—too softly to attract any listeners, who had dozens of Bardic Trainees standing or sitting all over the grounds, all vying for their attention. The dead rabbit was what had brought them together in the first place; she had brought her pet with her to keep her company, but it had been elderly and had died during her first winter here. Mags, who himself had not been at the Collegium for more than a few days, had found her sobbing out here alone with the poor thing in her lap, trying to scratch out a grave for it in the hard, frozen ground.

"Heyla," he said, plopping down on the grass. "Why th' long face?"

Lena sighed and brushed her dark hair out of her brown eyes. "Melting" brown eyes, Bear called them, with a sigh of admiration. Bear had taken to talking a lot about Lena when he and Mags were together and she wasn't with them. He said a lot of nonsensical things about her looks, always with sighs or a foolish grin.

Most of it didn't seem to make much sense. Fine, call her eyes "pretty," or "soulful," or "entrancing"— those all made sense. But "melting?" Mags didn't see how you could call her eyes "melting"; if her eyes were doing that, it would be hideously painful for her, and rather nasty to watch.

He grabbed his concentration back from where it was wandering among words in time to catch what was making Lena so sad. Funny thing about heat, it made your mind want to ramble off somewhere.

"It's the concert," she said mournfully.

"Aye?" That had him confused. "They gi' ye a solo ye don' like?" "They" being "he," actually; Lena's father, Bard Marchand, had been put in charge of the concert. Possibly because if he was put in charge, everyone knew that he wouldn't load the thing up with his own solos as some other Bard might be tempted to do. That was not because Bard Marchand was modest, nor because he was fair, nor even because he was generous. It was because there would be no one of importance at this concert—only the common folk of Haven and the parents and other relatives of the Collegium Trainees. The highborn, who had the Trainees of the

Collegia about them all the time, really had not given a
fig for the activities of this week with the exception of
the Kirball game. They could hear the Trainees any
time they liked, and many of the teachers made extra
money by playing at their parties. So for the notables
and wealthy of Haven, only the Kirball game had provided a variation in their usual schedules, and they
would much rather enjoy music in the cool and luxury
of their own dwellings than out in the sultry night in
the park.

And Marchand would really rather be there too. If
the audience didn't contain anyone important, Bard
Marchand was not particularly interested in putting in
more than a token appearance.

He'd have to do something, of course. He was the
famous Bard Marchand. There was no way he'd get
out of *some* sort of performance. But it would be short,
and there would be no encores.

"They haven't given me any solo at all," Lena said
tearfully. "I just found out today. All I have is my part
in the chorus."

The schedule still hadn't been set this morning.
There were a lot of Bardic Trainees, all of them wanted
solos, and it had been decreed that the only fair thing
to do was wait until the last minute to decide who
would be performing what to allow for people suddenly improving. Mags blinked. "What? Why?"

"They said it's because I froze at the Contest," she
said in despair. "And they said it's because I chose
such a simple song for the Contest. They said I'm not
ready for such a big audience."

Now, Mags knew very well that the only Trainees at

Lena's level who were *not* getting a solo were the ones who were performing in some sort of small ensemble or who had specifically asked to be let off. He tried to put a good face on it, although inwardly he was angry. If Lena had known she wasn't going to be given a solo, she could at least have gotten into one of the smaller groups. She was well liked among the Bardic Trainees, and when she sang in a group she never tried to overwhelm anyone else. People appreciated that. But he throttled down his temper and tried to put a good face on things. "Well, ye *are* summut shy," he told her. "Could be they thought they was doin' ye a favor, could be they reckoned ye'd be able t' enjoy the festival w'out getting' yerself all over pothered worritin' over yer piece."

She shook her head and wiped her eyes. "I'm probably just not good enough," she said shakily. "Not like Farris."

He drew a complete blank at the name. "Farris? Who be Farris?"

She left off pretending to play, and fished out a handkerchief. "Farris Grevner. He's new. He's Father's protégé. They gave him *three* solos."

Mags felt his temper flaring and threatening to escape the leash he had put on it. If Mags had had Bard Marchand in front of him at that moment, he'd have flown at him and broken his nose for him. It was bad enough that half the time Lena's father seemed to have forgotten that she even existed, and the other half used her to get to people he deemed important—like Mags himself, back when he'd saved Bear from that assassin and when he'd been the first "star" of a Kirball team.

But to take on a protégé? When his own daughter was right here and would have cut off her own hand to get some approval from him?

Then to give the boy *three* solos in the concert and Lena none?

It was beyond belief.

"Father can't show me any favoritism," she said, her voice sounding wretched. "I understand that. Everyone knows I'm his daughter, and he can't treat me differently than anyone else. It's not right—"

" 'S also not right t'give his Trainee *three solos*," Mags replied, voice thick with indignation. "Tha's th' same sorta favoritism!"

"Oh, it doesn't matter!" she exclaimed tearfully. "One, three, the only thing that matters to me is that I didn't get *any!*"

Mags patted her hand helplessly. There wasn't much he could say or do at this point. It was too late to ask to be included in a small group; even her best friends wouldn't do that without at least a little time to rehearse. All he could do was to let her cry on his shoulder and remind her that even if it had been meant as a slight, she was still going to get to enjoy the last day of the festival without getting all of a knot over her piece.

And to rein in his own temper, tight. He had to think of something to distract her. He wouldn't leave her to sink in misery.

Another of those welcome breezes sprang up, cooling his head and helping him to cool his temper.

"Jest go give yerself a wash," he suggested. Then, as he wished that Bear was here, something else occurred to him. One sure way to distract her would be to give her something else to think about. "One'a Bear's relations turned up. Dallen says 'tis his older brother. He got ambushed by some'a th' other Healers 'fore he could make a pother, but you gotta know he's gonna chew on Bear afore he goes home."

"That's true," Lena replied, looking faintly alarmed and drying her tears on her sleeve.

"Well, reckon Bear's gonna need some coolin' an' a friendly face, an' I misdoubt th' one 'e'll wanta see is mine." He put a little force into his words, and she nodded. He was thinking furiously now, trying to figure out if Marchand had done this to his daughter out of anything other than sheer lack of caring about what she thought or what happened to her. And what if it wasn't Marchand at all? What if this new pet of his was behind it all?

"An' look ye, if some'un *did* mean ye t'get hurt by this, well, if they see ye cryin', ye jest gi' 'em what they want. Eh? So don't." He made her look at him. "Mebbe 'tis Farris. Mebbe 'e wants ye t'feel like 'e's better nor ye. Mebbe 'e wants t'lord it over ye. Eh? Mebbe 'e's the mean-natured kind. We already *know* ye got all three Bardic Gifts. Mebbe 'e on'y got two. Or mebbe 'e ain't mean-natured, but 'e's feelin' pressed, 'cause *yer* th' one with the Marchand name *and* ye got all three Gifts an' ev'one knows it. So 'e pressed fer all th' attention. So. No matter what, 'e don't deserve no reward of makin' ye feel shamed an' bad."

She blinked, and looked at him in a way that suggested she was shocked. Certainly that had never occurred to her.

*Well, a'course it didn't. She never had t'fight fer nothin'
till she got here.* While this sort of thing was very different from the daily, frantic scrabble for food and shelter
and even the tiniest bit of comfort that Mags had en-
dured for most of his childhood as a mine-slave, the
motives were much the same, and he recognized them
for what they were.

"Now, best fer ye t'do is sit down an' have yerself a
hard think," he told her firmly. "Lookit how good this
is fer ye. Ye got *no* pressure. Ye want t' play fer folks,
well, ye kin sit down jest 'bout anywhere an' do it, like
ye bin. An' enjoy it wi'out havin' t' match up wi'
any'un else. So there. Git a wash. Make yersel' pretty.
Go take a nice corner an' git a liddle audience. Make
'em happy. *Be* happy. Then come git dinner wi' me an'
the rest and hev all yer favorites 'cause yer stomach
ain't in a knot, thinkin' 'bout the concert." He smiled
wickedly. "An' then—once yer fulla strawberry tart an'
cream, bacon-an'-egg pie, cake—*then* ye go by Farris.
Betcha 'e'll be green as grass, thinkin' 'bout that concert an' three solos, an' 'e won't hev been able t'eat. An'
ye smile at 'im, and wish 'im luck and mean it."

She blinked at him. "But—why would I do that?"

"Why? Ye mean it, 'cause ye're a good person. An'
'cause if this ain't his doin', an' 'e's scared 'alf t'death
over it, 'tis th' right thing t'do." He nodded as her eyes
widened. "Aye, think on that. An' if it *is* 'is doin', an'
'e's full of spite an' meanness, well, it'll put 'im in *knots.*
'E won't be thinkin' yer a nice person. 'E'll be thinkin'
whut 'e'd be doin' in yer shoes. 'E'll be mortal certain
ye got somethin' goin', some way t'mess 'im up when
'e gets up there. 'E'll be sweatin' then, lookin' ev' which

way fer trouble that ain't gonna come. An' the more it don't come, the more 'e'll look fer it. 'E's th' new lad 'round 'ere, an' 'e knows ye'll hev got allies—if 'e's mean, 'e won't hev no friends, but 'e'll allus be getting' allies, t' pertect 'imself. Flunkies. Suck-ups. 'E'll be lookin' fer yers. An' in a way it's kinda worse fer 'im 'cause ye're a pretty girl, an' ye kin use thet t'get boys t'do thin's fer ye."

"But I—" She looked shocked.

He interrupted her. "I know ye wouldn', but if 'e's mean, 'e won't e'en be able t' think like ye, an' it'd be the first thin' 'e'd think of. So . . . ye go be sweet an' nice t'im, an no matter which way, ye win. If'n 'e's nice, ye git a new friend, an' 'e'll be grateful, an' ye'll feel good 'cause ye was nice. If'n 'e's mean, ye'll make 'im miserable, an' ye kin still feel good, 'cause ye was nice an' showed ye was better nor 'im. An' look ye—ye gotta keep bein' nice. Cause if 'e's mean, ye cain't let 'im win by makin' ye miserable nor as mean as 'im. See?"

She nodded slowly. "I do see. You're right, Mags." She laughed a little. "And that is why you are a Herald Trainee, and I'm not."

He snorted, but secretly he felt a little pleased. It felt as if this was the first time he had actually put it all together—what he was supposed to do and how he was supposed to do it. The being a Herald, that is.

And for the first time, he didn't need Dallen to tell him he was right, because it all felt right.

"Shoo," he said, with a chuckle. "I 'spect t' see ye out there wi' a smile an' a audience. Bear's prolly safe 'nough till after dinner. So ye stick wi' 'im. 'e gits called, ye foller, so's ye kin be there after. Aye?"

"Aye," she replied, and got up. She brushed off her skirt and walked resolutely back to Bardic Collegium. Mags watched her go and nodded with satisfaction.

::*Pocket pie?*:: Dallen asked hopefully.

He laughed. ::*Aye, ye greedy git. I'll find ye a pocket pie.*::

::*Good. Make it two.*::

By the time dinner came, Dallen had been stuffed with pocket pies. Mags had found a herd of younglings hanging around the door to the Companion's Stable, watching the door yearningly. He made it known that many of the Companions from the Kirball game were inside recuperating, that they were all partial to pocket pies, and that as long as *he* was there, they were welcome to come in and offer treats. The kiddies shot off like so many barn swallows chasing insects and came back with their hands full of pies.

::You know you've been nominated for the status of a minor god, don't you?:: Dallen told him as he cleaned himself up a second time. Even without doing anything other than stand about answering Kirball questions or questions about being a Heraldic Trainee, he had been sweating, and he wasn't going to change into something nice without a second wash.

A second wash! Until he'd come here, he'd never had any kind of a wash except by accident when he got rained on. On a hot day like today he not only didn't mind a cold bath in the pump, he preferred it.

::I'll take it,:: Mags chuckled. ::Wouldn' mind bein' a god. Ye kin hev m' four an' twenny handmaids lay out me good uniform. Take it back, ye kin send twa out here t' wash m'back.::

He heard Dallen's snorting laugh even outside. ::If I sent even one, you'd be blushing so hard they'd think you'd fallen into a vat of scarlet dye.::

::Oh, thet's right. I keep fergettin'; ye're th' ladykiller, not me.:: He toweled off his hair vigorously. ::There. Reckon I won't offend no 'un's nose now, 'cause now I don' smell like you.::

::I take back all the nice things I said about you.::

::Thet's cause now yer stuffed too fulla pie t'move.:: He let himself into his room in the stable and got out his "good" uniform. Not his "best"—that was for fancy occasions like the special parties that Master Soren held. Or for use on the remote chance he would be required to attend some Court function or other, but that was about as likely to happen as for Dallen to sprout wings and fly.

This outfit was something new, something the Dean had decided he needed and had again found among the stored Trainee uniforms outgrown by highborn Trainees. "Best" was far more suitable for winter, being of warm materials. "Good" was for summer. The tunic and trews were light moleskin rather than canvas; they felt like soft leather but were thinner and cooler. The shirt was a very light linen of the same sort that highborn and wealthy ladies used for chemises. The boots were light leather, glove-weight. The tunic and collar and cuffs had very subtle embroidery at the hem— Lydia had told him it was called a featherstitch.

Everyone would be wearing some form of "good" clothing tonight at dinner. Most of them, except for the Bardic Trainees, would not be wearing uniforms. This was not a Collegium dinner, this was a family affair, and now that the Trainees had spent a full week with their families seeing them only in uniform, it was time for them to dress and act as part of their families for a few hours. Everyone with family visiting would be seated with them rather than among their fellows.

Dinner would also not be in the dining hall; it would be outside, in the gardens. It was the only way to accommodate all the visitors, though anyone who was not a relative was being gently ushered out the gates right now, since the big concert would be held down in Haven itself.

Mags wasn't sure he was going to attend that. He would have gone if Lena was playing a solo but now . . .

Well, he'd see how he felt after dinner.

He ambled up to the Palace, noting that the noise had died down considerably and that a small army of people was busy cleaning up the grounds. Not that they needed much cleaning; people had been very respectful, but there were places where flowers had been trampled, things had been spilled or upset, bits of ornamentation or half-eaten treats discarded. Given how fast the folks were working, though, it wouldn't be a candlemark before everything was set to rights. Finally, now that the sun was westering, the worst of the heat was over, and those fitful breezes had turned into a nice, soft zephyr of a wind. The picnic was actually going to be a pleasure.

He heard footsteps on the path behind him and recognized them immediately. Only one person he knew walked with that particular care, choosing each step with an eye to making as little noise as possible without actually sneaking. "We'd better hurry, or everything decent will have been snatched up," said the King's Own, Herald Nikolas, with a chuckle, as he came up even with Mags. "I swear, you would think these people had never had a decent meal in their lives. They've been devouring everything in sight all week."

If you had to pick Nikolas out of a crowd, you would never be able to. His hair and eyes were indeterminate brownish colors, his face was so unmemorable it practically fled from your memory the moment you looked away. Part of this was just Nikolas himself, but most of it was skill, a skill he was training Mags in with particular intensity. And only with a handful of people would he have let his guard down enough to have made a remark that was something other than innocuous.

Since Mags now knew very well that when a Trainee came from a family that was living in poverty, the Crown compensated them quite generously for the loss of a working pair of hands, he laughed. No Trainee from any of the three Collegia had to endure guilt, knowing how good his life had become while his family struggled. So—no, no one who had turned up here was actually starving most of the time.

"Might be, bein' as it's here at the Palace, makes 'em

think food mun somehow be better," he offered.
"Might jest be 'cause celebratin' means food t'workin'
folk. But most likely 'cause 'tis stuff they never seed
afore, an' figger never t'see again." He scratched his
head. "I mind when I got 'ere, I didn' even know what
t'call 'alf uv what they gi'e me."

"Very likely. Care to eat with me and Amily, Mags?"
his mentor offered. "Bear and Lena too, of course. I—
suggested to the Healers that they should keep Bear's
brother away from him for now. There's no way to
keep a confrontation from happening—family has
rights, of course—but there is no reason to ruin the
lad's day, or a triumphant week for that matter. Tomorrow will be soon enough. At the moment, I don't believe Bear even knows his brother is here."

Mags heaved a sigh of relief. "Good," he said sincerely. "Thet yer doin', sir?"

"In part, in part. I'd like you and Bear to come with
us to the concert as well." Nikolas sighed a little. "We
have a lot of work ahead of us, you and I, and this will
probably be the last chance you'll have for a lot of so-
cial time with your friends. You and I have a project we
will have to undertake that is going to occupy every bit
of your free time and probably some of your class time
as well."

Mags felt as alert as if someone had doused him
with a pail of ice cold water. He waited for Nikolas to
elaborate.

But it seemed he was going to have to wait. "I am
not going to discuss it with you right now," Nikolas
continued. "You might as well enjoy this last truly free
day without having to think about much of anything.

Just remember the relaxation exercises you have learned, put this aside, and enjoy the evening."

Mags nodded. He had learned a *very* great deal from one of the Healers lately, on Nikolas's advice, and one of those things was a series of mental exercises that allowed him to put something out of his mind and not merely appear relaxed, but actually *be* relaxed. It had made him that much more valuable to Nikolas, as someone with the ability to fit in and appear casual in virtually any situation, because he actually *was* relaxed and casual. The only time he really couldn't use the exercises was on the Kirball field.

"Should we go git Amily, sir?" he asked. It was a good question, since Amily was so lame as to be virtually crippled. The accident that had taken her mother's life had broken her leg in several places, no one where they were had known what to do, and by the time she'd seen a Healer, the bones had already started to mend all wrong.

Wonder if that ain't part'a why Bear's so hot on his healin' kits. Anyone with the basic knowledge that Bear was providing would have known at least how to immobilize Amily's leg in such a way that, though she might have been lamed, she would not have been crippled.

"No, she has a place set up for us," Nikolas replied. "We just need to collect some food and round up Bear and Lena. Speaking of which, there is Bear, just packing up."

They had, by this time, reached the row of Healers' teaching booths. Bear was putting the last of his demonstration kit back together and talking animatedly with a middle-aged woman. When he finished, just as they neared, he handed the kit to the woman, to her surprise and voluble thanks. He turned in time to see them approaching and waved. The woman took this as her signal to tender her thanks once more and make an exit, taking the kit, clutched to her chest, with her.

"Midwife," Bear said, without being asked. "Been here every day askin' good, sensible questions. Reckoned I could trust her with it. Heyla, Herald Nikolas. You kidnappin' Mags?"

"And you and Lena if you know—ah, there she is!" Lena appeared as if conjured, though Mags had the notion she'd been somewhere nearby, just out of sight, waiting for Bear to be finished so that she could "just happen" to come by as the dinner bell rang.

Which it did at that moment. "Your timing is impeccable, Lena," Nikolas told her, with a little bow that made her giggle. "I have orders from Amily to round up the lot of you so that you can make sure to get some of all her favorites from the repast on offer. We are not accepting your refusal." He did not mention Lena's father, nor the concert. Nikolas had been a Heraldic Trainee at the same time that Marchand had been at Bardic; he had been the one who uncovered one of Marchand's misdeeds that had earned him a terrible (but fully justified) rebuke. He knew very well that Marchand would have left Lena to wait for him in vain even if he *hadn't* been involved with setting up the concert.

I'm thinkin' might be Nikolas oughta get that god-hat Dallen was offerin'.

"Aha!" Bear said, pushing up his lenses, which were

always sliding down his nose. "*Now* the truth comes out."

"You have caught me out." Nikolas made a mournful face. "I am too old and decrepit to dash from table to table for my daughter's pleasure."

Mags laughed. "All right, Grandad," he said impudently. "We'll do yer dashin fer ye."

Nikolas shook an imaginary cane at him.

Someone—very possibly other Heralds, for Amily was much beloved—had set Nikolas's daughter up very nicely on the lawn nearest the entrance to the King's Own's quarters. She had sole possession of the one substantial tree there, which provided plenty of shade, and was seated on a comfortable pile of cushions against the trunk. There was a huge blanket, easily big enough for a dozen people to picnic on, spread out in front of her, more cushions stacked to one side, and a big basket which presumably contained plates and cups. "Hail, oh queen of summer." Bear intoned as they reached her, making a comical bow. "We, your loyal subjects, await your command."

Amily was, in Mags' opinion, prettier than Lena, though her beauty was so quiet and contained that hardly any of it was obvious. Like her father, she had brown hair and eyes that were of no particular shade— more like all of them, mixed. She shared his knack for blending in with the background when she chose to— though right now, she wasn't choosing to, and her lively expression when she saw them all made Mags smile. She blushed a little and laughed. "Well, my wish is for you all to get us food! You're the biggest, Bear, so you and Papa get our main course. Mags, you get the other dishes, and, Lena, you get the desserts," she said, but in such a way that you clearly understood she was grateful.

Mags dashed off, knowing exactly what it was he was going to be looking for. He had been snooping at the preparations, so he knew which of her favorites were going to be served up.

The cooks were more than prepared for people who were getting food for more than just themselves and had provided "baskets" hastily sewn together out of coils of grass, not intended to last past the picnic. And most of the food was intended to be eaten with the fingers. Mags returned in triumph laden with "baskets" heaped with vegetables in puff-pastry, a nice selection of cheeses, little individual loaves of bread, a clever "cup" of butter made of a cabbage leaf, and raw vegetables cut up bite-sized with a hollowed-out cabbage holding something to dip them in. He was the first to return, and Amily was laying out plates from the basket. As he put down his bounty, one of the Collegium servants left a pair of pitchers with water beading up on the glazed surface beside Amily.

Nikolas and Bear returned next, with cold ham, a bacon-and-egg pie, and a whole cold, roast chicken. Lena was very partial to ham, but Amily preferred chicken; Mag was amused to see that Bear had the chicken and Nikolas the ham. Last of all came Lena, with a "basket" full of pocket pies, honeyballs and strawberry- or custard-filled tarts.

Quickly the food was distributed, and there ensued contented silence, broken only by such quiet sentences as "Don' 'spose there be more'a them mushrooms?"

and "Anyone want ham?" Mags, for one, hadn't eaten since breakfast as he didn't like to have more than a bit of soup just before a game, and he was fairly certain Bear hadn't taken a break to eat all day. Between the two of them, they managed to inhale anything that no one else wanted, and when the last crumb was gone and no one wanted to send them off for another round, they reclined on cushions with identical expressions of satisfaction.

Nikolas looked at them with incredulity. "Where do you *put* all of that?" he demanded, as the girls giggled. "I am quite certain the human stomach cannot possibly contain everything you put into yours."

"They're growing lads, Niko," said the Dean of the Herald's Collegium, Herald Caelen, strolling up and sitting down on a corner of the blanket. "Don't you remember when we could eat like that?" He rubbed his middle with a mournful expression. "No more, alas. Too many honeyballs and I will *look* like one."

The breeze stirred the leaves of the tree above them; a page came by to collect the baskets, with another to pick up the dishes and carry them away. Nikolas sighed. "What do you want, Caelen?" he asked with resignation, echoing Mags' sudden suspicion that Caelen was not here by accident. "You would never drop yourself down on my picnic without a 'by your leave' unless you wanted something."

Caelen pretended to look offended. "It isn't what *I* want, it's what *you* want. Your little project with Mags will count toward his year in the field; the Circle approved."

Nikolas smiled with satisfaction; Herald Caelen was

another around whom he actually showed something other than a smooth mask. "And how much brandy-wine did that take? Am I going to have to restock your cellar?"

"Enough, and yes. Nothing like being able to choose your moment to make a request." Caelen chuckled. "It does help that they all feel guilty about assuming Mags was some kind of bizarre assassin planted among us."

"At least we won't have to worry about that again," Nikolas grumbled. "I swear to you, if I hear the words 'black' and 'Companion' together in the same sentence any time soon, I am going to use the speaker for mucking out Rolan's stall from now until the death of the universe."

"And I'll help," Caelen promised, then stole a cushion from Nikolas and stretched out on their blanket. "Curse Whites. I would love to lie down on the grass right now."

"Liar," Nikolas said, throwing a second cushion at him, which he confiscated and added to the first.

"Truth-Spell me," Caelen said lazily. "Then tell me about the old sticks. Are they coming around? Who do I need to cosset and coddle and coax?"

Amily and Lena ignored all this in favor of whispered conversation that involved a bit of giggling, but Bear, and especially Mags, listened with fascination. Mags filed every word away for later—Nikolas would probably ask him about it. This was how things were done, he had learned, at least among the Heralds—not in stiffly formal meetings conducted like religious ceremonies, but between two old friends who happened to be very powerful men.

Nothing they discussed was earthshaking, yet it was all important. What Nikolas knew was vital to the future running of this new Heraldic Collegium. Armed with this, Caelen would know where to put forth extra effort in bringing other Heralds, who did not approve of this new way of training the newly Chosen, around. He didn't know all of the "old sticks" all that well, but Nikolas knew everything about everyone. If he didn't know exactly what it would take to convince someone, he at least knew all the strings to pull to make the reluctant Herald dance.

Caelen could do the rest. When Mags had first gotten here, he had thought that Caelen was very intelligent, very kind, and rather unworldly. He had gradually come to realize that Caelen hid a very shrewd nature and sharp political savvy behind that unworldly exterior. While Nikolas knew how to make himself invisible, Caelen knew how to make himself look utterly harmless.

What Caelen knew about those in his care was vital to how Nikolas would continue to make use of the Collegium and the Trainees in it. Though he lived at Court, Nikolas rarely interacted with the Collegium. He didn't even know who all the Trainees were. Caelen was able to tell him—and tell him who their parents were and what, if any, important ties they had.

That was where Mags came in. Part of his "job" was to be Nikolas' eyes and ears among the Trainees. So occasionally—to Bear's eye-bulging surprise—Nikolas would ask *him* a question about one of the Trainees, and he would answer it in as much detail as he could. Which was often quite a lot.

Eventually the conversation went from quite serious to light and personal, and it was obvious Nikolas was not going to ask Mags any more questions. That was when Bear nudged him.

"What was all that about?" Bear whispered. Mags shrugged.

"You might as well tell me now. I'll pester you until you do," Bear pledged.

"Ain't nothink, really. Ye saw how Herald Nikolas likes t'know 'bout all the Heralds, on'y they's too many Trainees now fer him t' put eye on personal."

"So you're his eye. Huh." Bear regarded him thoughtfully and with a touch of admiration. "I 'spect this 'little project' of his means you'll be taking time off classes again. So—what? He's training you to be a spy?"

Mags blinked at his friend. He never, in a hundred years, would have suspected Bear of being that astute.

"No—wait—don't tell me. Just let me know if you need me to cover for you. Like get you class notes or something so you don't fall behind, or find out about the sorts of things I know about." Bear chuckled at Mags' expression. "What? You saved my life, and if you've forgotten that, I haven't. I owe you."

"'Twas more Barrett an' 'is crew than me," Mags said weakly.

"'Twasn't Barrett standing off a madman with a poisoned blade," Bear retorted.

"You know," Nikolas remarked conversationally, "You two haven't actually been whispering for quite some time."

They both froze. "Oh," Mags said, weakly.

Nikolas looked at Caelen. Caelen shrugged as well

as a man lying flat on his back with his hands under his head could. "You know I advised this some time ago," Caelen said. "You have your little gang, which includes me. It's time for Mags to build his own."

Nikolas nodded. By this point Lena and Amily had given over even pretending to gossip and were staring, listening avidly.

Mags glanced around. They were in an excellent position not to be overheard. Virtually everyone nearby had packed up and gone off elsewhere. Those who remained were not anywhere near close enough to hear them.

"Yes, we are surrounded, but at a distance. And they're all part of my 'gang,' as Caellen puts it," Nikolas said, as he followed where Mags was looking. He pointed with his chin. "That's Healer Sofrens, who came from my village. Rolan told me to bring him along when I was Chosen. Little did I know his father was beating him half to death whenever he was drunk, which was becoming distressingly often. Over there are three of my yearmates, who helped me when *I* was being trained as I am training you, Mags. And Bard Lita. Jakyr was part of my group too, but he'll not show his face where Lita is if he can help it." Now he sighed. "Jakyr, like Lita, still is a part of my network, in fact. I suspect my errands are part of the reason why he and Lita had a falling out."

Mags thought about that and decided to say something—because at this point, he knew quite a bit about Herald Jakyr, the man who had rescued him from the mines when Mags' masters would not allow Dallen anywhere on their property. Jakyr was a good man, he had to be in order to be a Herald, but if Nikolas thought that *he* was to blame for what had fallen out between Jakyr and his former lover, well, he needed to be told otherwise.

"Mebbe part. Not all," he said firmly. "I owes Herald Jakyr. Mun rescued me, eh? But 'e rabbits soon's 'e thinks a female's thinkin' temples and pledges. Dunno why, but that's 'is prollem, an' you got naught t'do wi'it, sir."

Now it was Nikolas' turn to stare. "How on earth did you work that out?"

Mags snorted. "Fust candlemark I was 'ere, fust pusson we met was Bard Lita. Don' need t'be Mindspeaker t'work *thet* out when 'tis in front'a yer face."

Caelen coughed. "Get to the point, Niko."

Nikolas shook his head. "Right. Look, you two— this is something Amily already knows. I'm the King's primary information gatherer—"

"—he means spy," Caelen said helpfully. Nikolas glared at him.

"I've been doing this as long as I've been King's Own. I was doing it before I was King's Own, in fact. This isn't usually what the King's Own *does* by the way, I just happen to be quite good at it." Where anyone else might have looked a little uncomfortable right now, Mags was struck by how—relaxed and *ordinary* Nikolas looked. He was so used to playing the role that now he probably couldn't remove the mask anymore, so to speak. "Now, of all the Trainees I have examined over the years, Mags is proving to be the best at doing the same things I do. So I have every intention of making him into my partner. If all goes well, he'll replace me eventually, but I sincerely hope this will be a partnership for a good long time."

"Good," Amily said firmly. "I won't worry as much if there are two of you mucking around doing secret things. And I think Mags has more sense than you do, Papa."

Caelen smothered a laugh. Nikolas sighed and rolled his eyes.

"Never have children," he advised Bear, "They either cause you to wish that you had smothered them at birth, or they turn into your mother."

"Grandmama has more sense in her little finger than you do in your whole body, Papa," Amily said. Nikolas looked aggrieved.

"To return to the subject," Nikolas said, severely, "no one can do this sort of thing without support. So you three are to form part of that support. Pick who else you tell carefully. Ask Caelen first. I'll tell *my* group, so they know to help you and to take you seriously if and when you come to them for help."

All four of them nodded. "Some uv th' Kirball team," Mags said meditatively. "Gennie an' Pip, an' mebbe Halleck. Lydia and Master Soren. Thet'll do fer now."

"Good choices, all," Caelen nodded as he spoke. "Lena, on *no* account are you to tell your father."

She gulped and looked a little guilty, but she nodded. "I promise, sir," she pledged. "Not a word to Father."

Caelen sat up. "Good. Because Tobias Marchand couldn't keep a secret if someone sewed his lips shut on it. I'm off. See you at the concert." He got to his feet and dusted himself off.

"Tell the boys to put the double saddle on Rolan, would you?" Nikolas asked, then glanced at Mags. "Unless—"

::Tell him yes,:: Dallen said instantly.

"Uh . . . .Dallen says to tell you yes," Mags relayed obediently. "Oh! He means to put the double saddle on *him!* So I'll—" he blushed.

"So no one will ever think twice about you being in my company." Nikolas smiled slightly. "We'll cement everyone's speculation that you and Amily are close by having you take her to the concert. Everyone knows how protective I am of Amily. They'll assume, when they see us together, that I am keeping a stern eye on her suitor."

"Which you *are*, Papa!" Amily giggled. "You can't fool me."

"Quiet, wench," Nikolas growled. "I still have parental rights, you know. A little respect, if you please!"

Mags didn't know quite where to look, so he settled for staring fixedly at a vague point in the distance.

Now Lena was giggling.

Bear elbowed him. They exchanged a look. Then Mags dared to look at Nikolas, who sighed and shook his head.

"I'll get Dallen and meet you here," Mags said hastily, using that as his excuse to escape.

But as he was getting the peculiar double saddle—not so much a double saddle as a saddle with a seat a bit more secure than a pillion pad—arranged to Dallen's satisfaction, something occurred to him.

::Why don't all Heralds know Nikolas's the King's spy?::
::Because whenever they think about it, we Companions

point out how ridiculous an idea that is,.:: Dallen replied immediately.

Mags was stunned. ::*I thunk ye couldn' lie in Mind-speech!::*

::*You can't,::* said Dallen. ::*It's not a lie. It is ridiculous. No other Monarch's Own in the history of Valdemar has been a spy. It's insane. It's impossible.::*

So . . . you can't lie in Mindspeech . . . but you don't have to tell the truth, either . . .

That was a revelation. It was one that could be useful.

::*All we do is tell the exact truth. We just don't exactly answer the question.::*

Mags thought about that some more. ::*Would ye ever do thet t'me? Not 'xactly answer th' question?::*

::*No.::* The response was so immediate, and so . . . forceful . . . that he was taken aback.

::*Why not?::* He had to ask.

But the answer was yet another he hadn't expected.

::*Because you could tell.::*

What?

Dallen nudged him in the shoulder with his nose. ::*Now hurry up and mount. Everyone is waiting.::*

4

The concert was fine. Lena acted like a trouper, singing in the chorus without a sign that she had been
slighted. Mags wanted to dislike Marchand's protégé,
but he couldn't; or at least, he couldn't dislike his mu-
sicianship. He didn't perform anything original, and if
he had Bardic Gift, he didn't display it, but he certainly
was a good musician. And his three solos were war-
ranted, Mags supposed; he did play three wildly different instruments—flute, fiddle, and trumpet. Nor
were any of his solo pieces overly long, more like inter-
ludes while larger groups got on stage.

So maybe Marchand wasn't trying to show off his
protégé, just doing something sensible to keep people
from being bored. Maybe.

But if Mags was any judge, probably *not*. Marchand
never did anything unless it had some possibility of
making him look good. Finding a young Bard with
that much raw talent and ability was going to make
him look good. That was what Mags figured, anyway.

Amily loved the whole concert, and afterward Herald Nikolas whisked them all off to a very enjoyable evening at an inn where a troupe of actors was performing short comic plays with performances by acrobats and tumblers in between. Mags suspected that Nikolas was trying to distract Lena; if so, it worked. She was still laughing and chattering with Amily about the funny lines in the plays as they all parted to go to bed.

But as he climbed into bed himself, after throwing all the windows open to the breeze, he was not thinking about the comic plays. Nor was he really thinking about the inevitable confrontation Bear was going to have in the morning, nor how Lena was going to deal with this newest slight on the part of her father. Oh, those things were in the back of his mind, but he had something more personal to occupy his thoughts right now.

::Nikolas' project—:: he said hesitantly to Dallen. *::I know ye all gossip worse'n bored kitchen help. An'I know Rolan tells ye things sometimes. Whatcha know 'bout it?::*

::Some. As you have already guessed, it's about the assassins.::

Well, that was scarcely a surprise. Although . . . *::They ain't exactly assassins,::* he pointed out. *::Fust time, they was just spyin', near's we kin tell. Second time, they was after thet book fer their code. 'Kay, they kidnapped Bear when they was pretendin' t'be envoys an' stuff, but we figger 'twas t'take care'a the 'un thet went crazy. There wouldn't'a been no killin' at all if they'd been able t'get off Palace grounds wi' 'im. 'Twas on'y bein' cornered an' caught made 'em dangerous. They mighta been bullies, but they didn' really hurt anyone till then.::*

::*And they might have remained merely kidnappers. Until they had no more use for Bear,*:: Dallen responded, a little tartly, as Mags tucked his hands behind his head and stared at the vague shadow of a bat flitting about the ceiling, catching bugs.

::*We don' know thet . . . .*:: he protested, then sighed. ::*But aye, prolly. Second time though . . . .*:: He shuddered at the memory of the ruthless, cold killer whose mind had brushed against his so many times. ::*Aye, that 'un, he was somethin' I'd'a called an assassin.*::

And he'd planned to destroy the stable full of Companions as a distraction while he stole back the book he needed to decipher the coded messages of his superiors.

::*Well, Nikolas intends to set the two of you up in Haven as a father and son in some shady business or other. I'm not sure what it is; it will be shady enough that you'll have a lot of contact with criminals, but also so no one will be surprised to see Guardsmen or Constables coming in from time to time.*:: Dallen seemed a little perplexed. ::*This is not my forte. I cannot imagine what that could be, but I am sure he has something worked out. What he wants to do is find out if there are any more of these people, either that there are some who haven't left, or new ones. To do that, he has to discover who set them up here in Haven. They knew next to nothing about Valdemar; someone had to give them local help. He wants to find that person—or persons. Once he does, with luck, we might have a better path to discovering what they wanted and where they came from.*::

And why one of them thought he recognized me . . .

A trace of that uneasy thought must have crept across to Dallen. ::*You do know that this could all have a very, very simple explanation, don't you?*::

He blinked. ::*An' what'd thet be?*::

::*Mistaken identity. They do say that everyone in the world has a twin somewhere. Perhaps he knew your "twin."*:: Mags sensed Dallen's mental "shrug." ::*The simplest explanation is generally the correct one.*::

::*Mebbe . . .* :: But Mags didn't really believe it. No, there was something more going on there . . .

But worrying at it was not going to solve it right now either. More interesting was that Nikolas was going to set the two of them up *together*, and that he had openly called him a "partner" in front of the others.

This . . . this was amazing. Yet, at the same time, it woke old aches. He knew one reason why Nikolas had chosen him for this life—it was because he had no family. If he vanished, there would be no repercussions, as there would be if, say, he were highborn or had other connections that could cause complications. The few people who knew him on sight would not let it slip if they saw him in an unexpected place, or out of uniform— not like someone with a hundred cousins who might bump into him and accost him loudly and publicly. There was no one that he could let things inadvertently slip to who didn't already know what he was doing.

He had no ties, no loyalties,except to the Heralds, who had saved him from what would have been a very short life of starvation, privation, and pain in the gem mines. He was related to *no one* in Valdemar, owed no one else anything, and no one owed him. He was the orphan child of two young people who didn't even speak the language and who had been murdered by bandits. The few things that had been left offered no clues as to their land of origin.

He could not have been more perfect to be trained as a spy if Nikolas had gone out and arranged it all himself.

And that was the ache. Although he made jokes about how he preferred being an orphan, the truth was, when he saw people who were happy in their families—Master Soren and his niece Lydia, Nikolas and Amily—he was raw with envy. Family brought along baggage, but it also gave support of a sort he'd never had . . .

Except for Dallen . . .

Stop whingin' 'bout what ye cain't change, he scolded himself. *Jest think; yer folks coulda been like Bear's. Or they coulda hated Heralds.*

Oh, his head knew that. But his gut, now . . . his gut knew what it wanted. Like salt-hunger, meat-hunger, this was family-hunger. In his rare moments of quiet thought, it always came back to him. What had his parents been like? Would they be proud of him now, or horrified by him? Had they been running from something? What? What kind of blood ran in his veins? What would he have been like if he'd had a real family, a mother and a father? Surely he had actual blood relations somewhere . . . if only he could figure out where they were . . .

Shet it, he told his gut sternly. *Mind whut they say. "Be careful what ye ast fer, yer like t'get it, an' in the wust possible way.."*

There was no point in looking for trouble. Trouble was all too inclined to come looking for *him*.

———————

::*Wake up, layabout!*::

Mags came awake all at once, the legacy of the years when you woke just *before* the kick came, so you could roll out of the way and pop up on your feet. ::*Wha—hey?*:: he replied, sitting straight up in bed and swinging his legs over to the floor before he was able to form a coherent thought. ::*Whut's th' 'mergency?*::

::*No emergency. Rolan just told me what you and Nikolas will be doing. He and Nikolas want you to be thinking about what you believe you'll need, based on when you were playing the blind beggar down in Haven. He's already got an identity as a fellow who deals openly in second-hand goods, who is secretly something they call a "fence." That's someone who takes in stolen goods and gets rid of them where no one knows they're stolen, or sells them in turn to someone who'll take them so far away the theft won't be known. You'll be his son.*::

::*Tell 'im I reckin I should be deef,*:: he answered promptly. ::*I be good at holdin' m'tongue, an' I kin make whatever signs an' Mindspeak whut I'm s'posed t'hev said straight to 'im. An people'll talk free 'round me, thinkin' I cain't hear 'em.*::

::*I'll tell them. If you can think of anything else, tell me. Nikolas wants to start tonight. These fence people usually don't work until after the sun goes down.*::

Huh. Takin' in stolen stuff. Guess thet'll be whut brings Guards an' Constables, an' I reckon we'll be passin' 'em whut we learn. Mebbe they'll be passin' whut they do. It sounded as if he was going to be doing without sleep for a while. Well, worse things had happened than a little lost sleep.

He washed up and pulled on his uniform. Nikolas

hadn't said anything about skipping classes. ::*Heyla, Dallen. 'Mind Nikolas thet I knows sparklies. Thet'd be th' reason for why 'e keeps me "bout.*::

::*Oh! Good idea.*::

He began mentally calculating what it was going to take to pull this off. Fortunately that exhibition game of Kirball was the last the teams would play this season. It was just too hot to play in that open field in all the armor and padding. Practice and games would resume in the fall, when it was cooler.

::*And Herald Caelen wants to see you about your class schedule.*::

::*Now?*:: he asked in surprise.

::*After breakfast.*::

Well, *that* was interesting. Perhaps he had better postpone making plans until after he heard what Caelen had in store for him.

Back at the mines, he'd loved and hated summer in equal measure. Hated it, because the longer days meant longer work. Loved it, because at least he wasn't freezing all the time, when he could snatch a free moment there were things you could eat to be grubbed up out of the woods, fields, and stream, and because even he, miserable creature that he had been, was able to see the breathtaking beauty in a summer morning.

Now he was well fed, healthy, and—yes—happy. And a walk up from Companion's Stable to the dining hall on a perfect summer morning was enough to make him want to sing. Not that he would. He would never shatter the quiet, full of birdsong and the scent of fresh grass and the flowers up in the gardens, with something that sounded like a mule in pain. There were many things that Mags knew he did well. Singing was definitely *not* one of them.

The Waking Bell rang as he reached the dining hall, but breakfast began there before the bell sounded. Plenty of people other than the Trainees ate here, and many of them started their day at dawn. He was, as usual, one of the first in the hall; he sat down at an empty table and ate neatly and quickly. Whatever it was that Caelen wanted to tell him, it had to be important, or he would never have had Dallen relay the order to him at a moment when most of the Trainees weren't even up yet.

He never ate so quickly that he wolfed down his food without tasting it, however. He had gone for so long eating what most of the folk in this building would consider not even fit for pigs that he never missed an opportunity to actually savor what he ate. And give a little silent thanks that he was getting it in the first place.

Just as the first of the Trainees began to trickle in, looking a bit rumpled and still sleepy, he was finished. He took his dishes to the hatch and ran down the hall and up the stairs to Caelan's office. The door was already standing open, and the Dean was putting away a stack of books. Like Mags, the Dean of Heraldic Collegium began his day early.

"I sometimes wonder if people who lie abed late have any idea what they are missing," Herald Caelen said conversationally, with a nod to the open window behind his desk. The office was in much better shape than it had been when Mags had first met the Dean. There were only half as many books and papers as had been crammed in here back then, and most of them were properly stowed in cubbys and on the bookshelves that lined the walls.

"Dunno, sir," Mags responded, and closed the door behind him. "Reckon they'd jest say 'tis same as sunset. On'y i' th' East."

"So they might. Well, sit down, this shouldn't take long. Nikolas has told me all about his plan and asked me to do what I could to make things easier on you. So I have. I have good news and bad news." Caelen waited while Mags took a seat, then seated himself. "The bad news is that I simply cannot wave my hand and make the classes you really need to take go away. It's possible it might take you more years before you are reckoned to be ready for Whites than the rest of your yearmates."

Mags' heart sank.

"The good news is—it might not. It's going to depend on how well you can keep up and what things the Circle ultimately decides that you need not take in order to qualify. And I *can* do things for the short term at least. Nikolas is fairly certain this little adventure is not going to be needed come the fall, and traditionally in summer we give students a lighter load anyway. So, this is what I've done. I've postponed some of your classes and moved the rest into a single block of time. So my question is, would you rather sleep from noon until sunset, then join Nikolas in the city, then return here at dawn and take classes in the morning? Or would you rather sleep from early dawn until noon, take your classes, then join Nikolas?"

Oh, now that was a good question. If he had only

himself to consider, he would take his lessons in the morning and sleep until nightfall. But he didn't have just himself to consider. He had friends. And if he did that, he would never see them.

It struck him, then, leaving him a little stunned for a moment. *I . . . hev friends. Real friends. People I wanter see an' talk to an' be with . . .* "Afternoon, please ye, sir," he replied, and laughed. "Reckon I kin get easier used ter eatin' nuncheon fer breakfast than breakfast fer supper."

"That's probably a wise choice," Caelen replied, making notes. "If nothing happens all night and you end up drowsing, you'll have a morning to catch up with the others in your lessons. And if you end up working all night, you will be very tired when you get back here. So tiresome of thieves and criminals not to keep regular hours!"

Mags managed a little laugh.

"All right, nothing for you today, you'll start the new schedule tomorrow. I'm glad Nikolas waited until the start of the quarter before embarking on this; it's much easier than trying to rejuggle everything after you'd already started."

That last was muttered as Herald Caelen began leafing through papers and making out schedules—not just Mags', but several others from the look of things. Since they'd all gotten their schedules before the week-long Event, these must be for newly Chosen Trainees who had just arrived, or were about to. Four of them, if Mags was counting right.

Good thing new Collegium's done.

He knew the Dean well enough by now to merely

murmur "Thankee, Herald Caelen," and take himself out. And once out in the hall, he realized that he had something he almost *never* had; a whole morning to himself. Only a morning, because he knew very well that his new schedule would be presented to him by nuncheon, if not before. If the Dean said he was going to start afternoon classes, the Dean would have him starting afternoon classes this afternoon.

Well, there was one thing looming that he probably ought to check on.

Bear. Bear's brother was not going to stand for being put off much longer.

::Erm . . . :: Dallen said. ::*If you were to stick your head outside, you would hear the rumbles of that very thing.*::

That didn't sound good. He hurried to the stairs and clattered down them, a lot more noisily than he usually did. He had yet to figure out how to be fast *and* quiet. ::*What's goin' on?*::

::*What you'd expect. Bear's brother and his father are ranting at him at the tops of their lungs. He's not alone with them. There is a great deal of . . . erm . . . presumed status flaunting going on.*::

Oh, Mags could very well imagine how *that* was—wait, what?

::*Status flaunting?*::

::*Bear has the four most senior Healers at Healer's Collegium and their Dean backing him.*:: Dallen was extremely amused. ::*Against that, the head of a House of Healing, no matter how old and well-established that House is, just doesn't measure up.*::

::*Huh.*:: Mags had been under the impression that Bear's father and brother outranked his teachers . . .

::*Certainly his father and brother are under that impression themselves.*:: Dallen paused. ::*Oh my. They are going to bring out the Very Large Hammer now.*::

::*Very Large Hammer? Ye ain't makin' sense, Dallen.*:: He shoved open the door to the outside and paused for a moment, casting a glance at the outwardly serene façade of Healer's Collegium.

::*Well, you might say that back when you and Bear had that little misunderstanding, I took one of the things he had said to heart. The part about us not getting him support against the arguments of his family from some of the more important people here.*::

There was a long pause. Mags didn't move. ::*And?*:: he said finally.

::*And I had a few words about him with Rolan.*:: Another pause.

::*And?*::

::*And Rolan spoke to Nikolas.*:: The third pause was too much.

::*If ye don' come t' the point, I'm'a gonna come straight t' the stable and shave yer mane an' tail bald.*:: He put a good deal of force behind his Mindspeech.

::*I was getting to it!*:: Dallen replied, sounding aggrieved.

::*Ye'd make a 'portant message inter a joke. Ye'd draw out anythin' with suspense so thet the telling uv it lasted all night. An' hev! Th' point!*::

::*The Healers will be presenting Bear's father and brother with the King's Edict that Bear is a vital resource and that he will remain at the Collegium to attain his Greens, then to train the unGifted Healers for the foreseeable future. In fact, they will be handing the Edict over about . . . now.*::

The explosion of anger was so powerful it jolted against Mag's shields. A moment later, two Green-clad figures stormed out of the Collegium, heading for the stable. Another powerful surge of mingled anger and impatience made Mags pick up his feet and sprint for the stables. But before he was halfway there, two sturdy cobs with those same Green-clad figures on their backs galloped out of the stableyard and down the road, heading for one of the gates to the outside world.

Mags slowed a little, but not too much. He wanted to make sure no one had actually done anything . . . egregious.

He only dropped to a walk when he reached the stableyard; the yard actually served three stables, with one open side. The Companions' Stable was to the left, with all of Companions' Field behind it. In the middle was the stable for draft and hauling animals. Riding beasts were served in the stable to the right. The yard was hard-packed dirt, but as clean as if a fanatic housewife kept it swept, and smelled of nothing worse than fresh straw and hay. The Stablemaster for the entire Palace was standing there at the riding stable door, shaking his head and patting one of his hostlers on the shoulder.

"Is ev'one all right?" Mags asked, and flushed. "I'm mortal sorry—them Healers, they was here t'get Trainee Bear, which he don' wanta go, an' Collegium ain't gonna let him go. So they kinda got—"

"Put in their place?" the Stablemaster said, with a lift of his eyebrow. He and Mags were very well acquainted at this point, since Mags was living in the

Companions' Stable and had been since his arrival here. "My thanks, Mags; we were warned they were likely to be temperamental when they left. They were certainly temperamental when they arrived. But thank you for making sure they hadn't caused anyone inadvertent harm with their—"

He groped for words. "Temper tantrum," supplied the hostler, pressing the heels of his hands into his temples. "Blessed Cernos, my head is splitting. If they'd been my littles, they'd'a both gotten such a hiding they'd'a been eatin' dinner standin' up for a week. Grown men an' Healers, actin' like that!"

The Stablemaster patted him on the shoulder again. "You go up to the Collegium and get your head seen to. They'll be able to put you right."

"Aye, I will. By *real* Healers, not poncy little brats," the man grumbled, and began to make his way, a little unsteadily, toward the Collegium.

Mags was torn between trying to offer up some sort of apology (since *they* surely wouldn't) and running after the man to make sure he got where he was going safely. He decided in favor of the latter.

Good thing, too, the man was losing his balance a little just as he caught up with him. Mags caught his elbow to steady him.

"You be a good lad, Trainee," the man said, thickly, through clenched teeth. "I got a very little touch of a Gift. Enough to make me good with beasts, not enough to be of any special use. So they tell me, anyway. So—"

"Oh, aye," Mags replied, as he kept the hostler steady. "Aye, I kin see what happ'd then. 'Tis like gettin' sunstruck, aye?"

"Exactly like. Or the time a beam fell on me and knocked me senseless." Now Mags was very glad that he had come with the man.

"I got ye, don' worry," Mags assured him. He half held the hostler up the rest of the way and maneuvered him in through the door. When he saw a Healer he knew making his way toward them, he hailed the man with a feeling of intense relief. The hostler would be in good hands now.

"Healer Juran!" he called. "This lad was down at stable when—"

"When two of my fellows who should have gotten a lot more spankings and a lot less being told how important they were when they were small came storming down there and blasted anyone with a touch of Gift and an unshielded mind with a display of their pique," the perpetually weary-looking Healer said tartly. "Yes, we all felt it, and I was heading out to see if anyone had been hurt by their carelessness. Come along, my good man." He took the man's arm, and Mags let go. "We'll get your splitting skull set to rights. And you—" he added over his shoulder, "You might want to go see your friend, young Bear. Standing up to a parent is a rather difficult thing to do at his tender age. Even when they are in the wrong."

Mags nodded, and he half closed his eyes, waiting for the sense of "Bear" to tell him where his friend was. It didn't take long, since Bear was very distressed. That sort of thing tended to make it easy for Mags to find him.

There were two other people with him, both full Healers in their most formal Greens, but by the time

Mags found the room he was in—an empty classroom from the look of it—they were on the way out.

"Ah, good," said the first, spotting Mags just outside the doorway. "Your friend Mags is here, Bear. Skip your classes today—or the morning ones, at least. This situation was very stressful for all of us, but it was a lot worse for you." He eased by Mags and walked briskly in the direction of the Infirmary.

"Take him out for a long walk," muttered the other to Mags as he passed.

Bear continued to sit where he already was, in one of the classroom chairs, looking drained. Mags decided the Healer was right. He walked straight up to his friend, grabbed his elbow, and tugged.

"C'm on," he said gruffly. "Outside, where th' air don't stink uv bad temper an' errer-gence."

"That's *arrogance*," Bear corrected, automatically, then smiled just a little. "Little did I know that Father planted a spy among the Healers here who has been reporting every time I breathed in a way that Father wouldn't like. Which explains . . . a lot. That was . . ." He shook his head. "That was like being beaten with words. If they'd wanted to punish me, they couldn't have gone about it more thoroughly. You know, I'd rather be tied to that chair with a madman about to kill me than go through that again."

Mags snorted. "Oh, I reckon they wanted t'punish yer. An' more'n ever now. Yer right, they be wrong, an' they got told so, an' I reckon folk like yer pa and brother don't get told they's wrong real often."

"Never, as far as I know," Bear said wryly.

"Then they ain't gonna fergive them's told 'em real

soon," Mags told him bluntly. "Well, reckon now thet th' King's put 'is oar in, ye won't hev'ta see 'em if'n ye don' wanta. Le's git a walk afore it gits stinkin' hot. Got stuff t'tell."

He hoped that telling Bear what he was going to be up to would take Bear's mind off his own problems, and it seemed that he was right. As they walked slowly down the road away from the Collegia, Bear listened attentively, nodding from time to time, but didn't interrupt until Mags was finished. It was still pleasant: sultry rather than "stinking hot," birds and insects making a cheerful racket, and the occasional breath of flower scent from the Palace gardens.

"Would you like to come 'talk' to a deaf person, so you can see exactly what you need to do to counterfeit it?" Bear asked, a little diffidently, when Mags was done. "And would you be pretending to be someone who was born deaf, or someone who lost his hearing because of a sickness or injury?"

"They's a difference?" Mags asked, surprised. "In how they act, I mean."

"Very much so." By this time the meandering course they had been taking wound them up at the Kirball field, and they both leaned against the fence and watched a Companion foal scrambling over some of the obstacles under the watchful eye of his mother. The little fellow was very intent. Mags wondered if *he* had dreams of playing the game.

"Which'd be easier?" Mags asked. "I mean, obvious, I wanta do what's easier."

"Someone who had once been able to hear, definitely," Bear told him. "Juran has a fellow like that

helping him. He does all the distilling for the Healers'
Collegium. Even I use him when I need more than a
single dose of something. He's very good and very
dedicated, and he has an amazing nose."

Mags nodded; that made sense. When people lost
one sense, the rest tended to get sharper. He remembered how his own senses had sharpened when he was
only pretending to be blind.

He followed Bear to Healers', taking the side entrance where the House of Healing was but bypassing
the rooms where the patients were. Still, you couldn't
avoid the sharp smell of the things they used to keep
infection away, or the feeling that if you cracked your
shields, you'd be bombarded with pain. It wasn't just
Heralds and folks from the Collegia and Palace that
were brought here. Anything anyone down in Haven
thought too serious for the Healers there was treated
here.

Bear ushered him around to the stillroom, where,
amid a bewildering array of odors both sweet and bitter, a relatively young fellow who had lost his hearing
in a fever walked him through what it was like for him
now.

Something Mags had not anticipated was that the
fellow could still speak. He sounded odd and a little
mush-mouthed, and his tone was flat, but he was perfectly understandable. *Should I try that? No, best not.
Might make people think I kin still hear some.*

The young assistant had learned to "read" what
other people were saying by watching their lips as they
spoke. Now Mags could see what Bear was talking
about; there were a lot of little behavior quirks that

Mags was going to have to think about adding to his character. The young man stared intensely at his lips when Mags spoke. He always had his back so close to a wall that no one could get in behind him and startle him. Mags realized at once that in someone operating in the criminal world, such a habit would be even more pronounced. In a world where he would (supposedly) not be able to hear anything, looking nervous all the time would not be out of character. Mags noted how the young man was acutely sensitive to any vibration, looking about immediately when the floor trembled the slightest bit as someone nearby dropped something heavy. He understood then that while he must never react to something that was purely a sound, he could, and should, react to anything that he could feel. As for the young man's sense of smell, well, it was clear by how he monitored the progress of the three different distillations he was running by scent alone that this was one of the strongest and most reliable of his senses. This very brief exchange told him *far* more than he would have thought of on his own. This would make life much easier for both him and Nikolas.

"Nights are bad for him," Bear said, as they left the young man. "A friend stays in the same room with him because he's terrified that something will happen in the night, a fire or something, and of course he won't hear an alarm, and in their haste to get out no one will remember him. I would expect anyone who couldn't hear would feel the same."

"Then I best never nap 'less Nikolas is about," Mags mused. "Heh. Not thet I would. Be crazy t'let down yer guard down there. This was a damn fine notion, Bear. Learnt more'n I coulda thought."

They walked out of Healers'—which somehow was always cool in summer no matter how hot it was—into the full strength of the sun. There was heat-shimmer above the grass, and the scent of heated rock instead of flowers. *Least we ain't goin' down there by day. Thet part'a Haven i' th' sun'd stink like a midden.* They ducked back inside, electing to face the Infirmary and sickroom spells rather than the heat.

"Well, good. Nice when I can be useful," Bear said, with what was almost a smile. Clearly, the fact that he had helped Mags had made him feel better.

"So," Mags ventured, as they left the Infirmary wing where the stillroom was, and faced the heat and full sun again. He squinted against it. "Ye wanta talk 'bout it?"

Bear sighed, and his shoulders sagged. "Nothin' much to say. You know this's been brewing for a good long time. Father's spy—his name is Cubern, by the way—is one of the Guard Healers, so I had no idea he was around; he was able to find out everything he wanted to know about what I was doing just by socializing with the teachers at the Collegium. He knew I wasn't planning to go home at Midsummer, even though most people do if they don't live too far from here. I've been trying to figure out a way to avoid going home at Midwinter.

"I know now that even though I never told them about the Event because I *knew* what would happen, they found out about it anyway thanks to Cubern. I suppose they got it in their head I was doing the healing kits in secret, without the by-your-leave of the Collegium and the Healers' Circle." He shook his head. "Deluded. That's all I can figure. They are so damn sure that they are right and everyone else is wrong that I suppose they thought once they 'exposed' me and showed the Collegium how dangerous my 'stupid notions' are, everyone would be horrified and wouldn't be able to get rid of me fast enough. Came riding up here figuring to drag me home for certain this time. Found out 'bout what I was doing at the Event when they showed up."

"Erm . . . I saw thet." Mags confessed. "Yer brother, I reckon. Thought 'e was gonna fall down inna fit there an' then. Dallen scared up some folks ter innercep' 'im afore 'e made a pother."

"Did he?" Bear looked interested—and grateful. "Well, I guess I owe Dallen a pocket pie. Yesterday was a real good day, and nothing they said to me today is going to change that."

Mags patted him on the shoulder, awkwardly. "Reckon Healers woulda kep' 'em away from ye, iffen they coulda. Reckon they tried t'talk some sense into 'em too, since they had 'em all yestiday an' last night. So Healers' on yer side, aye?"

"I know." Bear swallowed. "Parents still have rights. It's not as if they *beat* me or anything. They just think I'm—" He waved his hands, helplessly. "They can't see that anything I do is worth a fraction of what they call a 'real' Healer's work. Before I walked into that, the Dean had a long chat with me. Everyone tried to talk 'em around, but they just were not gonna listen, not to anyone, not even to the Dean. I guess m'father tried to—" He shook his head. "M'father has an exaggerated idea of his own importance. All right, our House of Healing is one of the oldest in the whole Kingdom, but that doesn't make him any more important than any other senior Healer. He just doesn't see it that way. The King's Edict, though . . . there was nothing he could say or do after that and nothing he can do to alter it. I don't think even he is stupid enough to try to claim that I somehow hoodwinked the King." He winced a little. "I've never seen him so mad. I thought he was gonna explode."

"Well . . . now yer safe," Mags said into the silence, as they both stood in the doorway of Heralds' Collegium. He sighed a little with relief to be out of the sun. "I mean, safe, they cain't drag ye outa here fer no reason. I don' mean I think they'd beat ye or nothin'." *Not with fists or sticks, mebbe, but words* . . . But he didn't say that out loud.

Bear scratched the back of his head.

"Reckon so," he finally said, sounding a little relieved but a lot bitter. "Probably be told I'm disowned as soon as he can find someone to bring the message here, but, aye, safe."

Mags looked at him askance. "Weren't *yer* doin' th' King reckoned ye was needed 'ere."

"You will never convince him of that," Bear replied sourly. "He'll find a way to blame me for it. Ever since he figured out that I wasn't going to spontaneously bloom a Healing Gift, he's been sure it was somehow all my fault."

"That's daft," Mags said flatly.

"Course it's daft, and he should know better. He does know better." Bear's tone had gone from bitter to exasperated. "He's a really, really good Healer. I don't think I've ever seen him fail. But to him, I'm a failure."

"But—"

"All my life, everything he has wanted to happen, has happened. Until me." Bear shrugged. "And now he has to go home and tell Alise or Avise or whatever her name is that I am not going to marry her. Or, more likely, tell her parents. He's gonna have to come up with some sort of excuse or reason. Another failure, this time because he couldn't control me and make me do what he wanted, and that'll make him look bad in front of everyone he told that I was gonna come home and get married. He's gonna hate that."

"Mebbe Alise'll be happy, though, if she don' know ye thet well." It was all Mags could think of to say. "Could be yer gonna make a lady real happy. Fer all ye know, she got some'un she's sweet on already, an' this'll leave 'er a way t'wangle thins."

He understood very well what poor Bear was dealing with. The Pieters boys had gotten the same sort of treatment from their father. He expected them to be copies of himself, obedient little copies that would do everything he told them to do without a murmur.

"Maybe." Bear finally stood up and straightened his back. "Let's get some nuncheon."

As Mags had expected, there was a new class schedule waiting for him in his room when he returned from eating. It wasn't at all bad, actually. Weaponry practice every day at the end of the day, although it would be a much shortened version of the class and would include no riding. Three days a week, classes specific to being a Herald—on this schedule, property law, criminal law, and surveying. Three days a week, classes common to all three Collegia—history, math, geography. Seven-day off, except that Mags knew very well that Seven-day was likely to be spent trying to catch up with things he'd miss because Nikolas needed him and he'd skipped a class or two.

Still.

He grabbed what he would need for his afternoon classes and made his way over to Bardic, which was where the history class was going to be taught.

It came as a pleasant surprise to discover that the class was going to cover the reign of King Bedwyn, which just happened to be a period he knew something about. He'd come across a book about that time that was written so well he'd borrowed it and read it for pleasure—the dog-eared state of the book had given mute evidence that he was not the only person to have felt that way. Math he had never had much difficulty with, and although geography was a new subject for him, it was just memorization. He could do that while he was down in Haven at night.

He went to weaponry practice feeling that he just might manage to survive this summer in a relatively sane condition.

———————————

That feeling of confidence vanished the moment he stepped into his room and found Nikolas waiting.

The sounds of the crickets outside coming through the open windows seemed suddenly as loud as shouts.

The King's Own tossed him a small saddlebag as he stood up, and Mags caught it. Since Nikolas was still in uniform and he was not suggesting that Mags change now, presumably the saddlebag held a change of clothing, and they would assume their disguises elsewhere. Mags felt his stomach tense up a little. He reminded himself that this was not the first time he'd gone into Haven in disguise for Nikolas.

But it was the first time he was doing so as Nikolas' partner. He shivered a little, despite the still sultry heat.

"Rolan and Dallen are saddled and ready. I've already established myself as a pawnbroker and clandestine receiver of stolen goods," the Herald said, holding open the door into the stable. "Time to add you to the mix. Now, it's been my experience in these situations that the simpler the story is the better, and the more you can get people to assume things, the stronger your disguise will be. Your notion of playing deaf fits into that perfectly. No one can question you, and you can listen to whatever is going on and no one will ever suspect you of eavesdropping. I'd prefer if you were mute as well—" He paused, waiting for an answer to the unspoken question.

"I'd already recked t'do thet." Mags nodded. "Bein' mute means I ain't got nothin' I need t'keep straight. Ev'body 'spects lad what's deaf t'be mute anyroad. We jest wiggle our finners at each other an' Mindspeak what we're sayin', an' nobuddy th' wiser."

He followed Nikolas out into the stableyard where

Roland and Dallen were waiting. Mags noticed something he hadn't, before. This groom was very familiar—in fact, every time that he recalled Nikolas going out clandestinely, it had been this groom who'd prepared Rolan. And now that he knew Nikolas had a special circle of assistants—

He'd be daft not t'hev a special groom.

They mounted up and rode out into the dusk. Fireflies danced over the lawns—it looked as if the King had planned for the Court to remain indoors tonight. Only lovers would be in the gardens at this hour.

The Companions' hooves chimed softly on the road, but there were always Companions going up and down at most hours. No one would notice two more. The evening breeze was just beginning to cool things off. In a way, Mags regretted this. It would have been a fine night to just laze about . . .

Once they were on their way, Nikolas resumed the conversation.

"I am going to tell anyone that asks a different story about who you are and why I have you," he continued, as they passed a Gatehouse with two Guards keeping a watchful eye on both sides of the wall. "The one thing I will *never* say is that you are my son. This will mean, of course, that virtually everyone will be sure that you are. If anyone calls you my son, I will deny it furiously, which will only cement their certainty. Willy Weasel is not the sort of man who would take in a deaf-mute for the sake of charity; only being my son could possibly prompt me to do such a thing."

Mags had to chuckle at that name. "Willy Weasel? Where'd ye git thet name?"

"Allegedly I look like a weasel," Nikolas replied, with an amused glance at him. "I am also very good at what they call 'weaseling a bargain.' People don't win unless I let them."

They were among the homes of the highborn and wealthy now. There were little garden parties going on in several. Mags was glad he had eaten, as savory scents wafted over the wall from one garden all lit up with tiny lanterns. One whiff and his mouth was watering a little even though he'd had dinner; if he'd been hungry, it would have driven him insane. "Aight. I be yer son, on'y ye ain't gonna say so. What else am I?"

Nikolas pondered that for a moment. "The Weasel wouldn't have a woman about, because he doesn't trust them, so your mother must either have abandoned you or is dead."

Mags shrugged. "Tell it both ways," he suggested. "Let 'em guess. Hev ye ever talked 'bout me afore?"

"I actually *have* spoken of you now and again," Nikolas said, and he turned slightly so Mags could see his grin. "I've been planning on getting you on this from the beginning. I'm usually grumbling that you are not there when I have taken in a piece of jewelry, or that you are asleep in the loft of the shop when I want something taken down off a high shelf. So you have been established as a young relative with an uncanny power for judging gemstones. No one will be particularly surprised to see you with me tonight. Although—" now Nicolas chuckled "—at least one person will be very disappointed. He has been passing me what I suspect to be inferior gemstones. You will put a stop to the practice."

"Should be able to, sir." Mags affirmed. Here he

knew he was on firm ground. No one was going to be able to get a flawed sparkly past him. And as long as he had one thing he was sure of, for now, that was enough.

"All right then." Nikolas and Rolan both nodded. "We've got enough of your persona roughed in that we can do a credible job of inserting you into my operation. Time for the next step in your education."

5

Mags was not quite sure what to expect at this point. Where would they don their disguises? How would they get to where they were going—they certainly couldn't take Rolan and Dallen with them. And where were Rolan and Dallen supposed to stay?

But going off to an inn, especially a very popular inn, instead of delving into the seedier side of town did not fit in with *anything* he would have anticipated.

It was the very large, very noisy inn that had featured the actors and players that they had been to last night. He assumed that Nikolas had a good reason to take them there, so he held his peace and asked no questions. Nikolas glanced curiously at him once when they had left Rolan and Dallen in a special area of the inn stables reserved for Companions but seemed satisfied with his silence.

Nikolas took a table in the common room; a small one right in the corner and out of the way, but well lit. He ordered drinks for both of them, looked very much like a man who was enjoying a rare night out, and spent about a candlemark talking to people he knew who came by the table.

"And this is Trainee Mags," he would say, as soon as the conversation allowed. "You will probably come to hear about him as a famous Kirball player if you haven't already, but he and I are getting acquainted away from the overly curious ears of my darling daughter." Then he would get an arch look on his face as Mags flushed. Then the newcomer would look at Mags, look at Nikolas, and get the "Oh—aha!" look on his (or sometimes her) face and say something like, "So that's the way the wind is blowing, eh? Well, she's of age for it—" and Mags would blush even redder.

That it was all true—except for the getting acquainted part—only made him more embarrassed. Which was, he supposed, the point, at least for Nikolas. Not that Nikolas specifically wanted him embarrassed, but that Nikolas wanted a consistently genuine reaction, since some of the people they were greeting were Heralds. And just when Mags was starting to wonder when they would actually get around to doing what they allegedly came down into Haven to do, one of the actors from the previous evening hailed them from across the room.

The man came to the table at Nikolas' gesture. "Niko, Arianna wants your opinion on her farce," he said. "We want it to be funny, but we don't want a repetition of the Bochter incident. Eh?"

Nikolas made a face. "No one wants to repeat that. It took the Constables most of the night to clear the inn. I can certainly help make sure no tender sensibilities are trodden on, nor tempers raised, nor insults taken."

He stood up. "Come on, lad. We get to be theater critics today."

"This will take a while, but you don't need to worry about Andels locking you in. You might as well leave by our entrance; it's closer to the stables, and there's someone on the door at all hours," the actor said, as they followed him through a side door. He wasn't pitching his voice in a way that made it *obvious* he wanted to be heard—but if Mags was any judge, he was making sure that anyone who wanted to hear him could.

Puzzled now, Mags still held his peace. The actor went one way at a t-junction in the hallway, but Nikolas went in the opposite direction, and Mags followed. Nikolas opened a little door that looked as if it led to a storeroom with a key he had on his person.

He opened the room, and somewhat to his surprise, Mags saw that a lamp was already burning in it. It probably had been a storeroom at one time, but now it held just two things: a rack with clothing on it and the lamp safely mounted on the wall. Without a word, Nikolas handed Mags a set of clothing not unlike what he had worn as the blind beggar and took down a similar set for himself. Very shabby and threadbare, but carefully mended. Shirt, jerkin, and some sort of loose trews, all in faded dust colors, with the faint remnants of stains on them. But clean. Mended clothing and clean—that put two more things in Mags' mind. He and Willie Weasel were supposed to care about how they looked, but Willie didn't spend a pin more on anything than he absolutely had to.

Things were beginning to make sense for Mags now.

This was where they would transform into their other identities—perhaps not every night, but given that Nikolas was a familiar creature around here, they would be using this room often enough. It was probable that someone had come to ready the room and light the lamp as soon as he and Nikolas had settled at their table. Then it had just been a matter of someone coming up with an excuse for Nikolas to go talk to the actors. Their comings and goings in an inn that was already frequented by Heralds in general (probably because of the plays) and patronized by Nikolas in particular would not be noted.

The actor who had accosted them was clearly one of Nikolas' confederates. Now that he had the general shape of things in his mind, Mags was confident that when Weasel and his boy left this inn, they would leave by a side entrance that no one would note.

Huh. Guess I been learnin' a lot I niver thought 'bout.

"All right, then," Nikolas said, very quietly, in tones barely above a whisper, as Mags hung up his uniform. "Tell me what's going on here."

Mags did, and Nikolas nodded with satisfaction. "I've built up confederates and places like this on a network that I inherited from my predecessor," he said. "This particular resource was his; he actually *was* an actor before being Chosen, and this inn belongs to his family. Remember the soapmaker you utilized?"

Mags nodded.

"I've recruited her," Nikolas said with satisfaction. "She's a fantastic resource. As you noticed, no one pays any attention to the person who comes to clean the ashpits."

Mags felt a sudden pang of guilt. This was all very well but—what if they were ever trailed back to these bolt-holes by someone dangerous?

"But—I wouldn' wanta bring danger on 'er—" he said hesitantly.

"That's another reason I am relieved to have you partnering me, Mags," Nikolas told him as he cracked the door for light, then blew out the lamp. "You should be able to sense if we are being followed, and in that case, we take another way back, one that will take us through a few cellars. That should effectively lose them. And if for some reason that doesn't work, we'll lead them straight into Constables or the Guard."

Mags felt much better about that as he closed the door to the little room and made sure that it locked behind them. He wondered if they would leave through a cellar this time. In fact, they left by a side entrance so lost in darkness and shadows that they had to grope their way along the alley it let out on to find a street. Not a nice street, either. Not a *dangerous* street, but there were a fair number of disreputable looking characters and establishments on it. Mags fell into his character immediately, sticking close to Nikolas and not reacting to sounds at all. Unlike the street of their inn, this one smelled. It wasn't rank, but there were faint suggestions that someone had been sick, overlaid with beer, cheap wine, and burning grease smells.

The neighborhood gradually became dirtier and darker. Not that Mags could see the dirt, but he could smell it. Places where cats and dogs (and probably people) had relieved themselves. A stink of unwashed bodies and unwashed clothing. Slops poured into the gutter only added to the reek, which would persist until a rain came and washed it all down to the collection basins. People living here weren't supposed to do this, but unless you actually caught someone at it, it was hard to tell who the culprit was.

Finally Nikolas paused at a shuttered storefront halfway down the street from one of the few streetlamps, took a key out of his belt pouch, and opened the door. The universal symbol of the pawnbroker, three coins, was painted beside and above the door. The paint was fading. The symbol was the visual representation that the pawnbroker would lend you two coins but would get back three, whether he got it when you redeemed your pledge or when he sold it.

It was as dark as the inside of a hat in there, and the place smelled musty. Mags held absolutely still while Nikolas groped around at the edge of the door. He came up with a tallow-dip, which he took to the dim little streetlamp and held it up until it took. He brought it back, sheltering it from the breeze with one hand, and Mags followed him and the light inside.

The shop seemed to hold a mish-mash of just about anything and everything; there were tables heaped with old clothes and shoes, battered tools and kitchen utensils hung on the walls, and above them were shelves with boxes on them. Everything on the wall had a paper tag on it. Only half the shop was open to the public; the other half was behind a wall with a barred window in it and a counter behind the window. It had another locked door, which Nikolas unlocked after lighting a lamp in the front. They both went inside, and Nikolas locked the door behind them.

This, clearly, was where the valuable things were kept. Tools in much better condition, silver plate, some jewelry in trays. There was more in labeled boxes on shelves along the walls. Mags didn't have a chance to do more than glance around when a bell over the door rang and a man entered.

"I hope that boy of yours came with you this time, Weasel," said the man, sounding irritated, as he pulled a small box out of a pouch and shoved it under the bars of the window.

"He ain't *my* boy, and aye, I got 'im," Nikolas half snarled. Since Mags had been standing away from the window looking at the things hung up on the wall when the man came in, he gave no indication that he had heard anything until Nikolas reached over and shook his shoulder, roughly.

He turned, hunching over in the same servile posture he used to take at the mine when one of the owner's sons accosted him. Nikolas pushed him toward the counter and opened the box, spilling out the rough-cut gemstones inside onto a tray. There was already a magnifying lens on the tray, waiting. Mags nodded, and Nikolas brought over a cobbler's lamp and lit it so that the clear light fell on the tray. Mags picked up the lens and the first of the stones, doing his best to ignore the man's beer-laden, foul breath, as he leaned forward to watch Mags sort.

There were about twenty of them. None of them were the rare sort: rubies, emeralds, or sapphires. There were some citrines, garnets, some quartz dyed to look like aquamarine and amethyst, and a couple of sunstones. Mags examined each stone carefully with the magnifying lens. All had flaws and inclusions; all had been cut to try to hide the flaws. He sorted them all into the cups at the edge of the tray. Nothing went into the one on the farthest right,which meant "worthless," but none of them went into any cup higher than "inferior," and the dyed ones he sorted out onto the counter.

The man was incensed. "What th' hell, Weasel?" he demanded. It was clear to Mags that he knew what the sorting cups meant. "Them's good sparklies! An' what's he sorted th' purples an' blues out fer?"

Mags made meaningless hand motions when Nikolas shook his shoulder, keeping his head ducked down as if he expected a blow.

::He's trying to pass off dyed quartz as aquamarine and amethyst. All of the stones have been cut to try to hide flaws. Nothing is even up to 'good' grade, but the ones in the farthest cup left have flaws that are interesting, at least, and could be recut and polished to take advantage of them,:: he Mindspoke to Nikolas as his fingers flew. ::My sense is that he knew very well these were fakes. They are worth just about as much as cut glass or paste.:: Nikolas nodded, then his face darkened with rage. As his hand shot out to grab the man by the collar and haul him up to the bars, Mags ducked and scuttled into a corner.

"Yer tryin' t' pass off fakes!" Nikolas snarled, and shook the man one-handed until his teeth rattled. "Ye rat bastard, yer tryin' t'pass fakes off on me!"

The man yelped and beat at Nikolas' hand. "No! I didn'—I never—"

Nikolas let go and spat at him. "Liar! I should take these'n get a Constable!"

"I didn' know!" the man sputtered, looking genuinely

terrified. "How was I t'know 'e'd be carryin' aroun' fakes? I lifted 'em fair an' square!"

::'E guessed. 'E don't know stones, but 'e guessed that these wasn't wuth much.:: Mags was positive of that. The man was terrified of the rage in Nicolas' eyes, because he hadn't expected it, so he was lying his head off, hoping to somehow wiggle out of this without Nikolas making good his threat.

::He jest admitted t' stealin' 'em,:: Mags added.

::I noticed that. Which would make me a receiver of stolen property. If I call the Constables now, I'll be in as much trouble as he is.::

"Ye damn fool, didn' ye figger 'e'd be holdin' a drop-pouch? Idjit! That boy has more sense'n ye do!" Nikolas spat again. He made no reference to the fact that the stones had been stolen, but he also was not talking about Constables now either.

"Well, they ain't all fakes, is they?" the man asked desperately. "I mean, the boy didn' sort 'em all out!"

"Nah, but they ain't wuth what ye was tryin' t'git outa me, neither," Nikolas snarled. "Not even close. Gold? Not a chance. Not even siller. Copper, I'll gi'ye. Two apiece, an' nothin' fer th' fakes."

"Two? Ten!" the man yelped, and they settled down for some serious bargaining. Mags had no idea that Nikolas was such a ruthless bargainer. Two copper was about what a glass or paste "gem" was worth. Even the fakes were worth twice that. But then again, these were stolen. While it was not likely that the Constables would be searching very hard for the thief who had taken something so small in value, there was still a risk for Nikolas in taking them. Eventually the man, worn down to nothing by Nikolas' sharp tongue and threats to expose him to the Constables as a thief after all, settled for five silver and twenty coppers for a pile of small gemstones worth, in Mags' estimation, about twenty silver.

Mags wondered what he was going to do with them.

Nikolas counted out the money reluctantly and shoved it under the bars. The man trudged away.

Nikolas pointed to a stool in one corner and handed Mags some horsehair, then made some meaningless signs. *::You have to look busy,::* he Mindspoke. *::Reading would be out of character, so I supposed you could braid some trinkets to sell here in the shop.::*

Mags nodded, scuttled over to the stool, and began to make a pretty, round braid for a bracelet. People came and went, some legitimate, some not. Mags soon learned that Nikolas was a moneylender as well, taking peoples' possessions as surety against a loan. Those who came in and repaid their loans a bit at a time got their property back. Those who defaulted lost it, and presumably Nikolas sold their goods. One fellow came in and joyfully redeemed his carpentry tools. Nikolas grumbled the entire time he was handing them over.

::This fellow's a good, honest man,:: Nikolas was saying in Mindspeech as he berated the carpenter. *::He just fell on hard times. I found someone who could take him on so he could get his tools back. He'll be fine now.::*

::Reckon ye didn' overcharge 'im, neither,:: Mags replied, keeping his face still.

::Well, it would have been out of character for me to be easy on him. Weasel is known as a sharp man, but fair, when it comes to a plain loan.::

But as the night wore on, people came in who were not honest. There was no reason why a fellow with dirt caked black under his fingernails and who clearly had not washed himself nor changed his clothing in a year would own six silver spoons, nor why a woman with paint caked on her face so thick it was cracking and a threadbare velvet gown so low-cut Mags was afraid her breasts were going to pop out of it should have a double handful of silk handkerchiefs, both plain and embroidered. Nikolas bargained with both of them as sharply as he had the gem thief, and with as little evidence that he cared where the loot had come from or how the possessor had acquired it.

Finally, as the trickle of customers slowed and dried up and Mags judged it was getting near dawn, the first man came in again.

"Here!" he said, thrusting something under the bars. "Now thet'll be worth somethin'!"

Nikolas gestured to Mags, who left off his braiding and joined the Herald at the counter. On the worn wood between them was a brooch set with carnelians and silkstone cabochons. Not worth much in and of themselves, but the workmanship of the brooch itself was incredible, made all of twisted wires of a metal that was so red it looked a little like copper—but which proved on application of the touchstone to be gold. And not plated, either.

Who would mount common stones in a setting of gold wires?

"Huh," Nikolas said, and stroked his chin. "Huh. I don't rightly know how t'value that. 'Tis gold. Carnelian and silkstone ain't worth a lot. But setting—'tis gold. I could gi' ye th' gold-weight value . . . I don' s'pose this's somethin' nobody'd miss." The last was said with so much sarcasm the words practically sank beneath the weight.

"H'actually, they won't," the man said smugly. "I got yon off a corpus. 'E won't be lookin' for it, and I misdoubt there's any sad relations about to shout thief."

"Grave robbin', now, are ye?" Nikolas cackled. "But if yon relations should come 'cross it in me shop—"

"They won't. Or if they do, they won't say nothin'." The man grinned smugly. "Furriners what weren't s'possed t'be here. Fool got hisself kilt by dray wagon this mornin', an' his friends lit out babblin' in some furrin tongue. I might've been follerin' 'em, seein' as furriners don't know city an' might need a guide."

"Big of ye," Nikolas said with a snort. "Right, then. I can gi' ye a bit now an' a bit more once I make sure this ain't gonna bring no trouble to m'shop. Here's gold-weight value—" He shoved a few silver pennies under the bars. "Come back termorrow an' ye'll mebbe get that agin." The man reached for the money, but Nikolas seized his wrist. "Not so fast. I gi' ye twice as much, if'n ye kin find out where these furriners be bidin'."

The man stilled. "Who wants t'know?"

Nikolas laughed. "Ye think I'm so daft as t'tell ye, so's ye kin run to 'em an' collect *my* fee?" He let go of the man's wrist.

::*He really does look like a weasel,*:: Dallen marveled, watching through Mags' eyes. Mags kept his shoulders hunched over and his head down. He was actually beginning to enjoy this.

Now, he himself wasn't at all sure that the brooch was from their murderous "guests." It wasn't of a style like anything he had ever seen before, but as he had come to know, there was a great deal of Valdemar out there, and beyond the borders of Valdemar, there were a lot of strange places and people.

Still, if the Weasel was known for taking in things like this, some other trinket might lead them to their targets.

::Is there any way you could tell for certain where this is from?:: Nikolas asked, as the thief rubbed his wrist.

::Not really. Not like stones got liddle maps on 'em sayin' where they come from. Might could be a Gift thet could tell ye where it's been, but I ain't got it. Mebbe I could look at them books the buggers left behind an' see if'n the designs look alike, but—:: He wanted to shrug, but didn't. No giving the game away by something out of character. ::I'd'a thunk an art-feller would be more like t'tell ye yea or nay on thet score.::

"I take all the risk, an' you get all the profit!" the thief whined. "Now I ask you, is that fair?"

Nikolas laughed nastily. "Oh, aye, a lot of risk ye took, takin' it off a dead man! Afraid he's gonna *haunt* ye?"

The thief looked around uneasily. Nikolas laughed again. "Ye got to do next thing t'nothing to get twice what ye got fer this trinket. Keep it in mind." He shoved the money all the way to the other side of the bars. "I buy lotsa stuff that ain't trinkets. People pay me t'find out things. I pay people t'find 'em out for me. Understand?"

"Aye, Weasel. But it still ain't fair—"

Nikolas snorted. "Ye want fair, go get yer friends t'gether an' make yerself a guild so ye can make yerself rules 'bout what's what! Fair!" He laughed through his nose. "A Thieves' Guild! Ha! That there might be funniest notion I heard all year!"

The thief looked at him sourly but did not dispute any further with him. He scooped up his money and left, looking entirely disgruntled. Nikolas slipped the brooch into a secure pocket inside his tunic. Mags went back to braiding horsehair.

Eventually Nikolas went to a cupboard with a lot of little drawers and rummaged around in it, coming out with a handful of curious beads. He handed these to Mags, who studied them.

No two were alike; they looked like something out of a magpie's hoard, if the magpie had excellent taste. There were carved stone, glass, enameled metal, and carved wood with a faint, exotic sweet scent to it. The one thing they all had in common was large holes, fully large enough for him to slip the round braided horsehair through. So he did just that with one of the enameled ones, secured it in the middle with a knot on either side, and finished the braid off with a loop and another intricate knot. He held it up to Nikolas, as if for approval.

::Very clever! Yes, that will give you an excuse to be here,:: said Nikolas. The Weasel, however, just grunted, snatched the bracelet, and hung it on a nail at eye level. Mags started a necklace.

By the time they left for the night, he'd made three pieces of jewelry and "sold" one—"sold" being relative, since another slattern, younger than the first and with only a smear of red lip paint, traded some of her offerings for a necklace with a porcelain bead covered in a garden of miniature flowers. It made him almost sad to see her put it around her neck; for a moment he could see what she might have been—and at the same time, what she was going to become.

He wondered how Nikolas could stand it, being in this shop night after night, seeing these people come in, some of whom were merely victims of appalling luck or very bad choices . . . .

::I stand it because there are some I can help,:: Nikolas said as if he had read Mags' thought. Or perhaps he had read the expression on Mags' face. ::That one—maybe. That bead is worth five times what I traded her for it, but I don't think she's going to let go of it easily, and it might be that little bit of beauty in her life will remind her that she can make other choices than she has.::

Mags was dubious . . . but . . . well, why not. Why not hope for her? So long as there was no expectation with that hope. Expectations, now, that was what bit you every time.

Hope for the best, expect nothing.

::Not that long ago, you hoped for nothing as well.:: Dallen chuckled.

::Aye, well, this big white mule seemsta hev corrupted me.::

He sensed Dallen's snort of derision at the same time that Nikolas straightened his back and stretched, then turned and cuffed him in the ear.

Well, made it look as if he had been cuffed. The fist merely grazed his ear and whiffed through his hair, but Mags had the sense to act as if he had been hit. He cringed and made a little animal moan.

Nikolas grabbed his shoulder and hauled him to his feet. "Come along, ye gurt fool," he growled. "Time t'be getting' home."

Nikolas blew out lanterns and locked up, making sure the foreign-looking brooch was in his pocket. Then he trudged up the street, Mags following with his back hunched. It was still as black as night, but Mags knew the "feel" of things, and dawn wasn't far off by his reckoning.

He was beginning to feel the effects of the long night; he was glad that he was moving, because he knew the moment he closed his eyes, he would start to nod off. He and Nikolas could scrounge something out of the kitchen, he was sure, though it was far too early for even the kitchen staff to be awake. Then he could actually get a good seven, maybe eight candlemarks of sleep. Much better than he had reckoned he would get; he had expected he would not see his bed until after dawn.

The inn was without lights at the back where they slipped in, and as silent as if it were populated only by the dead. They changed back into their uniforms and went out to the stable, where a sleepy hostler, awakened by the Companions, had just finished saddling them.

"They kept ye might late, Herald," the hostler said, though with no hint of complaint in his voice.

"Actors," Nikolas said in a tone of weary amusement, while Mags yawned ostentatiously. "They think because *they* can sleep all day and carouse all night, the rest of the world does the same."

"Aye, well, ye know what ye be getting into, Herald,

any time they ask ye to stay," the hostler said with a yawn of his own and a chuckle. "It ain't as if ye haven't been here afore."

Then he leaned over and whispered. *"New lad. Not sure he's asleep."*

"Good man," Nikolas whispered back and slipped him a couple of coins for his trouble. "Well, then. Till the next time my feelings of friendship overcome my good sense."

The hostler merely waved to them as they rode out of the stable doors.

Mags' whole thought at this point was for his bed. It appeared that Nikolas was like-minded, for the two of them practically flew up the hill to the Collegium, with both Companions moving at a very brisk trot, and there still wasn't any light showing in the sky by the time they parted at the stable door.

"I left word with one of the servants I trust to leave some breakfast waiting for you in your room, Mags," Nikolas told him as they hastily stripped the Companions of tack and stowed it. Fortunately so short a ride meant neither needed to be groomed, and although both of them had probably dozed some, it could not have been the sort of restful sleep they really needed.

"Thenkee, sir—" Mags began, but Nikolas waved him off.

"Part of what I do for you at the moment; when you make your own contacts among the servants, you'll handle these things for yourself. Now go and eat and get some sleep. You did will tonight. And, oh—" he handed Mags the brooch. "Study that while you are still awake, and give me your thoughts later."

He took it. "I will, sir, but—"

Nikolas just waved off his unvoiced objections, then headed for his own rooms and bed.

Nikolas had been as good as his word. There were pocket pies of the savory and sweet sort both, exactly the sort of thing that kept well and tasted fine cold. Someone had left a "sweating" crock set up for him as well—this was a sort of half-glazed vessel with a wooden spigot on the bottom that kept whatever was in it remarkably cool by evaporation through the unglazed portion. The cool water in it tasted as sweet as anyone could wish.

Following Nikolas' orders, Mags studied the brooch as he ate his pies neatly and methodically. The cabochon-cut stones were nothing remarkable, though the finishing was very fine. The rose-gold told him nothing. The designs . . .

He caught his eyes unfocusing and his head nodding.

Not gonna get anything more done t'night, he thought blearily, and left the brooch on the table to stumble over to his bed and fall into it.

6

The noon bell woke Mags, although the morning bell had not. It was already quite warm, despite having the windows open; a little longer and it definitely would be too warm to sleep in here. Now he was glad he had made the choice that he had, to sleep through the morning and get up at noon.

He threw on yesterday's uniform, since it would have to go down the clothing chute anyway, carried a clean set of Grays up to the Collegium, and had a good bath before going down to what remained of the noon meal. Things were pretty picked over, but he was quite able to put together a solid selection—and just as he was settling in at a newly cleared table to enjoy it, Bear came rushing in.

Bear looked even more untidy than usual, though the effect was mostly due to his hair standing practically straight up, as it did when he'd been nervously running his hands through it. And he looked distracted—so *very* distracted that he didn't even notice Mags was sitting there until Mags gave an unceremonious whistle. Bear's head swiveled as if it had been pulled by a string, and his face lit up.

Uncharacteristically, he *bounced* over to where Mags was sitting, with his round face so full of repressed emotion Mags worried that he was about to burst.

"Easy on, there, m'lad," Mags said, soothingly. "Siddown. Ye look like a runaway cart. What's got ye so riled up, eh?"

"Amily," Bear said succinctly, dropping down onto the seat next to Mags and helping himself to some of the veggies.

"Oh-*ho!*" Mags exclaimed with complete understanding now.

It had been determined that Amily's crippled leg, if rebroken, could probably be Healed again—not perfectly, but she would end up with a leg she could actually use, instead of one that was a twisted burden to her. Bear was the first one that had suggested this, based on the fact that he had rebroken and set farm animal's legs so that farmers didn't have to put them down. It probably could not have been done anywhere but here—but here at the Collegia, Healer's Collegium in particular, were some of the best and brightest in the Kingdom. And Amily was the daughter of the King's Own.

"So, they're gonna do it, an' they gi' ye a seat at front?" Mags hazarded.

Bear practically exploded. "They told me *I'm* the one to oversee it all, cause it's my idea! Well, not exactly *oversee*, but the one to figure out what's needed, get everyone together and agreed, and then be the one to keep everything running smoothly until she's all fixed and walking!"

Mags blinked. On the one hand—

"Uh, tha's good—" he said, feeling decidedly mixed about this. "But yer jest a Trainee—"

Bear didn't seem at all upset that Mags was dubious. Instead, he nodded vigorously. "Exactly, and I'll have the Dean checking over everything, and lots of people making sure that I don't make some stupid mistake. But I *have* done this before, and no one else has. And they tell me that when Amily is all healed, not even my father will be able to say I'm not a real Healer."

Now that he looked closer, Mags could tell something else. Under the excitement, Bear was scared. As well he should be, in Mags' opinion. This was going to be dangerous work—dangerous for Amily, that is.

Ah, but Mags already knew just how badly Amily wanted this. And who was he to stand in her way?

He wanted to help Amily more than anything in the whole world. He wasn't a Healer, and he knew nothing about Healing. So the only way he could help Amily in this was to help the Healers. To help Bear.

"Aight," he said, slowly. "So, this's kinda like plannin' a Kirball game. Aye? So. Fust thing i' th' game's gonna be getting' th' leg broke agin. But tha's like sayin' fust thing i' a real game's gonna be meetin' th' other team on field, an' we *know* thet ain't how't goes. Aye? So . . . fust thing . . . fust thing i' Kirball game's knowin' th' lay of the ground."

He quirked an eyebrow at Bear, who was listening to him intently. Bear's eyes flashed.

"Yes! That's it exactly! So the first thing is going to be to get some kind of . . . of map of where all the old breaks are, and how strong the mends are! Yes! And then get everyone familiar with it, even the ones that don't have the Gift to see it—"

"Sounds t'me like ye'll be needin' some'un who kin draw?" Mags hazarded.

"Yes! No . . ." Bear began running his hands through his hair again.

"No, whoever draws this has to be able to See what things look like and—"

"No 'e don'," Mags said patiently. "When we gets some'un in what got robbed an' 'e knows th' face uv th' feller what robbed 'im, we jest git Herald Rashi. She kin draw, an' she got Mindspeech, th' kind what sees pichers. She looks at picher i' feller what was robbed's head, an' draws it. So ye gets Rashi, an' she makes yer picher."

"Or better yet! She makes a *model!*" Bear exclaimed, face alight again. "We can get cattle bones the right size and shape, we can break them and cement them together—"

"Saw 'em," Mags advised. "Break 'on't be th' same as Amily, 'less ye saws 'em exact."

"Right, but we can put them together exactly the same as Amily's leg and—and we can make muscles out of stuffed cloth or something—and—" He was running his hands frantically through his hair now, but in a frenzy of ideas rather than frantic worry.

"Stop!" Mags laughed, holding up a hand. "That'll do fer now. Ye go tell yer Dean an' build yer field t'study. Like Dallen tol' me when I fust got here. One step at a time, aye? Jest take it all liddle bits at a time."

"Right! Thanks, Mags! You're a star!"

Bear bounced off again without even stopping to

eat. *Well, mebbe he et early on. An' if'n I don' eat now, I ain't gettin' nothin' till dinner.*

———————

Classes were a little confusing—and confused, as one of the teachers was not aware he'd been juggled into the history class in question, and there was even an enquiry sent to Herald Caelen before it got resolved— but things went a lot more smoothly than Mags had expected.

Except in one class. The Weaponsmaster was concerned that he not fall out of practice; Mags was, frankly, just as concerned. After all, he'd nearly been killed *far* too many times, and he really did not want to find himself facing down an armed opponent with skills gone rusty.

"Can you tell me why the Dean shortened your class?" the Weaponsmaster asked. "You should be spending a good three candlemarks up here a day. You'll only be spending one. You can't possibly keep in practice at everything with your practice time shortened to a third.

Mags shook his head.

"Can you at least tell me what you are doing in place of it?" the poor fellow asked desperately.

"Nossir," Mags said, and watched as the Herald tilted his head to one side, and got that "listening" look many of them did when their Companions were talking to them.

From the look of him, the Weaponsmaster was actually arguing with his Companion. Finally he sighed and rubbed his temple. "I don't know why I try," he said, a little crossly. "You can never win an argument with one of them, and they always have the last word."

Mags did his best not to smile. "True, sir," was all he replied.

"*Supposedly* this won't last past the summer," the Weaponsmaster continued. "But I want you to pledge me faithfully that you will do everything you can to keep your coordination sharp and your muscles conditioned."

That was an easy promise to make. Mags had no doubt that Nikolas would have him climbing up and down ladders all over the shop, moving heavy objects, rearranging things, cleaning things, to keep him awake if nothing else. He would stay fit, of that much he was sure. "Yessir," he promised.

"All right then. But any time you have a moment free and the inclination for a lesson, I want you to come to me. Whatever class I am teaching, I'll fit you in." The Weaponsmaster put one fatherly hand on Mags' shoulder, looking very worried indeed. "You have had far too many close calls, Mags. I would feel directly responsible if something happened to you that a little training and practice could have prevented."

At that point it was almost time to join Nikolas, and Mags escaped from the Weaponsmaster with another set of apologies and promises. He had just enough time to grab something to eat, shove the brooch in his belt pouch, and get Dallen saddled when Nikolas summoned him out to a different gate in the wall from the one they'd used the night before.

As they rode down to Haven, Mags related to his

mentor the Weaponsmaster's doubts and concerns. Nikolas was very silent for a while, as they passed through some quiet, residential streets in a modest neighborhood. Finally he answered as he led Mags down an alley to what seemed to be a dead end.

::*He has some legitimate concerns. He's right, you have needed to defend yourself far more often than our average Trainee. I'll see what I can do about this . . . .hmm. This actually might prove to be more of an opportunity . . . .*::

An opportunity for *what*, however, Nikolas did not say. Instead, he touched some part of the wall, and the entire end of the alley pivoted in the center. Mags would have liked to get a closer look at *that*—it was literally a brick wall, somehow pierced through the middle and rotating with hardly more than a touch when the locks were released. But he didn't get a chance, and Nikolas led him into a tiny, enclosed yard with a bit of roof over it. Hanging in an alcove at the back were outfits similar to the ones they had worn last night. There were also a pair of buckets full of clear, clean water. Nikolas took a bag off Rolan's saddle and filled two empty dishes with grain. He and Mags took off the saddles and set them aside, changed their clothing, and went back out through the pivoting door.

::*Did you consider that brooch?*:: Nikolas asked.

Since the wretched thing had been drifting in and out of his dreams all night, Mags nodded. ::*I dunno why,*:: he said finally, ::*But it made me think uv horses.*::

Nikolas didn't change his posture or his expression, but Mags *felt* his reaction, as if mentally he had smacked himself in the head. ::*Of course. It's Shin'a'in. Or rather, it's a Shin'a'in trade piece. They themselves rarely make anything that requires metalwork, but they're like magpies. They love jewelry. Members of a prosperous clan will hang themselves all over with it—and their favorite horses too. That's a bridle brooch.::*

Mags had to keep himself from frowning. ::*Does thet mean th' dead feller was Shin'a'in?*:: Somehow he didn't like to think that. He didn't know a lot about the Plains-people, but what he did, he liked. He rather thought he wanted to meet one, someday.

::*This far north in the spring? Not likely. You might— might—find one turning up at the Ashkevron Manor in the fall, when they cull the horse herds. But that's as close as they ever come to Haven. No, this is more than likely someone come up from the south who got the brooch in a trade or the like.*:: Nikolas sighed. ::*I think that's a dead end. I cannot imagine Shin'a'in having anything to do with someone like our 'guests.'*::

Mags stared at the back of Nikolas' heels and *did* frown. ::*Thet don' follow,*:: he said instantly. ::*Feller coulda killed a Shin'a'in an' took it.*::

::*If he did—well, that's why he's dead now,*:: Nikolas replied soberly. ::*But it's not likely. Shin'a'in on the Plains are almost impossible to find. Shin'a'in off the Plains are extremely suspicious of strangers. Rightly so, their horses are prized, especially the ones that they don't sell. I've heard that the couple of genuine Shin'a'in studs that the Ashkevrons own are valued at their own weight in silver.*::

Mags felt his jaw dropping. A horse's weight in silver? He could scarcely imagine that much money.

By this point they were at the shop, and Nikolas repeated last night's routine. When they were ensconced in the little room behind the barred window, and Nikolas had lit the lamp indicating they were open for business, someone came in almost immediately.

It was a Constable, a tall, burly, black-haired fellow with narrowed eyes and a clenched jaw, who said nothing to Nikolas, merely peered suspiciously around the store as if he was looking for something. "Evening, Weasel," he said, finally. "Been shown anything I should know about?"

"Whosir? Mesir?" Nikolas said innocently. "This's a lee-jit-a-mit shop, sir. Nothin' amiss here, no."

The Constable snorted. "And I'm a Master Bard."

"*Are* you, sir?" Nikolas' expression was of utter guilelessness. "Well, ye should take down one of them instruments on the wall an' give us a tune then! It'd be a rare pleasure to hear ye, sir."

"Leave off!" the Constable snapped. "You know what the law is about taking in stolen goods!"

"None better, sir, as ye remind me of it every time ye walk in me shop." Nikolas' tone did not edge so much as a hair into sarcasm, but the Constable glared at him anyway. "Now if I could be interestin' ye in some of me goods?"

"I'm more interested in that boy. Who is he?" The Constable thrust his face at the barred window. Mags considered many different responses, all in the flash of a moment.

'f I looks askeered, he's gonna think I'm askeered of Nikolas. Then he'll figger Nikolas' up to no good. Mebbe he'll try an' take me away. Same if I act shy-like. Mags decided that a bold approach was in order, glared at the Constable, and stuck his tongue out at him.

"That cheeky little bastard!" the Constable exclaimed, affronted. "Why I—"

Nikolas cuffed Mags, then grabbed his chin and thrust his head up so he was looking directly at Nikolas' face. "You show some respect fer the law, ye little demon-limb!" he said, enunciating carefully.

Mags sneered, then shrugged, and turned his back on the Constable. He sat down on his stool, still with his back to the man, and resumed his horsehair braiding.

"I'm mortal sorry, sir," Nikolas said, putting an edge of a whine into his tone. "Right little bastard's m'sister's son. He's been here afore, only I guess you was never here when he was. Deaf as a post from a fever. Promised her I'd take care of him."

"Well, see to it that you beat some manners into him," the Constable retorted, then Mags noted his footsteps retreating toward the door, and the jangle of the bell over it signaling his departure.

::*Good thinking*.::

::*Didn' want 'im reckonin' I was some kinda slavey ye'd bought, or th' like*,:: Mags replied. ::*Uh . . . meant t'ask ye somethin' . . . ye do know 'bout th' Healers Collegium an' Bear an'*—::

::*And that they plan to try and fix Amily's leg, yes, of course I do*.:: Nikolas sounded amused rather than alarmed. ::*You surely didn't think they'd keep that a secret from me, did you?*::

Nikolas took out the stolen gems from last night and unlocked a panel at the back of the room. There was a box inside, and inside the box were several small linen pouches. He poured each cup of sorted gems into a separate pouch, and shook them. ::*There. Good luck finding one set of stolen gems in a cup of stolen gems just like them.*:: He turned back to Mags. ::*Was there something else?*::

::*Bear's in charge!*:: Mags blurted.

His mentor nodded, slowly. ::*Amily told me last night. You think I won't approve?*::

Mags shrugged. ::*I didn' rightly know. I was gonna ast ye t'gi' 'im a chance. Not like 'e's doin' this wi'out supervision—*::

::*Exactly so.*:: Nikolas clapped him on the shoulder. ::*I trust the Dean, I trust the Healers' Circle, and I trust Bear. I'll let him know that myself, if you'd like.*::

Mags considered that. ::*Might steady 'im, sir.*::

::*Then I will. Now, knowing how you, Bear, and Lena are as thick as birds hatched in the same nest, I assume you've already had a hand in this project?*:: Nikolas handed Mags his horsehair and box of beads, and Mags sat down to work.

::*Aye. 'E's makin' a model uv Amily's leg as 'tis. Then him an' some senior Healers'll study it over, figger out what needs t' be done.*::

::*Slow, steady, and methodical. I approve.*:: Nikolas didn't ask if Mags approved; he already knew Mags did. As terrified as Mags was for Amily—what if this didn't work and she was left worse off than before?—he knew she wanted it more than anything. How could he stand in the way of that? The only "hold" he had over her would be to say, "I can't stand it if you try this. If you care for me at all, you won't do it." And that would be just wrong. She was brave enough to try this, to get the proper use of her leg back. She hated being a burden on people, hated that they would have to alter their plans to suit what she could and could not do. He also knew she worried for her father; she was the daughter of the King's Own Herald, which made her a potential target to be used to control her father. As long as she was fundamentally unable to escape a kidnapper, she represented a serious vulnerability, and it wasn't safe for her to go many places away from the Palace.

This was important to her. He would never stand in her way.

So, like her father, he knew he would worry and fret on the inside and never let his concern show.

::Reckon his fambly'll try an' stop it?:: he hazarded.

::If they find out about it, yes,:: Nikolas said, soberly. ::Mags . . . what do you think Bear needs to do? Not about Amily, about his own situation. I ask you this as a point of strategy, not as his friend.::

::Purt obvious, ain't it? Needs t'stand up to 'em.:: Mags finished the bracelet he was working on and started another.

::More than that. Because that will only alienate them, and in the end, he doesn't want that. What he wants is to be treated as someone with intelligence and valuable skills. To get that sort of treatment, he will have to discover why his father and older brother are treating him in this way. I'll give you a hint. It is not solely because he is the youngest son. After all, he has demonstrated that he can handle great responsibility.::

Mags shook his head. ::Dunno.::

::I don't either, but I do know this. When a person acts

this outrageously about something, it is because there is more going on than is showing on the surface. I think you and Bear need to find out what that something is and address it. In the many leisurely hours of your spare time, that is.::

Mags nearly laughed aloud at that.

::Now there is something that only you and Lena can do,:: Nikolas continued. *::Bear needs to learn how manage being under pressure. He tends to allow it to eat him alive. I think you can show him a better way.::*

::I'm tryin'. I'll put Lena to it. She does th' same; mebbe they'll learn from each other.:: He thought a moment. *::Better. I'll put him t'watchin' her on it. Reckon they concentrate on each other, they ain't gonna be thinkin' so hard 'bout thesselves.::*

The bell over the door rang, and Nikolas was all the Weasel again, Bear's problems, Lena's, even Amily's set aside for the moment.

It was the thief from last night.

"I want m'money," he said, abruptly. "Found out what ye wanted, and I want m'money."

Nikolas showed no signs of producing anything. "Got t'hear it first, don't I?" he said, with a sneer. "I dunno if it's worthy anything."

"But if I tell you afore ye pay me, ye can say it ain't worth nothin' when it is!" the thief protested.

Nikolas shrugged. There was a long, long silence as the man fidgeted on the other side of the barrier. Finally he couldn't bear it any more and blurted, "Feller that had the shiny was poisoned."

That got both their attention. "How d'ye reckon that?" Nikolas asked cautiously.

"I don' reckon it," the thief said. "Healer said so.

Feller's a guide. He was down in some city south, took some horse traders down there from here, that's where he got the shiny. Passed through there, picked up some other fellers t'guide back up here. Healer says he dunno what poison 'twas, on'y that feller was poisoned. Fellers he brung here, they was all kinda furrin. Bet they poisoned 'im."

Mags could smell the booze on his breath all the way from where he was sitting. He couldn't imagine how Nikolas could stand it. Nor could he imagine how Nikolas was remaining sober!

"An' where didja here all this?" Nikolas drawled, skeptically.

"Feller had a reg'lar 'oman at Peg's. Got it from her." The man kept looking furtively over his shoulder, as if he thought he had been followed into the shop.

"This woman gotta name?" Now Nikolas reached into the cash till, which was out of sight and reach from anyone standing at the barred window, and pulled out a few silver coins. He pushed them idly back and forth on the counter—still just out of reach.

"Senla," the thief said, all of his attention centered on the coins. He stared at them avidly.

"Senla at Peg's." Nikolas played with the coins. "Well, I 'spose she got nothin' t'gain from this . . . she ever see these furriners?"

"Nah. He just tol' her 'bout 'em." Mags watched the thief's eyes follow the coins, like a cat watching a fly. The coins made a soft scraping sound across the counter. It was the only sound in the shop aside from their voices.

"Well. That's somethin'. Ain't much but . . ." Nikolas

shoved the coins under the bars, and the thief grabbed them greedily. They made a chinking sound as he shoved then into a pouch that he thrust into his shirt. "You get me somethin' better, you'll get paid better."

The thief didn't reply to this; he skittered out the door as if someone had set him on fire. That was . . . odd. Mags wondered why he was in such a hurry to get out of there.

Nikolas drummed his fingers on the countertop for a moment. *::I'm torn . . . ::* Mags knew exactly what he meant. This was the middle of Weasel's business day. There was no way that Weasel would close the shop now, unless he was dying, or the shop itself was on fire. And maybe not even then. But he wanted to get to this woman now.

::I'll go, :: Mags said instantly. Sure, he was just a youngling. But there had to be plenty of reasons for a youngling down here in this part of Haven to be seeing a woman of that sort. Right now he couldn't think of any, but surely Nikolas could. *::Ye thin' of some reason fer me t'wanter see th' 'oman whilst I git there. Ye know where Peg's is?::*

::I do.:: Nikolas "showed" him the location, not in terms of a map, but the streets he would follow to get there. *::Going by rooftop?::*

Mags grinned at him. Of course he was going by rooftop. On the unlikely chance that someone had followed that thief here, the only person he would have to follow would be the same thief.

Nikolas nodded at a ladder in the corner. *::Hatch at the top.::*

Mags trotted over to the ladder and skittered up it,

feeling quietly gleeful that Nikolas trusted him to go after this woman. There was indeed a hatch at the top, bolted from this side. He pulled it up and dropped it down, poking his head up into the darkness above.

It was an attic. He hauled himself up into it, and in the light coming up from below, he saw the outlines of a roof-door.

::*Find the door?*:: Nikolas asked.

::*Aye. Lemme git 'er open, then ye kin close up from below.*:: The door to the roof opened outward; he checked and saw that it would lock again when he closed it. ::*Aight. I'm good.*::

He heard the ladder creaking, then the hatch closed and the bolt shot home. He was on his own. He levered himself out onto the sloping roof and shut the door quietly. No use alerting anyone to the fact that there was someone crawling about on the roof.

He took his bearings and started out, moving as quickly as he could. He just hoped that when he got there, he'd have figured out an excuse to talk to her. Or Nikolas would have.

Hmm. When he'd been snooping around as the blind beggar, he'd noticed that not all "house" girls stayed in the House to practice their trade. Trusted ones were allowed to visit clients. ::*Maybe Peg'll send 'er girls out, fer a price.*:: he suggested to Nikolas.

::*If the price is right, I am certain she would send her girls out to entertain performing bears,*:: came the cynical reply. Mags snorted. From what he knew, Nikolas was probably right.

::*I c'ld be errand boy, settin' somethin' up then.*:: That would make sense; a man with the means to hire a girl for the evening would also have the means to hire a boy to go out and make the arrangements for him.

This was an excellent part of town for roof-running. The buildings were crammed too close together for anything bigger than a rat to pass between them. Mags could basically scuttle along without anyone seeing him, as long as he didn't make more noise than a large cat. This was all very familiar: the feel of slates and tiles and the occasional thatched roof under his hands and feet, balancing on the slope, basically going on all fours with three points of contact on the roof at all times—

Since these roofs were inspected yearly for chimney issues—a fire in this part of town would be a complete disaster, because it would spread for blocks in no time at all—they were in good repair, even if the interiors left a lot to be desired. There weren't a lot of thatched roofs here; they were more prone to fires. Mags vaguely remembered that house and shop owners were being pressured to get rid of them. A pity, since they were easier to scramble across.

Then again, that was probably a reason that could be used to get them replaced. If he could do it, a thief would find it ridiculously easy.

Nikolas sent him another thought. ::*There's money sewn in the hem of your jerkin. It's enough to get Peg's attention. See if she'll send Senla to the Owl and Firkin. It's close, and I can be there soon enough. The Weasel has gone out to a tavern for food now and again on a slow night.*::

Mags gave his wordless assent. These roofs were absolutely ideal for what he was doing, even the ones that weren't thatched. Although they were steep, they were also broken up by chimney pots and dormers, to make the most use of the attic space. There was more than enough light for him to see his way up here, with a full moon and no clouds. He didn't even have to fight chimney smoke; any cooking was over and done with at this time of night.

He was mortal glad to get out of that stuffy shop and out in the fresh air.

And he took his time. It wasn't more than a few blocks to this house, and there was no real hurry to get there, so he could test each foot- and handhold, making very sure of them before he trusted his weight to roof or handhold. Down below, there were still a few people out and about. This part of Haven actually came to life after dark. Those who lived here worked from dawn to dusk and only had time to get their own business done when the sun went down.

He was literally on the roof of the house next door to Peg's when he heard a commotion below him. There was an altercation going on at the front door—but that wasn't what was interesting. What was interesting was that a few moments after the to-do started, he saw a back door open from the inside. A big, burly man held it open while a woman carrying a pack slipped out. It looked to him as if the altercation was being staged—there was a lot of shouting and some wild swinging of fists going on, but he wasn't sensing anger, and none of the swings were connecting. A distraction to keep anyone from going to see what was happening at the back door?

If it was, then the woman was leaving with the co-operation of at least some of the other inmates of the house.

Acting on a hunch, he followed her. She kept to the

alleys, and from the way she was moving, she was trying very hard to keep from attracting any attention.

If that ain't Senla, I'll eat Dallen's hay.

::*You stay out of my hay!*:: He sensed Dallen peering down through his eyes. ::*I would say you are correct.*::

::*Now why d'ye think she'd be runnin'?*:: he asked.

::*More to the point, why would one of the 'house enforcers' be helping her? The proprietors of such places tend to make sure that the loyalty of their men is firmly with the owner and not the women. After all, if there are going to be any disputes, the owner wants the ones with the muscles enforcing her will, not siding with the hirlings.*:: He sensed Dallen thinking some things over. ::*I'd have to say the owner knew about what just happened. There is no way it could be kept quiet. Not with all the shouting at the front, and the mock-fight.*::

::*Then this Peg person had t' hev ordered 'im t'help 'er git. An' ordered up yon fight, so's t'distract any'un what was watchin'.*:: That seemed the only possible conclusion.

::*Exactly so.*:: Dallen went silent for another moment, probably thinking. ::*Mind, it was probably not altruistic. If the woman was bringing trouble to the house, or even had the potential to bring trouble, it makes sense to be rid of her.*::

And thet might could be why th' thief was a-feared. The guide had definitely been murdered. The thief might think the same people would come after him. Perhaps because he had enquired about the woman?

Reckon th' gel thinks she's in danger, anyroad. Mags made a split-second decision. ::*Kin you git outa there?*::

Dallen clearly found the question amusing. ::*Easily. Rolan tells me our waiting places are deliberately made so we Companions can get out and come assist if we are needed. I see through your eyes where you are, I'll meet you somewhere. Just keep following her, and I'll intercept you at some point.::*

Mags oozed over to the next roof, and crept along the edge, keeping her in sight. She was moving so slowly and so furtively that it wasn't hard, even though the alley was in deep shadow. She was wearing light-colored clothing . . .

Not thinkin' real hard, I reckon.

He was very glad he had decided to try to get her himself; she obviously had no idea of how to get away from potential danger—other than sneak out a back door. And that might not even have been her idea.

She wasn't even looking up. From everything that he had experienced with the foreigners—if, indeed, they were from the same place as the killers who had tried to murder the Companions—they were skilled killers. They could just as easily have been up here on the roofs as he was.

With that alarming thought, *he* took stock of his surroundings, thinning his shields just the slightest bit. The quickest way to find out if there was someone lurking was to see if there were any thought-presences near him that were giving out bits of roof-image.

A moment later he was able to relax that part of his vigilance. No . . . no, there was no one there. All the human presences that he could sense nearby were definitely inside, and most of those were asleep; the only creatures on the roofs were cats and rats.

Dallen interrupted his thoughts. *::I'm almost there. I'm going to stop her at the end of the alley she is in now.*

Drop down behind her. We'll get her between us, so that she can't easily run.::

::Gotcha.:: He worked his way down the side of the building, which was in such a shabby state that there were plenty of finger- and toeholds. It was probably just as well that the inhabitants had so little worth stealing, because a thief who could climb would have no trouble breaking in. He clung to the side of the building and waited for Dallan's signal.

He never had been able to figure out how they did it, but when they wanted to, Companions could move like ghosts on the wind. One minute the end of the alley was clear. The next, it was full of a large, white beast.

The woman stopped dead in her tracks, her posture showing shock and uncertainty. She started to turn—

And Mags dropped down behind her, trapping her between himself and Dallen.

Things moved very swiftly then. Her eyes went huge and round, he heard her intake of breath. Without waiting for her to let it out in a scream, he rushed her, ramming her up against Dallen's chest and slapping a hand over her mouth.

She wasn't accustomed to fighting; she went limp, eyes terrified. Her hands were trapped by the bundle she refused to drop. If he actually *had* been there to kill her, it would have been ridiculously easy. She wouldn't even have put up a token fight.

"Whoa-up," he said softly. "I ain't gonna hurt ye. Ye knows whatta Companion is, aye?"

Her head moved under his hand, nodding.

"This here's a Companion. My Companion. Name's Dallen."

Dallen curved his neck around and nudged her with his nose. He did that thing that Companions could do and made himself glow slightly, so she could see him clearly in the dark. Her eyes went bigger. "I'm Trainee Mags," he continued. "We come here t'help ye. I'm agonna take m'hand away. Don' scream, aye? There's on'y th' two on us, an iffen ye got trouble on yer tail, I ain't sure jest the two on us kin keep ye safe." He took his hand away from her mouth. She didn't scream, though she was shaking in every limb. He looked her over as best he could in the shadows of the alley. She wasn't as slatternly as the women who had sold their stolen finery at the shop, but it was fairly clear what her profession was. Under the huge shawls she had wrapped about herself, her tawdry—and scanty—outfit was a clear advertisement for her services.

"Yer Senla, aye?" he asked. Her eyes widened again, and she nodded. "Aight. I know 'bout that guide whut was yer reg'lar, an' whut happen t'him. Here now— don' cry!" he added, with alarm, as her eyes brimmed with tears. "We ain't got time fer cryin'! I'm agonna git ye somewhere safe, so no cryin' till I does!"

He knew that Dallen would have been keeping Rolan apprised of the situation, and Rolan would have been keeping Nikolas up to date. So he simply Mindspoke Nikolas without a second thought. ::Got 'er. What d'I do?::

::Take her to the actor's inn. Keep her in the stable until I get there.::

Well, that was clear enough. And it was a good thing that he and Nikolas had left the Companions under saddle and bridle. He hauled himself up into the saddle, then held out a hand to Senla, pulling her up behind him. She weighed next to nothing. He revised his estimation of her age downward. ::*All right, you. Ghost us outa here. Make damn sure cain't nobuddy see us.*::

He felt Dallen's smirk. ::*As if I couldn't. Hold on.*::

". . . so when they murdered Giels, I knew they were gonna come after me," Senla sobbed, both hands wrapped around a mug of wine she held onto as if she were afraid she was going to drop it. "I told Peg. She told me she'd help me, but I had to leave, I couldn't bring trouble on the House."

Cleaned up, she was an entirely different person. Prettier, in Mags' estimation. He guessed she was about three or four years older than he was—but although in some ways she acted and thought as if she were much more experienced than her age, in others she was rather childlike. Annoyingly childlike. He had never quite realized how much he liked being around girls who thought for themselves instead of passively sitting there and waiting to be told what to do.

"Did you ever see these men?" Nikolas asked her.

She shook her head. "Giels told me that they spoke no language he recognized, and he's guided people all over the south, right down to that city the horse-people go to when they want to sell horses. Katashin'a'in, that's what it's called, I think."

Nikolas and Mags exchanged a look.

"He told me they had a lot of things he thought were poisons," she continued. "They'd put out baits when they thought he wasn't watching, and they'd check to see if the animals that took 'em had died. That was why when he just dropped dead in the street, I knew *they* had done it." She shivered. "I knew they knew about me, and I figured they'd guess Giels had told me about them." She started crying again. "Mistress Peg, she always likes her girls to make a nest egg an' get married, and Giels, he always said that was what we'd do. 'You make a nest egg, an' I'll make a nest egg,' he'd say, 'An' when we got enough that we can have that little tavern, you'll quit, an' I'll quit guidin', an' we'll sell beer, an' you'll wait on the custom, an' we'll have a grand old time of it.' That's what he said, and now—" She burst into tears.

Mags patted her hand, awkwardly. He wished that Giels had told his girl a little more than he had. Right now, given that there was a dead body in a Healer's hands and the Healer couldn't identify the poison used to kill the man, it was reasonable to figure this was the same lot as the ones that had tried to murder Mags and the King earlier this year.

That was really not good. Poison was definitely an assassin's weapon. Everyone around the King would have to be even more careful and alert about what he ate and drank now.

Giels had been commendably close-mouthed if he was trying to protect her. The only things she knew was that they were "foreign" and that there were no fewer than three of them.

"All right," Nikolas sighed. "Haven is not safe for you. We'll have to send you away."

She mopped at her eyes with the handkerchief he gave her. "Where?" she asked timidly.

"I don' know yet," Nikolas admitted. "You'll be safe enough here for a few days. I'll be back later today with someone who'll help you figure out where you can go and what you can do. Until then, don't let anyone in. All right? Open the door only to me. That was why I had food and drink brought up for you. You won't starve in the time I'm gone."

The girl nodded bleakly. Mags felt horribly sorry for her. But what could they do, really? They couldn't bring the guide Giels back. He hoped that there was *something* she could do besides sell herself, but in her rambling story she'd said more than once that she'd joined Mistress Peg's establishment when she'd come up from the country because she'd hated being a servant. So what else was there for her?

He and Nikolas went down to the stables and retrieved Dallen and Rolan, after changing into uniforms in the secret room. "What're we gonna do wi' 'er?" he asked Nikolas on the way back.

"I have no idea, and fortunately, that is not my problem," Nikolas replied, with just a hint of irritation. "Personally, I cannot think of anything she's suited for. I'll be bringing old Lord Kennely down with me after I get some sleep. It's his job to work out problems like this when we have someone whose life is in danger and who is assisting the Crown. He'll figure out what her skills are, find a place for her to go outside of Haven, and see to it she gets there safely. At least she doesn't have a huge family that has to be resettled along with her." He rubbed the back of his neck as he rode. "I tell you, Mags, it's times like this that I am mortally glad that I am *not* the one that has to make these decisions." He sighed. "I don't regret rescuing her. I just wish she'd told us more that is useful."

"Well . . . least we know one thing sure," Mags pointed out. "We know we got more'n the first lot 'ere now."

"Yes. And we know that this second lot is definitely not handicapped by being unable to read their orders." Nikolas' tone was grim. "You and I are going to have our work cut out for us now."

7

"**W**here's Lena?" Mags asked Bear as the latter sat down next to him with a tired thud. Mags passed him the bowl of butter and the loaf of bread without being asked. Across the table, Pip passed over a bowl of pickles, and Gennie stood up to snag a plate of cheese before it vanished down to the other end. Bear made himself a little ploughman's lunch and tucked in. "Driving herself to silliness in this heat," he said, in between bites. "Seriously. When she isn't in class, she's either playing or writing. And when I manage to drag her out, all she can talk about is Marchand's pet and sit there and fret because she wants to hate him and can't. Turns out the feller is all right, dead serious, dead grateful to Marchand for finding him. His family don't have two pins, they're from some stony spot on the Border, and he'd been learnin' on any sort of instrument that anyone would let him borrow. Now, coming up to Bardic, that means his family gets that family-stipend, which I guess is more money than they've ever seen, and he gets, well, Bardic." Bear finished what was on his plate and reached for the bowl of baby carrots—a rare treat, since you only got them when the young carrots were thinned out to allow the biggest to grow. "Off stage he's shy. Shy! Unbelievable." Bear shook his head. "So of course she can't hate him, so all she can do is try and figure out how to make Marchand take notice of her instead of the pet. I keep trying to tell her that she's wearing herself out for nothing, but she doesn't listen."

Well, that put an interesting complexion on things. Mags felt his thoughts disengage from the problem of *find the foreigners* to concentrate on Lena. And he snagged a few baby carrots to munch on himself while he thought.

No use in my tellin' 'er nothin', he thought. *She b'lieves me when I'm with 'er an' then fergets ev'thin' I tol' 'er when I'm agone.*

::*Exactly so,*:: Dallen replied. ::*Erm—not exactly. She would listen to you, as you said, but doubts always set it as soon as she is alone. But remember what you are trying to do about her and Bear.*::

::*Right.*:: So, what he should do is put in Bear's mind the direction things should take, and let *Bear* do the telling, and comforting, and so on. "Ye haven' been all that *around* yersel'," he told Bear, with just the tiniest bit of reproach in his voice. "Ye ken? So wha's she gonna do, wi' me runnin' about after Nikolas, an' *you* off doin', too. She gots nobody she talks to but us."

"Yes, but—" Bear faltered. "Damn it, why do you have to be right all the time? And the only time I can get her out of class is—"

"When I'm agone, aye." He nodded. "Nay, look, Bear, ye kin afford t'take a liddle time off Amily. Ye gots th' Herald what draws stuff she sees i' other peoples' heads, aye?"

Bear nodded and crunched a carrot. "She said she'd do it when I asked her this morning. Just have to get her an' Amily an' the right Healer together. Dean's finding me the Healer, an' Dean's gonna set it up. She says the best way is for her to make a bunch of drawings, then we use those to rough-saw the cow bones in the right places, then we all get back together again with her and the Healer and Amily and we make adjustments on the cow bones and pin 'em together exactly the right way. Then—I dunno, we're gonna have to figure out how t' do something more permanent than cement pins—we're gonna have a bunch of Healers handling the bones and turning them and studying them. I just can't figure out how to make 'em stand up to that much abuse."

"So who'd know how t'do stuff like stickin' bones t'gether?" Mags asked patiently. It was beginning to dawn on him what his job was in all of this. It wasn't necessarily to find answers. His job was to ask the right questions. Then even if neither he nor Bear nor Lena knew the answers, at least knowing the question would mean that they had a direction to go to find someone who did know the answers.

"Who sticks things together? 'Twouldn't be a Healer, the bones would have to be living. I dunno . . ." Bear ran his hand through his hair, making it stand on end.

Gennie noticed and smacked his hand lightly. "Quit that, you look like a hammerbird. Stick what together now?"

"Bones—bone pieces, I mean," Bear said, and explained. Now, anything that Gennie was interested in was bound to get the interest of the rest of the team, and they all leaned over to hear what Bear was up to. They were all gratifyingly encouraging in their enthusiasm, and not one of them expressed any thought that Bear wasn't up to the job; Bear began to brighten visibly.

And all of them began tossing ideas back and forth about how the bone-model could be made, until people at other tables started to notice. Ideas were tossed out and discarded. Glue obviously wasn't going to hold past rough examination. You couldn't nail the pieces together, the bone would split, and screws had the same problem. Pins by themselves were too unstable—

Finally one of the oldest people listening spoke up—not a teacher, but one of the servers. "Why does't have to be one thing?" he asked.

They all stopped talking and looked at him. He flushed, obviously unused to that much attention. "Oh—don't mind me—" he stammered.

"No, no, go on," Bear said, encouragingly. "Please. What did you mean by that?"

"Well . . . look, my ma is a seamstress for real special stuff for the Guard. Say she's got something that has got to hold up. Life or death. Uh—like the seams on the carry-bags they use to get sick or hurt people down off mountains, where you can't even get a stretcher. Well, she don't use just one thing to put that seam together. First, she sews it loose, so she can adjust curves and all. Then she sews three seams close together. Then she sews something to protect the seam on the outside. Then she glues the seam, then glues a layer of leather down, then she gets a saddler to stitch the leather down. So it's not just one thing . . . the loose stitches would pull out if that were all there was. One line of stitches might break. Three might get cut. The glue might give. The leather might get torn off if it was only glued. The saddle stitches might pop. But with all of that there, even if part of it goes, the rest is gonna hold it together . . ." The man flushed again. "Sorry. I—I shouldn't have—"

"Yes, you should have!" Bear exclaimed. "All right then . . . so, he's right. The pins only have to hold so we can do what?"

At this point there were three tablesworth of Trainees and other students involved in this.

"Well . . ." someone who wasn't in any of the three Collegia, who was up here taking classes so he could learn how to plan things like bridges and buildings, tentatively put his oar in. "What you need after you position the bones is something to hold them in place, temporary, aye? Well . . . look, is there any reason why your model has to be made of bone at all? Can't you just make a model directly?"

Bear frowned a little. "Sort of. I mean, I dunno of anyone who can mold the way the bone is out of clay, if that's what you're asking. The Herald that's making the drawings doesn't make sculptures, she told me so when I asked her to help."

"Right, that clarifies things. I'm Myca, by the way." He stuck out a hand, and Bear shook it. He tapped the server on the arm; the server jumped. "Introduce yourself, man. It's only polite."

"Pawel," the server said, diffidently.

They all nodded a friendly greeting. "Look, sit down—" Bear said, but Pawel shook his head. "I'm on duty, and if I don't work, the cook will have my hide and I might get my wages cut. Thank you, but I really need to get back to work—" He picked up some empty bowls and headed for the hatch to return them to the kitchen.

"Huh." Bear stared after him a moment. "Well, all right. So, Myca, I guess we could use something other than bone once we have the sketches, but there's no way that I know of to make a model that'll be accurate other than by pinning bits of bone together."

"Fair enough. Then Pawel was right. First pin. But then, go ahead and use carpentry glue, but glue the pins in first. Then glue the two surfaces. Then start working on something more permanent. I guess this is going to get a lot of handling, so it is going to have to be sturdy. I'd say to make a carpentry join, a dovetail or something like that, but that would be difficult to get right, and you're only going to waste time if you spoil it and have to start over. So—I'd use metal staples out of soft wire so you can set them in rather than hammering them in."

"Staples?" Bear wasn't the only one that looked puzzled, but this time it was a first-year Bardic student who suddenly popped his head up.

"Like a jeweler!" the boy exclaimed. He scrabbled in his belt pouch for a writing stick and began to sketch on the tabletop. "My cousin's a jeweler. Sometimes you have to join stone or metal together, and you don't dare put heat to it. So this is what you do. You drill a hole. You cement in one end of your wire. You bend that like so, and so, make it flat to the surface, you drill another hole, and you cement the other end of the wire in, make sure it's flat to the surface, and you can even burnish it into place, like inlay—"

Nods all around the table. "Oh, and you know what else I would do, once you have your staples in place all around the bone?" said Pip. "I'd get pliver-suede and fish-skin glue and sinew—"

"Or maybe horsehair, or gut, or harpstring wire—" put in one of the Bardic students.

"Aye, any of those. And I'd glue the pliver down, all the way around the break, then I'd glue the string and wrap the break. Just like fitting an arrowhead to the shaft. That'll hold the staples in place, the staples will hold the bone from shifting and the pins and the glue will keep the pieces from falling apart."

"I think that'll work," Bear said slowly, then grinned. "I think that'll work!"

"Might want to make two, and call on one of those fellows that makes the fancy colored-glass windows." It was Lord Wess, who had popped over from the Palace to have the noon meal with the team as he often did. "He might be able to do something with that copper foil and lead they use. Try that on the second model instead of the glue and leather and sinew."

"No reason why not," Bear agreed. "Then, if we can get one that'll hold through being used to make a mold from, we can make as many plaster copies as we like!" He looked around at the small mob that had gathered. "You're terrific!" he burst out, beaming like the sun. "You're all terrific!"

Mags smiled quietly to himself. *'Tis all askin' th' right*

questions. Then makin' sure when ye ask 'em, there's plenty of people about.

::*These are people used to thinking, Mags. You need people who are used to thinking. Otherwise you might as well go down to the kennel and ask the dogs, you'll get about as much help.*::

::*Eh, I 'spose thet's true.*:: Only partly true though. He reckoned you could get about anybody to think if you just coaxed at them long enough.

He finished his lunch quietly as the chattering died down. Someone brought some paper so the one lad could copy his rough drawings of stapling onto something more portable than the top of the table, and Bear could put everything else into coherent notes, and things generally got back to normal. "So," he said, once Bear had tucked his precious notes into one of his books. "Now, 'bout Lena."

Bear sighed and shook his head. "What about her? Mags, I—I don't know what to tell her, really. And she cries, and I feel like breaking something because I don't have anything good to say, or anything at all really, and—"

Bollocks. Ev'body knows how they feels 'bout each other but them.

"Whoa-up," Mags stopped him. "Goin' at this all wrong, like. Ye oughter ask yersel'—what the hell is goin' on here? This's Marchand we're lookin' at. If th' attention ain't on 'im, 'e finds th' center of attention an' sits on't. If there's a more self-centered feller i' th' whole damn Kingdom, I never heerd of 'im. So now 'e goes and picks up this raggedy tad-bit what's got a lot of what makes a Bard an' brings 'im 'ere, an' why? Goodness uv 'is heart?"

Bear stared at him. "Put that way—"

"There's somethin' in't fer Marchand," Mags said firmly. "I know it. I jest don' know what 'tis. All I know is, gotta be somethin' 'e can't git from Lena, so—" he made a dust-off motion with his hands. "'E knows 'ow she feels. Ain't like 'e's gonna lose 'er no matter 'ow 'e treats 'er. So 'e gits whut 'e wants from this pet, an' then Lena gets a crumb or so when 'e reckons 'e wants somethin' from 'er."

Bear looked at him in mingled admiration and despair. "You're right. That feels right, it matches the man perfectly. But I can't tell Lena that!"

Mags tilted his head to the side. "So? I thin' I know what yer thinkin'. Sure, tell 'er, she likely won't b'lieve it. So what'll make 'er believe?"

"I don't know," Bear said slowly. "But I can think about it."

"Good." Mags smiled. "An' i' th'meantime, 'stead uv tryin' t' think uv some daft thing t'say, which you ain't good at, ye know, jest tell 'er—no, show 'er, thet she's as good a Bard as anybody else up 'ere, an' then get all stern wi' 'er and tell 'er that it ain't 'er pa she needs t'please, it's 'er teachers. 'Er pa ain't gonna grade 'er—they wouldn' let 'im, even if 'e'd teach, which 'e's too bone-lazy t'do."

"Amen to that," Bear sighed, then managed one of his old grins. "All right then, I'll take all this to the Dean. He's made it clear that once I find solutions to things, he'll see to it that they're implemented. He told me he wasn't going to give me an excuse to skip class and go larking about Palace, Collegia, and Haven."

"As if ye would!" Mags laughed.

Bear reddened a little. "Well . . ." he admitted. "Maybe a little . . ."

Mags smacked him in the shoulder and left him to finish his meal. He headed for the kitchen. If Lena hadn't eaten, and he was pretty sure she hadn't, bringing her a basket was a good excuse to work his wiles on her.

────────────

Mags did not go to Lena's room himself; for a start, that would have been improper, and for another, he wanted a little bit of backing before he tackled his friend. So, counting on the fact that she encouraged people to come to her, he presented himself with not one, but two baskets of nuncheon at the door of the office of Master Bard Lita Darvalis, Dean of Bardic Collegium and head of the Bardic Circle. The door, as he had been told was usual, was open. The Dean liked her students and teachers to know that she would ever shut them out or refuse to see *anyone*, regardless of rank and status. Lita was oblivious to the quiet cacophony of her Collegium—people practicing anything and everything in their rooms, in the practice rooms, with their teachers, alone or in groups, voices lecturing in classes, people just talking. A lot. Bards seemed to do that.

The very air of Bardic hummed. He had the slightly confused impression that if all the people were suddenly snatched away, Bardic Collegium would still murmur quietly to itself, like a bell that hums on and on after it has been struck.

He tapped politely on the doorpost, and the Dean looked up. Her brows creased. "Mags?" she said. "What brings you here? Shouldn't you be—"

"Got a candlemark," he assured her. "I brung ye nuncheon, Dean Lita." He held up a basket with a sprig of rosemary tucked under the lid. "Cook put in whut was on offer 'e knowed was yer favorites."

"Knew," she corrected automatically. "And *brought*. Thank you Mags . . . now what's your *real* reason for being here?"

Lita did not look all that imposing sitting behind her cluttered desk, with an open window framing tree branches behind her. She just looked like an ordinary middle-aged woman, handsome rather than beautiful, dark-eyed, with dark, graying hair. Her Bardic Scarlet outfit was no uniform—unlike the Heralds and Healers, the only thing "uniform" about what Bards wore was the color—and it was not particularly fancy. She generally favored a split skirt, a belted tunic and shirt tailored like those that the Heralds wore, and at the moment, both were made of very lightweight, breezy material, so she looked just a bit gypsylike. There were ink stains on her writing hand, and the only sign that she was the Head of the Bardic Circle was the Seal of her office in the form of a ring on that hand.

But Mags had seen her perform, and he knew that the moment she put her hand to the strings of one of her favored instruments, you would forget everything about her, and be caught up completely in whatever story she was telling you. Afterward, if someone were to ask you what she looked like, you would probably use words like "goddess," and "regal" and "queenly."

Mags chuckled, not taking offense in the least, and put the Dean's basket on the least cluttered corner of her desk. "Lena," he said, simply.

The Dean rolled her eyes. "That girl . . . how Marchand threw such a child, I will never know. He lives to please himself, she lives to please everyone but. On the other hand, I could wish all my students gave me the sorts of problems she does. I tell you, it is far from comfortable presiding over a Collegium where by rights we should count double enrollment."

Mags had been about to say something about Lena, but the comment caught him off guard. "Ah, what, ma'am? Double enrollment?"

"My Trainees and their egos," she said, making a face. "All right, what can I do to help you?"

"Twa thin's," he said. "Fust one, git some'un t'drag 'er outa 'er room so's I kin feed 'er and talk to 'er."

Lena nodded. "And?"

"Second one, I dunno whut 'tis, but ye gotta hev some way uv showin' 'er ye figger she's as good nor better'n Marchand's new pet," he pointed out. "Ye know Lena. Ye know thet boy is gonna make 'er feel like 'er pa's wrote 'er off as a failure. Tellin' 'er ain't gonna talk to 'er gut. Ye gotta show 'er."

"Oh, bother," the Dean said, torn between exasperation and amusement. "You would say something like that. I'm a Bard, young man, we're all about words, not deeds."

He dared to raise an eyebrow at her.

She raised one right back at him, trading him look for look.

"I can keep this up all day, you know," she said conversationally. "I am the past mistress of the admonishing brow. You cannot hope to beat me. Besides, I agree with you. But I am *not* going to coax and cosset her. That was all very well when she first came here and was terrified, lonely, and shy. She's older now, and I am not going to allow her to fall into the trap of being weak and bleating like a little lost lamb because she wants attention. It's not attractive, it's not appropriate, and it's not Bardic."

"Yes'm," he said obediently, resuming his normal expression.

"Unnatural child," she complained. "You have the looks of someone barely old enough to be admitted and the mind of an old man. A conniving, calculating, scheming, plotting old man."

"Yes'm," he admitted. "Schemin' kept me breathin' i' the' mine."

She made a wry face. "I imagine it did. All right, I'll tuck your second demand in the back of my poor overworked, enfeebled brain and let it simmer. Perchance the Goddess or the Angel of Music will take pity on me and stick an answer in there for me, before my mind melts of the heat. And I'll summon a Lena-extractor now—no, wait. I'll get her myself. I haven't been out of this chair in candlemarks. You wait here."

Suiting actions to words, the Dean got up and left him standing there, basket handle in his hands. The

Dean's office was on the same floor and corridor as the rooms for the female Bardic Trainees—for reasons that would have been obvious to anyone with the least knowledge of restless young men and women, all of them very far away from the parental eye. In no time at all, she was back, with Lena in tow.

He was relieved to see that Lena didn't look *too* bad. She'd been getting some sleep, since her eyes weren't red or dark-circled. She did have that slightly distracted air she usually had when she'd been working too hard, though.

"There, now. You see? Even the wretched Cook is worried enough about you missing meals he sent one of your friends over with a basket. You should be ashamed of yourself, Lena," the Dean scolded, gesturing at Mags as they came in. "What is the very first thing we tell you youngsters when you get here? Hmm?"

"Your body *is* your instrument," she said without thinking.

"And what would I do if you neglected your instrument, let it get shamefully out of tune, didn't keep the wood oiled and polished, allowed the strings to break?" the Dean asked sharply, with a fearsome frown on her face.

Mags stilled his feelings of alarm. The Dean was acting as she had said she would, and he couldn't fault her. She had been teaching Bardic Students for a very long time indeed. He had to believe she knew how to handle someone like Lena.

He waited for Dallen to say something, but Dallen

remained silent. So . . . he hazarded that this meant Dallen agreed with the Bard.

"Take it away from me until I deserved it again," Lena whispered, her head hanging.

"Well, I can't exactly take your body, can I?" The Dean sniffed. "But I *can* take you out of that room and tell you that if you don't stop driving yourself into the ground, I am going to suspend you from *all* classes and assign you to the stables for a moon. No music. Plain ordinary labor. Nothing that would harm your hands, of course, but other than that, subject to the orders of the Stablemaster."

Lena looked up sharply, her mouth agape with shock. "You'd—what?" A faint flush of outrage passed over her pretty face. Mags felt encouraged to see it. The Bard might be right. It might be that what Lena needed to make her stronger was a bit of opposition, not support.

The Dean crossed her arms over her chest. "I am responsible for you, for your health, for your well-being. If you refuse to take care of yourself, I will give you no choice in the matter. A month of good healthy work carrying water and feed and shoveling manure should undo all the nasty things you've been doing to yourself. When you see your meals, you'll devour them because work made you hungry. And you'll be so tired at the end of the day that you'll fall asleep whether you want to or not. It's not as if you have anything to fear in your studies; you're so far ahead now that you'll probably get your Scarlets a year early, if not sooner than that." The Dean shifted her weight to one foot and raised an eyebrow so eloquently that Mags was ashamed of his own effort earlier. "So. What is it going to be? Start acting like a perfectly normal girl, study and create, yes, but also eat and play and sleep? Or am I going to have to put you to stable duty?"

Lena stared at her, eyes wide and shocked, and finally remembered to close her mouth. But what had startled her was not the parts about stable duty. "Get—get my Scarlets—a year early?" she stammered.

The Dean threw up her hands. "What, am I speaking Karsite now? Didn't I just say that? Haven't your teachers been implying as much? Yes. Or sooner than that. *You don't have to worry about falling behind.* You're making the rest feel rather badly, actually, which is scarcely fair. That poor little brat Marchand brought in is terrified of living up to your standard. He's sure that if he dares say a word to you, you'll somehow magically and instantly see him for a fraud and have him thrown out."

"I—what?" Lena's jaw dropped again.

"I must be speaking Karsite," the Dean muttered, loudly enough that both of them could hear her quite clearly. "No one understands a word I say today. Lena, there is only one thing in which you are not so very far ahead of your yearmates that they would resent you if you were not a pleasant and friendly person. You need to work on performing in front of large audiences alone. And to be absolutely honest, I've put people into Scarlets that *never* mastered that. There are plenty of Bards out there who won't play for more than a dozen people at a time."

"There are?" Lena said, dazed.

"There are—however, do not take that as permission

to slack. I want to see you trying, and trying hard, to overcome your stage fright. And since you are so far ahead, believe me, much more will be required of you than your yearmates. But for now, I want to see you learning how to be a person. You can't create if you don't have experience." She none-too-gently turned both Mags and Lena around and shoved them at the door. "You. Two," she said, enunciating with exquisite precision. "Out. Eat. Play. Do not come back before your next class. Or I shall visit great wrath upon you."

Lena still seemed stunned, so Mags grabbed her elbow and towed her out of the office.

From there it was a short trip down the stairs and out the door. The coolest place he could think of to have their impromptu picnic was a kind of cave-grotto down by the river. Most of the time it was entirely too damp to be pleasant, but he was pretty certain it would be nice today. And he didn't particularly care if someone else was there, either.

Which was just as well, because there was: a couple of young highborn fellows from the Palace, one in brown linen with all the edges piped in red, and one in a dull green of much better quality than the first. They were engaged in a spirited game of hares-and-hounds, laid out on one of the little stone tables this place held. They looked up when the two Trainees came in, waved in a lazy fashion, pointed at the other side of the grotto, and went back to their game.

The cool in here was a fabulous relief from the heat outside. There was just a bit of a damp smell, but with an overtone of green that made Mags think it came up from the river. Moss thickly carpeted the floor, the artifical "cave wall" of the grotto was cold to the touch, as were the stone benches on either side of the three little stone tables. Mags set the basket down and took a seat as Lena did the same.

By this point Lena was mostly over her shock. *She won't b'lieve it, a-course, not e'en when 'twas th' Dean hersel' what tol' 'er she was thet good. Not once she starts t'thinkin' bout it.* Which would be where Bear would come in. Once Bear started showing her what the Dean had just *told* her, Lena just might, slowly, start to accept that it was nothing about *her* that made her father treat her like something he'd scraped off his boot. No, it was all about Bard Marchand and what Bard Marchand wanted.

I gotta figger out whut 'e's getting from thet boy . . .

Mags unpacked the basket. There was a *lot* of food. More than two people could eat, and only one of them was going to actually be eating. There was so much that it caught the attention of the two fellows at the portable game board. They looked, and looked away, looked, and looked away, and finally one of them caught Lena's eye.

"I suppose you're going to eat all that?" that one finally said, wistfully. "Erm . . . we got up too late for luncheon, and the Palace Cook told us to 'take your lazy carcasses out of my kitchen, dammit.'"

Mags was amused at that. They could, of course, go down into Haven and have whatever they wanted at any inn in the city. Or they could go visit the stately manor of some friend, who would have father, mother, or housekeeper order them up something. Clearly, however, they were disinclined to move very far in this heat.

Prolly figgered on waitin' till Cook fergot 'bout 'em, then gettin' a page t'fetch summat fer 'em.

That startled Lena into speech. "Oh, no!" she laughed breathlessly. "Please, come help yourselves."

With glee, they did, coming over, and when Mags assured them that it was all right, that he had already eaten, taking everything that the two Trainees pressed on them. They were very polite about it and thanked them both profusely before returning to their game with their booty.

"Lissen," Mags said, when the young men were immersed in the game again, munching on the food in one hand while they moved counters with the other. "I didn' come over t' git ye in trouble wi' yon Dean. I come over t'git yer help wi' Bear."

Immediately her brows knitted with concern, her own woes set aside for the moment. "Is it the whole business of fixing Amily's leg?" she asked, and then answered herself before he could say anything. "Of course it is. He has to be worried sick about it. He's in charge, which is an awfully big trust and an awfully big responsibility. It's bad enough that it's a fearfully dangerous thing to do, but Amily is our *friend*. That just makes it all worse."

Mags nodded. "Now look. Reckon them what's in charge got a pretty good hold'uv this. *I* think, akchully, thet th' reason they put Bear i' charge 'ere, is on account 'f a coupla thin's. They wanta gi' 'im th' chance t' *show* 'is pa 'e's got th' stuff. They wanta put 'im inna place where 'e ak'chully sees fer 'isself thet 'e's got th' stuff. Aye? Gi' 'im whatchacall—self-confidence. I don' think they knowed 'ow much 'e's like t'fret hisself t'pieces on account'a 'e cain't think'v answers. Eh? Then 'e cain't think'v answers on account'a 'e's frettin' hisself t'pieces. Jest goes roun' an' roun'. I kin 'ep 'im some, an hev, but the frettin' part, I cain't do nothin' 'bout thet. So. Thet's where *ye* come in."

She nodded, slowly. "I can see that. I need to make sure he eats, because—" her eyes flickered to the strangers for a blink. "—he'll take it better from me than from you."

Good girl, Lena! "Aye. 'E'll say I'm bein' a nanny an' 'e' don' need one." He grinned at her. "'E's said as much already."

"And I need to make sure he sees some sun and thinks about something other than Amily." She smiled. "And, of course, when he starts complaining about his family, I listen and let him run on and then tell him that they are idiots and don't deserve him. Which they are, and they don't. so it won't even be a little lie."

"Teach him hare-and-hounds," said one of the young men at the game board, unexpectedly, turning and looking at Lena. "Or if he already knows it, play it with him. I know they teach you Bards the game straight off—I've lost plenty of pocket money to you Trainees. It's a good excuse to come down here in the cool. If we're here, we can even trade off partners. If you don't mind that, that is?" He looked up and flushed a little, as if realizing he had been just a bit rude for eavesdropping, and even more for butting in on the conversation.

But Lena beamed at him. "That would be a lovely idea—Lord—?"

"Charliss," said the speaker, with a foolish grin. He

was a very affable looking fellow, with blond hair that flopped a bit into his deepset blue eyes and a generous mouth that looked as if he smiled a lot.

"Moron," said his friend, who was a thinner, slightly harder version of the first young man, aiming a cuff at him. "Lord Pig With No Manners." Now he turned toward the two of them. "And after you were so nice as to feed us too. I'm Grig. No Lordishness attached. I'm the poor-and-pitied cleverer cousin, assigned to make sure Char keeps from putting his foot in his mouth too often." He sighed and shook his head. "As you can see, it is a never-ending and utterly thankless task. And yet, I endure."

"Grig, Lord Charliss." Lena somehow managed to give an impression of a curtsy while still sitting. "I'm Trainee Lena, this is Trainee Mags."

The two young men started, their eyes popping, taking Mags completely aback. "*The* Trainee Mags?" gasped Charliss. "The Kirball player? For South team? The one with the Companion that runs like a cat with twelve paws?"

::*A cat with . . . twelve paws? That's an ungainly image,*:: Dallen snorted.

"Erm—aye?" he said.

The two young men exchanged a gleeful glance. "Benter is never going to believe us," said Grig, grinning as if he was never going to stop.

"Oh, he'll believe us. He'll just never *forgive* us," replied Charliss, with the air of someone who had just taken all his opposing player's hounds in one go. "So, Trainee Mags . . . just what strategy would you recommend to get on a Kirball team?"

So thet's where th' wind blows! "We-ell," he said, with a glance at Lena to make sure it was all right with *her* to start this particular conversation—because, after all, he had come here with her, not them. "T'start with . . . ye gotter git th' right horses . . ."

8

::*When I proposed this business, I thought you would be sitting here in the shop with me, not climbing about rooftops all night,*:: Nikolas said, ruefully. ::*Mostly, I thought you would be watching me work these people, and watching out for my back. And you have done that. But I never imagined I'd be putting you out there on your own.*:: He was not happy with this, but . . . and this had given Mags such a thrill that he almost forgot how dangerous this was going to be . . . he had not argued at all.

::*Somebody gots t'be i' shop, buyin' what-all,*:: Mags replied briefly, with a glance down at Nikolas' worried face, as he pushed open the hatch in the ceiling. ::*Somebody gots ter foller th' lads as sells ye th' words. Nobody'd b'lieve ye'd leave me i' charge'v shop, even if'n I weren't s'posed t'be deaf, so reckon I gotter foller.*::

Nikolas was going to start second-guessing himself in a moment, if Mags didn't say something to lighten the mood. He climbed up into the attic space and dropped the hatch back in place. ::*Asides, yer too big t'climb 'bout like yon roof-rat.*:: The "word" he used was "big," but the mental shading that came with it was unmistakably "fat."

::*Oy!*:: Nikolas replied, with mock outrage. ::*I'm not that big!*::

::*An' yer jest not limber 'nough, either. Reckon yer bones git creaky. Cain't hev ye breakin' yon tiles an' fallin' through some'un's ceiling,*:: Mags continued, mockingly. ::*That'd land ye in gaol fer certain-sure, they'd figger ye fer a thief. An' then whut?*::

::*And would you dare take me and Rolan in a challenge race, you unwashed brat?*:: came the "growled" reply.

::*Nossir,*:: he said promptly. ::*Wouldn' dare, sir.*::

::*Because you know we'd beat you like a hand-drum,*:: Nikolas told him.

::*Nossir. Cannot lie, sir. 'Tis cause yer not on'y big, yer me elder. Wouldn' be fittin', t' challenge a gran'ther, sir.*::

Not only "fat," but "old."

He suppressed his giggles at Nikolas' reaction of outrage. He wasn't just goading Nikolas for the sake of it. The King's Own was seriously worried about him, and if he had to do his part of this evening's work with an undivided mind, he had to shake off his concern for Mags. It was true, he *did* have a dangerous job. He was going to lie in wait above the door until a couple of men who said they had information to sell about the foreign spies arrived, sold their information, and left. Then Mags was going to follow them. It wasn't the full moon now, it was the dark of the moon. And he wasn't merely making his way across the rooftops to get from one place to another, he was going to have to follow someone, which meant keep up with people walking on the flat, open street, and it wasn't going to be people as oblivious as Selna.

Wunner whut happened t' Selna . . .

Further talking with her had uncovered the rather disconcerting information that she'd gone into the "profession" with Mistress Peg because she'd come up from the country to be a serving maid and hadn't liked all the hard work. Now, Mags knew that not all households were like that of Master Soren, where the servants were treated fairly, and if she'd been treated as a slavey, well, he could sympathize. But she'd come up from the country in the first place because she'd been under the delusion that being a maid in the city meant huge wages (compared to the country) and a life of ease . . . after all, there could be dozens of servants in a household, and with that many hands, she had told herself that no single one would have to work very hard.

Guess't musta come pretty shockin' when she was put i' scullery, he thought ruefully, arranging himself in the shadows above the door and watching for movement up and down the street. He himself had firsthand experience of what working as a scullery drudge was like. And just because there were dozens of servants in a household, it didn't follow that this was going to make for leisure. Not when the master and mistress would entertain thirty or forty guests at a time, when they constantly had houseguests, and when the houses themselves were so big. Only when the highborn and wealthy were away from their town manors, off in the country on their estates, did things slow down, and the skeleton staff left behind could expect some of that leisure.

Well, he just hoped that the poor old fellow in charge

of such things managed to find her someplace where she would be content. He rather dreaded to think that it might be another establishment like Mistress Peg's.

But he didn't have any time to think about it now, not when the two men he had been told to watch for had just come around the corner. One of them was holding something.

He went very still. ::*They're 'ere,*:: he warned Nikolas.

He did not like the way they moved; they were aware of everything around them and prepared to attack at the first sign of trouble. But at the same time, they held themselves with an unconscious arrogance, as if the assumption that they would prevail in any fight was something so ingrained in them that it was unconscious. Their walk said all of that. It was . . . it was the walk of a predator. It was the way the man who had nearly slaughtered a stableful of Companions had walked.

That alarmed him. If they even suspected that Nikolas was not what he seemed—the previous lot had proved they would kill without thinking twice about it. Quickly he passed that information on to Nikolas. ::*Amily'd never f'rgive me if—*::

::*And she would equally never forgive me if anything happened to you,*:: Nikolas replied somberly. ::*I have a knife on me and I've bolted the door. There's a shutter I can slam down over the pay-window if I need to, and that will give me time to come up the hatch and join you.*::

The men had reached the shop. Mags froze, not even breathing. Unlike Selna, they were making a quick scan of *everywhere*, including up, before either of them even touched the door. Mags knew he was in full shadow. He knew that at most, only the top of his head showed from where he was crouched. But he felt a cold chill spread over him as their gaze raked the roof, and he didn't relax at all when they finally opened the door and entered the shop.

Assuming all went well in there . . . he was going to have to be very, very careful when they came out.

Carefully, he opened his awareness some. Not like dropping shields at all, but enough to see if he could just read something on their surface.

He couldn't, not like he could with ordinary folk. There was something in the way, and he pulled back. This was *not* the point at which to make them wary, because men like these two reacted swiftly and decisively when something made them wary.

At least he had not felt that bewildering kinship with either of these men, the way he had with the rage-filled assassin. Nor did there seem to be any inexplicable link with them. He still had no idea what could have caused such a link. It had almost been as if—

—no, that was utterly ridiculous. And he had better not let his thoughts wander, not now, not at this juncture.

He didn't move, not a muscle, as he concentrated on sensing what he could, passively, without letting his shields down too far, and without impinging on Nikolas. The last thing the King's Own needed right now was to get his metaphorical "elbow" jiggled.

Well . . . they were talking. Small things leaked past those shields-that-were-not-shields. There was no sense of animosity . . . a bit of contempt for the lowly creature who was purchasing their information. Information . . . they wanted to be known? They were *planting* this information?

He couldn't shake that impression. Whatever it was these men were here for, they *wanted* what they were selling to be generally known. Generally? No . . . no they wanted it to be known to the people who were interested in it. Now, since "it" was the whereabouts of the foreign assassins, it followed that they wanted the people who were trying to track them down—the Heralds, the Guards—to know this deceptive information. Of course. They were trying to throw the Heralds and Guards off the trail. That, at least, made sense.

Now they were amused, as Nikolas reacted to a bit of intimidation with fear he tried to cover with bluster. The bargaining concluded quickly after that. They pushed something through under the bars. Nikolas pushed a great deal of silver back, and he added the Shin'a'in brooch that had told them nothing on top.

They didn't react to the brooch. They gathered it up and left. The emerged into the street, examined the entire area for anyone who might be following, and turned and walked away, going in the opposite direction from which they had come.

Mags watched them. He was going to keep as far back from them as he could.

::What'd they say?:: he asked Nikolas, as the two strode off, positioning themselves in such a way as to cover each others' blind spots.

::That the spies left Haven,:: came the reluctant reply. ::They say they arranged passage with a traders' caravan going into the East, into Hardorn. They said that the foreigners *had paid them with almost everything they had, and they sold me another one of those poetry books and a few odds and ends.*:: Nikolas hesitated. ::*It's a very plausible story. Why don't I believe them?*::

::*'Cause yer smart.*::

::*Or I have good instincts.*::

::*Wut I think I got from 'em is thet this's tryin' t'throw us offen th' trail. They got that funny shield t'other one had, so I cain't be sure. I got little bits, 'cause whatever thet shield is, I dun want it pickin' up on me. So I cain't be certain-sure.*::

Now Mags left his perch and followed the men. He had the "flavor" of their thoughts, even if he had not probed deeply enough to read anything. With that, unless they worked their way into a crowd, he would be able to find them.

::*Oh, I think you're right. These men were better prepared than the first lot—they speak Valdemaran extremely well, and they're dressed like locals in old clothes—but they can't hide what they are, and they are too well-trained to be local thugs.*::

Mags continued to gather what he could from them, passively. Whatever else these men were, they were not insane—or at least they were not as full of rage as the other assassins had been. Cold, definitely. Calculating. Purposeful. And literally nothing *meant* anything to them, not even each other, except the job. The first two assassins had been the flawed copies of which these two were the perfect originals. Mags didn't want to get too close to their minds, though, because he sensed that they were very much like the second assassin in another aspect. They were not Mindspeakers— but they could be. They were not shielded—but that *something* was protecting them. So long as he hovered passively, that "thing" wouldn't notice him, and he could pick up bits of what they were thinking. Images, feelings, mostly. Unlike the first and second assassins, they did not hate Valdemar. Nor did they like it. They were entirely indifferent to the place. For them, it was just another place that held a job, and it was always the job, not the surroundings, that mattered.

He followed on the roofs; he wished he could have gone down to the ground, but he didn't dare. These men were too good. They just might spot him.

There was a definite purpose in them, not just whatever the long-term job they had come for. They had an immediate task, one that had to be performed very, very soon. He balanced on a rooftree and scuttled down the slates while his mind oozed around them like a weasel circling something very dangerous, but asleep. The task was to take care of something unfinished. There was contempt. Contempt for the task? No. He crossed between two roofs as he followed that faint wisp of contempt. Not contempt for the task. Contempt for . . . for . . .

There was a flash of an image, but because he had seen this man with his own eyes, and more than once, he knew it immediately. The supposed "head" of the phony "trading envoys!"

The contempt came strongly with the image. Contempt for him—contempt, presumably, for the rest of the men who had been with him. Disgust . . . .

Mags negotiated a drop to a lower roofline, then scrambled up it to reach a higher one. Disgust. They had . . . they had . . .

Well, he already guessed at that. These men were disgusted with their predecessors because of their performance—or more correctly, lack of performance. They'd failed at the task, the greater task that these two had taken over, and failed at it twice.

Oh, but there was anger as well. Why anger? It was cold and distant. It wasn't for the failed agents. It wasn't for anyone in Valdemar. Someone else. Someone had—no, he couldn't make it out, it was too abstract.

But now they had stopped; he couldn't hear their footsteps on the street ahead, and he felt himself getting nearer to their "presence." He slowed his own pace and slipped up on them at a crawl, careful to remain below the roofline on the opposite side of where they were. When he was as close as he dared get, he hugged the slates, his chin pressed into the roof, and closed his eyes. He let go of everything except the need to listen, with his ears, with his mind. Like a sponge, he soaked up everything around him.

He could hear them talking, but not clearly. He didn't think they were speaking Valdemaran now; the cadence, the accents were wrong.

What were they doing besides talking? Why had they stopped? Did they realize they were being followed?

No.

It was this place, this building that he was on. It wasn't much, one of those narrow two-story houses that was a scant two rooms up, two rooms down, and an attic. There was no one in it. But this was where they had to take care of that . . . unfinished business that

was smaller than the greater task the other assassins
had left undone.

. . . an image of a broken trail.

. . . a little cruel pleasure. The sense that punishment
had been meted out.

One went to the front door and unlocked it. The
other stood guard in the street. The strange not-shield
tightened over both of them, letting nothing out now.

Whatever it was that he went in to do, he was done
quickly. He came out, conferred with the other, and
then, the two—

Burst into a run from a standing start, with absolutely no warning.

They ran like deerhounds; Mags could scarcely believe how fast they were. They ran so quietly that he
actually hadn't realized they were moving at all until
their "presence" shot away.

They were already at the end of the block before he
had gotten to the edge of the roof. He gazed after them
in disbelief and crushing disappointment; he couldn't
hope to catch them or even keep up—already the
mind-traces were fading with distance, and in a moment—

While he tried desperately to keep hold, the faint
traces slipped from him and were gone.

::Nikolas—:: he said with despair.

::I was following,:: came the reply. ::Dallen let me "ride"
his link with you. It can't be helped. See what they were doing in that house, if you can.::

Well, one thing for sure, he was absolutely *not* going
in the front door. If he'd been in the shoes of these men,
he would have left a trap on the door. But they might

not be aware that most of the buildings in this part of town had rooftop hatches; that was what he would look for first.

It was easier to find than he had thought. The owner must have had reason to be up here more frequently than most, for he had installed a real hatch with a solid door, the kind that was in Nikolas' shop, rather than a makeshift thing you had to move tiles to find. It was locked, but only by a sliding bolt; working by feel, Mags got it open and felt around the edges for any sort of triggering mechanism for a possible trap. It was risky, brushing his fingers around the edges like that, but he kept his body out of direct range of anything that might shoot him as best he could.

There was nothing. He gave the frame of the hatch a more thorough examination and still saw nothing.

All right, he was safe so far; holding onto the edge as long as he could, he lowered himself down as far as his arms would reach, then dropped the remaining distance onto the attic floor. There he crouched, listening.

Nothing. The house was absolutely silent. He couldn't even hear any vermin.

. . . light would have been nice.

Then again, he was used to working in the dark.

On hands and knees, he felt his way along the attic floor, searching for the hatch that would lead down into the house itself, using the dim patch of sky and stars where the roof hatch was open as his guide in the search, crawling in an ever-widening circle until his hands encountered something raised off the surface of the floor. A hatch identical to the first, also locked.

He listened with mind and ears, then pressed his ear
to the hatch. Still nothing.

Odd. No rats. No mice. Wunner why?

It *could* be that they were extraordinarily vigilant
about vermin. It could be that they'd actually had a
ratcatcher in recently; once a ratcatcher had gone over
a place with his ferrets, it usually took the surviving
rats and mice a fortnight or two to work up the courage to come back.

He worked the second latch open as he had the first.
This hatch opened downward, and he peered into the
darkness—and this time, he saw a glimmer, a faint
shimmer, of light, at the farther end of the house. He
thought it would be coming the ground floor, at the
back of the house.

He dropped down onto the floor and made his way
toward that faint glow, confident now that the house
was empty. He thought these might be bedrooms; there
were large, bulky objects on the floor, and a musty, bitter smell. It was nothing he could identify. Not exactly
a perfume, but not exactly a *stink*, either. The closest he
could come was some sort of bitter herb.

The light was coming up a staircase at the back of
the house.

Damn. I hate this.

There was no good way to get up or down a staircase when you didn't know what was waiting for you
on the next floor. All he could do was lie down flat on
his belly and scoot himself awkwardly down the stairs
a little at a time, hoping that if there *was* someone there
after all, and his Gift had gone completely unreliable,
he would see them before they saw him.

But he saw the source of the light first.

It was a candle, left burning atop what looked like a heap of clothing and bedding. This was where the smell was coming from. It looked as if the cloth had been drenched in some sort of oil, it was stained and dark, and there was a sort of dull sheen on it.

Once the candle burned down—which would not even take a candlemark—the clothing would catch fire. With all that oil the place would be ablaze in no time. Was this what the assassin had come into the house to set up?

::Probably,:: Nikolas confirmed. *::It's a good way to ensure that you are long gone when the fire starts.::*

And that candle was awfully slim and short—

Mags didn't bother with getting to his feet; tumbling down the stairs was faster. At the bottom he bounced up and ran over to the pile of clothing and snatched the candle out of it.

This looked like the kitchen: fireplace with some pots, the table on which all the clothing had been heaped, some chairs, implements on the counters. He wrinkled his nose; the smell of the oil had covered up the stink of spoiled food. But it was old; he went to look at the pots, and they were half full of mold and spoiled food, all of it dried and cracking.

No one had been here in a while. Why bother to burn it down?

Then he recognized another smell.

He knew that smell . . .

Absolute dread rolled over him, and he shuddered. He remembered that smell from the mines, when Col Pieters and his boys had hidden things they didn't want anyone to ever find, knocked out the supports of the tunnels their secrets had been left in, and buried them in the waste rock that held no gems. But the rock never stopped the rot, and the smell would permeate through the mine and get into everything, and all you could do was tie rags around your mouth and nose and try to breathe through them until time and vermin took care of the problem. And try not to think too hard about what was making the smell, because if you did . . .

He didn't want to go into the next room. He didn't want to see what was there.

He didn't have a choice.

::*Wait—Mags—*:: Nikolas' mind-voice interrupted him.

This room had a door between it and the next; Mags propped the candle in a little wax, pulled off his shirt and jerkin, took the shirt and wrapped it around his face, making sure to cover his mouth and nose, before putting the jerkin back on. Then he tried the door.

::*Am I yer partner, or not?*:: he asked fiercely, telling himself not to be sick.

::*You are. But you don't have to do this.*::

::*I'll haveta do't sometime. Ye knows thet. Fust time might's well be now.*::

He sensed Nikolas' resignation. ::*I'll send the Guard. When they take over from you, get out the same way you got in.*::

The door wasn't locked, but it had been jammed shut. Not caring now about noise, he rammed it repeatedly with his shoulder, hearing something crack every time he did, as if he was breaking some sort of seal. Each time he did it, more of the stench puffed out around the frame. Finally the door gave, and he stumbled into the room.

The candlelight flickered over a scene of grotesque, even macabre, horror.

Even through his shirt the stench was appalling.

The stench of four bloated bodies sprawled across the furniture in bizarre poses of ease, as if they were all relaxing. Their clothing wasn't disarranged, there was no sign of a fight, no sign even that they had been carried in here. They looked exactly as if they had come here together to pass some time before bed.

But they weren't relaxing. They were dead.

Dead, without a mark on them to show how they had died.

The Guardsmen had sent some of their most experienced and hardened men, but even they had been overcome with nausea and had had to leave the building. Several had been violently ill. And the curious thing was—at least in Mags' mind—there was not a man among them, himself included, who would not happily have seen these men hang. At the very least these "victims" had conspired to wipe out a stableful of Companions; they were spies, they had colluded in kidnapping a Healer Trainee and probably would have killed him when he was of no further use to them. But your head could tell you all that a thousand times, but your gut was going to react to the visceral stench in the time-honored fashion, and that was all there was to it.

Someone dispensed mint-soaked scarves to wrap around their faces, and that helped. But after the initial group arrived and set up a line that no one would be allowed to cross, there was a wait for a Special Squad, a wait during which the Guard Captain insisted that no one could touch or move anything.

Finally the Special Squad arrived, laden with bags and implements and lanterns, and the others dispersed to hold the curious outside an established perimeter, their faces reflecting their relief. Mags remained, partly out of curiosity and partly in case any of this new group wanted to ask him anything.

They had stronger stomachs than he did, that was certain. For all that he could tell, the stench didn't bother them at all. They examined the bodies in place, minutely; they confiscated every used dish and pot, then, after (finally!) having the bodies closed up into waterproof bags and transported on a cart somewhere, they allowed all the windows to be opened so that the place could air out. Mags was intensely grateful for the brisk breeze, and felt very sorry for anyone nearby who was downwind of the house.

Two of the Special Squad combed over the room of death like misers searching for a lost gem while the rest accompanied the bodies and the confiscated objects back to wherever they were being taken. One of them actually was picking up small things and carefully bagging them, and when Mags finally gave in to his curiosity and came to see what he was doing, he saw to his surprise that the young Guardsman was picking up dead bugs.

The fellow looked up and saw Mags staring at him in disbelief. "Didn't you notice there weren't any flies?" he pointed out, and held up a dead one.

Mags blinked. "Ye mean, them flies is all dead?"

"As dead as last year's leaves," the fellow replied. "And I will bet that is why there are no mice or rats here, either. It might have been poison in the food, but given all the dead insects, I suspect poison fumes or smoke of some sort."

"Ye kin do thet?" Mags gulped. That was altogether nasty. How could you guard against something like that? "Ye kin poison summun with stuff they breathe in?"

"It's not easy, and it's rather difficult to get people to sit there and breathe the stuff, but, yes, it can be done. Of course, if you drug them first, it's trivial, and judging by their relative positions, they were either drunk or drugged when they died." The Guardsman went back to picking up bugs. "Whatever it was, it would have to work quickly. It might have been a poison in the food or drink, but that wouldn't account for the dead bugs. We can test for most poisons, but not the sort that are inhaled, and the men who did this might have been trying to prevent anyone from finding out that these men were murdered rather than died by accident. I do think, however, that the room was sealed after they were dead, rather than before. Probably to keep the stink from leaking out and betraying whoever did this until they were ready to burn the house down."

"'Ow long've they bin dead?" he asked, a little repulsed, but a little fascinated by someone who would talk so matter-of-factly about grisly corpses.

"More than a day, not more than two." The reply was prompt. "It's been warm, the room was sealed— normally bodies don't bloat until the third day, but the room probably got rather hot during the day, and that would speed things up."

Mags relayed all this to Nikolas.

::Hmm. So it appears that they died before or about the same time as the guide,:: came the reply.

::Reckon so.:: And that begged the question—how long had these new killers been in Haven before they rid themselves of the first lot? And why? *::Ye've been askin' 'bout strangers fer long?::* That was a good place to start.

::The Weasel is an established persona of mine, and he's always bought and sold information,:: Nikolas said thoughtfully. *::But I have only been asking specifically about foreigners for a week.::*

It would have taken a few days for that particular piece of information to get around . . .

The same thought must have occurred to Nikolas. *::Damn. By looking for them, I killed them. I wanted to catch them, not kill them.::*

That puzzled Mags—not that Nikolas was unhappy about these men being killed, but that he blamed himself. *::I'm purt sure ye didn' toss poison i' their fire, sir.::*

::I might just as well have,:: Nikolas replied bleakly. *::If—::*

::I'm purt sure they was gonna get kilt anyway, sir,:: Mags interrupted, as he watched these odd Guardsmen finish combing the room, then spread out to the rest of the house. *::Thet was how them others thet I was follerin' was thinkin' anyroad. Ye fail, ye die, leastwise, if this new lot gits sent t'clean up yer mess.::* He paused. *::Coulda jest been coincidence too. Or they coulda bin killt, an' then these others heard 'bout you lookin', an' figgered t' pass on that th' fust ones'd got away an collect them some money at same time.::*

::Maybe,:: Nikolas replied, then went silent.

Well, Mags had done his best, and if Nikolas was going to brood about this, there wasn't much he could do about it. All things considered, through, if *he* were a ruthless killer who could not only send searchers on the proverbial wild hare hunt *and* make some money at the same time? He'd do just that.

That *might* have been why they decided to burn down the building with the bodies in it rather than just leaving them for someone to find. Having someone find the bodies of four people who were supposedly leaving the country at a brisk pace would certainly alert the authorities that there was someone else in town who not only had provided the misinformation but had probably done the murders in the first place.

These Guardsmen fascinated him, despite their grisly avocation. Obviously they expected to learn something from the things they were collecting, but what? He followed the bug collector up to the second story. The air was much better up here. He didn't even need his mint-soaked scarf.

There were plenty of lanterns up here as well, which gave him a very good look at the two Guardsmen who were left. They looked remarkably alike—not as if they were from the same family, exactly, but as if they had been picked precisely to be unmemorable. They both had hair and eyes of the same neutral brownish, faces that were neither round nor square, short nor long, both were of middling height and weight, neither had any distinguishing features. Rather like Nikolas in a way, although with Nikolas, a good deal of his ability to be "invisible" rested with his training.

It seemed that the fellow Mags had been talking to wasn't just a bug collector. When Mags got there, he was helping another man go through the dead folks' belongings, and not just sort through them, but take them apart. Hems were opened on clothing, linings torn out, mattresses were cut open, any object was picked up, examined minutely for—

What? Why were they poking and prodding, closing their eyes and running their fingertips over things?

The bug-fellow opened his eyes to see Mags staring at him, perplexed. He cracked a very slight smile. "Secret compartments," he said, without waiting for Mags to ask him the question. "And if you have Mindspeech, would you kindly tell Nikolas that if he eats himself up over this, I am going to drag him out of his bed later today and beat him senseless? That seems to be the only thing that gets through his thick skull."

The other man uttered a smothered chuckle.

"But—how?" Mags asked. "How're ye lookin' fer stuff that's s'posed t'be hid?"

"Well, if we had found one, I could show you, but in general, we look for something that seems to be solid, or solidish, but is a little too light. That's why we are weighing these things in our hands. We look for drawers or compartments that are too short. We close our eyes and use our fingers, hunting for concealed seams and test to see if what seem to be solid panels will actually move. Thus far, I am sorry to say, we have found nothing."

"This place has been cleaned," the second man said, with an air of one pronouncing a judgment. "I don't think we'll find anything unless these lads thought they might be betrayed and hid something, or the killers made a mistake. I don't think either is likely. That fire was cleverly and carefully set. The room was sealed to keep the stink from getting out too much; there's pitch all around the doors and windows, and it would have set up around the front door once they closed and locked it. They didn't need to break the seal to set the fire; you said they came in the back way. There would have been remains, but nothing that could have been identified, and anyone investigating would have seen four drunks in the front of the house, and what was left of the table in the kitchen, and figured a perfectly ordinary bunch of fools left a candle stuck to a table soaked in grease and were too drunk to notice when it set a fire. I don't think anyone that thorough is likely to have been careless with his victims' belongings."

"Me neither," Mags said glumly. He explained more-or-less what he had picked up from the killers, and the second man nodded, as if not surprised.

"I don't know what we have here, exactly," he said, closing his eyes and running his fingers over the back of a hairbrush. "Spies, I've seen before; caught one or two. Killers for country or for hire I've seen, though we usually don't intercept those, the King's bodyguards do. But I have not encountered anything like this. The first lot that came in—the ones that I believe you and your friends uncovered, Mags—were well trained to a point, but most of them were gentlemen trained as spies, not professional spies, and they were just not prepared for Valdemar. It was bad enough when one of their number went mad, but it got worse when that second madman popped up."

"Got *no* ideer where 'e come from," Mags said ruefully. " 'Tis like mebbe when 'e was s'posed t'be hangin' 'bout th' others, but whatever made th' fust mad sent 'im mad too. An' they didn' know 'e was conkers till they got 'im t'ketch Bear so's Bear c'd take care'a th' mad'un, an' then 'twas too late."

The second man shrugged. "That's as good an explanation as any. Well, whoever sent them in the first place didn't make the same mistake twice. They found out about Valdemar, they got people who could pass as natives, and gave orders that the mess be cleaned up as thoroughly as possible." He paused as he put the unlit lamp he had been examining aside, after he had emptied it of oil so he could be sure there was nothing hidden in the bowl. "They planned. They took their time. They were absolutely methodical. They might not have arrived with exact orders but with the discretion to do whatever had to be done. I think—no, I am sure—they knew they were going to kill these four within moments of talking to them and realizing what a hash they'd made of things. They probably had been given contingency plans and a free rein when they left—wherever they came from. But these four never saw it coming. They thought they were passing the job on to a new team and that they could go home."

::Ask him how he knows that,:: Nikolas said instantly.

"Nikolas wants ter know how you knowed thet." Mags waited, head tilted to one side, watching the two Guardsmen. "But I reckon 'tis thet." He nodded at the empty pack that lay crumpled at the head of the bed.

"You see—" said the first to the second. "That's what Niko's been waiting for. Not just Mindspeech. Not just someone clever and agile. There are Trainees by the dozen who have those qualifications. He's been waiting for someone who can observe and think and not just assume things."

The second nodded. "You're right," he told Mags. "It was the empty pack. And do you know why?"

"'Cause it don't b'long there," Mags said. "Pack should'a been stowed, prolly wi' th' others, outa th' way. Who needs packs, iffen yer settled in? Iffen feller had it *with* 'im fer some reason, like 'e were keepin' somethin' needful in't, it'd be at foot of bed, not th' head, or off t' side, mebbe i' corner." He thought of all the times he'd been briefly in the rooms of other Trainees, all the packs he'd seen. Always, empty ones were stowed on a shelf that was awkward to get to, anywhere out of the way. Always, if they held something the owner wanted to keep in them, they were at the foot of the bed, where they wouldn't get kicked or tripped over.

Never where that one was. Unless . . .

"Reckon 'e were packin' up," Mags said thoughtfully. "Mebbe him an' t'others cooked up a big meal t'git rid'a stuff that'd spoil. Thet's when th' others done 'em, after thet meal. Then they come up here an' went through ev'thing, jest t'make sure. Prolly where they got thet book an' stuff they sold Nikolas."

"Good," said the second with satisfaction. "And that is why I am fairly certain they heard the Weasel was making inquiries *after* they did this, not before. Probably shortly after. They would have made several passes through this place, making sure that nothing was left behind. If they hadn't heard that someone was asking about their victims, they would simply have left this as a mystery—four men, dying after a big meal in this neighborhood—the Guard would have written it off as accidental. Maybe some of the food had gone bad. Maybe they picked the wrong mushrooms. If we tested for poison, we wouldn't have found anything. No one would have been called on to investigate, the men would have been buried in the Poor Grounds, and that would have been that. But then they heard that someone was snooping about, and they realized they were going to have to clean up a bit more thoroughly than they had first thought, because someone would be smart enough to put four dead bodies together with the fact that the Weasel was looking for information. So they planted the story that these men had left town and set the fire, figuring it would take some time before the Weasel found his buyer. By that time the fire here would have destroyed all signs that there was anything other than four common laborers living here, and no one would associate what the Weasel wanted to know about with this place."

Mags turned all that over in his head, and nodded slowly. That made plenty of good, sound sense. ::*Hope yer feelin' unguilted,*:: he told Nikolas.

::*I would, if that were even a word,*:: Nikolas retorted. But he sounded more like himself, and that pleased Mags no end.

"Gods, I am never getting the stench out of this uniform," the first muttered.

"Toss it," advised the second. "I can't think of any good way to get it clean. It's not as if they won't give us more. It won't be the first time I've tossed a uniform that reeked of death."

Swiftly, Mags put two and tow together. "You're not Guard," he said flatly.

"Well . . . we wear the uniform. We get paid by the Quartermaster like everyone else." The first man grinned at him.

"D'ye work fer Nikolas, or t'other way round?" Mags was very interested to hear that answer.

"Let's just say we work for the same person. And since you do too, we probably ought to be polite and introduce ourselves. I'm Tal Merrick. This is Kan Betler. The other three members of our team are Jun Lysle, Ref Graden, and Serj Karmas." Tal put his hand on his chest and made a little bow.

"Jest Mags," Mags said, bowing awkwardly. "Got no other name."

"We know," said Kan, and waved a little. "Hello, Dallen."

::Well! How thoughtful!:: Dallen sounded surprised and pleased. ::Tender my greetings please.::

"Dallen says 'lo." Mags smiled a little. "Aight. Anythin' I kin do?"

"Not really," Kan told him. "Takes a bit of training to do what we do, to know what to look for. We investigate any death in Haven that doesn't seem straightforward. Sometimes we investigate when we are asked to do so by relatives. Rarely we go outside Haven. We work with Nikolas a great deal because he has things we don't."

"Mindspeech," Mags said instantly. "An' Truth Spell."

Tal touched one finger to his nose and pointed the same finger at Mags. "Sharp one. And he works with us because deaths that aren't straightforward sometimes involve threats to the Kingdom and the King."

"If you aren't going to die of boredom, you might as well stay and watch," Kan continued, going back to his methodical sifting of the foreigners' belongings. "It will save us having to have the Weasel arrested so we can talk to him, and Nikolas will appreciate that we are educating you."

::That's only so they can get out of sharing some of the special brandy they keep down at their headquarters,:: Nikolas retorted.

"I ain't bored," Mags replied—and it was the truth. He was anything but bored. He watched carefully, making note of what they did and did not do. This was a skill worth having . . . .and now that the bodies were gone and the house was airing out, it was becoming more tolerable to be here.

As expected, they found nothing, and finally, at a point well after midnight, the Special Guards packed up the things they wanted to take away and departed, leaving Mags alone in the house.

He climbed back up on the roof per Nikolas' instruction—but then something told him not to leave. Not just yet. There was something tickling around the edges of his awareness. A presence—no, several.

For a moment, he was afraid it might be the other assassins, come back to make sure the house had burned as they had planned. But as whoever it was neared, cautious as a feral cat, he knew immediately it wasn't them.

There were three . . .

They were young. Very young. He sensed their hunger—very physical hunger. They might be young in age, but in the way of poor children, they were old in grief and experience. They were creeping up on the house full of anticipation, but as soon as they saw the doors and windows standing wide open, they stopped in their tracks, hidden in the alley, their anticipation turned to despair.

Mags crept across the roof to the point nearest where they were and strained his ears.

::*What have you got, Mags?*:: Nikolas asked him urgently.

::*Dunno yet. Mebbe somethin' worth chasin. Kids, but they was comin' here fer a reason.*::

"Hoi!" came a whispered voice. "They done a runner!"

There was a whimper. "We ain't a-gonna git paid naow! I'm *hungry*, Merrow!"

"Shut it!" said a third voice. Mags identified it as belonging to the oldest of the three. "Mebbe they done a runner, but they left house open. Lessee what we kin find. Mebbe they's still stuff i' there."

With infinite caution the three slipped up to the back door. One skittered up to the door and peered inside.

"Ain't nobody 'ere," came the whisper. "Pew! Stinks!"

The youngest whimpered again, this time sounding terrified, and the whimper rose to a thin wail. "Noooooo!" the child cried, backing up from the door. "Don' go in there! It's Death! It's Death!"

And despite the hunger that Mags sensed gnawing at her belly, the little girl fled.

The other two paused.

"She's—" there was an audible gulp. "She's right. Ma smelt like this, arfter a day . . ."

The older one was indifferent. "So? If they's dead, they ain't a-gonna need their stuff. Doors and winders open, must mean Guard's been an' gone, an' ain't nobody else aroun'. We'll git first pickin's. Gotta be somethin' we kin use er sell."

The younger hung back. "What if they's—ghostes?"

"Then them ghostes kin pay us," the elder said defiantly. "We done what we was 'sposed to. We kin take what they owes us outa their stuff."

The two figures slipped inside the house, one boldly, one reluctantly.

Oho. So them bastiches got thesselves some errand-runners, eh? An' th' new ones don' know 'bout 'em, or they'd'a tidied up the kids afore they bolted.

Mags weighed the notion of confronting the children—but they might manage to elude him and run, and even if he caught them, they'd probably lie. What to do? He wanted to find out just what sort of errands these youngsters had been running . . .

It made perfect sense for the assassins to use children for almost anything that didn't require strength. A hungry orphan would do just about anything, no questions asked, if you approached him right, didn't frighten him, made sure he thought he was getting the better of you.

I surely would've, back at th' mine.

And if you needed to be rid of them, a couple of stray children would never be missed.

All right. Then the best thing to do would be to

eavesdrop on them now, follow them back to whatever place they called home, and figure out exactly where that was. If he tried to intercept them now, they'd run. After all, they could tell by the stink that *someone* had died here. Anyone they encountered would likely be involved in a killing or be a rival looter. Better to approach them later, when he could figure out how best to get at them without spooking them.

He slipped back inside the house and stayed well out of sight, but not out of hearing. One of the two found a candle and the means of lighting it, and they carried it with them as they went from room to room. Once inside, when they thought they were alone, they were not exactly stealthy. Unfortunately, he didn't learn very much from listening to them, since most of their comments were restricted to evaluating how much they could carry away and what was likely to bring the most money if they sold it.

When they moved their search upstairs, he pulled himself back up into the attic and listened from there.

Adults might have been disappointed, even angered, by the lack of things of real value—what the Guards hadn't taken, he suspected that the pair of killers had carried away—or by the fact that garments had been ripped up and things taken apart. But these little fellows were not dismayed—and he certainly felt kinship with them when they discovered a pile of warm stockings and exclaimed in glee to find that not one had a hole in it. He remembered a time when finding a stocking of *any* sort was cause for rejoicing.

Eventually they staggered out, laboring under the burden of two full packs apiece, one carried on the back and one in the front, with whatever else they thought salable tied on the outside. It made them ungainly and ridiculously easy to follow, and they were so concerned with their burdens that they were not paying any attention to their surroundings at all. He was even able to follow them down on the ground, ghosting along behind them near enough that he could still overhear their occasional mutterings.

But such disregard for their surroundings was not only to his advantage. It also made them targets.

He spotted the thief about the same time that the thief spotted them. A ragged youth in his teens, he was lounging in a doorway near what Mags figured was an ale shop when he saw the two children. Mags sensed his greed and glee as soon as he spotted the easy targets, and knew then what the fellow was. He was probably a little younger than Mags, but he was several years older and much taller and heavier than his potential victims. In fact, he was not at all unlike—

The flash of memory overcame Mags for a moment.

Mags sensed the cutpurse who was hiding in the alley ahead; then sensed that the thief had spotted the assassin that Mags called Temper. The surface thoughts of the thief, desperation crossed with greed, alarmed Mags, and he stopped, bending over to fumble with a shoe while he tried to figure out what was going to happen and if he could do anything about it.

The would-be thief was a boy, not a man, a boy no older than he was. A boy with a master to answer to, and who, so far today, had nothing to bring back to him. Coming back meant a beating or worse, and no supper. The boy looked at Temper with the eyes of a hunter and saw good clothing, a man well fed, with no obvious weapons. That was enough; the thief made his decision. Before Mags could even think of something to try to stop him, the boy was moving.

His was the cut-and-run style, rushing at the victim from under cover, cutting the bands of the belt pouch, and dashing off with it. Effective only when conditions favored a swift escape, it was well suited to a night thief and to thefts where crowds thickened and thinned again, hampering pursuit.

The boy thought he had such conditions—night, the alley, and a half a dozen escape routes on the other side of the street.

He was wrong.

The man heard the running footsteps; his instincts all came alive, and an unholy glee came over him.

The rest was a blur to Mags, caught as he was between the thoughts of the cutpurse and the thoughts of Temper. Temper threw off such violence that it rocked Mags back on his heels, but it was precise and calculated violence, and an acute pleasure in what he was about to do that was very nearly pain in and of itself.

The man moved at the last minute; the boy's outstretched hands missed the tempting purse. There was a moment of anger and bewilderment on the part of the thief as his hands closed on air.

Then a flash of terrible pain and incredulity.

Then nothing.

And in the street ahead, all that anyone would have seen was the thief make a rush, the man step aside, and the thief falling to the ground as if he had stumbled. Except the thief didn't get up again.

Temper passed on, leaving the cooling body of the boy in the street. It happened that quickly. One moment the thief was alive, the next, dead.

Mags shook off the unwelcome memory, and this new thief faded back into the shadows and waited for the two laden boys to pass, figuring to take them from behind. Burdened as they were, they wouldn't be able to run or fight effectively.

Mags swarmed up a drainpipe and got onto the roof; he waited for the older boy to come out of the shadows and paced him while he followed the children, making sure that they didn't have an adult protector anywhere about. When the thief was positive they were alone, he made his move.

That was when Mags dropped down on him from above.

All that training at the hands of the Weaponsmaster culminated in a move so perfectly executed that he thought his mentor would probably be beside himself with pleasure if he could have seen it. Mags managed to knock the boy cold without damaging him too much, and do it so silently that the children up ahead of him were not even aware that anything had happened.

Mags dragged the young thief into the shelter of an alley, pulled him behind a pile of garbage, and left him there. *Bad luck, tosser,* he thought, as he resumed tailing the children. *Mebbe that'll teach ye not t'rob kiddies.*

The children staggered into what looked like an enormous abandoned building; it was hard to tell in this light, but part of it looked fallen in. Burned out, perhaps?

::*I believe so,*:: Dallen told him. ::*There was a building around about there, a big building that held several apartments. There was a fire there four or five years ago. No one could sort out who it belonged to afterward—probably the actual owner didn't want to come forward, thinking he'd be up on charges for letting it get into that state. So it's been abandoned, and no one can do anything about it until an owner is found or the city confiscates it. I suppose there are all manner of squatters in it now.::*

They plunged into the warren; he followed only far enough to determine that their "home" was an intact part of a cellar—and that the little girl who had fled was already there. He left them then, as the oldest of the boys sorted out some of the things that were likeliest to sell and hurried off with them to get some money and buy them all the food they had been promised as the reward for—whatever it was they had done for the assassins.

::What are you thinking?:: Dallen asked curiously.

::Tryin' t'think how t'get at 'em,:: he said briefly, as he headed back to the Weasel's shop at a trot. *::Reckon I'll sleep on't. I dun' think they're gonna go anywhere soon.::*

It had been a very long night, full of exertion, and once he got back to the shop and Nikolas' congratulations, he was yawning. And starving. He didn't say anything about the latter to Nikolas; after all, he would be getting food soon enough.

If he could stay awake for it.

He managed to have a coherent conversation about the Special Guards with Nikolas, anyway, once they got the Companions and headed back up the hill. It was quite enlightening; evidently there were more suspicious deaths in Haven over the course of a year than he had dreamed.

". . . so the rule of thumb is, figure out the motive, and you generally find the killer, if there is one," Nikolas was saying, as they rode in through the back gate near the Kirball field.

"Wisht we could figger out the motive of them twa new bastiches," Mags fretted. "An' if there's more'n two. I cain't b'lieve all they been sent fer was t'clean up t'others' mess. I reckon they're s'posed t' finish what t'others started, an' we still don' know whut thet was. I dun' like it, sir. I dun' like it one bit."

"That makes two of us, Mags," Nikolas replied, and sighed. "All right. I need to report to—whoever is awake at the moment. It won't be the King; probably the Lord Marshal. Then I need to write a report that the King will get as soon as he *is* awake. There's nothing much that you can do, lad, so get yourself fed and get some sleep. We'll be on this tomorrow."

Dallen paused, in response to Mags' unspoken command. "Sir? Reckon this's th' time fer me t' take a bit uv leave from classes?"

Nikolas pondered that for a moment. "It might just be," he said, slowly. "Your Gift isn't going to find these men from up here on the hill, not without opening yourself far too much and endangering yourself. You did that once already, and we were lucky you didn't go mad. The odds are not good that we will be lucky twice. We might have to repeat what you did last time—moving through the city until you can sense them, then narrowing down our search until we find where they are." He gnawed his lip. "I'll know better after I report to the King—but yes, be prepared. We might be settling in for a long job."

An' there goes any chance'a seein' Amily fer a while. He sighed. "Yessir," he said obediently. *This's too important. Even wi' her Healin' thing a-comin' up. Nikolas knowed it, an' 'e's 'er pa. An' she'll know it too.*

She's 'er pa's daughter, after all.

Mags woke from a dream of the mine knowing exactly what he needed to do to get to those three children down in Haven. It pained him—but it was absolutely the surest, fastest way. They would never respond quickly enough to kindness—that was what the dream had been about. In the dream he'd outgrown being allowed in the kitchen. He'd been just old enough to have been tossed in with the rest of the kiddies to learn the business of chipping out sparklies, and one of the older boys had immediately latched onto him. He had become the lad's personal little slavey, which was generally the norm with the very youngest of the children. He'd been bullied and hit, and at the end of the day, half his sparklies went to his "master." Only later, when the older boy had died of a fever, had he figured out that he had been better off with him than without him. Maybe he'd had his sparklies taken, but he never went without food—the older boy had always seen to it he had his bowl of "soup" and his slice of bread and never let anyone take it from him. He might have been bullied, but he had never had to fight—the older boy had protected him.

That was how he would approach these kiddies. They likely thought they were safe from discovery in their little cellar; he would ambush them there, give them a good fright, and tell them that they were working for him from now on. A cuff or two would get them in line fast enough. If he'd had time, he would have tried wooing them with kindness; he didn't have the time. Maybe later he could make it up to them; right now he had to get them cowed, under his thumb, and compliant enough that he could worm their recent activities out of them.

And in the process, he would be able to protect them and see that they were adequately fed. The combination of care and bullying should do the trick.

He explained it all to Dallen as he washed and dressed. The Companion listened without interruption until he was done.

::*I don't like it*,:: Dallen said, slowly. ::*Oh, not the plan, the plan is sound enough. I just don't like that it puts you in the position of hurting those children even a little. I can see why you think* you *have to—I just don't like it*.::

::*No more do I*,:: he confessed. ::*But kin ye see another way?*::

::*No*,:: Dallen admitted. ::*Not an expedient one*.::

::*Aight. I'll arsk their f'rgiveness later. Make it up to 'em. Mebbe thet Lord Somethin' what took care a Selna kin find 'em someplace good t' go. Now, I gotter find out what they was doin'. Maybe it weren't nothin' but runnin' t'fetch stuff, an' they don' even know what 'twas they was fetchin'. But mebbe it were somethin' important fer us t'know. Either case, I gotter find out*.::

Instead of going straight to lunch, he went to Nikolas' rooms—and walked straight into a storm of tears.

Nikolas nearly opened the door to his rooms in Mags' face; they were both shocked, Nikolas that he was there, and Mags because Nikolas hadn't sensed him before he opened the door. But Amily was wailing, and Amily never wailed, her voice thick with tears and pitched high with frustration.

"But why?" she sobbed. "Why?"

"I can't tell you, sweetness," Nikolas said, in a tone of voice that suggested to Mags he had used this very phrase several times now. "I'm sorry, but I can't."

"You can, but you won't!" she wept. "That's not good enough! I got myself all ready for this! I can't bear dragging myself around any more! I want to get it over with, and I want to get it over with now! What if something happens? What if Bear's parents drag him off? What if the other Healers get tired of waiting about and get assigned somewhere else? What if it never happens?"

Mags quickly deduced what was going on: for some reason, the complicated procedure to straighten Amily's leg had been canceled, and she was justifiably upset, the more so because her father wasn't telling her why. Somehow, something had changed, and changed drastically, between last night and this morning.

"The King has already issued the order that Bear is to stay here," Nikolas reminded her, an edge of exasperation in his voice. "And the cancelation has nothing to do with Bear."

"They don't trust him!" she cried. "I trust him! That ought to be good enough!"

Nikolas pinched the bridge of his nose between his thumb and forefinger. "Amily," he said sharply, "I have been over this with you a dozen times now. We will fix your leg. I don't know when, but this is just a temporary delay. You have to stop this; you're going to make yourself sick—"

"As if you care!" she cried, burying her face in her arms.

Nikolas gave Mags a look of frustration. "See if you can calm her down," he said, in the tone of someone who was quite at the end of his rope. "I'll be back."

Oh . . . great . . . How was he supposed to do that?

He closed the door behind himself, quietly, and crossed the room to where Amily wept, draped over the arm of a settle. He sat down beside her. He didn't know what to say, so he opted to say nothing; he just patted her shoulder now and again, awkwardly.

Finally she stopped crying and sat up and looked at him with eyes red and swollen. "I don't understand!" she said blotting her face with a handkerchief. "They just came and told me that they were putting off fixing my leg! They won't give me a reason, and they won't tell me *when* they will allow it! They won't talk to me about it *at all!* Don't they understand how scared I am to do this? Don't they understand how hard it was to decide to go ahead? Why won't they just—"

"I dunno either," Mags said, feeling utterly helpless. "This's the fust I heard of 't. There's gotta be a reason . . . I dunno, mebbe they wanta give Bear more time t'get ever'body all coordinated like? Mebbe Foreseers figger there's gonna be a summer plague or somethin', an' they're gonna need alla th' Healers? Mebbe—" Well, he could think of dozens of good reasons, but not any that meant they wouldn't tell Amily the reason why. And there was a reason; he'd seen that in Nikolas's face, in a brief flash of guilt when Amily demanded the reason of him and he'd said he couldn't tell her.

Couldn't. Which meant he was under orders. If he hadn't known the reason, he would have said something to that effect.

What on earth could cause him to be under orders like that?

Amily knew all of this as well as he did.

And if the answer had been, "It can't be done now because the Foreseers think it will kill you," yes, she would be told that too.

The only thing he could think of was that it had something to do with the new spies—or assassins—that he and Nikolas had uncovered, and that made absolutely no sense at all. As Mags was very well aware, although the King would do so with tremendous regret and a guilt that stayed with him the rest of his life, he would not hesitate to sacrifice anyone, not even the daughter of the King's Own, for the greater good of Valdemar. And what difference could this procedure make to the safety of the Kingdom anyway? That was like saying the safety of Valdemar depended on whether or not a particular orchard had fruit this year.

"You can come up with maybe's until you turn purple, Mags," she cried passionately. "So can I! I'm not a child; don't I deserve to know what the real reason is?"

"Reckon yer pa jest wants t'pertect ye," he said, for truly, what else could he say?

"But I don't *want* to be protected!" Now she flushed with a little anger, which was good—at least she wasn't crying anymore. "All right, I am going to be as afraid as anyone else if there is a good reason to *be* afraid, but I can face whatever it is! I *can!* I don't *need* to be protected!"

Mags thought about how Nikolas looked whenever he thought Amily was going to be hurt, even a little, and the lengths he went to in order to keep that from happening, and clamped his mouth shut.

"Look, I'm certain-sure it ain't 'cause they don' think they kin trust ye," he said finally. "An' I don' think it's 'cause they reckon ye'd ever do summat thet'd cause a mort'a trouble. But mebbe they ain't tellin' ye, 'cause if ye knowed, ye'd do summat that'd bollix things all up, wi'out realizin' ye was doin' it?" He shook his head. "I jest dunno—but I'll try an' find out."

She dried her eyes some more. "I *hate* not knowing things," she said fiercely. "Father used to keep all sorts of secrets from me, because he thought I'd be afraid, or I'd fret too much about the danger to him, and I fretted more because I didn't know what was going on! He knows that! He knows it better than anybody!"

Mags could see that. "I'll jest see what I kin find out," he pledged, which was, after all, all that he could really do.

———

". . . and they won't *tell* me!" Bear fumed, his anger underlaid with anxiety. Of course it was. Poor Bear— the first thing he would think was that this delay was because "everyone" had realized that his father was right, and it was the height of madness to have put him in charge of this project, only no one would tell him that because they were all going to be polite about it.

Then he would be certain that the truth was that they all knew, and they were talking about him in pitying tones behind his back.

Pitying or scornful.

Bear had an active imagination. His next leap would be that shortly his father would be sent for, and he would go home and—

And he would never see Lena again, nor any of his friends. He'd become an animal Healer, dispensing herbs for sick sheep. *Maybe* his father would allow him to take a human as a patient, so long as it was nothing serious—or was purely mechanical, such as setting a bone or stitching someone up prior to the "real" Healers doing their work.

"Look—" Mags said, desperate to hold off the inevitable cascade of "and-then-they'll-do-this." "Has anybody said anythin' 'bout this, 'cept 'tis bein' delayed?"

"No—but—"

"How d'ye know it ain't some Foreseer seein' a summer plague i' Haven?" Mags rubbed his temples. Getting Amily calmed down had been hard enough. Getting Bear calmed down was giving him a headache. "Hellfire, iffen there was one'a those, they'd be needin' alla beds an' ev'ry hand."

Bear gave him a *look.* "There hasn't been a plague in Haven for over two hundred years."

"Then yer overdue," Mags retorted. "It don't have'ta be a plague. Could be a fire." He thought about what a disaster that fire the assassins had set could have been if there had been a wind. "Hot, dry, big ol' windstorm, some'un's lantern goes over, whut happens then? Bad time t'hev some'un laid up i' middle uv a complisti-cated Healin'."

"That's not even a word," Bear said crossly, but he was listening at least. "So why not just *tell* me that?"

"Cause Foreseers got caught lookin' stupid 'bout me?" Mags replied. "Mebbe 'cause—look, yer part'a my crew, so I kin tell ye. They's a couple new lads from thet merry band'a killers, an' they are *whoa* better'n the first lot."

Quickly, he told Bear about the situation he and Nikolas had unearthed. As he had hoped, it at least got Bear's attention and got his mind off his own troubles. "So what'f they seen this new lot doin' somethin' that hurt a buncha people? So, aye, they tell head of Her-alds and head of Healers, and they find out Nikolas knows 'bout 'em already. But they ain't a-gonna bandy this 'bout. Iffen it gits out, people'll panic, start seein' assassins ev'where, next thing y'know, there's people beatin' up people on account'a they got a funny way'a talking, or they *look* furrin' or—well, you know peo-ple."

Bear nodded, slowly, reluctantly. "But wouldn't Nikolas tell you?"

"Not iffen 'e was ordered not to. 'E's kept plenty'uv things from me. Hellfire, I'd wanta go tell Master Soren an' my other friends down i' Haven, an' they'd wanta warn their friends, and sooner or later, some'un'd slip." By this time, he was half convinced himself. It made perfect logical sense.

"I mean," he continued, "Le's go ahead an' get *real* crazy. 'Cause these fellers don' know what kinda weather we'll get, mebbe they cain't count on the right sorta stuff to make a big fire, an' they *know* we got the Foreseers what might See somethin', an' Heralds that'd get roused up right quick iffen they ran 'round settin a *lot* of fires. But mebbe they got a new kinda plague where they come from, new t'us, mebbe. An' mebbe they know what spreads it. So mebbe they come 'ere wi' thet i' baggage, an' are getting' ready t'turn it loose."

Bear shuddered, the anger in his expression fading, being replaced y alarm.

"I ain't sayin' 'tis thet," Mags hastened to add. "I'm jest sayin', could be. Aight?"

"All right," Bear agreed. "But where does that leave me?"

"Where'd it leave ye afore ye got tapped fer Amily's fixin'?" Mags countered.

"Well . . . ." Bear rubbed the back of his head ruefully. "Keeping Lena from feeling bad, as much as I could. And classes. And doing my work with the healing kits. I feel bad for putting some of that aside, but I have the basic kit now, and that part is out of my hands . . ."

"Aight. So figger 'stead'a runnin' 'round tryin' t'be three people, ye got leave t'jest be one fer a change." Mags punched his shoulder, lightly. "Wish't I c'd say th'same."

::*Mags*,:: Dallen interrupted. ::*Time to go. Nikolas has arranged that leave.*::

"I gots t' git," he said, feeling both a bit of thrill and a lot of apprehension.

". . . and not to go to class," Bear said after a moment, studying his face. "You're going to be down in Haven all the time now."

"Mebbe." Mags shrugged. "Dunno yet. Mebbe we'll move inter thet shop fer a while. I dunno. Might could be e'en Nikolas dunno. Jest know I gotta go now, cause we gotta be down there long afore sunset t'day. I gotta start huntin' fer this new lot."

Bear gave him a long and measuring look. "These people almost killed you," he said, somberly. "Three times, they almost killed you. And the ones that almost killed you, you say weren't as skilled as these *new* ones."

"Aye, I figgered thet part out," Mags said dryly. "Might've been no bad notion t'have some other Gift, aye? Too bad we don' get t'pick, I'd'a picked one thet made it so I had t'be treated like King hisself."

"And what Gift would that be?" Bear asked.

"Dunno. Kingdom's Luck? Thet a Gift? Whatever, I'm th' one thet kin hear these lads, so I'm the one gotta go." He honestly wished it could be anyone but him right now. Or better yet, that there were two of him.

Bear made a face. "Just—"

"Don' say 'be careful,' aye? I ain't goin' inter this plannin' on doing stupid shite." Mags gave him an evil stare.

It had the desired effect. Bear laughed a little. "Point taken. And I suppose you had best get on your way before Nikolas gets annoyed with you. Go on, I'll—try not to let my imagination get the better of me. I'll definitely keep Lena sane, and try to do the same for Amily."

Mags thought about advising him to do—or not do—any number of things. But in the end—would any of it do any good? Probably not. "I'll let ye know when I kin, what's what," he said instead. "Iffen ye see me t'morrow, least ye'll know I ain't fightin' fer bedspace wi' bugs down i' Haven."

And he had to leave it at that.

He met Nikolas at the stable and knew immediately by the size of the packs that Dallen and Rolan were carrying that he would not be seeing his friends over lunch—not tomorrow, and maybe not for a while. A moment later, Nikolas confirmed his guess.

"I can't say that I will be terribly unhappy at not having to deal with my daughter for a while," the Herald murmured as he tightened the girth on Rolan's saddle, and made sure that everything was comfortable for the Companion. "Maybe by the time I am back up here, she'll have decided that I am not the worst father in the Kingdom."

"I—" Mags tried to think of something to say, and couldn't. He finally just shrugged. "Ain't nothin' I kin say, sir. Iffen yer unner orders, well . . . an' I reckon ye cain't even tell me thet much. An' iffen ye cain't tell me, aye, ye cain't tell Amily. I don' like it, an' she don' like it, an' it ain't fair, though. Ain't like we'd tell any'un, an' any'un thet thinks we would's daft."

Nikolas just gave him an opaque look. "Let's just say that events in the past have proved that Foreseers sometimes interpret what they See incorrectly, no one wants to chance that happening this time, and leave it at that. Amily *will* get her leg mended as soon as can be managed, and Bear *will* be the one overseeing it. I just can't tell you, or her, or him when that will be. Now let it go. That's more than I should have told even you."

"Yessir," Mags replied, and got into the saddle. "So . . . any notion 'ow long we'll be livin' o'er yer shop? Attic's like t'be mortal warm t'sleep in. I dunno, might could wanta think 'bout sleepin' elsewhere?"

"We'll actually be living in a squalid little basement—or rather, what *was* a squalid little basement before I smoked out all the vermin and made some improvements," Nikolas told him, though he didn't look at all happy about this. "I couldn't do too much without exciting attention, however, so it will be rough."

I don' think 'e 'as the least little idea of rough, Mags thought to himself, but with more amusement than bitterness. Maybe it was a good thing that even Nikolas forgot, now and again, just who he was talking too. "'Tis a basement. Be cooler than attic. Might could be cooler nor up 'ere. Dunno whut yer room's like, but mine's been a-getting' warm."

"There is that," Nicolas admitted, and hoisted himself into the saddle as well. "So, off we go to our grand adventure of sleeping in a cellar, bathing in a bucket, and eating dubious sausage and hoping it isn't so dubious that we need a Healer afterward." He shook his head, and Rolan echoed the gesture. "Oh, the grand and glamorous life of the King's Own! I've more than half a mind to kidnap Marchand and show him what *our* work is like on an intimate basis. Maybe then he

wouldn't be so cursed jealous of me." He led the way
out of the stableyard and onto the road.

Jealous? Huh. Thet might 'splain a few things . . .

"Oh, I wouldn' do thet, sir," Mags said aloud as they
passed through the gate and moved down among the
Great Houses. "Fust time 'e felt a mouse run o'er 'im i'
th' night, 'e'd bloody scream so loud 'arf Haven'd
think we was stranglin' a cat. Then, there goes us bein'
all quiet-like."

"It would be *worth* it," Nikolas said, fervently. "Can
you imagine his face?"

"Oh, aye." Mags chuckled. "Huh. Mice. Cain't say I
like hevin' m' face run over i' th' night meself. Reckon
we better git us a cat?"

Nikolas sighed. "Yes. I'm afraid so. It's been a while
since I smoked the vermin out. The bugs haven't returned, not even the black beetles in the cellar, but
there isn't much there to attract them. Mice are another
matter, and they're probably back already."

::*I'll help you find a good mouser,*:: Dallen said.

"Aight," Mags said. "I'll sort it."

Nikolas cast a ghost of a smile his way. "I rather
hoped you would."

"Here's the problem. This cellar was really only meant
as another escape route, or a place to hide while someone searched the shop," Nikolas said aloud, as he
shoved the crate that Mags usually sat on aside, reveal-
ing a hatch.

'E's talkin' out loud 'stead'a Mindspeakin'. Which prolly

means he don't want me t'chance getting a liddle bit of what-ever 'tis 'e ain't s'posed t' tell us. 'cause 'e knows I kin git stuff that kinda spills over. Well, if that was what Nikolas wanted to do . . . it wasn't as if Mags had any grounds for objecting. He thought about it carefully, and decided that he didn't mind. Because Nikolas knew that Mags knew that Nikolas—Mags caught himself before he started snickering. *Hellfires, ain't like he's insultin' me. Jest doing whut he was tol' t'do.* Furthermore, Mags had the oddest feeling that if Nikolas thought for one moment that Mags actually *needed* to know what was going on, he would violate those orders and tell him.

So I'll make't easy on 'im an' not fuss.

"I 'spect most shops 'round 'ere hev thet," Mags observed dispassionately. Or at least, with a good imitation a cheerful indifference.

Nikolas pulled up the hatch; instead of the ladder Mags expected, there was a good solid—new-looking—set of stairs. Nikolas handed him a lit lantern; he went down first.

As a home, it was pretty primitive. There were a couple of straw mattresses stacked up against the wall, with some bedding rolled tightly atop them, and that was about it. Mags sniffed; no mouse stink, nothing but damp, but he was glad he and Dallen had acquired the new shop cat anyway. If they started bringing food here in any quantity, mice would follow.

The walls were extremely crude slat-wall wood, the floor was either hard-packed dirt or soft rock, the tunnel leading out of one side was cut through the dirt, but had been expertly shored up. It *was* cool. "It'll do," Mags pronounced. Nikolas looked vaguely relieved.

Guess 'e fergits what I come from.

The only problem was . . . the floor space was minimal. Not bad for one, not so comfortable for two. "Where's tunnel go?" he asked, shining the lantern in, but not venturing down it too far.

"The basement of the shop next door. The empty one. We bought it when we bought this one, to keep it empty."

"Huh." Mags considered that a moment. "Might could sleep o'er there, iffen ye don' like sleepin' down 'ere. Thet place got heavy shutters an' bars over t'winders, ain't nobuddy gonna see in t'know."

Nikolas looked thunderstruck, as if the idea simply hadn't occurred to him. Mags allowed himself a ghost of a smirk.

See? I ain't entirely useless.

"If it's cool enough," Nikolas replied. "I have no idea if that place is going to be a stifling hellhole or a reasonable space to use. But I feel like an idiot for not thinking of that myself."

"Outa sight, outa mind," Mags said philosophically. "So, ye know them liddle 'uns I was follerin' last night?" he continued, instead of gloating. "I reckon t'take 'em over an' find out what they was doin' fer the dead fellers."

The King's Own turned to look at him, wearing a slight frown. "By take them over—you don't mean—" Nikolas began hesitantly.

"Nay, ain't messin' wi' they heads, but I ain't got time t'lure 'em neither. I gotter git 'em under m'thumb right quick. Iffen them others know 'bout 'em, ye kin bet they ain't gonna be breathin' too long." That, too, had occurred to him this morning. "I reckon t'take over thet gang'uv theirs." He quickly explained what he had in mind; Nikolas listened carefully. "Reckon I kin hev most'a what they know in a couple nights. Then we figger what t'do wi' 'em."

"You're probably chasing nothing, Mags," Nikolas cautioned. "I very much doubt that those men were so stupid as to entrust a couple of children with anything important."

That might be true. On the other hand, Mags knew firsthand that adults, men especially, tended to forget that children had minds and ears of their own. They might have overheard something useful. They might have deliberately eavesdropped. And they might not even be aware that what they had heard was important.

But there was no point in bringing that up just now. It would just sound as if he were trying to dig up specious reasons to go track those children down.

Mags just shrugged. "Dunno till I find out. Which I reckon t'start on t'night. Reckon I kin cast 'bout fer them new fellers while I'm bullyin' the liddle 'uns."

Nikolas winced—rather as Dallen had done. Mags reflected that it was rather odd that they both felt so squeamish about frightening and intimidating a group of street urchins who were probably already criminals and yet were utterly matter of fact about other, far nastier things.

Maybe it was because Nikolas was a father and saw his own child reflected in the eyes of every child. If so—

—*'e needs t' get over thet.* Not every child was innocent.

Not every child was good. Mags knew that one, first-hand. Always seeing a child as the innocent left you open to not seeing when the child was scheming to take you down.

It remained to be seen what these three were—innocent, half-innocent, or nasty little monsters. Although the fact that they had banded together and were loyal to each other was a mark in their favor.

"I won't need you that I know of," Nikolas said, "You might as well go see what you can do about these children once we have a look at the other shop." He looked sheepish. "I haven't been there, except to make sure all the exits were in order."

Mags ran over what he knew of the shop next door in his mind. If this shop was small, the one next door was scarcely more than a hole in the wall. It looked to him as if it had literally been built between two existing buildings, and how the builders had gotten away with that, he could not imagine. Nikolas led the way into the tunnel, which was short and ended in a ladder. While Mags held the lantern, Nikolas climbed it, and opened the hatch at the top.

Mags passed up the lantern and followed.

The space he climbed up into was dusty, narrow, and absolutely empty—from inside it was clear that what he had taken for a shuttered window was actually a shuttered hatch. In fact, it looked exactly like a serving-hatch. There was no front door, only the rear and another ladder to a hatch directly in the roof above. There was nothing in this long, narrow room but a single barrel. The good thing was, it was not nearly as warm in here as he had feared, though it was stuffy. It would make a decent place to sleep. And there was a privy in the tiny patch of walled yard that this place and Nikolas's shop shared.

"What was this place?" he asked.

"Alehouse," Nikolas said briefly. "Or, really, more like an ale stall. You brought your own tankard or pail, bought the ale at the hatch, either took it home or drank it standing at the front. When the owner was prospering, he probably also sold bits of things to eat. Meat pies, sausage, that sort of thing. There are not a lot of these places anymore. It was one thing when this was a busy street during the day and people would snatch a bite and a drink on the way to a job or on the way home from one. But this part of the city stopped prospering, and when you are poor, you drink water, or what you can brew out of what you can scavenge, and you don't pay someone else to cook your food. And in the rare good times, you want to go somewhere that you can sit down to drink your ale."

There was just enough room for them to put their mattresses here without blocking the exit. And this was probably better than the cellar, where it was likely that they'd kick or step on each other a couple of times a night. They spent a little time hauling their bedding over and setting up; by then it was dark, so Nikolas opened the shop, and Mags went out over the roofs.

He didn't immediately seek out the children, however. They were secondary to the reason why he and Nikolas were here, after all. He settled in the coolest spot he could find, one with a bit of breeze and nothing digging into his backside; he rested his back against a cold chimney and carefully opened his mind.

Not a lot. And slowly.

Nearby thoughts brushed against his. Ordinary folks, settling in for the night after a hard day of work, for the most part. Nikolas' shop notwithstanding, most of the people in this neighborhood were pretty law-abiding. They'd steal a little if they got the chance, just as he and the mine-kiddies had stolen and for the same reason—not out of greed or avarice, but to eat, to live. But most of them wouldn't steal from a neighbor, and most of them wouldn't do anything to harm another person who wasn't trying to harm them. He didn't probe; probing was wrong, unless he had a compelling reason to do so. He simply let surface thoughts brush past him. There was a lot of anxiety about money, some hunger pangs that drinking water wouldn't still. Restless children who had not worn out their energy at *their* jobs (for everyone worked here), exhausted parents who had come home exhausted and only wanted to stuff a crust into their children and themselves and sleep. Some bright spots of happiness—someone had done well, there had been a good meal, a promise of prosperity, a bit of luxury. Someone was in love, someone was heartbroken, both were not much older than he was. Many were a little drunk, several were very drunk, some were in pain, physical or emotional. A few were ill. Several someones were—he shied away from that particular activity, a little embarrassed. Nothing was so terrible that it required his intervention or that he call for help via Dallen. It was "noisier" here than up at the Collegium; Dallen had explained that as the existence of many old and new shields, and the buffering efforts of the Companions.

But nowhere was there that peculiar half-emptiness that marked the presence of the foreigners. Which didn't mean that they weren't in Haven, it only meant that they were not within a block or so of where he was. That was the problem, the farther he reached, the more mental voices started to press against him, and the harder it became to lock them out. Now, if he was "talking" to a single person, or a few, he could reach quite far indeed without danger. But if he had to do something like this, open his mind to every stray thought that passed by, well— That was a great deal more difficult. Partly, since they weren't Mindspeakers, it was more difficult to make sense of what they thought, and their thoughts didn't have the force behind them that caused them to reach farther.

Which was just as well, since this was rather like being in a room full of people all talking at once. He had to concentrate to sort out what anyone was saying. The farther away *he* reached, the noisier it became, because it wasn't possible to block out the nearer folk while reaching for the farther.

Such things had driven people mad in the past. And they probably would again. He was just fortunate that he had Dallen. The more he came to understand Heralds and Companions, the more it became obvious that Dallen "helped" him far more than most Companions aided and taught their Heralds.

He put up his shields again, "resting" for a moment in the peace and silence that followed the incessant chatter.

::You aren't exactly the normal sort of person we Choose,:: Dallen commented dryly, ::As you already knew.::

::*Quit joggling m'elbow*,:: he chided, with amusement. ::*I think I jest figured out you got in an' dumped a whole lotta learnin' in m'head back when I was lettin' ye keep me from havin' fits.*::

When he had first been Chosen, he had understood nothing. Quite literally, nothing. He had been one short step up from a feral thing, and if he had not accepted Dallen's offer to buffer him from the rest of the world, and to simply supply him with exactly the information he most needed about his new life—well, he certainly wouldn't have done very well.

::*It was things you would have learned anyway if you had been Chosen when most are, instead of when you were ready,*:: Dallen replied. ::*And anyway, most of it was about the managing of your Gift. You had a great deal of information and a great many skills you needed to acquire in a very short time. The consensus among the Companions was, why add the burden of learning how to handle your Gift, too, when I am an expert in Mindspeech and Empathy, you and I have a uniquely strong and open bond, and I could just give you the benefit of what I knew directly?*::

::*So thet's how come I never needed too much trainin' in m'Gift?*:: he replied.

::*Exactly so. You didn't need attention from an outside teacher, because you had the knowledge already.*:: Dallen paused. ::*It was for your protection, too. What if you'd had Temper impinge on your mind when you first arrived here? As it was, we all had to work hard before we understood that there was a powerful outsider disrupting your thoughts and your sleep.*::

::*Huh. Kinda seems like cheatin'.*:: He waited for Dallen's answer.

::It would be, I suppose, if we could do that with every Chosen. But we can't. You. A few of the Monarchs' Owns of the past. Some of the Herald-Mages. Not Vanyel, interestingly enough. It requires a peculiarly receptive and open mind, and a point in time where everything comes together so that they are not only receptive, but their minds are prepared to accept everything we give them without question.:: Dallen paused. ::And now you think about this and . . . ::

His thoughts were already racing through the implications. ::Ye coulda just dumped in whate'er ye wanted to.::

He sensed Dallen "smiling." ::Yes.::

::Like . . . makin' me think 'bout things a certain way. Makin' up m'mind for me, pushin' me t'think one thing's good, 'nother's bad.::

Dallen seemed delighted. ::Yes.::

::Ye didn'.:: Actually, he was delighted too. There it was, proof that he was still his own person.

::Tempting, especially when you were wallowing in a swamp of delusions of inadequacy, but no. You had— have—to remain you, Mags. All I ever did was give you very, very rapid training so that you didn't go insane as your Gift blossomed. And at any rate, the time when I could do that so freely is passed; I can still teach you things if I have to, but never with that freedom and ease.:: He sensed mixed feelings now, both pride and a little regret.

He decided to blunt the regret with a joke. ::Huh. Well, hellfire. I was hopin' ye could git me through them Courty Graces horsecrap wi'out hevin' t' strain m'skull.::

::Perhaps we can work on your speech,:: came the sarcastic reply.

Mags smiled even broader. ::My dear old Companion,:: he said, his mental voice reflecting letter-perfect diction and grammar. ::*I fear I must disagree with you. What you are taking for ignorance is part of the persona of the thick-as-a-brick games-player that Nikolas wishes me to cultivate. The less cultured I sound, the more people underestimate me.*::

He paused, eyes still closed, grinning at the mental silence. ::*'Tis also harder'n hell,*:: he admitted. ::*An' it don't seem like me, if ye take m'meanin'.* ::

:: *. . . what about those words you make up?*:: Dallen finally asked.

::*It's on account'a I'm a bonehead, an' don't allus 'member what th' right word is, so I come's close as I kin.*:: That comment nettled him a little. He really *did* try, after all. ::*People figger it out!*::

::*I suppose they do.*:: Dallen sighed. ::*All right, I don't think that our quarry is anywhere around you, and at the moment we have no real direction to go in, other than that you sensed they still had a job to do here and were not going to leave until it was done. I am going to try to put my thoughts together and think in what part of the city they might be. You pursue those little thieves.*::

::*Not thieves, so much,*:: Mags corrected him, opening his eyes, and starting to stretch to get all the kinks out. ::*The bastiches owed 'em an' not like they was gonna get paid.*::

::*Point taken.*::

Mags stood up, careful to remain in the shadow of the chimney. ::*How you plan to try and figger out where them new bastiches is?*:: He paused. ::*We need a name fer 'em. Think on't wouldja?*::

::*All right.*:: Dallen sighed. ::*This is the part of the job I never really enjoyed. I'm going to do something that—eventually—you are going to be able to do as well as I can. It's just not very pleasant in this case, and you don't have the experience that I do to do it yet.::* There was a pause. *::I am going to attempt to put myself inside their skins and think as they do.::*

Mags froze. He was getting better at *thinking*, because the implications of what Dallen had just said were all racing through his mind.

::Tha's . . . ugly.::

::Yes.::

::Tha's kinda how I figgered out how t'get t'them kiddies.::

::It's exactly how.::

::An' how I handle Bear an' Lena an' Amily. I could—::

::Not yet. You have the raw talent, the reasoning ability, you just don't have the experience. You will, and when that day comes—::

He waited. Finally Dallen finished the thought. *::When that day comes, I will be both proud, and terribly, terribly sad.::*

He let that roll over in his mind a moment. *::Sad 'cause . . . when I know how the baddest of bad people think . . . when I kin think like they do . . . I ain't ever gonna be completely happy or . . . comfortable . . . or . . . .::*

::Secure,:: said Dallen, sadly.

::That. Not ever again.::

::Yes,:: said the creature closest to him in the whole world. *::And you can decide you don't want that—::*

::Why would I?:: he said, somberly. *::Some'un's gotta. Hellfires. Might's well be me. I got you t'keep me from goin' crazy, eh?::* He blinked, as a moment of epiphany

came upon him. ::*Hell . . . fires. Thet is the kinda Herald I'm a-gonna be. Not th' runnin' about country. Not th' tellin'a laws. Not—all the rest of't. This. This is gonna be m'job.*::

 ::*And that, O my Chosen, is why I Chose you.*::

11

Mags lurked outside the abandoned building and waited for his quarry to return. He had already scouted his way in and had already trapped all their clever little exits. Well, they were clever if you were a little child; not so clever if you were an adult and a predator. He wished he had more time; he didn't want to do things this way, but in the long run, he'd have done them a favor. Tal and the other men in that special unit of the Guard agreed. The first adult that wanted to put any effort into taking them would have them, just as he would have them. The bunnies would not be escaping this warren.

He even knew where they were: at a rag-and-bone seller, someone who would accept the clothing that had been unceremoniously ripped apart by the Guard. He knew what they planned to do—sell enough to buy a meal and eat it on the spot, because it wasn't safe to have food here now that it was summer. More gleaning of their surface thoughts proved that they had learned summer could be as perilous a time as winter. They'd learned that they couldn't hoard food in warm weather the hard way twice, once by getting sick on food that had spoiled and once by being swarmed in the night by mice and rats.

It *was* safe to store what they'd gleaned from the Agents' house—and although they had gleaned what they had thought was the best, the boys had gone back to the house again and again until they and the rest of the neighborhood looters had picked it clean.

In one way, they were right to feel relatively safe. The part of the cellar they'd claimed as their own was very difficult to get into if you were adult-sized, and it was hard to work your way through the half-collapsed walls to get there. You had to know exactly where you were going, or you ran into dead ends. An adult determined to trap them would probably do one of two things: either catch them as they went in or came out, or set fire to the whole cellar, clearing the way. They weren't thinking of that, of course. To their minds, it would be impossible for anyone to know they were in there in the first place.

Of course, they had not come up against someone like Mags: small, agile, trained. He would have been able to pull this off even without Mindspeech. With it? This was not so much a challenge as a chore to be gotten over with. He was not looking forward to what he was about to do to them.

These children weren't good—but they weren't bad, either. They would steal anything they thought they could take, but they were also living on the edge of survival, and what they stole meant the difference between living and dying. They had no love and no loyalty to anyone or anything outside their own little family, but they had no hatred for anyone else, either, except the brief, bright hatred that burned when someone cheated them or robbed them—because being cheated or robbed meant an empty belly. He certainly understood them. They differed from the Mags of the mine in only one way. Up until last winter, they'd had a mother.

She might not have been a good mother, but she fed them before she fed herself, and she gave as many kisses as cuffs. That counted for a great deal down here.

As he had learned when he was here as a blind beggar, Haven wasn't perfect, even as Valdemar wasn't perfect. There *were* places these children could have gone for help, but they either didn't know about them or didn't trust them. That was true of a lot of the sad stories down here.

And . . . if everyone who needed help came for it, would the help run out? The places that distributed food as charity often did. Shelters frequently had to shut their doors in bad weather, because there literally was no longer room inside to move. How would— how *had*—three small children who could not even hold their places in line fare?

When your options were steal or starve . . . you couldn't exactly call those "options."

But right now, Mags needed to focus.

There were plenty of hiding places around the remains of the basement that gave him a clear view of where the children would come in. It was dark, but not completely, and the children would probably have a rushlight with them. Even they couldn't thread their maze at night without some kind of light. So Mags crouched in a space where two tottering wall fragments had met, a space where it was unlikely he'd be seen in the dim illumination of a rushlight.

Mags waited, hunched down and resting, patient, every so often allowing his shields to drop a little so he could look for those Agents. That was what Dallen had decided to call them, and it was just as good as any other name to Mags.

He got no brushes of that now-familiar feeling of the shield-surrogate they wore, but as the moments became candlemarks, he finally *did* sense the children approaching.

He froze in place. They didn't seem particularly sensitive, but there was no point in taking chances. If they guessed he was going to ambush them, they'd bolt, and it would take days for him to track them down again.

They weren't talking today, but he sensed the sleepy content in all three of them that came from a full belly. Good. That was exactly what he wanted. He needed them to be off guard and unready. If there had been a real predator hunting them now, they'd be tied up in sacks before they even reached the entrance to their maze.

They wormed their way into their shelter, thinking of nothing but the comfortable pallets they'd made out of the bedding that the Guards had taken apart. He followed behind them, silent as a snake. They started whispering to each other now, feeling completely secure. And in their minds, why shouldn't they? So far no one had found them in here—except the mice, the rats, and the bugs. And even if someone did, there were three ways of escape besides the way in. Mags felt them letting their guards down further.

There was even a better source of light than a single rushlight in their shelter, as he had discovered to his amazement. You couldn't see it until you were in their hidden corner, but they'd managed to create a little fireplace, and there was still plenty of wood in this building to scavenge. It was how they had survived the winter.

That was going to work in his favor.

Even though he felt a sickening guilt for what he was about to do to them. They had reached their "home" and were settling down on the beds. He heard them talking, not bothering to whisper. They were making plans on where to take some of the ruined boots and shoes tomorrow. Not the same rag-and-bone man that they had just sold things to; they were smart enough not to make anyone think that they might have more loot cached. He listened with his ears and his mind, pausing just inside the last twist of the path while they bickered. The eldest wanted to go quite some distance away; the girl whined that it was too far. He waited until they were fully engaged in their little argument, then slipped into the room.

"Shet it!" he shouted, before they even realized there was someone else with them.

Three pairs of startled eyes met his.

"Ye'll be takin' it where I tell ye," he growled, contorting his face into a snarl.

They froze, but only for a moment.

The girl moved first; with a high-pitched shriek of terror that nearly split his head in two, she dashed for one of their exits, and she screamed again when she found it blocked. Well, actually, it was more than merely *blocked*; Mags knew tunnels and tunneling, and it had not taken him long to find the way to collapse the rubble so that the exits had literally vanished. The little girl didn't know what to do; she only stood there and screamed in terror. The two boys rushed him.

He backhanded the younger into the pile of bedding, taking care to throw him rather than hit him, and grabbed the elder by the throat, pulling him close so the boy could see his face. "There'll be none'a *thet*," he growled, and used his free hand to pinch the boy's mouth shut when he squirmed and tried to bite. "Nor thet, ye demonspawn. Yer *mine*. Sooner ye decide thet's th' way it's gonna be, th' less I'll heveta beatcha."

Now the girl and the other boy swarmed him; it was brave, but pathetic. He felt sick inside as he deliberately terrorized them. This was a horrible thing to do to anyone. This was what had been done to him—

'Cept the blows an' the beatin's were real and meant t'hurt, he tried to remind himself. But the rationalization felt . . . hollow.

He did the best he could to turn what looked like blows into deflections, always sending them tumbling to keep from hurting them too much, but it was almost a candlemark later when the three of them finally stopped fighting or trying to escape and huddled together on the pile of bedding, cowed and terrified.

He looked them over. The two boys moved to protect their sister. Good. That was the control he needed. He reached for the sobbing girl-child, slapping the other two out of the way, and before she knew what was happening, he'd snapped a collar and leash on her.

"Now," he said, squatting down on his heels to glare at the three of them. "This's how it's a-gonna be. Ye do what I say. Ye do ev'thin' I say. Yer *my* gang now. An' iffen ye don' do what I say—" he pulled abruptly on the leash when the child was off-balance, and the little girl sprawled onto the floor. "—then this bit has some'pun 'appen to 'er." He let his lips curve in a lazy smile, while inside he cringed and felt so sick it was all he could do not to throw up. "Now, I dunno what that some'pun'll be. It'll d'pend on where we is, an' what ye was s'posed t' be doin' fer me. Mebbe she don' get no supper. Mebbe she gotta sleep i'dirt. Mebbe I fin' some'un then likes liddle wenches . . ."

They were old enough to know exactly what he meant, and all three of them froze in terror.

"So," he said blandly. "Yer gonna do what yer tol'. An' right now, thet's t'come along'a me."

With the little girl crawling on hands and knees ahead of him and the boys, now thoroughly cowed, trailing behind, they emerged from the ruin.

"Where're we goin'?" the eldest quavered, when the younger boy crawled out and stood up.

"Shet it!" he snarled. "Ye'll see, soon 'nough."

There were a number of places he could have taken them, including the shop, but he knew that Nikolas would never tolerate how he was going to handle these children. If it had been an adult—given what they needed to know, Nikolas would have terrorized them himself.

But not a child.

So for now, he had a different goal in mind.

The same house where the Agents had killed their predecessors.

The little girl began to fight and utter a thin, high wail when she saw the place. He grabbed her by the back of the neck and shook her a little. "I said, *shet it.*"

"Bu-bu-bu—" she blubbered. "They's—they's gh-gh-gh-"

"Ain't no ghosts," he scoffed. "I been squattin' 'ere an they ain't no ghostes. So shet it."

Before he had gone stalking the children, he had prepared his squat, thanks to Tal and his squad. Tal had been far more pragmatic about the plan than he had been.

"Look. You're going to scare them. Well, they're scared that much most of the time, and if they're not, they should be. When it comes right down to it, unless you do this, they've got three futures. They die of privation. They die by someone's hand. Or—maybe—they survive. Like you survived in the mines. Reckon up the odds for yourself."

There was a good, sound cellar here, one with only one door in and no windows. It was perfect for his purposes. He had already gotten the keys to the place from the Guard—anyone coming around now was going to have a rude awakening to find the place locked as tight as it had been open before. The turning of the key in the lock caused a thunder of deep barks to erupt on the other side.

The little girl would have screamed if he hadn't had a precautionary hand at her throat. Instead, she shook where she stood.

"Down, Dammit!" he growled, reinforcing the command with a mental one. The dog—a huge fawn-colored mastiff, whose name really was "Dammit," dropped to the ground. He shoved all three of the children inside and locked the door. "You—" he barked, pointing at the younger boy. "Kitchen. Git th' food onna table. *Now."*

The boy scuttled off and returned with the old, splintery basket full of broken meat pies and burned sausages and grease-soaked loaf ends Mags had bought from a vendor. Mags pulled open the hatch to the cellar and gestured roughly. There was a lamp burning down there; the two boys went down the stairs, followed by Mags, followed by the girl on the end of her leash. When they got to the bottom of the stairs, Mags whistled, and the dog came down in a rush.

There were three pallets down here, a couple of empty buckets, and one full of clean water. There were also iron rings in the wall over the pallets. Mags hauled the girl over to the pallets and shoved her down on one, then tied her leash to the iron ring above her.

"Guard!" he told Dammit—who had been borrowed from Tal. An exceptionally well-trained animal, he would no more harm these children than fly, but they didn't know that. And he would guard them. Nothing would get past him.

Dammit whined, his thick tail thwacking the dirt floor. Mags turned to the children.

"Ye got food an' water an' bed," he snarled. "Use 'em. T'morrow, yer gonna *work."*

Then he thumped his way up the stairs, slamming the cellar door closed, shooting the bolt home.

Now he had them. It was just a matter of—not breaking them, but bending them.

And he felt so sickened by all he was going to have to do that he could not wait for it to be over.

––––––––––––––

The next three days were exhausting for the children. Without letting them know what exactly they were doing, he had the boys running all over the city, carrying meaningless messages until they could barely stagger, while the girl was put to such simple household tasks as her strength would manage. He had a plan, and he figured it was a good one.

On the night of the third day, the Guard "stormed" the house.

"His" Guard, of course. Mags "escaped." Tal was in the lead and took charge of the children immediately. And the little ones, who would have run like rabbits at the sight of a blue uniform three days ago, literally flung themselves at him.

They were so grateful for rescue that once the questions started, they couldn't stop babbling—even though most of the time neither they, nor Tal, had any idea of what they were actually talking about. But Mags, who was in the next room listening to the thoughts that spilled out like gravel from an overturned bucket, found himself practically struck dumb.

He didn't believe it at first. The overheard words as the three waited for their rewards, night after night.

"Our men on the Hill."

He was certain they could not have heard it correctly—or the assassins had meant something else entirely. But, no, there was another memory, sparked into
life by one of Tal's gentle questions, and another, and
another—none of them saying directly that the plants
were in the Palace, the Collegia, or both—but the code
words couldn't *possibly* mean anything else!

That was . . . insane. Not possible. Everyone was
vouched for! How could—

He sat there, thunderstruck. Even Dallen was
speechless.

Time and time again, these three children had been
sent to pick up messages that came from "Our men on
the Hill," or take messages to them. Never directly, of
course; they came via message drops, places where a
message could be hidden until someone who knew it
was there came to collect it. Thanks to the memories,
Mags had the locations of these drops, of course, but
there was no use going to them now—with the original
Agents dead, they wouldn't be in use. The new Agents
would have established a new set of drops—and they
wouldn't be so lazy as to send half-feral children to
fetch the messages for them, either.

::*This is insane,*:: Dallen said, finally.

::*Tell me 'bout it,*:: Mags retorted, feeling as if the floor
had dropped away beneath him.

At least he could count on Dallen to relay all this,
because right now it felt as if he were so rattled he
couldn't move.

And then—he was metaphorically knocked halfway across the room.

The door to the little room next to the one in which Tal was questioning the children opened, but it wasn't one of the Guard that was standing there.

It was Nikolas.

"Time to go, Mags," the King's Own said, tense, but quietly. "We're leaving."

"Ye heard?" Mags blurted. "Ye heard, right? Dallen relayed, aye? Ye—"

"I heard. So did the King, and—well, most of the Circle. We all heard. And we all agree. It's impossible."

Mags stared at him. Surely Nikolas had not just said—

"We're going, Mags. This is a dead end. We'll find another way to track down these Agents. But this isn't working." Nikolas's face was a mask, unreadable. "Maybe you somehow infected those children with some—fantasy of what you *thought* was happening. Maybe this is coming from some other source than the children. Maybe they are hallucinating. I don't know, I only know that what they are showing you is impossible, and we've been told to pack up and come back. It's over."

"But—"

"It's over."

He clamped his mouth shut on any further words. He listened silently while Nikolas gave directions about the disposition of the children—being sent off to a home for orphans somewhere outside Haven, he gathered. He hoped they'd be happy. He was laden with sorrow and guilt for what he had done to them—he'd terrified them completely, and they might never get over it—but at least they were still alive. If the Agents had gotten hold of them, they wouldn't be.

He could scarcely believe that Nikolas, of all people, was dismissing what he had heard from these children. Nikolas knew very well he hadn't somehow "infected" them! It didn't work that way!

Dammit, I know it don't work thet way!

He had not projected so much as a stray food-thought at those children! There was no way that he could have influenced them!

He turned his mind to Nikolas, but was met with an absolute, rock hard barrier.

Finally, he let out his breath in a sigh, as Nikolas stood there with his arms crossed over his chest, waiting.

"Aight," he said, feeling bitterness so profound he could taste it. "It's over. Le's get back."

He lay on his back in his bed, staring at the ceiling. He hadn't had anything like an appetite when they got back; he'd had a hot bath and gone straight to bed. Nikolas . . . he could scarcely describe *what* Nikolas was being like. It wasn't as if Nikolas were angry at him, not even for putting those kids through a pretty bad experience. And it wasn't as if Nikolas were blaming him for anything—

No, it was as if Nikolas wasn't even . . . there. As if something had pulled every bit of his mentor's attention away so completely that there was nothing to spare for Mags.

As if there was nothing that Mags could possibly say

or do that would contribute in any meaningful way when Nikolas was being so totally uncommunicative.

Dismissed, that was the word. Mags had been dismissed.

Did I fail? he wondered bleakly. *Hev I so messed up thet there ain't no possible way I kin get back t' th' way ever'thin' was?*

But . . . he *hadn't* influenced those children. He *knew* he hadn't! Why would he ever even *think* even in his most fearful fantasy that the Agents had people planted *here?*

But . . .

But if not, what could the explanation possibly be?

Is't me? I mean, it was me, list'n t' their thinkin'. Mebbe it weren't them thinkin' it, but me thinkin' it was them thinkin' it . . .

Now his head was splitting, trying to second- and third-guess himself.

::*I'm not any happier about this,*:: Dallen said fretfully, startling him. ::*I trained you. I gave you my training, and it is the best. I'll stand by it. I cannot imagine any way that you could either have misinterpreted the children, or influenced them.*::

::*Then what?*:: he replied in anguish. ::*How? How kin it be true an' not-true?*:: He pressed the heels of his hands into his temples and tried to think. It was tempting—so tempting—to just give in on this one. He wasn't in disgrace. No one blamed him for anything, and certainly no one *suspected* him of trying to make trouble. And no one was accusing him now of being some foreign agent himself . . .

When he opened himself to the stray thoughts up

here, there was none of that suspicion and accusation there had been before . . . although there was a lot of heavy shielding going on that was new. It was harder to shield emotions, though, and he wasn't getting any animosity under all the shields.

Think. It ain't th' end uv th' world.

It was like he'd told Bear. What did he have before all this started? He was still a Herald Trainee. He had his classes, he had Lena and Bear and Amily, he had the Kirball team. He had Kirball itself, and he had plenty of things he was good at. He could just let things . . . be things.

After all, he was only a Trainee, he wasn't supposed to be able to do the same things as a Herald. He didn't have the experience, he didn't have the knowledge . . . wouldn't it just be smarter to let it all go and let other people deal with it?

Of course it would . . . .

He sighed. *Problem is, I ain't very smart . . . .*

. . . and I ain't gonna let it go.

After a long and restless night, he still found himself with no appetite at all. And since the Dean had not given him his new class schedule—only the third one this quarter—he found himself feeling a little sick, very headachey, still wracked with guilt over what he had put those children through, and with nothing to do.

He stared at the ceiling, as the light in his room grew. He felt the breeze die, and the air become heavier with heat.

Well . . . he might have nothing to do, but that just meant he could go see someone who could at least do something about the headache.

He got up, washed under the pump—the water was lukewarm—and got dressed in a fresh set of Grays. The headache wasn't any better. In fact, it was a little bit worse.

He did not expect to see Bear on the path approaching *him* as he left the stable, however . . .

Bear looked as if he had spent a similarly unhappy night. Mags looked him up and down for a moment, taking note of the dark-circled eyes, the pinched look to his face. "Iffen I look like you—"

"You do," Bear said abruptly. "Lena's coming here in a bit. She's not doing real good either."

He sighed. He had hoped that at least one of them was managing to get along without problems.

Faint hope, evidently.

"What's wrong wi' Lena?" he asked.

Bear rolled his eyes. "There's . . . a rumor. Something someone says someone they know heard someone they know say Marchand said." He looked as if he had bitten something sour. "I hate gossips. I really, really, hate, loathe, and despise gossips."

"What this time?" Mags' irritation with Bard Marchand rose. Sometimes it seemed as if every problem Lena had could just be solved if Bard Marchand would get hit by a runaway cart.

Bear looked away, and flushed a little. "Marchand thinks he may not be Lena's father."

Mags felt his mouth dropping open. " 'E akchully *said* thet? Wi' 'is own mouth?"

Bear waved a hand in irritation. "I don't know! All I know is the rumor started, and Lena is taking it predictably. One moment she's crying because she's a bastard, the next she's sure everyone is looking down on her, and the next, she's thinking about leaving the Collegium because she's here under false pretenses."

Mags shook his head violently. "Now *thet* is plain stupid! It'd be false pretenses iffen she was pretendin' she 'ad th' Gift an' didn't—it ain't yer name that gets ye in, it's what ye got!"

"I know, I know, and we all managed to make her see sense on that one, but she's still all in knot over this." Bear's jaw tensed. "And I haven't heard *anything* back on the field trials of the first lot of the healing kits. I mean . . . nothing. It's summer! People get hurt in summer! People get sick from bad food, people eat the wrong mushrooms, people fall out of trees, chop off their own hands—you'd think by now I'd be getting reports back! But . . . nothing!" He sighed, and pinched the bridge of his nose between his thumb and forefinger. "I keep thinking . . . I was wrong. M'father was right. People *are* too stupid to be trusted with something like that. What if the reason I haven't heard anything is because people are killing themselves with it? What if they're killing *other people* with it? What if—"

"What if you share some of that headache medicine you promised to give me if I got out of bed?" Lena asked, coming around the side of the stable and looking every bit as miserable as the two of them. "You are the cruelest person in the entire world, Bear."

"Maybe," Bear retorted. "But you aren't crying, and you're out in the sun."

"Which is stinkin' hot, an' we all have wuss head-aches an' prolly none of us et," Mags interrupted. "How 'bout we take thet medicine an' all go someplace cool an' play 'my life is miserabler than yours'?"

"I could do that," Lena said, snatching one of the potion bottles from Bear and downing it on the spot.

"I know jest th' place," said Mags, doing the same. "Le's go."

Bear swallowed the last bottleful and left the empties on the side of a stall, as he and Lena followed Mags.

"Miserabler?" Mags heard Bear say to Lena. "Is that even a *word?*"

There was no one in the grotto. And it was blessedly, blessedly cool in there. They all flung themselves down on the moss—Lena with a sigh, Bear with a grunt, and Mags utterly silent. It felt good to lie on the cool, soft moss, the three of them forming a sort of triskele with their heads in the middle, not quite touching.

For a while they all just lay there, waiting for the headache potion to take effect. When his headache finally began to ebb, Mags was able to feel all the muscles that had been tensed up, making it worse. One by one, he coaxed them to relax, keeping his mind blank and thinking of nothing else, just staring at the artificially irregular rock of the ceiling. He wondered how this grotto had been made and who had made it. Whoever had—well, Mags was grateful. And he was equally grateful that no one from the Palace was down here when they had arrived.

"Well," Bear said into the silence. "You first, Mags. What happened?"

"Nothin' good," Mags sighed, but slowly, picking his

words carefully, he related everything that had happened, from the time that he and Nikolas had taken up residence to the moment when Nikolas told him that they were leaving. He hid nothing: not what he had done to those poor children, nor what Nikolas had said.

"Huh," Bear said. "Well . . . you probably should have gone for the long way with those younglings. At least then you wouldn't be feeling all guilty now, and you'd know that . . . no, wait, that's not true either."

"What's not true?" Lena asked.

"Even if—in fact, *especially* if Mags had spent days getting those little'uns to trust him, then bringing them to the Guard for protection, everyone could *still* say he'd somehow influenced them. And they would have. And Mags, you'd have even less reason to trust your training." Bear made a rude noise. "Which is stupid, given what Dallen told you. Companions are better Mindspeakers than any human, or almost any. You're sure you didn't somehow taint those younglings, Dallen is sure . . ." His voice trailed off, but Mags knew better than to interrupt Bear when he did that. Something had just occurred to Bear, and he had to think it through before he said it out loud. "I have to wonder if Nikolas isn't just as sure that you didn't influence the little'uns as you are. And—and everyone else agrees with him, but they don't dare tell you. That's why they pulled you out so fast—something is going on that this just fitted into, and they *can't* tell you outright, and they hope you never find out. And *that's* why all the people in the know are shielded so tightly. They believe you. They don't want anything to get out while they try to figure out who it is."

Mags sat up and stared at Bear, who was still on his back with his hands behind his head, looking up at the rock arch of the grotto. "But tha's impossible!" he objected.

"Nothing's impossible," Bear retorted. "Improbable, maybe. But the second you assume something is impossible, you pretty much open a door for it to come in and happen, because you won't be guarding against it."

"There's a lot of people up here, Mags," Lena pointed out. "A *lot*. I know everyone is supposed to be vouched for, but what does that mean, really? Just take the courtiers and the Guard, for instance. Somebody's uncle who knows their family told the people up here he was reliable, and that's all there is to it. Same for the servants. Certainly most of them are from families that have served the Crown or the highborn for decades if not centuries, but families die out, and someone has to replace them. That's just the Palace servants. Some of the highborn who have Palace apartments instead of their own manors bring their own servants. The Hill operates on trust; if you shake that, you upset a lot of people. Do you want to put everyone up here through a Truth Spell to prove they are loyal?"

"No!" Mags retorted, revolted at the idea. Lena was right; the Hill did operate on trust.

"Heralds get a pass because of the Companions, but there are two more Collegia, remember. If you want an example of someone who's up here all the time and would probably fall right into someone's hands and babble everything he heard to them if he thought it would get him more adulation, you don't have to look any farther than Bard Marchand," Bear continued, with more than an edge of bitterness to his voice. "I'm not saying that he'd work hand in hand with these Agents of yours, not if he knew—but if he thinks they're just incredibly wealthy and could make him more popular or something, and he thought they were just trying to get a little more influence in the Court, he'd tell them anything he heard and probably help them get on the grounds of the Palace as a bonus. Or take that new protégé of his. Where's he from? We don't know. How old is he, really? We don't know that, either. He could be like you, Mags, undersized, and be a *lot* older than he looks."

"Any Trainee could, except the Heralds," Lena replied. "And besides the two Collegia and the servants, there're all the courtiers, who are always bringing in poor relations, trying to get them advantageous marriages or Crown appointments. For that matter, let's be *really* afraid and consider that someone might have murdered a new Guard on his way to take a post at the Palace and taken his place! It's not as impossible as it seems."

Mags scratched his head and lay back down. "Reckon not," he said slowly. "An' thet business 'bout a Guard . . . not so crazy neither. Iffen I was t'try an' git in, reckon tha's a pretty good way. Guard uniform lets ye inter anyplace on th' Hill."

"You know what else I think?" Lena said. "I think the reason Nikolas went all rock-faced on you and you both came back is that what you told him ties right into why they canceled the Healing on Amily's leg. I don't think he would have reacted so strongly otherwise."

Mags opened his mouth—and shut it, without saying anything. It was an unlikely theory—but so was the notion that there were enemy Agents or spies somewhere in the Palace or the Collegia.

And it certainly would explain Nikolas' stiff attitude.

"Huh," was all he said.

"I am not gonna tell you to leave it alone, Mags," Bear said, while he thought about that little tidbit. "But I don't think you're gonna get anything out of Nikolas or another other Herald."

::Rolan certainly hasn't been forthcoming,:: Dallen put in. ::Which, when you think about it, is interesting. It's very difficult, even for us, to lie mind to mind—which argues that he is refusing to talk about it because I will certainly know there is something not quite right about a denial.::

"I've been thinking about other things too," Lena said, after another long silence. "I think we're getting nowhere trying to sort out our own problems. You know, proving that Bear is as good or better than any other Healer, proving that my father is wrong about me, and finding your enemy Agents. I think maybe we should trade problems."

". . . just how's that s'posed t' work?" Mags asked dubiously.

"Well . . . look, I have a *lot* of chances to go just about anywhere up here on the Hill that I want to," Lena pointed out. "Even Trainees are welcome anywhere they want to go. I know you've been training in how to be sneaky, but I've been training in how to be welcome. I can literally look everywhere up here for those Agents. What's more . . ." her voice hardened. "What's more, I can *make* people trust me."

"Wait, what?" Bear asked, startled.

"You know my f—Bard Marchand uses Projective Empathy. They say *I* have it too, I just didn't want to . . . to be so manipulative, so I haven't gotten much past the most basic use of it, in case I have to use it some day to control a crowd in an emergency." She lost some of the hard edge to her voice. "So if I really start training in it and use it to make people trust me, the way he does, I can find out a *lot*."

An' ye prove ye gots th' exact same Gifts's Marchand too. Aye, I see where this's goin'. But he didn't object. On the contrary, this was one of the better ideas he'd heard. And using Projective Empathy for a purpose like this? Not only was it ethical, it was probably something that everyone in the know was wishing Marchand would get off his behind and do himself.

"Ye know what," Mags said after a moment. "Might could be I kin find out what's goin' with yer healin' kits and mebbe find out why Amily's Healin' got canceled too."

"You aren't—" Bear began.

"Not a bit," Mags replied. "They're expectin' me t' snoop an' listen wi' m'Gift. Well, I'm still gonna, when I git a chance t'go down inter Haven, but I bet they find reasons t'keep me up 'ere. An' I ain't gonna use m'Gift fer that up 'ere. I'm gonna go lookin' at comin's and goin's and records. Gonna chat wi' Guards. Dependin' on what I find out, might could tell me if'n some'un makes a lotta liddle trips down inter Haven thesselves that nobody else does. Gonna watch who's watchin important thin's—who gits thesselves duty so's they kin be at partic'lar place. An' I reckon whoever this is, they ain't all doin' th' same thing . . . so who's meetin' up on the sly wi' sommun odd."

Bear was very quiet. "Well, I had a notion . . . there's a City Healer who belongs to one of those charitable orders that came up to talk to me about the kits. And he's asked me a couple times if I'll come down a few days a fortnight and work with him down there. There's a lot more people who'd trust a potion than a Healer down there. Now . . . I could do that. And people talk when they're getting helped. Heck, they babble sometimes. I could have you come along as my helper, Mags, and you could—"

"Aye, could do," Mags said, seeing immediately where he was going. "Yer right, people, they sorta rain bits'a thinkin' when they're hurtin'." He perked up at the thought. "Now thet there's a fine notion, Bear! An—ye know what? Ye do thet, yer gonna show ev'body i' th' whole damn Healer's Circle thet yer gonna shove right up an' do th' dirty work, not jest the stuff where yer fiddlin' wi' yer plants an' all an' niver touch a real human patient."

He heard the life come back into Bear's voice. "Aye. I'll show I not only can accept responsibility, I'm willing to take it on my own."

"And I'll *prove* I'm my father's daughter, but . . . without being so self-centered," Lena said, firmly.

"An' . . . an' I'll show I kin figger stuff out wi' jest usin' m'head. An' Dallen," Mags said.

::Thank you for that.::

::Yer welcome. Yer half m'brains anyway.::

::Only half?:: Dallen teased.

::Ah, hush.::

Slowly, Mags felt his stomach unknotting, and the tension behind his eyes easing. It felt good to have a plan again, and better to have one that didn't involve torturing children.

He felt his eyes starting to drift closed . . . and became aware of something else.

Bear and Lena. They were probably unaware of it themselves, but now that they had something they could actually do about their situations, they would be a great deal happier if he was elsewhere at the moment. Mags was always careful to screen out stray thoughts around these two, but nevertheless, a great deal of *feeling* swirled around them . . . and . . .

"I'm a-gonna find Amily an' tell 'er what's goin' on," he said, trying to keep it from sounding abrupt as he sat up. "Reckon she needs ter know right off, aight?"

"Oh . . . damn, I can't believe I forgot about Amily!" Bear exclaimed, "Definitely, she can use some good news. She's kind of gotten over being mad at her pa, but . . . she's not happy."

He got to his feet. "Mebbe I kin change thet," he said with a smile; he started to leave the grotto but then turned back a moment.

He caught Bear just reaching for Lena's hand and suppressed a grin at Bear's flush. "Lena—ye mind what yer Dean said. Aight?"

She looked confused. "What my Dean said?"

"'Bout playin'. Reckon t'day ye kin skip class fer once. Or at least, fer a liddle." Without waiting for their answer, he strode off.

He regretted the brisk stride within a few steps as the heat hit him like a hammer, and the headache threatened a return. ::*I'm a-gonna cheat. Dallen, where's Amily?*::

It had occurred to him that Dallen seemed to be able to locate Amily just fine, even though she was not a Herald. And Dallen did not challenge this observation. ::*Well, that's interesting . . . .*:: the Companion said after a moment.

::*What is?*::

::*I'll have to show you.*::

Following Dallen's mental instructions, Mags found himself going into the Palace, which was not a surprise since Nikolas and Amily had their rooms in the Heralds' Wing there—but then, following further instructions, he went down a half-hidden set of stairs he never even knew were there, into what must have been a basement, and from those stairs down a long, dim—and blessedly cool—corridor. There were several doors leading from it; the place had a definite feeling of age and was plain, without being shabby. He stopped where Dallen indicated, and tapped lightly on the solid oak door there. "It's Mags," he called softly. "Kin I come in?"

"Mags?" the door muffled Amily's voice, but the surprise in it was clear. "Yes, of course! I wasn't expecting anyone down here—"

He opened the door to a room scarcely larger than a closet, round and with a round table in the center. It was lit by one lantern, heavily shaded, suspended from the ceiling above the exact center of the table. Beneath it, resting on a padded base, was a sphere of crystal. The table itself was surrounded by padded benches with backs to them. As the door closed behind him, the "dead" feeling to the room showed that it was so well-insulated against outside noise that a small riot could probably take place outside the door without the occupants of the room being aware of it.. Amily was sitting on one of the benches, and it seemed she must have been staring into the sphere.

"What—"

"What is this place?" Amily asked. "It's a workroom for doing things at a great distance. It's one of the most shielded rooms on the Hill, and the shields are tremendously old. It's said Vanyel made this place, though no one remembers how or why. We're right underneath the Royal Suite, in fact."

"I was gonna ask, what're ye doin' down 'ere all alone?" he said, with a half smile.

"Just . . . thinking, I suppose," she replied, as he sat down beside her. "It seems easier to stay calm down here. And it doesn't hurt that it's cooler than upstairs."

"Aye t'thet." Her hand lay quietly on the table; he considered it, then put his over it. This seemed as good a time as any to ask her about something that had been on his mind for a good long time. "Y'know, yer pa started up this thin' 'tween us t'gi' me a reason fer hangin' about. We were friends an' all, an' thet was fine, but now, ev'body seems t'figger we're courtin'. Even yer pa. Nobody seems t'hev asked you how ye feel 'bout thet. An' nobody seems t'hev asked ye if ye fancied the courtin' be fer real."

Amily looked right at him, no blushing or faltering. He liked that about her so much—she was so straightforward.

"I was hoping that you holding my hand right now meant you were happy with the idea," she said, with a faint smile. "Because I don't think I would care to be courted by anyone else."

He grinned hard enough to make his face split and squeezed her hand. "Reckon we feel 'bout th' same, then," he said warmly. He was about to say more when Amily held up her free hand, stopping him.

"But Mags, that was one reason why I wanted to have my leg fixed—don't you see?" she said, anxiety now coloring her voice. "I've been such a burden on Father all these years, I don't think I can bear to be a burden on someone else!"

He blinked, taken by surprise. His first reaction was to tell her she was no kind of a burden, but that wasn't true and they both knew it. His second was to say nobody minded, and that was partly true. People were only people, patience ran out—

—well, just look at the prime fit that she herself had pulled when her Healing had been canceled. And she was one of the most patient people he knew.

The silence lengthened, and he knew if he didn't say *something*, she was going to think the worst. He scratched his head. "Ye know, there ain't no good answer t'thet. 'Cept thet I unnerstand. An' it ain't like yer never gonna git yer leg fixed, right?"

Her eyebrows furrowed, but she nodded.

"An' it ain't like nobuddy *wants* ter help ye. Ye know thet. Right?"

Again, she nodded.

"So ye ain't hateful, an' this ain't gonna be ferever. It's jest fer a liddle while longer. I think th' world'a yer pa, but I think he's a damn fool fer not tellin' ye what's goin' on, though—an' not jest cause it ain't right." He smiled crookedly. " 'E's a damn fool fer thinkin' we'd all jest sit there wi' our hands folded nice an' not try an' find out what's what fer oursel's."

She managed a little smile. "Or maye he does know you're all going to try, and he figures to let whoever ordered him not to tell find out that keeping you lot from chasing after a secret is like trying to keep kittens in a basket."

"Ye're in thet, too," he reminded her. "Ain't jest me an' Bear an' Lena. Bet ye've been snoopin' a bit on yer own, aye?"

She blushed. "Well," she temporized. "People do tend to forget that I'm around when I'm quiet. Can I help it if they say things I'd rather not hear?"

Something about the way she said that, gave him a sudden notion . . .

He knew part of what made Nikolas so good at what he did was that he *did* have a subtle Gift—maybe a variant on Empathy, Mags didn't know enough about Gifts to guess—that made people forget he was there.

And it sounded as though Amily had the same Gift.

I thought Companions always Chose people with Gifts?

Well, maybe not. Maybe it was only that the people they Chose, had to have a Gift, and you could have one but not be Chosen . . .

"I'll tell ye this," he continued, abandoning that particular line of thought. "E'en iffen yer leg never gits fixed, it'll be wuth dealin' wi' it t'be wi' ye. An' thet's th' plain truth. I ain't gonna say it ain't gonna be a pain, but it'll be wuth it." He grinned crookedly. "Iffen you kin put up with me getting' beat up playin' Kirball and moanin' and whinin' 'bout it after, reckon we'll be even. Aight?"

Whatever she had been expecting him to say, it hadn't been that, judging by her reaction. But judging by that same reaction, she was just as happy with it, if not more.

She looked puzzled for a moment, then suddenly just beamed at him as if he had given her the best present of her life. She looked as if she, too, was searching for something to say, but he had the sudden intuition that words were probably not the best reply at this moment.

So instead, he reached for and captured her other hand, leaned over, and kissed her.

Yes . . . that was the best reply. The best possible reply.

Bear was right. People did babble to Healers. Mags had learned an amazing amount just by being the one who handed things to Bear while he patched folks up. He was becoming an expert on other peoples' children, how they should be raised, other peoples' love lives, other peoples' grievances, other peoples' pain, other peoples' neighbors. Unfortunately, none of this information was leading to where the Agents were.

Mags had solved the possible problem of being forbidden to help Bear with his charity Healing by simply not asking for permission. Bear went down into Haven one out of every two or three afternoons, and if anyone asked Mags where *he* was on those occasions, he would reply with absolute truth that he was with Amily.

Which he was. *She* was helping Bear as well. Women were sometimes shy around a male Healer, even at the best of times. If they'd been abused or—as Bear delicately put it—"interfered with," having to go to a male was problematic at best. So it was Amily who asked them questions, while Bear stayed a nonthreatening distance away, Amily who soothed them, and Amily who dispensed advice and herbs in equal measure. And if there was anything that was a testament to how successful Bear's idea of allowing folk with training but no Gift to do Healing work could be, it was Amily's work with these poor victims of abuse and assault.

Here, her leg was a help rather than a hinderance. These women saw it, saw her as someone even weaker and at a greater disadvantage than they were, and did not react to her as they would probably have reacted to another woman who was obviously better off in the world than they were.

As for Amily herself, although she would often come back up the Hill bowing under a mingled burden of compassionate grief and anger, Mags could see that being there, *doing* something that he and Bear could not, and accomplishing something good, was making a slow but profound change in her. She wasn't just a cripple anymore in her own eyes; she wasn't just the Herald's daughter who had not been Chosen herself. She was Amily, whom Bear and Brother Killian relied on to handle the heartbreaking cases that would not respond to them. She was Amily, who had managed to get three women in the past fortnight to leave their abusers and allow the Brothers of the Well to get them away to the sanctuary of their corresponding Order of women, off to the north in Amberdeen—which was more than Brother Killian had been able to do in six months.

Mags only wished he'd had as much good fortune. He hadn't gotten so much as a hint that the Agents were anywhere in the city at all—neither rumors nor brushes of their presence. Up the Hill, absolutely no one had been acting out of character. If he had had absolutely nothing to do but listen to and watch folks, perhaps he might have gotten somewhere, but as it was, he wasn't even running up dead ends, because he wasn't finding any beginnings.

Nikolas and the other Heralds were similarly baffled, if the stonewalling on Amily's Healing and the stoney faces were anything to go on.

He reflected on this with a feeling of dull urgency as he and Bear, with Amily on Dallen, made their way back up the Hill after another of Brother Killian's charity afternoons.

"Bloody hell," Bear said, with feeling, flapping the loose neck of his sleeveless tunic to cool himself. "I never thought I'd miss winter. I swear, the hardest part of doing this stuff for Killian is the climb back up afterward."

"I'm sorry," Amily immediately said, contritely, from her perch on Dallen's back. "I—"

"Nah, never mind 'im whingin'," Mags interrupted. "The walk's good fer 'im. He'd ne'er get any exercise otherwise, wi' 'is nose i' book all th' time."

He kept his tone light to cover his disappointment—and his growing unease. He couldn't help but get the feeling that time was running out to find the Agents and their plants. They *had* to be planning something soon, he just felt it, like a storm about to break.

Bear snorted. "As if—" he began, as they passed through the gates with a wave to the Guards standing sentry, who looked only slightly cooler than Bear.

That was when whatever he had been about to retort was lost in the stampede of Heraldic Trainees bearing down on Mags.

Dallen backed up quickly to avoid having Amily jostled. The Trainees were all talking at once, asking him if he'd heard, if he knew—since none of them bothered to say *what* it was they were so roused to a fever over, all he could do was shake his head.

That was when Gennie and Pip came fording through the throng, good-naturedly pushing the rest out of the way until they got to Mags.

"Where have you *been?*" she demanded. "We've been looking all over for you ever since the announcement!"

"Off wi' frien's." Mags said, gesturing vaguely toward Haven. "Wha' 'nouncement?"

"Well . . . it seems that half of Valdemar has gone mad for Kirball," Gennie told him, so excited she was bouncing a little on her toes. "But they don't just want to see it, they want to *play* it too."

"Wait—" it was Bear who spoke up before Mags could, frowning and combing his fingers through his hair in agitation. "That's insane. The only reason hardly anyone gets hurt now is because you're playing it with Companions. That field is a nightmare! You go using ordinary horses, and you are just begging for broken bones and maybe someone killed!"

"Everyone knows that," Pip replied. "That's why the Guard's been working with some of us to come up with a simplified version—one that uses a flat field and doesn't need Heralds. We've been training two Guard teams for a moon or so now. We even have two versions, one with riders and one using all foot."

Bear stopped making his hair stand on end. "Ah," he said, calming down. "Oh. Well . . ."

"The point is," Gennie interrupted, "The King himself authorized a Kirball Festival! He's going to have us demonstrate our style and then have Guard teams demonstrate the new styles! He's checked with the Healers and the Guard, and everyone agrees that we can start training again even though there's a lot of summer heat—*with precautions*, Bear, so don't start making your hair look like a hedge—and have the Festival in time for the start of Fall Quarter! Isn't it fantastic?"

Mags didn't quite know what to say. "Aye," he managed. "Fantastic."

Fantastic t' think there's three enemies up 'ere, we dunno who they be, there's at least two more down i' Haven we cain't find, an' we're gonna do . . . games.

::*That was my reaction*,:: Dallen said, ::*until Rolan pointed out that the Agents will certainly think we are unaware of their presence, will certainly try to take advantage of this opportunity . . . and . . .*::

Mags waited. Dallen's Mindvoice was . . . smug. Really smug.

::*And?*:: he prodded sharply, when Dallen had let the silence go on for too long.

::*And he as much as admitted that yes, you were correct, there are three operatives up on the Hill somewhere, no, they still don't know who they are, and they are hoping to use this Festival as the means of smoking them out.*::

On the one hand . . . that was absolutely insane. No one in his right mind would do something like this . . .

On the other hand, the three—spies, operatives,

whatever they were—did not know that the Heralds knew they were there. The Hill was going to be thrown into a games-mad frenzy for the next moon or so. Schedules would fly right out the window, people would become unpredictable in actions and habits, and that would put the Agents under a tremendous amount of pressure. They might snap under it. They might make mistakes.

They might reveal themselves.

"It's *fantastic!*" Mags said with more enthusiasm. "Which teams'll be a-playin'?"

"All of them. East against South, us and North," Gennie said with great satisfaction, rubbing her hands together with glee. "This is going to be amazing!"

It'll be amazin' iffen I kin get through this next moon wi'out droppin' over wi' exhaustion. An' ne'er mind them Agents tryin' t'kill me iffen they ever figger out I'm lookin' fer 'em.

Helping Bear was completely out of the question now; there was no way he would be able to do that *and* keep up with the training schedule that Gennie had imposed on them.

Training was in the morning, before the full heat of the day was on them, and with all four teams needing field space, they were beginning at dawn. The Dean had thrown up his hands in defeat as soon as this Festival had been announced. Those Trainees who were on the teams had been put into their own classes, which were more like big tutoring sessions, lasted all afternoon, and dealt with all subjects together. Instead of attending formal classes with lectures, each of the players was given daily assignments by his or her regular instructors and was expected to turn them in completed by dinner. Teachers came and went during the afternoon, and the Trainees were expected to help each other. Strangely enough, it worked well, at least as far as Mags could see—though he could also see the potential for slacking off, so he doubted this novel approach was going to last past the Festival.

But this approach pretty much decreed an end to his "snooping" up on the Hill. He simply did not have time. By the time dinner was over, the Collegia kitchen staff and the few servants were gone—because *their* working days began before dawn and ended as soon after dinner as possible. He had no reason to be poking his nose over into the Palace staff and absolutely no reason to be found among the courtiers. The Guard had been tolerating his presence by day, but by night, those who were not on duty were not in the least interested in socializing with a "boy"—and at any rate, most of that socializing was going on down in two or three specific taverns in Haven, where, again, he would stand out rather than blending in. If he'd had time, he might have been able to slip in posing as a potboy, but by the end of the day, he was far too weary to spend his evening delivering drinks and clearing tables.

The closer the time came for the Festival, the more agitated he felt. He was getting nowhere alone. He had no idea if Nikolas and the others had had any more success than he had—but he rather doubted it.

Finally, the week before the Festival, he made up his

mind. So far as he knew, he was the only person, Herald or Trainee, who had exactly the right combination of Gifts to find the Agents, if they could be found at all. He'd had one brush with their minds; in theory at least, he *should* be able to find them at a middling distance . . . if . . .

He thought about this all through the afternoon tutoring session, and instead of going to supper and sitting down with the rest, he went out to Companion's Field to consult with Dallen.

::*Whatcher think?*:: he asked, without preamble, when Dallen ambled up to the fence and put his nose over it. While occasionally it was a bit irritating to have Dallen "looking over his shoulder," so to speak, virtually all the time if he didn't specifically work to keep the Companion out, this was one time out of many when it was a distinct advantage that Dallen knew what he had been considering.

::*I think it will work,*:: Dallen replied. ::*With a few changes. Nothing drastic. But it will make a great deal of difference. Do you remember that room with the crystal sphere in it?*::

He blushed a little. As if he could forget! He and Amily had gotten rather beyond just kissing before prudence and Dallen's reminder that the room was not a private one had brought them both to their senses.

::*What 'bout it? I mean, 'tis shielded, so that'll help, I s'pose—*::

::*It's more than that,*:: Dallen said, raising his head and flagging his tail. ::*Much, much more. If you were being Gift-trained like the rest, you wouldn't even know the thing exists, much less what it can do, for years, maybe not ever. But I am your instructor, and it is my determination that—::*

::*What thing?*:: Mags interrupted him. ::*Ye mean, thet glass ball?*::

Dallen snorted and shook his head so his ears flapped. ::*That 'glass ball' is not glass at all and—well, never mind. The point is that one of its functions is to allow anyone to focus a Gift with great precision, providing that the Gift us under conscious control. For instance, it helps Mindspeakers to focus right down on a single person at a great distance.*::

Mags saw where he was going immediately. ::*So, since I already know what these bastiches feel like an' look like, what wi' thet whatever 'tis thet's watchin' over 'em, I kin find 'em wi'out havin' t'drop shields an' kinda roam around open.*::

::*Exactly,*:: Dallen replied and fixed Mags with an intense gaze, his blue eyes practically boring a hole into Mags' brain. ::*You'll have to be careful—I honestly don't know what is shielding these people, and we already know that it reacts poorly to any perceived meddling. For all we know, if it thought there was something about, it might lash out. And the danger isn't only to you, it's to anyone about that might somehow be open to it.*::

::*Aight. I'm headin' fer thet room now.*::

He patted Dallen's shoulder, turned, and—

Well he *would* have trotted toward the Palace, if it hadn't been so hot that it felt as if he were being weighed down by bags of baked salt. He concentrated on the fact that it was going to be a lot cooler in the shade and grimly forged his way toward the buildings.

Getting inside the Palace was a relief. The side door

was in shade, and the stone walls of the Palace held out a lot of the heat. The cooler he got, the more energetic he felt, and he began to feel less like a baked brick as he made his way down the dim stairs and into the lower level. By the time he reached the door to that mysterious little room, he was feeling as if he could take on almost anything.

He opened the door to find that the room was empty, and there was no sign that anyone had been in it recently. That shaded lamp was still burning over the center of the table. Was it ever allowed to go out? Maybe not. If Dallen was to be believed, and the crystal sphere could make your Gift work better, then you wouldn't want to have to wait around for someone to come light the lamp for you when you needed it. How many people knew about this place? He'd bet, not many.

::*It works best with specific Gifts,*:: Dallen said. ::*Mindspeakers don't bother with it, much. For sending a message quickly to a Herald at a distance, it's easier just to ask the Companions to do it.*::

He entered and closed the door behind him, then sat down carefully on one of the padded seats. ::*Now what?*::

::*I want you to understand that because you are going to be using your Gift in a very intense way, it is going to take a great deal out of you,*:: Dallen cautioned. ::*Your Gift is like any other thing you do; it takes energy to use it. This will be exactly like playing the most energetic game of Kirball you ever have in your life, followed by two more. And that's if you're lucky.*::

::*Nothin' comes fer free, I got it,*:: he replied, leaning over the table. ::*What else?*::

::You will not need to keep your shields up. The room will shield you in part—to be brief, it will shield you from everyone up on the Hill. For the rest, as you hunt, I will shield you, as I did before you learned to shield yourself. Save your strength for the hunt.::

::Aight.:: He relaxed and let the shields down, a little at a time, and—

Huh.

Dallen was right. The shields on this room were incredible. He wondered how that had been done, since most shields evaporated when the person who held them in place died.

::Now just let your eyes rest on the crystal. Remember what those Agents looked like when you saw them, either with your own eyes or Nikolas'. They were probably not bothering to disguise themselves at the time. Then remember how their minds looked to you, and when you are sure of what you are looking for, start hunting. It will be like sifting gravel to find a gemstone.::

He braced his elbows on the tabletop, cupped his chin in his hands, and stared at the crystal. After a moment, he realized that he couldn't look away. Something was holding his gaze.

The crystal was holding his gaze.

He made no attempt to fight it. Instead, he did as Dallen had told him to do and concentrated on the two enemy Agents he had seen. Height . . . roughly the same as Nikolas, one shorter than the other. Build . . . powerful, but lean. Their faces though . . . there was something like a distant family resemblance there. Both had lightly tanned skin, dark hair, dark eyes—by candlelight he couldn't vouch for the exact color. Thin lips, strong cheekbones, deep-set eyes. Expressions that were so neutral they were masklike. Eyes like shiny dark pebbles and just about as cold and lifeless.

Things started coming up in his memory, things he had not consciously noticed at the time. A scar at the corner of the shorter one's left eye. That their hands were gloved, but the gloves had no fingers. That the fingertips looked oddly flat, the fingers had a cross-hatching of faint scars on the backs.

When he had them firmly in his mind's eyes, he added the memory of how they had "felt" in his head. How dispassionate and cold those stray thoughts had been, as if everything were a factor in some calculation that only they knew the answer to. And how utterly indifferent they were to whether something or someone lived or died. They were nothing like the man who had somehow driven his dreams and feelings into Mags without realizing it. And yet . . . they were clearly cast from the same mold, fired in the same furnace. The one that Mags had called Temper had been flawed, though the flaws had never been on the surface, and those who had sent him had had no idea that what they had sent out would crack so easily under pressure. These two were the perfect specimens of . . . of . . . of whatever it was they were supposed to become.

Weapons. They were supposed to become weapons.

Mags felt something fall into place as he recognized what they were. And he had names for them now—"Ice"—that was the older, slightly taller one. He was colder than the other, and experiences and emotions simply slipped off him. "Stone" was the other—not as cold, but harder. Nothing got past his surface. The first froze his own feelings. The second never allowed them to escape.

And that shield, that shadow that enveloped them. No, not exactly a shadow . . . a fog? No, that wasn't it, either. It was just as cold and dispassionate as they were, which probably made it easier to obscure their thoughts. Despite being a separate *thing* from them, and despite the fact that it definitely reacted to an intrusive presence, Mags didn't think it was exactly alive. Not as he knew things were alive. And despite the appearance of intelligence, he didn't believe it could actually think. Could it be it was like a clockwork toy that gave the *illusion* of life by doing several things in a lifelike manner?

Never mind. He knew what it felt like, too. He could hunt for it as well as for them.

::*Ready to hunt?*:: Dallen asked.

He answered with a wordless *yes*.

He felt his eyes closing, and yet, he could still see the sphere. Odd . . . but he didn't have time for musing. Because—because at that moment, "he" wasn't sitting at the table anymore. "He" was floating . . . somewhere. If he concentrated quite hard, he "saw" parts of Haven beneath him, but the buildings were like sketches of buildings, while the people in them varied from dim ghosts to perfectly normal looking people to creatures that burned like stars.

And without thinking about anything but the need to hunt, he began to move. It was something like flying dreams he'd had, and the dream-landscape below him took on a hint of familiarity.

Well, the only analogy he could make was that "he" became a hunting falcon, circling up over the Palace, searching, searching . . . Herald Jakyr, the Herald who had rescued him from his life at Cole Pieters' mine, was an avid falconer and had taken him along on a few hunts on the rare occasions he was in Haven. And this was exactly like being one of those hawks, circling, soaring, keen eyes looking, looking everywhere. Walls were no barrier to those eyes, as he circled farther and farther outward. He "saw" the people beneath him and somehow saw them outwardly and inwardly too. He could have read their thoughts, but that wasn't *right*, and besides, it was not why he was out here. He only needed to recognize what they were—see that they were *not* what he was hunting for—and move on.

It was anything but effortless. He felt exactly as if he were playing a hard game of Kirball, and he was hunting the ball. Energy drained out of him; Dallen had spoken nothing less than the truth. At least it wasn't stinking hot . . .

This was like the search he'd done for Bear, only so much more precise! And there was none of that mental clamor he had to shut out all the time under ordinary circumstances, the clamor that had come so close to driving him insane the single time he'd been forced to rid himself of all shields. If he'd had to hold his own shields against that, this task would have been out of the question; he could never have done it.

Mags sensed his quarry in the distance before he "saw" them, sensed the chill of the thoughts that wisped away from them. That was what made them stand out in this vague and ever-changing landscape.

There was nothing, and no one, as cold and emotionless as they were.

They were on the move. And the thing that shielded them made it impossible to say exactly where in the real Haven they were.

::*Damn*,:: he heard Dallen say, as he sped toward them. He wasn't sure if that "damn" was because that sheltering thing obscured their location or because of what they were doing. For as he neared them, the real landscape of Haven solidified around them, as if by their very presence they were dragging it into this world of ghosts and shadows. A moving, irregularly shaped spheroid of reality surrounded them.

He could "see" it all quite clearly, and he watched in amazement and grudging admiration. He'd thought *he* was good going over rooftops. Now he was glad he'd never encountered these two up there. They moved like nothing human that *he* had ever seen: fast, agile, making insane leaps that not even a cat would try. The only way they could have gone faster over these rooftops would have been if they had grown wings.

Well, at least he knew they were in the city.

He didn't need Dallen to tell him to stay with them for as long as he could. Those shield-things weren't perfect. Thoughts—the most intense thoughts, at a guess—leaked out. He had to stay with them and concentrate on listening so he could catch those thoughts.

His focus narrowed again. He stopped being aware of anything except the two shields and the whispers that slipped out and evaporated away.

He was getting hints, but not in words. These two were concentrating on what they were doing to the exclusion even of coherent thoughts. But he was getting *something*. They had just left their allies on the Hill! But . . . who were these allies? He strained for a hint, since their escaping thoughts bore hints.

Scents, glimpses, traces of sound—

He was too far. The thoughts were too tenuous to catch from this far away, and he tried to get closer—

Suddenly, something bright and dark together exploded in his face.

He was flung halfway across the "sky." He felt Dallen enclose him for just a moment, protecting him.

He was stunned; it felt as if he'd been hit in the head hard enough to crack his skull.

When he could "look" again, they were gone.

Dammit! I got too close! The shield-things had sensed him and—well, now he knew what they could, and would, do.

He hovered in an empty space, an empty "sky," with the world beneath him, blank for the moment. Thanks to Dallen, he knew what had happened. Even through Dallen's protection, they had shocked his system, and he had lost his mental image of the world.

Should he try to find them again?

Could he? What if those shield-things recognized him and went straight into an attack? Could Dallen protect him a second time?

Before he could make up his mind, another unshielded thought—not from Ice and Stone, but someone else entirely, echoed across the ghostly spaces where he floated.

An image. Amily. Amily, bound and gagged, terrified and alone.

::Mags!::

It wasn't an image in the present—he knew immediately that Amily was safe in her own bed. This was something someone had seen . . . no, Foreseen.

::Mags!::

He ignored Dallen and focused on *that* thought, on *that* mind, fear and anger turning his will into a rapier with a tip of diamond, searching until he found the mind that held that vision.

He didn't have to "follow" anything this time—he was there, *right* there, in a room here in the Palace, catapulted into the midst of a small group of people. Nikolas, the King, a Herald he didn't recognize, three people in the robes of three different Temples, the Lord Marshal, a couple of Healers.

". . . I thought perhaps we'd averted it when we canceled the procedure on Amily's leg," the strange Herald was saying. "But all four of us got the same vision within an hour of each other. These people are going to try again to take Herald Nikolas' daughter and hold her to force him to do what they tell him to. Last time we got a vision, they were going to take her either just before or just after her leg was reset. We couldn't tell which—"

"Probably because *they* didn't know which; it was going to be a matter of opportunity," the King said, face impassive. "But now?"

"As you must have expected, Your Highness, they *are* going to use the Kirball Festival, and the crowds and the confusion . . ."

Nikolas groaned. "There's no hope for it. I can't allow her to be used as a tool to manipulate me. We'll have to find somewhere to send her—"

"Niko, where would that be, exactly?" the King interrupted sharply. "The first lot were bad enough, and one of them nearly murdered a stableful of Companions, but *these*—there doesn't seem to be anything that will stop them. And it isn't Amily that they're after—not really—they have some broader agenda that begins with breaking you. And we don't know what that agenda is. We don't even know who they are or where they're from!"

Mags was furious, a swirling, seething anger that washed over everything for the moment, since its real target was out of reach. It erupted into a torrent of pure emotion that left no room for the tiniest of thought, turning him into a fireball of rage and hate.

A fireball that burned out as quickly as it had erupted, as his chin hit the hard surface of the table and he came abruptly back to himself.

He was shaking, shaking with reaction and with weakness and, a little, with cold. His head felt fit to burst. Pain throbbed behind his eyes; his mouth was as dry as a handful of sand.

And he truly, deeply, wanted to kill someone.

::*Mags?*:: Dallen whispered.

::*Aye. 'Tis all right*.:: Well, now the mystery was solved. He knew why the Healing had been canceled. And he thought . . . maybe . . .

One of the images he'd gotten from the Agents was of a keystone pulled from an arch, and he thought he knew now what it was they were here to do. Amily was just the keystone. They had correctly identified the weakest—and yet, the strongest—spot in the grand construction that was the Kingdom of Valdemar.

The King's Own.

Take the daughter of the King's Own, and the King's Own crumbles. The King is without his prime support, and confidence in the Heralds is eroded Kingdomwide—after all, if the Heralds couldn't protect Amily, who could they protect?

Opportunistic outsiders take advantage of that uncertainty, and with the right strikes at the right time, the entire Kingdom falls apart.

He sensed Dallen's shock.

::*Well, that's how it'd look t'outsider, ye ken,*:: he said grimly. ::*But they don' know Heralds.*::

With shaking hands, he pushed himself up and away from the table.

::*I'm gonna go hev me a liddle talk wi' King's Own.*::

14

Mags was still shaking with fatigue when Nikolas entered his own rooms to find him, Amily, and Bear there, waiting. It had taken some strong potions from Bear and what seemed like a bucket of salted honeywater, but at least his head wasn't splitting, and he could think clearly. Bear had asked to come along when he talked to Amily; he welcomed the support.

Nikolas already looked shaken as he entered his rooms; when he saw the three of them together, his face went white.

"We know," Amily said, calmly. "We know everything. Mags told us about your meeting."

Nikolas's gaze flashed to Mags, and there was a moment of recognition on his face. So, interesting. Nikolas had sensed that Mags was in the room a few candlemarks ago—had the King?

Probably.

Nikolas cleared his throat carefully. "Then you know—"

"That I am not moving one inch from the Hill," she

interrupted. "I'm just the lever to overset you. They know if they kill you, someone else will be Chosen as King's Own within a week. So what they want to do is weaken you—or better still, break you."

"Of course," Nikolas said harshly. "That's obvious. And when the news got out that my own daughter had been—" He shook his head. "People would say, if the Heralds can't keep one girl safe on the Hill, why should we trust their judgement, their ability, anywhere else? Pressure from within, pressure from without, the Heralds start to fall apart. From there it's only a matter of time before the Kingdom falls apart, divides into little warring factions. That's why I have to get you away from here, you have to go into hiding. Right out of the Kingdom if—"

"No," Amily and Mags said together. He took her hand in his.

"Thet ain't gonna do it," he said. "I went huntin' fer these critters t'night. Ye send 'er away, they'll hev 'er afore she's halfway t'next city. They're more'n good, sir, there better'n anythin' ye've ever seen at what they do. They jest don' *stop* till they git what they want, an' they don' let nothin' stand i' their way." He tried not to sound as if he were accusing Nikolas but he wasn't sure if he managed it. "Admit it; ye knew th' moment I tol' ye 'bout the spies up here thet I was right."

Nikolas flushed a little. "You were right. The Foreseers had already gotten that much the first time. I'm sorry, all of you, sorry I was not allowed to tell you."

Mags nodded a brief acknowledgement of the apology. "So ye wanta send Amily away—well, there's people spyin' fer 'em, planted right up 'ere. So they'll know yer sendin' 'er away. Mebbe they won't know when she leaves, mebbe they won' even know tha's what yer gonna do, but they'll know soon's she's gone, an' they'll find 'er. It ain't gonna work. They'll track 'er down. Ain't no way ye kin keep 'em from findin' 'er."

"You should have told us what was going on in the first place, Father," Amily continued, as Nikolas looked as if he wanted to dig a hole right there and stuff his daughter into it to keep her safe. "It wasn't *right*. And if you'd told us, we could have been thinking of ways to catch these men all this time."

" 'Idin' 'er 'ere i' th' Palace, an' startin' a rumor she bin sent off ain't gonna work, neither," Mags pointed out, divining the next turn Nikolas's thoughts would take. " 'Ow's thet gonna help Amily, by makin' 'er a prisoner? 'Sides, s'pose ye kin keep 'er safe i' dungeon, say, wi' a mort'a Guards; these bastiches ain't stupid, they'll swap t' some other target. An' ye won't know who 'tis."

"I want some say in this," Amily said, her voice shaking. "This is my life we're talking about. I don't want to spend it locked up like a prisoner, or watching over my shoulder in some strange place I've never heard of. In fact, I *don't* want other people making decisions *for* me anymore. Not even you, Father. Not even you."

Mags squeezed her hand. She squeezed back. Mind you, he hated this. But he couldn't deny her this, either. Guarding her back was one thing. Protecting her like a child did no one any good.

"You said yourself that you know what all this is

about. Well, the way to stop it is to stop them cold right at the beginning of their plan. Thanks to the Foreseers, we *know* what they're going to do. So we *let* them. Or we let them try, anyway." She raised her chin and looked her father square in the eye. "You are not the only one in this family that is willing to risk everything for Valdemar."

"No—Amily, I can't let you do this!" Nikolas protested.

"You mean, you can't stop me from doing this," she corrected. "We've spoken to the King and the Lord Marshal, and they both agree this is the smartest plan." She smiled a little, shakily. "Or, as the Lord Marshal put it, 'There is nothing that ruins a bad person's day quite as thoroughly as an ambushed ambush.'"

"Amily—"

She shook her head. "We may have discussed this only briefly, but it wasn't difficult to come to that conclusion, Father. They are not aware we know of their plans. That makes this our best chance to catch them off guard. You've put both yourself, and Mags, at far greater risk in the past. Yes, you are very highly trained, but Mags is only a Trainee. And I have been thinking about this while we waited for you. The logical time for me to serve as bait for this trap is going to be during the Kirball games. That's when there will be the most noise and confusion, the best time for them to take advantage of the crowds. They will believe they have the upper hand, when in fact we are the ones in control."

Now all three of them, Bear, Mags, and her father, stared at her aghast and in disbelief.

Then they all began talking at once.

Mags was frantic. How could he protect her if she was among the spectators and he was on the field? When she'd told him her intention of going ahead and acting as bait, he'd agreed because *he* planned to be right there to guard her. It wasn't something he would trust to anyone else. Besides, he *knew* how Ice and Stone "felt," and he would know if they got close!

He tried to make himself heard, but after a moment of babbling, he finally shut up and let Bear and the King's Own rattle on while he thought—hard.

Finally Nikolas and Bear both ran out of objections and left him a chance to put in his own oar.

"Look, Amily," he said, trying to sound reasoned and logical, "Kirball's dangerous, aye? I mean, th' game. Ye've seen it. Ye saw Corwin took off wi' smashed arm."

Taken by surprise by the apparent change in subject, she nodded.

::*Sir,*:: he said, wincing a little at the *ache* in his head that using Mindspeech was giving him at the moment. Dallen was right; using that crystal took an awful lot out of whoever was crazy enough to try it. No wonder there wasn't a line to use it in front of that room! ::*She's made up 'er mind, an' ye ain't gonna talk 'er outa doin' this. But lemme try an' show 'er why hers ain't the best plan.*::

Nikolas bit his lip, but he didn't interrupt.

"Kirball's dangerous. Ev'body knows thet. Nobuddy'd think nothing if somethin' happened an' *I* ate serious dirt. Like, I go down an' I don' git up. But there'd be a big to-do, an' ye'd not be thinkin' 'bout bein' carried off right then, ye'd be askeert an' tryin' t'git t'me, an' th' crowd'd be millin' an' shoutin' an' tryin' t'see an' ev'body's attention'd be on me an' not on *you*. Ye kin bet they'd figger thet out. Prolly plan t' do somethin' t' make me eat dirt so's they'd git thet chance t' grab ye."

As he saw her eyes grow wide, he drove home the last nail. "An' iffen they wanted ye all quiet an' not fightin' an not thinkin', while they was seein' 'bout makin' me eat dirt, they might think about how t'make it permanent. 'Cause ye ain't gonna be in no shape t'do nothin' if ye done passed out or somethin' an' I ain't gonna be comin' fer ye if I'm dead."

"If it was me, I'd set it up so I had some way to *make* her faint," Bear put in. "I can think of a couple just off the top of my head. No one would be surprised, and if you had people in Healers Green come carry her off, no one would stop them, either."

Amily was white now, to match her father, and slowly nodded.

"Now . . . playin' bait durin' t'other Kirball games . . . tha's not a bad thought," Mags continued. "Jest not durin' mine. I kin stick wi' ye—hellfires, ye know how t'ride Dallen, an' 'e knows you, ye kin be on 'im, ain't noplace safer, an' I don' think these fellers really unnerstand what a Companion is. I thin' they thin' Companions're jest extree smart horses. Even iffen they got some ideer Companions're more'n thet, I don' thin' they got ary notion jest 'ow special they be."

::*You say the sweetest things,*:: Dallen said dryly. ::*But I like the idea of her being on me. She will be safest there.*::

"Ev'body'll say, 'So sweet, lookee there, them two mun be t'gether,' aye?" He nodded a little. "None on 'em are gonna thin' ye know howta *really* ride 'im." He blew out his breath. "Now, look ye, I *know* th' way them fellers minds feel. I'll know iffen they even get close. An' I kin give a mind-shout *when* they be, an' *where* they be. Like when I mind-shout th' ball i' the game, on'y they be th' ball."

For a plan he'd come up with on the fly, it wasn't bad. It let Amily do what she wanted to do, when she wanted to do it. And it let him be there to stick by her, because no one was going to get her without eliminating him, first.

Nikolas took a deep breath, and some of the color came back into his face. "All right then. Amily, you are right, I have no business telling you that you cannot do something only you *can* do for this Kingdom—even though I hate the bare thought of it. I'm sure the King and his advisers are still trying to work some way out of this predicament; I will go and tell them what we've decided, and they can put together a coherent plan."

::*Should we tell 'im we already did?*:: Mags asked Dallen. ::*Well, except for th' part 'bout doin' it durin' th' Kirball game . . .*::

::*No. Let him keep some shreds of his dignity.*::

Nikolas got up, still shaking a little, and looked down at the three of them. "I think you are both very brave, and very insane," he said to Mags and Amily.

"Says the man in the 'Here I Am, Shoot Me' uniform," muttered Bear.

Mags shrugged. "Reckon best way t'keep Amily safe's t'let 'em think they got high ground when it's us's got it."

"I hope you're right, Mags," the King's Own said, and left.

"It'll be all right," Pip said, as Mags fidgeted with his gloves for the twentieth time. "No one, and I mean *no one*, is going to try to get her where she is right now."

"I wouldn't try it," Gennie agreed. "She's out in the open, and there's a stiff wind, so that means these people can't use some sort of smoke or powder to incapacitate everyone. If they had incredibly powerful Mind-Magic, they'd have used it already. There're Heralds all around the ring. There's absolutely no way you could eliminate all those dogs. You might be able to do something to, oh, *maybe* half of them. And the ones you didn't—" She shook her head. "They're boarhounds and deerhounds, sure, but Herald Sorald told them to protect her while she's there. When Sorald tells an animal to do something, it generally gets the job done."

Right now, Amily was judging a dog contest. She was, indeed, surrounded by wolfhounds, boarhounds, deerhounds, and bearhounds—not to mention a nice selection of the enormous mastiffs trained from puppyhood to guard children. She was in the middle of a riding ring, set up for horse and hound judging. A Herald with the Gift of Animal Mindspeech had—so Mags understood—made it quite clear that besides behaving themselves and ignoring anything that might be a distraction, the dogs were all required to protect Amily from *any* threat.

This, or so those whose expertise in this sort of thing said, was likely to drive the Agents and any help they had hired on insane. There she was, out in the open and untouchable. They all felt that this would make the Agents snatch at the first opportunity that presented itself to make their play.

Mags wasn't so sure about that. If the Agents really had recruited local criminals for this—certainly. But to his mind, they were much, much too cool to be irritated into acting before they were ready. No, he was pretty certain that, despite all their plans, *something* would happen where, for a moment, everyone would be caught off guard, and only *then* would the kidnappers move in.

As he saw it at this point, his job was not so much to keep them from taking Amily himself but to buy time for the rest of her protectors and the ambushers to get to them. It was one thing to tell himself that there was no way they would get to Amily except through him— but the reality was the very best he and Dallen could do, if Ice and Stone were as good as he thought they were, was to delay them until the odds were just too great for them to succeed.

::Are you sensing anything?:: Dallen asked.

::I'm thinkin' mebbe I put m'foot in't when I bumped them shields,:: he admitted ruefully. *::I'm thinkin' now them things knows me, an' they closed up even tighter nor afore.::*

::If you did, there's nothing we can do that will change that, so you have to watch for the shields themselves,:: Dallen admonished. *::And if you didn't, then they'll be leaking away, and you need to watch for the telltale signs of* them.*::*

"Hate it when yer right," Mags muttered.

"What?" Pip whipped his head around.

"Jest—Dallen."

"Right." None of them really had their heads in the

game today. Mags wished he'd been able to divulge what was going on, but even if the only ones he'd told were his fellow Grays, that still meant there was a chance that Ice and Stone would get wind of the plan. Only the specific Heralds guarding Amily knew what had been predicted. *I'd still feel a hella lot better iffen t'others knew . . .*

Even as he was thinking this, he noticed something . . . odd.

The Trainees on his team stiffened. So did those on the opposing team. Was some sort of message being passed? Then why hadn't *he* heard it? And why was every Gray on *both* teams turning furtively to look at him?

A Mindvoice that was completely new to him "spoke" inside his head. ::*Mags. It's Riker.*::

Riker? But he was the Captain of—

::*We all just got told by our Companions what's going on.*:: Mags looked up, *startled*, to meet Riker's solemn gaze. ::*Gennie's blocking everything at the moment, I think she's a bit stunned at the mere idea that Amily could be in serious danger. Ask her to come over and talk to me quick, please.*::

Mags gave an abrupt nod and turned to see that Gennie was looking at him with a horrified gaze before she got herself under control. "Gennie, Riker wants ye t' go talk to 'im," he told her. "Not sure why, 'cept 'e says you an 'im need t' talk 'bout what's goin'."

She nodded brusquely and moved out of the pack, heading for the other side of the Kirball field.

"What's going on?" asked Jeffers, puzzled. "Gennie—"

"Huddle up," Pip said sharply. "I'm going to tell you."

When they had huddled, Pip and Mags together explained the situation as best they could. A shocked silence filled the space where the team huddled together when they were done.

No one objected, though. Everyone remembered what had happened a mere few moons ago. And when Mags said that Ice and Stone were more dangerous, and more skillful, than the man who'd nearly burned down Companion's Stable with Companions locked into it, the team was inclined to believe him.

"I . . ." Halleck rubbed his helmet absently. "This is insane. How can we play a *game* when—how can *you* think to play, Mags—"

Gennie came trotting back over to the huddle. "That's what we were just talking about. We aren't going to play a game. We're going to give a show. Riker and I will call the moves, Mags will tell the rest of you. We'll end in a tie. Stay sharp. Mags, keep most of your attention on the crowd, keep watching for those men. All we need out of you is the occasional brilliant move that I'll plan for you, and relaying orders to the non-Gifted. So long as you do a few plays that look like our star Kirball player, no one is going to notice that you're nothing more than Dallen's passenger the rest of the time. That suit?"

There were no dissenters.

"Right, then. First play out of the box, scrum a bit, and whoever gets the ball, kick it to the twisted elm and let Riker's bunch run it up and down the sidelines for a while. When the crowd gets tired of that, we'll break for a new play. Hup!" She pulled the face-guard down over her helmet; they did the same. Both teams headed for the middle of the field, and the start of a game-that-wasn't.

::*You just stick tight, and I'll make it look as if you're actually playing,*:: Dallen told him, as the pack scrummed over the ball. ::*Concentrate on watching for those devils.*::

Mags hunched down over his saddle horn obediently, while Dallen was seemingly everywhere. It probably looked very exciting to their audience, and Dallen *was* working up quite a sweat. But it was all running and leaping and fancy footwork that didn't actually accomplish anything, though it wasn't likely anyone would notice.

Meanwhile, Mags cast his mental net wide, searching for either a hint of those cold, cold thoughts or the shields that guarded the two.

::*Mags!*:: A cautious call from Gennie got his attention. ::*Ball coming, right right back. Give me a brilliant hit down the center toward the goal. Now!*::

He swiveled in his saddle, saw the ball coming at him at exactly the right angle for him to give it a boost onward—of couse, the other team also had a Fetcher, which was probably why it was flying so true—stood up in his stirrups and hit the ball with all the pent-up fury over this situation he had dared not otherwise express—

He hit the ball so hard he came close to bursting it. Probably the only reason that it didn't was that it was already moving and he just boosted the speed. It screamed toward the opposing team's goal with a force that surprised everyone, including him. Pip just got out of its way instead of giving it a helping whack. The goaltender stiffened, then dove to the side, not even pretending to try to intercept it.

The ball hit the back of the goal, in the deep black shadows of the little stone building. Hit it so hard that the tiny building echoed with a hollow *boom*—

"Did the ball just explode?" Halleck asked in the sudden silence.

The goaltender peered inside. And signaled for a new ball.

One of the judges rode up to the goal, brought out the flattened remains of the Kirball, and held it over his head.

The crowd went insane, as one of the sideline helpers brought in the new ball.

His entire team was staring at him.

::*Well* . . . :: Mags managed. ::*Ye wanted a brilliant move.*::

::*Bastard,*:: said Riker, with no rancor whatsoever. ::*How the hell are we supposed to top that?*::

Mags didn't manage to top that move himself, although he did execute three more showy plays, one in each quarter. That was enough to make it *look* as if he was playing the game brilliantly, when in fact he wasn't playing the game at all.

It was just as well, because early in the second quarter he knew that the Foreseers had been absolutely right. He sensed the odd blankness of those shields somewhere beyond the watching crowd. He caught faint hints of Ice, thought none of Stone, during the last quarter. He relayed all of that to the Heralds guarding Amily.

They were all glad to exit the field at the end of the last quarter. Mags had a throbbing headache, and they were all drenched with sweat. Riker walked over to the horse trough and fell into it, armor and all, then got out, pumped his helmet full of colder water from the pump and dumped it over his Companion's head.

"I hope we never have to fight a battle in heat like this," he said aloud.

"Weaponsmaster says heat kills more fighters in a summer war than anything else but disease," Gennie observed. They both cast a brief but penetrating glance at Mags. He shook his head slightly.

::Where's Amily?:: he asked Dallen.

::Still judging dogs. They're restless. Herald Sorald says they sense something out there, but they haven't managed to locate it.:: Dallen sounded worried.

::Then they're better nor me. I'm jest gettin' liddle flashes. So she's still judgin'? Hev I got time t'—::

::Yes, just as we planned. I'll go to the judging ring, Nikolas will put her up on me and we'll meet you there.:: Dallen tossed his head impatiently. *::Go!::*

Mags stared at him, askance. He was filthy, covered in sweat and sweat-caked dirt. *::But ye look—::*

Dallen gave a quick glance around, as if to make sure no one was watching. No one was. He shook himself vigorously, and for a moment the sun winked off him as if he were made of something reflective.

And in the next moment, he stood there looking as if he were fresh from the hands of the groomers.

Mags gaped.

::*What?*:: Dallen said, with irritation.

::*Ye—*::

::*Yes, I did.*::

::*Why don't ye—*::

::*Because you'd get lazy. Now move, if you please. The dogs are not happy, and my skin is crawling. Something is about to happen. There's something important about this whole situation we don't understand, and—something's about to happen. I can feel it.*::

Mags moved, pulling off his armor as he ran to the stable. He'd left a clean set of Grays at the pump; he stripped off, washed, and changed in record time, then ran toward the dog-judging ring.

He crossed the end of the new Kirball field, where the remaining members of the Trainees' teams were chatting with the Guard teams before their game, and he spotted Amily on Dallen, coming toward him.

And that was when he sensed Stone. Nearby. *Very* nearby. Practically—

But wait—there was Ice! Ice on one side of him, Stone on the other! But why were they here, instead of focusing on Amily? Weren't they—wasn't it Amily they wanted?

But he felt it now, felt their concentration on *him*, felt a chill of real fear lance through him.

"Lady Amily! Lady Amily!" A middle-aged man ran up to Amily waving his arms wildly. He looked vaguely familiar; Mags tried to place him. Guard? No, he didn't have a fighter's build. He wasn't in the uniform of any of the Collegia—

"Pawel!" Amily said, in surprise.

Course. Pawel. One'a th' servers at Collegium— Of course Amily would recognize him and remember his name. Like her father, she made a point of being able to recognize almost everyone she had ever been introduced to.

"What—Pawel, what is it?" she asked. Loudly. Loudly enough to make heads turn toward both of them.

Not nearly as much attention as Pawell's shouting attracted. "Lady Amily, don't—don't go to the Kirball field!" he shouted desperately. "It's a trap, Lady Amily! It's a—"

Mags had wormed his way through the pack at the end of the field and felt a surge of icy anger that stabbed right through his head and made him double over with the unexpected pain.

Which was why the man who had been following him stumbled right into him. Fear joined the pain—

It was Stone! How had he gotten so *close?*

Instinctively, Mags ducked under him so that the man rolled over his back and landed on the ground. Mags got a startled glimpse of something in his hand that glittered, reflexively kicked it away, spun, and ran toward Amily.

::They're 'ere!:: he mind-shouted. *::They're 'ere and they're after both of us!::*

Evidently the group going after Amily had not discussed things in advance with the group going after Mags. Or perhaps, vice versa. Mags sensed Stone behind him, dropped, and rolled out from under his grasp, coming right back up on his feet again as rescuers came running from all directions.

Someone in a Guard uniform had knocked Pawel to

the ground and was reaching for Dalen's bridle. He was *saying* "Lady Amily, this man is demented, allow me to escort you away from here." He was *saying* that, but Mags read his thoughts, and they were not that of a Guard.

::*Tha's not a Guard!*:: he shouted to the rescuers, as Dallen half reared, lashing out at the man with wicked hooves. ::*Trus' Dallen!*::

As Amily clung to his saddle like a burr, Dallen put his head down and charged an entire small group of "Guardsmen," barreling right through them and heading for the *real* Guard and more of the Heralds.

Mags sensed Ice coming at him from the side. This time instead of dropping and rolling, he abruptly changed direction, heading for the piled supplies for the stables. He vaulted over a stack of hay bales and switched direction again. Ice followed him—out of the corner of his eye he saw that Ice was wearing a Guard uniform. Stone probably was, too.

Another three men in Guard uniforms had converged on Amily. Two were hanging onto Dallen's bridle, forcing his head down by their weight. One was shouting something about getting that horse under control. Obviously they hadn't yet figured out what Dallen was. Mags did another tuck and roll, this time starting with a leap. Ice and Stone nearly collided, saved themselves, and pelted angrily after him.

He looked for a weapon, spotted a hayfork. That would do. He glanced at Amily—already Herald Caelen was charging up to Dallen's side, his Companion ramming one of the men trying to "coax" her out of the saddle and sending him tumbling.

Mags grabbed the hayfork as he ran past it, ran on a couple of paces, felt Ice and Stone breathing down his neck. He turned his headlong run into a fast turn, holding the hayfork like a quarterstaff. He managed to clip Ice across the face with the handle-end. Ice went down, his nose spewing blood.

Stone danced back, and the two of them stared at each other for what seemed like forever.

The shields over both of the men were so tight it was as if they weren't even there. And the shields themselves—

If I touch 'em ... they'll kill me. He sensed the shields roiling with the same sort of energy that had stunned him the last time he got too close. All *he* could do—all he dared do—was hold his own shields up and tight.

Stone's eyes stared into his, and the most frightening thing at that moment was that there was no anger, no animosity, no emotion whatsoever in his expression. There was only calculation. He was being assessed and measured for the next time.

And there would be a next time.

Then Stone reached down, hauled Ice up to his feet. The two moved so fast Mags could hardly believe it. Stone glanced around quickly, pulled on Ice's arm, and they bolted, running straight at the mob milling around the Guard's Kirball field, the mob of people who were only now beginning to understand that something strange was going on.

And then they were gone, melted into the crowd.

Frantically Mags searched for the "sense" of them, but those wretched shields had clamped down, and all he got was the faint impression of the two of them retreating, faster than any human should be able to run.

Mags leaned against the wall, arms folded over his chest, face impassive. There were some captives out of this fiasco: the group in Guard uniforms who had gone after Amily.

Unfortunately, questioning them only led to a dead end.

The men in the stolen Guard uniforms had been nothing more than hirelings, who had been in the generous pay of Ice and Stone for fortnights. Oh, but they were clever hirelings, able to slip in and pass as Guards because, it seemed, they had done it before.

Many times before.

Often enough, in fact, to have been recognized by several of the Guard officers actually stationed here at the Palace, who assumed that since *they* were in uniform, and on the grounds, they belonged here.

It was stunningly clever. There was always some turnover here, the men had been supplied with the right people to reference, the right things to say, even the passwords.

"Which are not that hard to get," one of the captains said in disgust, "We've gotten lax. Anyone with a right to be on the Palace grounds could just loiter near the gatehouses when we change and overhear them. We never thought to guard against someone on the inside."

As the men were questioned under Truth Spell, they

revealed that they even mingled with the Guards in their chosen taverns down in Haven until they were able to swap the right gossip. These were very clever men indeed—and Ice and Stone, who ordered them to do all these things, who kept them so well paid they were not the least bit interested in looking elsewhere? They were brilliant.

Unfortunately, the false Guards not only didn't know who had hired them—other than vague descriptions—they also had had no idea that the girl they had been sent to fetch was the daughter of the King's Own. They had thought this was all some ransom scheme when they'd finally been given their target.

Once they discovered *that*, they couldn't confess fast enough. The Truth Spell wasn't even needed at that point. It was clear they were terrified of what the King's Own—and the King—might do to them if they didn't cooperate. It was just too bad that they knew so little.

Pawel, however, looked to be a very different proposition, and Mags had taken his place in the interrogation room with hopes that he would learn *something* useful.

Like—why Ice and Stone had wanted to kidnap *him*.

The room was crowded to the poing of being stifling. There were four Guards, two Healers, a Herald whose name Mags didn't know who was in charge of the questioning, Nikolas, who was not being permitted to do anything but glare, and Mags.

Pawel sat on a hard wooden chair with his head in his hands, weeping. Mags wasn't even trying to read him; he was pretty sure all he'd get was a flood of inco-herent emotions.

"I'm sorry," he said, brokenly, over and over again. "I am so very sorry."

He'd been saying that for the last couple of candle-marks now. Mags was pretty sure he meant it. So was the Herald who had administered a Truth Spell to him—the kind that *compelled* you to tell the truth. So were the two Healers who had come to make sure he didn't do anyone any mischief and see to it that the Truth Spell didn't harm him any.

Right now, it seemed, all it would let him do was say how sorry he was.

Mags finally got tired of it. He walked over to the man, grabbed his shoulder, and shoved him back in the chair so that he had to look up. "Mags!" the presid-ing Herald snapped, warningly. "Let him be. You won't get anywhere by bullying him."

Mags ignored the Herald for the moment. "Fine," he growled into Pawel's face. "We unnerstan'. Ye're sorry. Now *tell us what yer sorry about!*"

He put a good deal of mental force into that com-mand, and it seemed to snap Pawel out of the weeping fit he'd been caught up in.

Pawel gulped, coughed, and began to stammer. "I—I'm—"

"Sorry, I know." Mags glared.

"No, I mean . . . It wasn't supposed to happen this way. This—this was all wrong. I was supposed to go home. I was—I was supposed to become a priest. Of Vkandis."

"Karsite?" someone gasped.

"What's thet s'posed t'mean?" Mags growled.

Pawel seemed mired in his own thoughts and memories; his eyes were glazed and swollen and not really focusing on Mags.

"When I was a child, I wanted to be a priest. I've always wanted to be a priest. But I didn't have the money for the love-offering to become a black-robe, or the Sun's Blessing to command demons to my will as a red-robe. So . . . so they told me, if I served the Son of the Sun in another way, they'd—they'd—" He shook his head. "All my life, all I ever wanted was to serve. All my life. And this was my chance. They sent me here. They told me how to fit in. They got me a position in the kitchen. All I had to do was wait."

"Wait a moment." The presiding Herald was leafing through some papers. "It says you've been serving in the Palace and Collegia kitchens since you were thirteen! That's a good twenty years ago!"

Pawel nodded, then hung his head. "I thought they'd forgotten about me. But I stayed quiet. I did what I was supposed to. I prayed, I waited for signs, I stayed quiet. I began to think that this was just their way of getting rid of me, or that the Sunlord had chosen another path for me. Maybe I was supposed to learn that you were not so bad after all. I never saw the demons that they said you commanded. I never saw all the evil things they said you White Riders did. You weren't oppressing your people, or forbidding them to follow the Sunlord's teachings. Down in Haven, things might not be that good everywhere, but they weren't any worse than in Echtsten. Maybe *I* was supposed to come back on my own, and tell the priests myself what I had learned. But I was faithful to the duty I had been given, and I stayed. Then those foreigners—the trading delegation—one of them gave me the sign. I didn't think there would be any harm in just doing what I'd promised! All I ever did was tell them what I saw and heard! There's no harm in that!" His tone grew increasingly desperate, and then he sagged back down over his knees. "It was nothing, I never saw anything that was important! I never heard anything but what the Trainees were gossiping about! I didn't know any secrets! Where was the harm in telling what I knew?"

Th' harm? Tellin' 'em ev'thing 'bout how t' get on up here? Pawel had given those men what they needed most, the intimate knowledge of Palace life. *That* was how they had been able to come and go at will, and who knew how much they had been able to learn with their own spying?

"They told me they were from home. I didn't know . . . I never traveled much beyond Echtsten on the north Border until the black-robes sent me here. They told me they were from the South, so I believed them, even though they didn't pray to the Sunlord at the proper times or—" Pawel shook his head like a weary beast. "But I told myself that this was all because they were in disguise, as I was, so of course they wouldn't give themselves away. But then—there was something wrong with them. The magician started seeing demon-eyes everywhere; he said the eyes were watching him."

"Magician?" someone said, sounding puzzled.

"What—" but whoever it was never completed the thought.

Pawel's shoulders shook. "I began to think maybe I was wrong about you, that you were hiding something after all. And when the magician went mad, I was sure of it."

"That wasn't us, Pawel," said one of the Healers, as the Herald in charge whispered to Nikolas. "We don't know what that was—"

"You don't understand," he wept. "I realized that when they tried to hurt the boy Bear and then when they tried to kill all the Companions. After all this time, I saw—I finally saw it, I finally believed it, completely, you're good people. The priests are wrong about you. Oh, sometimes you treated me like I wasn't there, but . . . wasn't I trying to act as if I wasn't there? So you wouldn't notice me and I could see more? I tried to make myself angry about that, but then one day when I spoke up, because I wanted to help Lady Amily, those youngsters listened to me, respected me, even though all I ever did was clean up their plates."

Mags blinked, remembering when Pawel had helped with the solution to Bear's bone-break modeling problem.

"They told me that you were demon-summoners, that the Companions were demons, and for a while I was afraid of them. Until I saw the truth. The Companions, they aren't demons, they're *nothing* like the demons that the red-robes command. Lady Amily was always kind to me. The worst that has ever happened to me here was the cook shouting at me when he was out of temper. You're all good—you do good things."

He shook his head violently. "So when the newest ones came and they told me that once I answered all of their questions and did what they asked of me, I could go home, I thought—I thought, this is why I'm here after all. I'll finish this and go home, and if I just tell the truth, if I just tell them back home what you're really like, they'd see that they're making a mistake. And once I got back home and they made me a priest, I could keep telling our people about you, and there would be peace."

He broke down again, weeping. "But then—then they told me I had to get them Guard uniforms. So I did, a piece here, a piece there, out of the laundry. I tried not to think about what they might want uniforms for; I told myself it was just to slip out of Valdemar safely. Then they told me that I had to help them take away Lady Amily and the Magpie Trainee. I told them I wouldn't—and one of them—he got into my room! A locked room! He got into my locked room in the middle of the night! He told me that he was a red-robe and a demon-summoner, and that if I didn't help him, he'd bring his demons to eat my soul, and the demon would wear my body and I would never see home again, I would die forever and never walk in the Sun's Light!"

He was shaking with grief and fear now. The Herald in charge looked at Nikolas. "Isn't there a Temple of Vkandis Sunlord somewhere down in the city?" he asked.

"Yes . . . ah, I see where you're going. I'll Mindspeak one of the City Heralds to bring a priest up here."

But Mags was shaking Pawel's shoulder until the man

looked up at him again. "Fust thing, thet bastiche ain't no priest'a nothin'," he said, sternly, putting all the force of his mind behind his words to make the servant *believe* him. "Neither of 'em is. Ye know thet, Pawel! Ye seen 'em do stuff no priest ever did! Ye ever heard tell'a priests learnin' t' run rooftops like cats? Heard tell'a priests thet'd sneak 'bout like thieves? Heard tell'a priests thet fight as good as Weaponsmaster?"

Pawel shook his head.

"Wha's more, you ever ask 'em fer a blessin'? Bet they wouldn' do it, right?" Pawel nodded, slowly. Mags snorted. "What kinda priest won't e'en say a liddle blessin'? E'en th' *wust* priest, the falsest priest, he'll say a blessin' t' any that asks! Not them. It's cause they weren't no priests, an' they weren't no Karsites. They knew they didn' know 'nuff t'even fake a blessin', an' ye'd know thet when ye heard 'em. Mebbe yer people *hired* 'em. They knowed ye was here and knowed th' right signs, an' they got ye t'help 'em, an' they had t'learn that from some'un, so I reckon they got told when they got hired. But they ain't Karsites. They ain't priests. They're jest . . . fancy killers."

Mags turned on his heel and walked back to the wall, leaning against it with his arms crossed. His head burned. He hadn't much liked using his Gift that way, but neither Nikolas nor the other Herald had stopped him. And it wasn't as if he'd put anything into Pawel's head that wasn't already there. All he'd done, really, was make Pawel see and acknowledge what he already knew.

Still. It didn't feel wrong . . . but he wasn't sure it was entirely right, either.

::*Well done*,:: Dallen said, as the Herald in charge took over the interrogation again, alternately coaxing and stern. ::*Well done for handling him, and well done for doubting, Chosen. You must walk a very narrow path, and you know it. Never forget how narrow that path is.*::

Mags acknowledged him wordlessly, and he pondered the man before him. Not a good man . . . not a bad man, either. Just . . . just a man. He didn't hate Pawel, how could he?

But he didn't much like him at the moment, either.

How could Pawel have been here for so long and fail to see how wrong the people who had sent him were? Had his very faith made him don blinkers of his own free will? And if faith made people do that, then how did you get them to abandon what blinded them without breaking them?

Right now, Mags wasn't sure he cared for religion of any sort. Plenty of priests had seen what was going on at the mine and done nothing. Priests had blinded Pawel to what was right in front of him, day in, day out.

But . . . then there were the priests that Bear worked with . . .

Eventually they had everything useful they were likely to get out of him, and he was taken away. Mags didn't know what was going to be done with Pawel—he wasn't entirely certain he cared. Pawel and the drop-points for his orders were both compromised now, and he would have to be gotten away somewhere in case Ice or Stone decided to make sure he couldn't reveal any more than he already had.

"We know why they wanted Amily," Nikolas said,

after Pawel was taken off. "But why did they want Mags? They *did* want him—the two men that Mags calls Ice and Stone were after Mags themselves."

"Maybe to keep Amily quiet?" hazarded the Herald in charge. "If they intended to hold her for any length of time, they would have wanted a significant hold over her; something or someone they could use to coerce her without actually hurting her. They could threaten you, but she would know that was hollow. But if they had Mags, they could do anything they liked to him to make her cooperate."

Well, that was an ugly thought. But it did fit in with Stone and Ice's personalities.

The problem was . . . that just didn't *feel* right to Mags. He had no evidence at all, other than his instincts, but—

Well, there was one thing. There had been that moment when Amily was safe and he was not, when he was staring into Stone's face—watching the man calculate and assess—

Iffen he'd thought he could git away wi' me, he'd'a grabbed me an left Amily.

Mags wasn't sure how he knew this. He only knew that he was as certain of the truth of it as he was of his own name.

And that somehow, this was directly related to the fact that the *really* crazed assassin, the one that had taken Bear, had recognized him.

The hell is goin' on? Had they somehow mistaken him for someone else? It wasn't the first time the thought had crossed his mind. And it drove him frantic that he had no more idea now than he had then.

There was one useful thing they had gotten out of Pawel. There were two more spies up here . . . he didn't know who or what the first one was, but he was absolutely certain that one of them was either a Bard or a Bardic Trainee.

15

It had taken the better part of a candlemark to relate everything that had happened. "Tha's it," Mags finished. He had gotten Amily, Bear, and Lena to all come out to his room after supper; with the Companions standing a watchful presence, he was fairly certain no one was going to be able to overhear anything he told them. Amily had the single comfortable chair, and Mags paced restlessly. Lena and Bear sprawled on his bed. "Tha's all I know. Amily, yer pa wants ter wait till it's a mite cooler afore they do yer leg. Nobody wants ye t' be hurtin' an' swelterin' at th' same time. An' there's other reasons . . . sorry, I weren't half listenin' . . ." He shrugged, finally sat down on the floor at her feet, and she reached for his hand.

"Infections. Easier to get 'em in hot weather. And it'd be easier for you to get heat sickness too." Bear pondered it all. "Well, I reckon we can get you mostly done before the snow if we do it before Harvest Moon."

"If you don't, well, then I just get to be pampered and lie about like a spoiled child next to the fire all

winter and have people fetch and carry for me," she
said with a smile.

Mags snorted. "Like I kin see ye doin' that. Not
hardly." He decided to risk getting teased about it later
and stole a kiss. Right now, he wanted all the kisses he
could get. He was still getting the shakes when he understood just how close their escape had been. If Amily
hadn't been on Dallen . . . he'd have been too busy
fighting off Ice and Stone to help her. All those men
dressed in real Guard uniforms had looked very con-
vincing. Bear had been right, they'd had the means to
knock her unconscious, and they could have carried
her off under the guise of getting her help.

He tried to remind himself that they had all been
prepared for something like that. She'd have been
swarmed by Hera;ds and Companions. But all he
could think about was Amily's terrified face.

How close he had come to never seeing her again . . .

"But the spy in Bardic—" Bear's brows furrowed.
"It has to be Marchand's pet. It *has* to. Who else could
it be?"

Mags expected Lena to agree with Bear immediately. So, obviously, did Bear. They were both shocked
when she shook her head.

"It isn't," she said decidedly. "It can't possibly be
Farris. For one thing, there isn't a deceitful bone in his
body. For another . . ." She bit her lip. "For another . . .
I know why Father picked him, now."

Mags had a horrible, vile thought. And something
of that must have shown on his face, because Amily
took a quick glance at him and paled.

But Lena was continuing, twisting a bit of her hair

around one finger. "This is going to take a long, long explanation."

"We got time," Mags pointed out. "I really wanta hear this."

She nodded. "You probably would never have noticed . . . I actually don't think anyone but me has noticed . . . but Father's compositions seem to come in lumps. He'll do a lot of new music, then there won't be anything new for a while. Then he'll do a lot more new music. It's not just that he's working on something long and complicated. He doesn't work on anything *at all*. He'll do concerts and performances, he'll go to parties, he'd even come home to visit, and when I was in his rooms, the only music that was there was whatever he was learning. I mean, I've known that forever, and even though I don't know any other Bard who works that way, I never actually thought it meant anything— until a few days ago. You see, I've been helping Farris learn composition—"

Bear gave her a look of incredulous surprise. "You . . . what? But I thought—" He glowered a little at her. "I told you I thought you oughta avoid him altogether."

"I was just taking Mags' advice!" Lena said. "Mags said, if I was nice to him and he was horrid, people would notice, and he would look bad. If I was nice to him and he was nice to my face but horrid behind my back, people would notice that even more. But if I was nice to him and he was nice back, and grateful, then I'd have a friend. So no matter what, I won if I was nice to him."

Bear scrunched up his nose, pushed his lenses back

up, and thought about that a while. "Remind me never to cross you," he told Mags finally. "You seem so perfectly ordinary most of the time, then you turn around and come up with something like this that's—it's political-level scheming is what it is! Where do you come up with these things? Sometimes I wonder if you're manipulating me like that!"

"I wouldn't call it scheming," Amily said mildly. "He wasn't telling Lena to do anything but be nice, which is what she would rather do anyway. He was just giving her the reasons why it was to her advantage."

Mags shrugged uncomfortably. What could he reply to that? He wasn't really trying to be manipulative, but it was so easy now for him to see how people worked, take that apart, and put it back together in a way that made things better. Being such an outsider was turning out to be as much of an advantage as it was a handicap. "I'd rather hear what Lena has t'say. I *really* wanta know why she's so certain-sure th' spy ain't Farris."

Lena took a deep breath. "I know this is roundabout, but it's important, and it all has to do why I know it's not Farris. When I was helping him with beginning composition, I realized right away that he's good. He definitely has Creative Gift. His melodies are wonderful, and they just flow out of him naturally. And he works the way everyone else I've seen works—he *always* has songs he's working on. Even when he says he's finished, something will set him off, and he'll look for a piece of paper to jot the music down on. He can't stop and take a rest from it any more than he could take a rest from breathing."

"So? That doesn't mean he can't be a spy too," Bear said stubbornly. "In fact, that would make him a better spy. He could write things down in musical notation, and no one would be the wiser. And anyone suspicious of him would see he really *was* someone who belonged in Bardic and not think any more about it."

"That's true," Lena agreed. "But—look, you have all been trying to figure out why Father brought him here. You assumed he was a spy and were and thinking it was because he somehow tricked Father into it. But that's not what happened at all."

"What?" Amily asked, skeptically. "He told you what happened?"

"He didn't have to, once I figured it all out." Lena frowned unhappily. "He's not some kind of scheming adult in a youngster's body. He didn't trick Father. It's the other way around. Father's tricking him. Father's *using* him."

"Aight." Mags scratched his head. "Lena, I cain't see ary way Bard Marchand could be usin' a youngling." Well . . . not true. He *could*, but evidently that wasn't the sort of using that Lena meant."

"I'm getting to that," she replied. "Three days after I helped Farris with one of his own original melodies, I heard Father use that *same* melody for one of his own new songs! Or what he claimed was his new song." She looked as if she had swallowed something bitter. "And when I asked Farris about it the next day, he was all, 'I know! Isn't it fantastic! It's such a great honor! My stupid little thing in one of Bard Marchand's songs!'" Lena shook her head. "I tell you, I thought I was going to be *sick* when he said that."

It took Mags a few moments to unravel what it was that Lena was saying. He started to ask a question to make sure he understood her correctly, but Amily beat him to it.

"You mean . . . your father is stealing his protégé's work, and claiming it as his own?" Amily asked incredulously.

"Oh . . . he does change things, rearranges it a bit, and adds a lot to the melody. He puts it into his style. And he is certainly writing all the lyrics," Lena amended, though she was still looking sour indeed. "But . . . the melodies aren't his. The hardest part—coming up with the bare music—he's not doing that. And he's making Farris think that he's doing Farris a *favor* by stealing his music! He's *using* Farris! And it isn't the first time, either."

Amily made a shushing motion at Bear. "How would you know?" she asked.

"Because I did some checking in the archives. Every single one of those bursts of songwriting has been when he's had a protégé, or he's been somewhere *way* off away from Haven amd come back with a whole new book of songs. And his protégés? I checked. They're always very poor. He carts them off with him when they are about ready to produce their Master work. He says it's to give them the space and isolation they need to work. They mysteriously get offered a really comfortable permanent position somewhere far off and never come back, and the work they send back as their Master piece is just barely good enough to get them full Scarlets."

Mags looked at her askance, his mind full of nefarious

things that Marchand could be doing. "Ye don't thin'—
'e ain't murderin' 'em—is 'e?"

Lena looked at him, shocked, and shook her head.
"No! Uh . . ." Then she blinked. "Actually . . . in a way
he *is* murdering them . . . not physically but . . ." She
bit her lip. "He takes someone who adores and ad-
mires him. He takes the best of their work. I *bet* the
closer it gets to them getting their Scarlets, the more
horror stories he tells about how hard life is on the
road. They were poor, for the first time in their lives
they've been living in plenty, and now he's telling
them, 'Oh, and by the way, once you get your Scarlets,
you'll probably be poor again.' But then he takes them
on one last trip with him; he probably tells them that
he's doing them this huge favor, taking them somewhere quiet and luxurious so they can put all their energy into their Master piece. But that's not *why* he's
taking them. He's found a wealthy household off back
of beyond of nowhere that *desperately* wants a Bard of
their own, like a sort of prestige pet. And he's already
been priming them with his visits. So this last time, he
brings his protégé with him and says, 'Look, see how
much I esteem your regard for me, I am bringing you
my very own student! Offer him the position!' "

Amily's eyes flashed anger. "Oh, that . . . *snake!* So
of course they do! And of course after all of March-
and's terror tales, the poor thing can't believe his luck
and takes it!"

"And Father 'helps' him with his Master piece.
Which is, of course, just barely good enough to pass.
And everyone says, my goodness, poor fellow just
never lived up to his promise, so sad, but at least he

has a position! And *he* settles into to that position never realizing Father used him all those years and now has just dumped him in a backwater to become someone's fat little house Bard, happy to sit by the fire and be a trophy and write songs about horses and cows!" Lena was clearly very angry by this point. Mags wasn't *entirely* certain why she was so angry—though he could certainly understand that it was extremely unethical for Marchand to be stealing his protégé's work and claiming it as his own—but he had the feeling that Amily understood perfectly, and he figured eventually she could help him figure it out.

That wasn't what was important at the moment.

"Aight, I know ye know Bard business," he said. "An' I'm purty certain-sure thet iffen ye say Marchand's doin' this, 'e is. What I don' unnerstan is why this means 'e ain't a spy."

"Oh . . ." Lena deflated a little. "Well . . . I suppose it doesn't. It's just . . . *this* is why I know he's not using my father, my father is using *him*. Farris isn't the conniving one, it's Father. You see?"

"Aight. So . . . gimme 'nother reason." This wasn't just baiting her. Mags trusted Lena's instincts. And he knew that if there was another reason . . . she'd articulate it, once she thought about it.

"I . . . hmm." She sat there with her brows furrowed with thought, while Bear held her hand. "Well . . . he never leaves Bardic, much less the grounds, except to eat. If you think I work hard, you should see him! All he ever thinks about is music. I just don't think he'd have any *time* to pass people messages. He's very naïve. He desperately wants to think the best of everyone.

His people may be poor, but they are awfully kind, and he's very good-hearted." She sighed. "I don't know how to say this, Mags, but him being kind is something you just can't fake."

"Aight." Mags nodded. "I 'spect some'un's gonna find a way t' get Truth Spell on 'im t'make sure'a thet, but . . . I 'spect yer right. So . . . whatcher gonna do 'bout what yer pa's doin'?"

A thin little smile crossed Lena's lips. "I already have done something about it," she said. "You know that a copy of everything a Bard does is supposed to go in the Archives here, right?"

"No, but I'll take yer word fer it," Mags replied.

"Well, I took the copy of that new song, *and* I took the copy I'd made of the composition work—" She paused a moment. "Well . . . blast. I need to explain something else now. Whenever we work on composition, we take it to the teacher that same day, and he or she dates and initials it. This isn't just to prevent someone from stealing your work, it's to prevent anyone from claiming *you* stole *his* work. So Father's song had the date he left it in the Archive, and Fariss' work was dated, and it was pretty clear what came first. I put them in a folder, and I left them on Bard Lita's desk." Lena looked like a very satisfied kitten . . . one with a mousetail sticking out of the corner of her mouth and a smudge of cream on her nose.

Mags blinked, then turned to Bear. "An' you said *I* was bein' all poltical-connivin' an' manipulational!"

"Oh, hush. And that's not a word." Bear kissed Lena's hand, and she blushed. "That was *fearfully* clever! It could have been anyone who left that on the desk!

It's not like Marchand hasn't irritated a lot of people around here."

"I'm half tempted to tell Bard Lita it was me," Amily said thoughtfully. "But she won't ask. All she needs is the evidence, it speaks for itself."

"Tha's a fact," Mags agreed. "But . . . ye had that other prollem . . . didn' ye?"

This time it wasn't a blush that reddened Lena's cheeks, it was a painful flush. "All I ever heard was the rumor," she said. "No one would ever tell me directly they'd heard him say that. And . . . now that I know what I know about his composition . . ."

"Look," Bear interrupted, "let me just ask this outright. Do you *want* him to be your pa? Cause I'll tell you right now, if *my* pa claimed I wasn't his, I'd send the old blowhard a smoked ham and a thank you letter!"

"Bear!" Lena exclaimed, shocked, as Mags and Amily laughed.

"Well, look, what's he done for me? Nothing but give me gray hair before my time! Look!" Bear pulled a lock of very dark hair away from his head. "See? And what's Marchand done for you? He didn't even get you into Bardic! Your grandpa did that!"

Lena wavered. "That's true—but it's not me that I'm worried about. Mama would . . . if the rumor got home, Mama would never dare go out in public again. It would be horrible for her. Everyone would be trying to figure out who my real father was. Grandpapa would be mortified, and he'd blame Mama . . ." Tears sprang up in her eyes at the mere thought.

Bear hastily put his arm around her. "Hey, there, it

hasn't happened yet. It's just been a couple of whispers. Your friends are pretty good at squashing 'em. Lord Wess has been real good at that. He says he just looks down his nose and drawls that—no, wait, let me see if I can do this right."

Bear took his arm from around Lena and stood up. He slouched indolently against the wall and looked down his nose at all of them "My dear old creature, of *course* Marchand would say something like that. The fellow cannot *bear* the idea of anyone having more talent and adulation that he does when it's a *stranger;* can you imagine what he's thinking about being eclipsed by his own *offspring?* And a *girl* at that? He's already done what he can to keep her out of the public eye, but that won't hold for much longer. He's probably writhing in *agony* on his pillow at night at the mere *thought* that the words 'The great Bard Marchand' would be applied to anyone but him. Since he can't do anything about the poor girl's brilliance, he probably decided to see if he couldn't separate her from the name, and damn the consequences."

Bear gave one of those odd laughs that Wess did . . . a sort of wheezing snigger. "Of course, the man is so wrapped up in his own consequence that he hasn't thought things through very well. Because if Lena wasn't his, then for all of his claims about how irresistible he is to women and how clever he is, his own wife found him quite inferior to someone else altogether, and he's been played the fool! It's something right out of one of those tavern songs where a woman bids goodbye to her husband at the front door and brings the lover in the back, and when the husband asks about strange boots under the bed, she tells him something ridiculous."

Bear wheezed again. "Just wait. As soon as it dawns on him that he's set himself up to look like the doddering old man in a farce, he'll deny ever having said that."

Mags applauded slowly as Bear bowed and sat down—both for the performance and for Lord Wess's cleverness.

"I imagine that got around pretty quick to Marchand, because according to Lord Wess he hasn't let out a peep about you not being his since," Bear continued. "Backed himself into a bad corner with that one."

Lena nodded slowly. "I just—I—" She let out her breath in a huge sigh of mingled frustration and unhappiness. "I think about him using all those other Bardic Trainees, and I just want to—I don't know. But he *is* immensely talented. He's also immensely self-absorbed. For so long, all I wanted was for him to take notice and be proud of me and now . . . now I just don't really know what I want . . ."

"You'll figure it out," Bear said with confidence. "You can do anything you put your mind to. I've seen it."

"Not everything . . ." She shook her head. "But . . . Amily, Mags, are you *safe* now? Is it over?"

"Gotta be," Mags said. "They'd be insane t' try t' get Amily after thet. Completely bonkers. Oh, I don' thin' they're *gone*, they took on th' job uv doin' fer th' Karsites what th' Karsites ain't been able t'do wi' armies. Ev'thin' I read offen 'em tells me once they git a job, they stick on't till thet job's done, 'less they kin figger out how t'break t'contract. But they gotta be smart 'nough to know that snatchin' Amily ain't gonna git 'em what they wants." He tried to imagine himself into Stone or Ice's head and failed utterly. "I dunno what they're gonna do next. They ain't like thet crazy one, nor th' feller what tried t'burn t'stable. They . . . think. Tha's all they do, actually. They be thinkin', calculatin', alla time. They gotta be thinkin' what they kin do, an' I cain't reckon like they kin."

"Well, good. Does this mean you're going to go back down into Haven to spy with Nikolas?" The light from the lone candle that was all Mags was willing to have for light in this heat flickered across her face.

"Dunno. Well, I know Nikolas' keepin' the shop goin', 'tis one uv 'is main ways t'get 'is own spyin' done. But I dunno iffen I'm gonna go back down there soon. Things are kinda all of a muddle right now." He frowned. "We still don' know who t'other two plants are up 'ere on th' Hill. We gotta figger thet out quick, an' I don' think makin' ev'body take a fealty oath unner Truth Spell's the best ideer for fndin' out."

"Someone's suggesting that?" Bear said, surprised.

" 'Course. It's purt well guaranteed thet if there's a right bad idea, *some'un* on t' Council is gonna suggest it." Mags grimaced. Interacting with the Court and the Council was one part of being the King's Own that he was just as glad he didn't have to do. He might well envy Nikolas the attendance at those fabulous High Feasts he had heard about, and wish he could see some of the fabled entertainments—but dealing with anyone highborn except those he knew were his friends and allies?

No. At least, not for a lot of years.

"Mags . . . I'm not so sure about that," Amily said into the silence. "You said yourself, these aren't the sort of people that give up, and the one thing they *know* they can use to get to Papa is me . . ."

He frowned a little with irritation, but frowned more when Bear gave an exaggerated sigh. "Amily, that doesn't make any sense," Bear began, and Amily got a stubbon look on her face and started to talk over him in a higher and slighty whiny voice. And the more she talked, the more he began to feel . . .

Well, he wasn't sure what he felt. Very irritated, as she started out from the reasonable assumption that Ice and Stone were frighteningly clever, appallingly inventive, and terrifyingly well trained, and spun that into a wild fantasy of strange, unstoppable killers with one foot in the spirit world who had, like some weird Pelagirs creature, gotten her "scent" and would not rest until they carried her off. Her tone grated on him and set up a headache just behind his cheekbones. He began to harbor the exceedingly uncharitable notion that—well, although she had not liked all the restrictions, she *had* liked being the center of attention and the praise she'd gotten for being willing to play bait— and now that attention was going to be taken away, and she didn't want that to happen. The attention she would get for having her leg worked on was passive . . . and it was centered on a defect. The attention she had gotten for being essential to laying the trap was active and centered on her *bravery*. Oh, he could see that all too well.

And he didn't *want* to listen to the convoluted,

paranoid fantasy of someone who had turned into an attention addict. Not when it was distracting him from real danger and obscuring how he was supposed to solve it.

The room seemed way too hot. He wanted to lie down or get a drink, but most of all, he wanted to be alone.

And suddenly, as Lena added *her* voice, much more shrill than usual, the gathering turned from supportive and friendly to argumentive and confrontational. And Mags had no idea *how* it had gotten that way.

Or *why*.

Wait—

Yes, he did know. He just couldn't do anything about any of it. Because despite having survived the kidnapping, nothing had changed. Well, nothing, except that right now the bare thought of how narrow their escape had been was making him feel sick; paradoxically, as more time passed, he was getting *more* obsessive and anxious about that narrow escape. In the short term—he would stand by what he said; there was no way that Ice and Stone would make a second kidnapping attempt, not this soon, not when the whole Hill was on alert.

But for the long-term, paranoid fantasies aside, Amily probably was still in danger, and she still could not defend herself or even run away with her leg the way it was.

Now, on the one hand, if the "short-term" could just extend to getting her leg fixed, she would at least not be a literal sitting target. But that bizarre story she was spinning around herself was the equivalent of the tale

of the little boy who yelled for help in the woods once
too often . . . the more she talked, the less anyone
would even pretend to listen. The less they listened,
the wilder her story would become. Eventually no one
would take her or the danger she was in seriously. And
that would be when she was in the most danger of all.

He couldn't think . . . he just could not think of a
way to tell her this without making her angry.

Everything else was, oh, gods, the *same old problems.*
Nothing had actually been done about them. Bear and
Lena *still* were unable to grow spines and just *deal* with
their parents.

And he *still* hadn't done anything remotely useful
about these killers except to uncover that they were
(probably) in the pay of the Karsites, and that had been
by purest accident.

Nothing had changed. They were all circling the
same stagnant problems, accomplishing nothing. And
from the way things looked, they would *keep* circling
the same stagnant problems forever.

At that moment, Lena's voice hit a particularly
piercing note, at least to his ears, and a lance of pain
stabbed through his temple. He clapped one hand to
his head and swore.

At least that shut them up.

"Mags?" Amily said. "Are you all right?"

No, I ain't all right, an' anybody not completely balled up
i' 'er own liddle center uf 'er own little universe 'd see thet!

"Headache," he said, between clenched teeth. And
when Bear started to get up and come over to look at
him, he confronted Bear with a snarl, making him back
up a pace. "Don' *touch* me, Bear! I ain't some whinging

li'l soft thing whut's never had wuss'n a broke nail, all right? It's *jest* a headache."

Bear fidgeted with his glasses. "Sometimes headaches come from something worse—you might have—"

"I been looked over," he snapped. "I been looked over good. Nobuddy found nothin'." He squinted at all of them. "I jest need somethin' right now that ain't squallin' an' whingin' an' argufyin'. Like mebbe some peace."

Bear frowned. "That's not a—"

"Don' say it," he growled. Bear backed up another pace.

"I think we should go," Lena whispered. She looked—scared. Did he look that ferocious?

Evidently he did. Amily looked as if there was something about him she was suddenly unsure of.

So unsure that she picked up her crutches from beside the chair by herself and struggled to her feet without any help from him. "I think we should go and let Mags get some rest," she said, but she did it with a look at Lena that somehow managed to imply that it was Lena who was at fault.

Or at least, that was the way that Lena reacted.

But mercifully, before they could get into it again, Bear got them all out the door.

Mags started to throw himself down on the now vacant bed, when he realized that Amily—

::I've got it,:: Dallen informed him. ::I'm not letting them past me till Bear boosts Amily up on my—there we go.::

For one moment, Mags was even feeling a surge of resentment against *Dallen* for interfering, but he throttled it down and cursed himself for letting pain get to him that badly.

But this was, without a doubt, the worst headache he had ever had in his life. For a moment he was tempted to call Bear back and beg him to have a look—

But he'd *been looked at.* Four—five—six Healers? He'd lost count. They'd all gone over him to make sure he hadn't been poisoned secretly or cracked over the head or something else. And they'd all said he was fine.

Gotta be the heat. This was the worst summer he could remember.

::Thanks,:: he told Dallen briefly, and even that single word hurt his head to project.

Quarrelsome voices and hoofbeats moved out of the stable. It seemed as though now they were arguing about which of them had given Mags the headache.

Except, of course, that was not what they were fighting about. It was just the excuse to fight. They might not recognize, as he had, the underlying causes, but they certainly *felt* those causes. They knew, all three of them, that they were getting nowhere. But at least two of the three weren't willing, or weren't ready, to do what they had to to solve their situation,

"Treat th' cause an' not th' symptom," he muttered. But if you couldn't make yourself face the cause?

"Hellfires," he growled. He levered himself up out of his bed and laid down on the floor. At least it was cooler there.

A lot cooler.

He closed his eyes and prepared to wait out the pain.

That, at least, was something he was good at.

But the next thing he knew, it was morning.

Morning, sadly, did not bring much relief. His room still felt stifling once he stood up. His head throbbed, and he felt vaguely nauseated. He began to wonder if he had eaten something bad—or if those murdering bastards had somehow managed to poison him after all. Was this how that guide had felt, and just brushed it off as something that would go away?

He didn't feel all that *bad*.

But he didn't feel all that *good* either.

Dallen whispered something into his mind—too faint to make out. *Th' hell?* he thought with irritation. ::*What?*:: he replied. ::*Cain't hear ye.*::

This time, though still whispered, the sense was clear. ::*You've over-taxed your Gift. It took both of us to fend off the attacks of Ice and Stone's shield-constructs. Holding your shields against it took more than either of us would have thought. You were shouting for help so loudly that the Gifted heard you down in Haven. Then you helped interrogate Pawel. Now you're paying for it.*::

Bah. Well, he wasn't going to use Mindvoice then

until it stopped hurting. Doing so would probably only make things worse. He looked down at himself, realized he was still dressed, and opened the door into the Stable.

He marched straight over to Dallen's stall. "Is there anythin' I kin do fer this?" he asked aloud.

Dallen regarded him with his head tilted to the side, then managed to make a strange sound. After a moment, Mags recognized it as snoring.

"Sleep't off, eh?"

Dallen nodded.

Well, he wasn't going to get any sleep in that room. All the things that made it so nice and warm in the winter were turning it into an oven, and he was the bread.

"Look, tell—whoever—I'm a-gonna find somewheres cool t'sleep. Don' care iffen I miss class. Don' care iffen I miss food. Cain't eat anyroad."

After a moment, Dallen nodded, then rattled the chain on his water bucket. That was easy enough to understand.

Drink plenty of water.

"Aye. I will."

He stopped long enough to take a pillow and one of his leather water bottles. He filled the latter at the pump and trudged up through air that was positively leaden with heat and humidity to the Palace. That lower level where the crystal sphere was had been cool enough . . . maybe there was another room down there he could borrow long enough to get some sleep.

But all the doors were locked except that one.

He opened the door and stepped just inside, and the

cool felt like a gift from the hand of a god. Even the lamp didn't seem to be giving off much heat. He considered the room. Considered the crystal with a wary eye. True, he was not intending to use it, but what if it . . . oh . . . used itself? He drank from his water bottle while he considered the risk.

After all, there was probably a reason why the thing was down here all by itself, hidden away in a room hardly anyone seemed to visit . . .

On the other hand, it hadn't done anything when he and Amily had been here. The benches were padded, and with his pillow one would be as good as a bed.

But the breath of cold from the room finally persuaded him. He closed the door behind himself, sat down, then laid himself down on his side, fitted his back along the curve of the bench, shoved his pillow under his head and closed his eyes.

It just felt so good . . . even if he didn't actually get any sleep, the cool made his head throb a lot less.

He drifted off into a semiconscious state that was not quite sleep and not quite wakefulness.

It felt as if there were something, or someone, in the room with him. Uneasily, he tried to move but found he could not. Under other circumstances he might have panicked—

But he was in the Palace. Whatever it was, it would have had to get past so many protections, it couldn't possibly be a danger. And it wasn't actually doing anything. It wasn't even paying any attention to him. It was just there. As if it had been there all along, and he was only just noticing it.

He slowly became aware that it wasn't anything

alive—at least, not as he understood the state of being alive. Finally, he knew what it was, what it had to be.

It was the stone.

The stone became aware of him as soon as he became aware that the stone was what it was. He felt it regarding him in a detached way.

Perhaps he should have been alarmed, but he wasn't. And yet, he knew he had sensed something similar recently, from a source that *did* alarm him. What was it? Where had he seen this before?

The shields. The shields on Ice and Stone. This was like those shields. Except for the part about *trying to kill him*. So what were those shields, and why were they like the stone, anyway?

He felt the stone noticing, becoming aware of that thought. It didn't *respond* as such, but . . . something floated to the surface. The stone had seen this before.

There was a strangely peaceful indifference to the stone. It wasn't responding to him or to his emotions so much as responding to the mechanical stimulation of his question. As he not-quite drowsed, the stone presented him with an answer.

Ice and Stone were each wearing a talisman. This did not mean what *he* thought it meant. To his mind, a talisman was a religious token, something meant to bring one closer to one's god, and make it easier to reach the god when asking for help. But to the stone, a talisman was an item created by magic to protect, hide, and defend the bearer from attacks that were not physical. Like mental coercion, or magic.

Magic? he thought involuntarily. *Protects them from* magic?

The reply wasn't a thought, exactly. It certainly wasn't framed in words. But his own mind put it into words, somehow.

Of course, magic. Just as the stone protects everything within its influence from magic, from even the *thought* of magic.

That—don't make any sense—

It doesn't have to, not to you.

The reply had come with such . . . cheerful indifference . . . that he couldn't take offense. It would be like taking offense because the leaves were green instead of blue. Well, if the stone knew so much and was answering questions—

So where are they?

Near. Their talismans interfere with the stone. The stone interferes with them. The result is a pattern of confusion. This means the stone cannot locate them.

Oh.

Mags drifted a while. The ache in his head ebbed and was soothed as the stone became disturbed by it and moved to rectify the situation.

He came a little more awake—or maybe just aware—when he sensed . . . conflict. It was nearby. He groaned a little when he realized it was Amily and her father, fighting. Or rather, Amily was fighting; Nikolas was just standing there, helplessly letting the tirade pour over him.

A brief flash told Mags what had triggered it. Nikolas had suggested Amily might be better off leaving Haven for a while. He *had* been going to suggest that she go with an entire group of her friends—Mags included—and just for the summer until it was cool enough to fix her leg. But she hadn't let him get that far.

She had worked herself up to the point of hysteria with her terrifying theories anyway. This had just triggered some old, old resentments. *"You just want to be rid of me!"* The words were distorted by sobbing. *"You think I don't know, that I've never figured it out? You've always been angry because I lived and mother died! And you've always been guilty because you weren't there! You've always resented me because you have to take care of me, and that's a burden on you that the King's Own doesn't need! And you've always been disappointed in me because I wasn't the son you wanted and I was never Chosen!"*

And Nikolas wanted to say, no—no—but he couldn't. Because that would be a lie. Amily had poured out the bitter truth. It wasn't *all* the truth, how could it be? He loved his daughter. He was proud of her, prouder than ever after she willingly made bait of herself, even though she was terrified. But every word she said was also true . . . how could it not be? He had adored his wife, and her loss was an ache inside him that would never heal. How could he not but feel guilt that he was not there? And . . . at the times when the ache was the worst, how could he not look at Amily and think, *why was it you and not her?*

As for Amily being a burden—she was. There was nothing she could do about that. There was nothing he could do about the fact that he was not just a Herald, he was the King's Own, and that brought with it an entire load of additional responsibilities. And he knew, because he winced when he thought about it, that there had been so many times when he had been laden down already and *she* had needed something, and he had thought, *Oh, if only you were not here . . .*

As for not being a son . . . every man wants a son. Every man is filled with fear and unease, along with delight, at being presented with a daughter instead. Daughters belong to that strange, delightful, but incomprehensible woman-tribe, but a son . . . ah, a son is a member of the man-tribe. A man can understand a son. A man doesn't have to be afraid for a son . . .

And not being Chosen? Oh, that opened up a world of mingled relief and disappointment—what father doesn't want the best for his child? And there was nothing better than having that perfect friend, that perfect support, that was a Companion. But relief that she would never know the endless self-sacrifice required of a Herald, never have to look at someone she loved, and think *If only you were not here . . .*

Mags pulled away from the fight, feeling queasy. That wasn't anything he wanted to know . . . and how in hell was Nikolas going to reconcile all of that? How could anyone? Suddenly, Mags felt a *lot* more sympathy with Jakyr, who fled any hint of connection, much less commitment.

Maybe that was why Nikolas had practically thrown Amily at Mags when he realized the two were attracted to each other. Mags . . . could take her, take the burden onto himself and leave Nikolas free to only be the King's Own, and not Amily's father. Mags could protect her, when Nikolas could not—as Nikolas had not been able to protect her and her mother. Mags would shoulder the burden, and Mags certainly wasn't disappointed with her . . .

No, Mags didn't want to know any of this.

Not when he had felt that burden, felt Amily desperately clinging to him, trying to infect him with her crazy theories so that he would make protecting *her* and being with *her* his priority.

And he felt the same frantic smothering that Nikolas did. The same desperate bewilderment as he faced two duties with only enough time, energy, and attention for one.

He blocked out the fight. He didn't want to know any more, didn't want to hear any more. And somewhere deep inside him a little voice whispered that this might not be so bad . . . he would miss her company if he used this as an excuse to break off the never-official betrothal . . . but would he miss the burden?

But in turning away from one quarrel, he was drawn to another.

Lena was sitting in a little wilted heap in the herb garden, talking, while Bear tried to get cuttings. From the look of things, she had started talking when she sat down, and had not paused since.

"Will you stop whining!" Bear snapped. *"For Cernos' sake, Lena! You're not a little girl anymore! If you don't like what your precious father is doing, tell him, tell Lita, tell both of them to their faces! Tell that little rat Farris how he's being used! If you don't like how you're being treated, say something. Get up on your hind legs and have it out with them, for once in your life!*

Lena stared at him, tears starting up in her eyes.

"And stop crying!" Bear spat. *"That was cute when you were a little girl and passable when you first got here, but*

*hiding in your room and sulking and weeping until you're
sick are just . . . .juvenile! Grow up!"*

The tears dried up as if a desert wind had sprung
up. Lena glared at Bear with her fists clenched at her
sides. *"Grow up? Say what I feel? Have a confrontation?
GROW UP AND FACE MY FATHER JUST LIKE YOU
DID?"*

Bear froze, lenses slipping down on his nose, mouth
half open.

*"Just like you? Just like you stood up to your father?
Because you make such a shining example to follow!"*

Mags winced frantically away from that fight as
well. What was *wrong* with them all? Why were they
ripping into each other?

The stone stirred at his unhappiness. It sensed his
question.

It had an answer.

Stagnation equals death.

Well, that "answer" had come right out of nowhere
and made just about as much sense. What was that
supposed to mean, anyway?

They are not dying.

Mags felt a stab of irritation. Of course they weren't
dying. That was pretty obvious. What exactly was the
stone trying to get at?

Change is painful. Birth is painful. Creatures in pain
lash out without knowing why, and often without caring what they strike.

What are you, anyway? he thought at it, resentfully.
*The storage room for every cliché and worn-out motto that
was ever spoken in this Kingdom?*

Yes.

Uh . . . what?

Among many other things.

Right. Now it was having a philosophical dialogue with him. He was talking philosophy with a rock. Had this just gotten very, very strange?

It already was. You just hadn't noticed.

How could he have not—

You are looking outward so steadfastly you are not looking inward anymore.

Now you sound like some sort of mystic.

Yes. You are all out of balance.

How would you know?

I *am* balance.

Well that made him pause.

How can I . . . how can we . . .

I am past and present. I am not future. There is no knowledge stored in me of what you *will* do. Only what you *can* do and what you have done in the past, all of you.

So . . . you're a library?

Among other things. Many other things.

At this point he wasn't quite sure if he was hallucinating, dreaming, or the stone actually *was* communicating with him. He wasn't using his mind-voice, that much he was certain of, because it would have hurt if he had been. This was deeper than that, at a level where he thought very clearly, but very slowly—where he was articulate, but it wasn't exactly in words.

Why are you talking to me?

You are a Herald. You are part of the Web. I am the heart of the Web.

The Web . . . he thought he remembered that concept, that all Heralds and all Companions were connected in a vast network like a spiderweb—and like a spiderweb, something touching the Web was felt by everything in it.

Can you help me?

You must ask the right questions.

Well, wasn't that *always* the case . . . He sighed in his sleep, if it was sleep. That was the problem: What was the right question?

Who am I?

That was it. That was the one question that was never answered. The one that lurked under the surface of everything he did, just as Amily's knowledge of her father's feelings lurked, and Bear and Lena's fear of confronting what they most desired approval from.

That was what lurked inside Mags. Everyone else he knew, *everyone,* had a plan, a map, for what they were doing, and every map had the same sort of starting point. *This is who you are. This is what you came from. This is where you are going.* People might refuse to follow the path on the map, but they still had the map itself, and it gave them the foundation for their entire life—whether that life was spent in rebelling or in conforming. No matter what, they always had an anchor to keep them from drifting away entirely.

He had nothing. He was only what other people thought they saw. Cole Pieters had thought he saw a piece of human trash, valuable only as long as it dragged rock out of his mine. The priests that had visited had seen the offspring of bandits—likely bad blood himself. Here at the Collegium—he was the star

Kirball player—he was the pig-ignorant little slave boy who nevertheless fought tooth and nail to learn—he was Amily's human crutch—he was Bear's rescuer—

But none of these were him. Or, were all of them?

Who am I? he asked again.

Who do you want to be?

What?

Who do you want to be?

I don't understand . . .

What you want is an anchor. But an anchor can be at the end of the line as well as the beginning. Who do you want to be? Make that your anchor.

Oh . . . .Oh!

Yes. Sleep now.

He slept.

———————

Someone was shaking his shoulder. He batted at whoever it was and tried to bury his head deeper into his pillow.

"Mags," said a voice. One he knew, but couldn't put a name on. "Mags, wake up."

He really didn't want to wake up. Not when he was finally comfortable for the first time in days. Weeks. He hadn't realized how poorly he'd been sleeping until now. Classes could go hang for one day. He was finally going to catch up—so there.

The voice got sterner. "Mags, you can't stay here. Wake up, that's an order."

Oh, well. If it was an order . . . but dammit, it wasn't fair. Why shouldn't he be able to sleep late just once? The only other time he got to sleep late was when he was in the infirmary.

He dragged himself up out of sleep and levered himself up off the bench with the help of the table. Herald Caelen stopped shaking his shoulder and offered a hand to help him up. He took it, knuckling the eye that had been squashed into the pillow with the other hand.

"Sorry, sir," he said contritely. "M'room's like a damn furnace. An' I don' thin' I got a decent night's sleep this whole fortnight."

"Yes, well, there's a lot of that going around," Caelen replied, pushing him forward a little, past the threshold and closing the door firmly behind them both. He motioned to Mags to keep going along the corridor. "Even those who were not in on the plans for Amily were aware that there was *something* going on. It made for a lot of uneasy sleep, and the heat is not helping."

"Mebbe you oughter give people a turn down 'ere, then," Mags said with a chuckle. "I was sleepin' a treat." He gave his hair a hasty comb with his fingers to settle it.

Caelen gave him an odd, sideways look. "Most people would say the opposite."

Really? That seemed uncharacteristic of Heralds or Trainees. "Uh—why? Sir? Them benches're purty soft. Good as a bed."

Instead of answering, Caelen responded with a question. "Did you have any dreams? Sense that you weren't alone? Anything at all out of the ordinary?"

Mags made a face. "Jest a good solid night. Since most'a my dreams is nightmares, I s'pose not havin' bad ones is out'a th' ordinary." A very vague memory seemed to come near to the surface of his mind, like an ornamental fish in a pool of green water—but it retreated again before he got the shape of it, and he shrugged it off. "Nay, sir. I jest slept, slept real good."

"Interesting. Well, I'm tempted to tell you to continue to sleep down there until the weather breaks," Caelen said dryly. "You're the first cheerful person I've spoken to today. Everyone is quarrelling with everyone else. It's the same down in Haven, and there would probably be fighting all over town, except that no one can muster the energy to fight." He rubbed the back of his own neck. "I never thought I'd miss winter."

By this time they had reached the stairs going up. "Reckon iffen ye ain't gonna lemme sleep down 'ere, I'm a-gonna sleep out i' Companion's Field," he said, following the Dean up the stairs. "Druther get et by bugs than bake."

"You may regret saying that," Caelen replied absently. "There are some nasty surprises out there, and being covered in no-see-um bites is no joke. I left your new class schedule in your room. And while I hesitate to make personal recommendations—if I were you, I would avoid my friends for a while."

Mags winced. He might have no memories of what he'd dreamed of—if anything—before he'd slept, but he had very vivid memories of Amily spinning fanciful tales of near-hysteria, and Bear and Lena breaking into a quarrel before they'd left. "They was achin' fer a fight when they left m'room," he said carefully.

"Well . . . let's just say they all got one." Caelen shook his head. "Nikolas is down in Haven, and he was said to have left so quickly that even Rolan was taken by surprise. Lena and Bear had what was described to me as an 'epic' and very public battle, parted ways, then Bear promptly stalked down to the Guard barracks and for reasons unknown to me had a shouting match with a Guard Healer by the name of Cuburn. Lena spent the entire afternoon mewed up with Master Bard Dean Lita, at the conclusion of which Bard Marchand was sent for, and there was more shouting, and Marchand was forbidden any further contact with one of the other Bardic Trainees."

Mags whistled. "An' I slept through alla thet?"

"Consider yourself lucky," Caelen replied. "This way you weren't asked to take a side. That is why I advise you to avoid them if you can."

When they emerged, Mags blinked in surprise. The sun was going down.

"I slep' all day?" he exclaimed.

"Which is why I came to find you." Caelen slapped him lightly on the shoulder. "When you didn't appear at class and you were not in your room, people were worried. The only reason no one went into a panic was because Dallen was not in the least bit disturbed. Dallen told my Companion where you were and that you were sleeping off Gift overuse."

"Aye. Tha's what Dallen tol' me. Said t'sleep 'er off." It was so amazing *not* to have a headache!

"Try to get something to eat, I order you to get plenty to drink, and it won't hurt you to sleep more," Caelen told him. "Now, I need to go break up another contentious argument in the library. Remember my advice about your friends. Even Amily, at this juncture."

Caelen stalked wearily off without even saying

goodbye, Mags stood in the doorway, feeling the heat pummel him, and felt his refreshed spirits wilt and sink.

Bear and Lena at each other's throats in public? Amily driving her father off?

Here he'd thought they'd at least solved their big problem for the short term—but solving it only seemed to have made everything else worse.

He groaned. Any appetite he'd had was gone.

::Dallen?::

::Ah, you sound better.::

::Aye. Sleepin' he'ped. Reckon mebbe I better do some more on it. Cause from what Caelen says, jest by sayin' "heyla" I c'ld start a war.::

Dallen snorted. ::Not just you. Come on along to the field. I'll show you a cool place for a lie-down. One with nothing in it to bite you.::

::Don' haveta ask me twice.:: The mere thought of more sleep was intoxicating. ::Jest gimme time fer a wash-up an' clean stuff. I could sleep fer 'nother day.::

The next few days were spent in catching up with classwork and some very careful watching of what he said so that he didn't launch anyone else into a fight. And tempers were very short. No one seemed to be getting enough sleep, everyone was dozing off in class, and the grotto was full of people all the time. So was the bathing room, as people tried to cool off with baths. The river was full of splashing bodies. Any place there was a marble or stone floor, you could expect to find someone lying on it. Permission had been given to everyone in the three Collegia to wear as little clothing as their modesty and the sensibilities of others would allow.

But it wasn't just the heat. Perhaps it was that so many people up here were Gifted, and irritation tended to spread. But after the blowup in his rooms, and after learning about the subsequent fights that Lena and Bear, and Amily and her father, had had, Mags was determined not to contribute to the situation. No matter what happened, no matter what the provocation, he refused to discuss anything other than classwork, the weather, and Kirball. He managed to sidestep every single potential quarrel that started brewing in his vicinity that way; some, though not all, he was able to completely avert.

As for his friends—well, things were not exactly "friendly," although *he* hadn't quarreled with any of them. He'd just snapped at them, he'd been a bit impolite, but he hadn't actually said anything that bad. But the other fights . . .

He had a confused "memory" of actually being there at the time of the other altercations—he hadn't been, of course, but finally he decided that someone who *had* been in earshot must have told him about it when he was feeling heat-sick and the memories had leaked over. Certainly a lot of people knew the quarrels had taken place, and certainly none of the parties had been making any attempt to keep their voices down.

Lena and Bear avoided him, out of embarrassment, maybe. Or maybe they had been advised by their respective Deans not to go to him or Amily until things calmed down.

Amily—he couldn't explain her silence. She made no attempt to contact him for several days, not even after he had a batch of mint drink that the Cook was experimenting with sent round to her. One the one hand, he felt deeply hurt, but on the other, if he was going to follow Caelen's advice—which he was—he shouldn't be trying to talk with her anyway.

It was hard, though. They'd always been able to count on each other for sympathy and at least a ready listener. He wasn't really having *conversations* with the rest of his friends so much as he was being a referee, which wasn't any fun and just drained him.

He felt—well, not *miserable*. No matter what, if things didn't sort themselves out by the time Ice and Stone were finally dealt with, Mags was determined to *get* it sorted out. But aside from the enervating and irritating effect of the heat, and the constant need to pick his way carefully among potential fights, and missing his friends and *really* missing Amily, his spirits were decidedly low. Melancholy, that was it. He went to sleep in that relatively cool spot out in the Field at night with a headache; he'd wake up without one and with the hope that things would be better. He'd endure the heat and the quarreling all day, Lena and Bear and Amily wouldn't even turn up at the same meals as he did, and the drain of the heat and the headache would build all day long. He'd go to a fretful sleep feeling just a little sick from it.

Nevertheless, he was absolutely determined not to end up moping and hiding with Dallen in Companion's Field.

Besides . . . he wouldn't be *that* alone out there. Trainees and their Companions were camped out all over the wretched place. He kind of resented whoever it was that had staked out the chapel in the middle; it had stone floors. Though it *was* said to be haunted by Tylendel's ghost, at this point he was thinking a ghost just might be better company than some of the living.

He had already found out the same day what Lena had been doing, closeted with Dean Lita; there had been plenty of people listening avidly when Marchand was called in, and there were enough who disliked Machand that the story spread, in a great deal of detail, rather quickly. As Mags had rather cynically expected, Marchand claimed that he had been doing his protégés a favor, and they had asked *him*—indeed, he claimed they had *begged* him—to use their melodies in his songs. From all reports he went on at great length about how he had taken simplistic little "apprentice tunes, not worthy of a moment's notice," and improved them out of all recognition.

Of course . . . all the protégés he had stolen work from were "conveniently" so far away that without using a Herald to relay the testimony, no one was going to learn the truth soon. Ah, but Marchand had a hidden card to play. He had young Farris brought in to prove his case.

This had not done him the good that he had thought it would—though that might have been because another Bard had taken pains to explain that stealing someone else's work and claiming it as your own was a serious breach of Bardic ethics. So, perhaps with his hero-worship shaken a bit, Farris must have been less than successful at proving Marchand's innocence. He did go on at some length that he considered having his tune used by Marchand was an honor he didn't deserve, however. So they got a contradictory answer. Farris wasn't certain that he'd given Marchand the melody and the permission—but he *was* certain that it was an honor, and in his confused way, he indicated that if Marchand had asked, he would have offered the tune with both hands.

Mags would very much like to have heard Lita's

thoughts about that. As Mags understood it, teachers *did* use student work all the time, but it was *always* with permission beforehand and with full credit. Not appropriated without, or with ill-informed, consent, and not without credit. But with Farris partially backing Marchand's claim, there wasn't a great deal she could do other than rebuke him sternly for his "carelessness" in not giving full credit. Then, according to the sources, the volume of the discourse had been reduced to muttering.

More than that, he didn't know, since no one was there except Lita, Lena, Farris, and Marchand himself, Lena wasn't talking to him, and no one else was talking at all.

Mags was quite certain that if outright theft could have been proved, Marchand would have been in very serious trouble indeed. He suspected that Lita was going to ask the Heralds for a quiet little investigation into the matter, but until they came back with answers, Marchand had skated by again. As it was, he was ordered to keep away from Farris and not to take on a protégé again. Ever.

Whether or not he would actually *do* that . . . Mags was dubious. Marchand spent a lot of time away from Court and the inquisitive eyes of his fellow Bards. It would be quite easy to aquire another Talented youngster out there and just keep him away from the Bardic Collegium entirely. He could teach this unofficial protégé himself, even find a position for him in some place that knew nothing of how the Bardic Collegium worked, where if Marchand said the protégé was a Bard and he wore Scarlets, well, then, he must be one.

Marchand would have someone to steal tunes from, and no one the wiser.

It just remained to be seen whether getting caught was enough to frighten him into doing his *own* work again and not resort to what would be fraud.

So much for Marchand. He was someone Mags would rather not think about.

Except, of course, it seemed that Lena had finally been goaded into standing up against her father openly, and that could only be a good thing.

Meanwhile, the search for Ice and Stone went on. Down in Haven, Nikolas was not only hiding from his daughter's temper, Mags knew he would be extending himself and his resources as far as he could to find the two Karsite agents. But these two were cut from a cloth that no one in Valdemar had any experience with. What had always worked before was not going to work now.

Some people surrounding the King thought they had probably left already; after all, they had been thwarted in a very public manner, and their identies had been compromised. But Mags wasn't so sure of that. He'd had a look at some of their thoughts; these weren't men who would take even that grave a setback as the reason to retreat.

For one thing, even if they went back to Karse rather than going back to wherever they called home, they wouldn't find much of a welcome when they got there. They knew enough about Karse to threaten a Karsite native with demons . . . which meant that they knew very well such things were real and deadly. The Karsites would not tolerate failure from an unbeliever;

they barely tolerated it in their own ranks. Mags was damn certain that *he* wouldn't risk it.

For another, the fact that *they* had executed their predecessors for failure indicated that they knew that were altogether likely to face a similar fate if they returned without fulfilling their contract. And maybe they were the very best of their kind—they were certainly better than the first batch that had gone out—but even the best can be overwhelmed by sheer numbers, and even the best have been trained by *someone*. Mags recalled the images he'd caught from Temper's mind— the harsh environment, the rigid rules of behavior, the unforgiving nature of Temper's superiors. No, Ice and Stone would find no sympathy there. And it was—at least according to all the history he had been reading—a time-honored tradition for the Master to eliminate the student who failed.

If Mags had been in their shoes . . . he would lie low, wait until vigilance was relaxed, and try some other way to at least give the appearance of destabilizing the Crown or harming Valdemar in a significant way. What that could possibly be . . . he had not a clue. Amily was probably no longer a target; there really was no good reason to make her one. Even with collaborators on the Hill, everyone was looking out for her now. If she so much as stabbed herself with a needle, there would be people checking to make sure it had been an accident and the needle wasn't poisoned.

For all he knew, though, these men had some way of unleashing a plague on Haven, and summer was certainly the time to spread disease. A plague could wipe out thousands very quickly, and the highborn would

certainly not be immune unless they left Haven. Even
if the King and his family didn't sicken and die, it
would lay low many of those also responsible for ruling the country.

Or—hot as it was, dry as it was—if they spread
across the city one night, setting fires, they could en-
gulf the entire city in flames. Would the Hill be spared?
Possibly . . .

But in his nightmares, he could imagine only too
well a scenario in which it would not be. Where Ice and
Stone set delayed fires of the type they'd tried to set
before, using candles—and meanwhile, had brought
wild rats up to the Hill and the homes leading up to it.
Affix a box full of smoldering tinder to the rat and turn
it loose—eventually it will be somewhere that will
burn—inside walls, in stables full of hay, in a storage
room. Do that fifty, sixty, seventy times—and the manors on the Hill, if not the Palace, will catch and burn.
The privileged seldom know how to deal with an
emergency themselves. They would be relying on the
Guard and the Constabulary Fire Service. But *they*
would already be down in Haven, and stretched thin.

And then what? Everyone flees to the Palace? And
in the confusion, in the crush of panicked people running from their burning homes, it would be easy for Ice
and Stone to get inside the walls and start fires there.
They might not even need to murder the King or try to
manipulate him through the King's Own at that point.
With Haven in ruins, centuries of records destroyed,
an entire city homeless, Valdemar would be in chaos
for decades, and Karse would have exactly what it
wanted.

He tried not to think about such things. Or rather, he tried not to think about such things after tentatively Mindspeaking Nikolas one night about the time he knew the shop was generally empty, offering with great diffidence that these ideas had occurred to him and then waiting for an aswer as a properly respectful student should.

::We'd considered both of those scenarios,:: Nikolas replied. ::But you're the one who has actually picked up some of their thoughts, which gives you an edge in understanding how they might react to this setback. We'll put a higher urgency on those possibilities. Thank you, Mags.::

Mags wasn't at all sure what "higher urgency" meant, but at least someone would be on guard against those possibilities, which allowed him to sleep a little better at night.

He *did* find out what had happened with the Guard Healer Cuburn; that particular spectacle had been very, very public. Bear had stormed down to the barracks and in front of a large group of the Guard (and more who came when they heard the altercation) confronted the man about spying on him for his father. Then he had unleashed a long tirade on the theme of "Old men who want their sons to be nothing more than copies, but vastly inferior copies, of themselves, so they can preen about having a boy who duitifully follows in his father's footsteps, yet never have to worry about finding rivals in their own houses."

According to Corwin, who had actually been there, Bear's rant had not only been scathing, it had hit home with no few of the Guard. Evidently Bear's father was not the only man who wanted to keep his son under his paternal thumb, bound body and soul to whatever the family business or tradition was, regardless of whether the boy was suited to it. Bear had gotten quite a few sympathetic hearers that he probably had not expected.

Enough that when Bear was done and had stormed back to Healers' Collegium, the Captain of the Guard had taken Cuburn aside and suggested that his men were going to find it difficult to completely trust in someone who had taken the position with the Guard for the purpose of spying on someone. How could they trust anyone who was "no better than a nosy old gossip?"

Cuburn had vigorously denied he was doing any such thing and swore that he had taken the job because he wanted to serve the Guard, who were the first defense of Valdemar. He swore he would prove it any way that the Captain wanted.

He probably hadn't reckoned on the Captain calling his bluff.

"In that case," the Captain had said, "You won't object to my arranging a transfer."

Mags didn't know if Bear had heard about that part. He also didn't know if the Captain had actually gone through with asking for that transfer. Corwin had told him that transfers could take several moons, so . . . well, he supposed they would only know the truth when Cuburn was gone.

Officially, Bear had been given a stern lecture by his Dean. Unofficially—well, who knew? He was still acting as disgruntled as his namesake after a long winter's hibernation. Mags was perversely proud of him, actually, as proud as he was of Lena. Bear didn't have his father in reach, but he *did* have his father's spy, and he could be certain that every word he had spoken would get back to the man he *really* wanted to have words with.

But he couldn't tell them that, because he hadn't seen so much as a thread of Bardic Trainee rust or Healer Trainee pale green since he'd sent them out of his room.

All Mags could do, really, was concentrate on his studies and on research in the library and the Heralds' Archives to see if anything like Ice and Stone or the shields they wore had ever come up before, and, if so, had there been any way of finding such things when the ones who were being shielded didn't want to be found. He frequently found himself looking back with nostalgia on the time when the most urgent reason to be here was to find out who or what his parents had been. Then it had only been to prove that he was not the child of thieves and murderers. Now there was, potentially, an entire city at risk.

And he prayed for the weather to break. Because just maybe all it was going to need was a good hard rain and cooler weather to clear peoples' heads. Since he was pretty sure that virtually everyone else in all of Haven was praying for the same thing, it was a wonder that the gods hadn't answered before this.

Which, Dallen'd tell me, an' prolly any good priest, ain't how gods work. Which don' seem fair t'me, when all we're askin' fer is a liddle rain.

He was up in the Archives alone when the sound of light footsteps in the corridor warned him that he wasn't going to be alone much longer. He sighed. He really, truly, did not want to be bothered right now. It was late enough that his daily headache had bloomed nicely behind his forehead and cheekbones, and it was only the fact that it was still too hot to sleep in the Field kept him up here in the Archives.

And they were female footsteps from the sound of it, unless it was a page. Pages usually didn't come up here unless they were sent. So either some female was coming here, or a page had been sent here, and in either case it was more likely that the desired object of the person's search was Mags and not a random volume of Heraldic Reports.

He abandoned the passage he had been working on and waited, knowing he might as well. If that unknown someone was coming here to do research herself, he could go right back to what he was doing. But if she was looking for *him*, he wouldn't be allowed to get back to work without hearing what she wanted and probably coming up with an answer for her. He just hoped it was something trivial—like an answer to part of the classwork.

But when Lena came in through the door, he was actually shocked. He would have expected to see almost anyone *but* Lena. "Lena?" he said incredulously.

She ducked her head a little, diffidently. "I hope I didn't interrupt anything important . . ." At the moment there wasn't a trace of the bold little tiger who had faced down her father.

He closed the book and pushed it aside. "Importat, aye. Urgent . . . not s'much."

"Oh, good. I need advice," she said, sitting down at the little table across from him.

Oh, bugger. Here it comes. She's going to ask me for advice about—

"It's my father." She sighed heavily. "He wants me to talk to you about an invitation for you and Amily."

Mags eyed her dubiously. "What sorta invitation? T'what? Why me'n Amily?"

"He wants you and Amily to come to one of those private concerts," she said, with decidedly mixed emotions warring in her expression. "It's in one of the mansion on the Hill. I . . . just don't know what to think about him anymore."

"Ye think 'bout him th's same way ye think 'bout any other thief. But why'd 'e ask fer me i' the furst place?" He looked right into her eyes so she could see the sincerity there.

"You're—well, you're *Mags*," she replied, as if that was answer enough. "You stopped that madman from burning the stable, you're a *brilliant* Kirball player, and you saved Amily."

"Lotsa people saved Amily," he pointed out with perfect truth. She rolled her eyes.

"You are either incredibly modest or incredibly dense," she said crossly. "You act as if you aren't anyone special, but you saw how those young highborn treated you *before* you rescued Amily—like a hero. And now? Every single person at that concert is going want to talk to you, flirt with you, ask your opinon on things." She shook her head slightly. "Anyone who is there is going to lord it over everyone who wasn't if you turn up there.

Which, of course, Father knows. He acts like a spoiled adolescent who just *knows* no matter how much trouble he gets into, he can charm his way out of it. This is probably part of the 'charming his way out of it.'"

"Because it gets 'im more people what think 'e's next thing' t' a miracle worker. I'd be sick 'cept it'd take too much energy." Mags actually did feel a little sick. Did Marchand ever stop trying to manipulate people? Was there ever a moment in his day that he wasn't scheming and plotting a way to make an already fabulous existence even better? The man had adulation, hordes of followers, he was wealthy, he could have virtually anything he wanted within reason. But it never seemed to be anough for him.

"He's asking Amily too, because you are the romantic couple, the hero who risked his life to save her and all of that rot." She paused. "I think."

"Whazzat s'posed t'mean?" he asked.

"That . . . I don't *know,* because he could actually have taken Lita's lecture to heart this time, and this could be a demonstration of good intentions. Or he could be even more crafty than I thought, and it's the *appearance* of good intentions, designed to throw any sort of suspicions off." She frowned. "I just don't know. I can't tell. And . . . oh, damn, anyway!" She scrubbed fiercely at her eyes. "He's being *nice* to me after I was the one that told Lita what he was doing! He *thanked* me for 'bringing him to his senses.' I don't know if it's real, or if it's because he knows he won't be able to get to you except through me. I *want* it to be real. I still want it, even after all I know about him!" She looked up at him, shoulders hunched. "Do *you* think it's real?"

Mags tried to figure out how to be sympathetic without being overly sympathetic and failed utterly. "Erm . . ." he said.

"And I am *not* going to cry!" she said fiercely. "Bear was *horrible* about it, but he was right. I am not going to cry over this! He doesn't deserve one bit of my concern, right?"

"Ah," was all he could manage. He studied his hands. And thought. "Well," he said tentatively. "Amily could stand ter get out. I don' mind bein' shown 'round like a prize, 'cause I kin git a chance t' do th' whole *boy ain't too bright* act thet Nikolas wants me ter do. So, hell, Marchand's motives don't even come inter what I decide, practically speakin'."

"I suppose . . ." she replied. She didn't sound convinced.

"An' 'nother thing. Git 'im t'invite Lord Wess. Feller has a eye on 'im, an' 'e's sharper nor a good knife. *I* cain't go sniffin' 'round Marchand's head w'out he's doin' somethin' 'gainst th' law. But Wess? Wess kin watch yer pa, an' lissen, an' prolly git 'im t'say thin's 'e'd ruther not. Iffen yer pa's fakin' it, reckon Wess'll winkle it out."

He smiled, rather pleased with himself for thinking of that, and made a mental note to add Wess to his little company of helpers. He didn't have anyone among the highborn, just the people around Master Soren. Wess would be exceedingly useful, and he'd gotten the impression that Wess would enjoy being exceedingly useful. The young lord had often complained that as the third son, he had about as much utility as a third leg.

"But—" she began.

He shook his head. "Don' e'en bother tryin' ter fig-ger Marchand out, 'cause it don' matter what 'is mo-tive is. Point is, we make 'im useful ter *us*, an' nothin' else hasta matter. Jest keep yer head on thet. 'cause oth-erwise, 'e's gonna get t'yer, yer gonna want 'im t' be a real pa t'ye, an' yer back where ye was."

"But—" Her eyebrows creased. "What if he really *is* trying to do right?" She thought a moment. "Well, this concert thing does look rather bad. There's no reason why he would want you and Amily there except to in-crease his own prestige. But maybe someone is going to be there that he thinks you or Amily should meet!"

"I dunno iffen 'e's finally doin' right. You dunno. Likely 'e don' even know." Mags shrugged. "We got ter wait for it t'play out. Till then, we jest make sure we use 'im, cause damn sure iffen 'e ain't walkin' th' straight path, 'e's tryin' t'use us. An' iffen anythin', 'e *owes* us fer bein' sech a piss-poor father. Fair?"

She sighed. "Fair."

He held up a cautionary hand. "Now, I ain't said yes yet. This's fer two, and I gotta go talk t'Ami—" He stopped, looking at the faintly guilty expression she wore. "Ye already did, didn' ye?"

She sucked on her lower lip and looked at him out of the corner of her eye.

He didn't know whether to be cross or amused. But amused was a lot less trouble than cross. "Wimmin," he sighed. "I dunno *why* I'm a-tellin' ye 'bout tuggin' yer pa 'round, an' makin' 'im inter *yer* game-piece, when wimmin do thet natural as breathin'."

She gave him an affronted look. "No we don't!"

"I ain't a-gonna argue. 'Tis too bleedin' hot t'argue.

All right, ye kin tell yer pa we're gonna go get trotted 'round like a couple'a breed-horses at 'is stupid party. When is't?"

"Three days from now," she said, and kissed his cheek before she stood up. "Thank you, Mags."

"Don' thenk me," he replied, turning his attention back to the chronicle he'd been picking through. "I'm figgerin' t'get plenny outa this. Le's jest 'ope th' 'eat breaks afore then, or there'll be folks pickin' fights there too."

Bad enough that the heat hadn't broken, but Mags was going to have a to really push it to keep from looking like some sort of rude boor by turning up late for the wretched *thing* that Marchand had arranged.

He'd said yes assuming it was one of those evening concerts Marchand liked to stage. Which would have been just fine, no trouble at all. But it wasn't. It started with a party in the garden—a garden that was supposed to be something special even by highborn standards, with all sorts of cooling fountains and water features. Then dinner would be served at dusk, the fountains would be hushed, lanterns would be floated on the still surface of the water features, and Marchand would perform.

One small problem. Or not so small, since Mags didn't want to look as if he didn't care when the event was taking place. Classes were going to go practically right up to the time Marchand's "little gathering" was supposed to start; Mags was going to have just enough time to change into his good set of Grays before throwing himself on Dallen and literally galloping down to the event. Of course Marchand had not bothered to see what Mags' schedule was before setting the time of the gathering . . .

If he'd been taking Amily pillion on Dallen as he always had before, this would have been impossible. But Amily had told him that she didn't mind going ahead of him, especially since Marchand was supplying her with a carriage and a burly footman to get her into and out of it.

So all he needed to worry about was getting himself down there. And it turned out there actually was a legitimate connection with him, and an equally legitimate reason why Marchand might be doing him, and the highborn, mutual favors. This was the home of one of Marchand's highborn patrons, an avid—one might almost say fanatic—follower of Kirball. Fanatic enough that he was supplying horses to the Riders in the interest of having the best possible games to watch.

Now, supplying horses to one team was one thing; Lord Wess's father was doing it for Mag's team because his son was on it. But supplying horses to all four? That argued for someone who really *was* interested in the game as a pure game, and wanted to make sure that one team didn't win over another because of superior "equipment." Mags was very interested to meet this man and talk to him.

It would be a fantastic change from talking, and thinking, about potential killers.

Mags sprinted through the furnace-heat from his last class to the stables. It felt as if he were wearing his Kirball armor, the heat weighed him down so much. It also felt as if he were running in a dream, the sort where you are running as fast as you can and getting nowhere at all.

Dallen was already saddled and waiting; the grooms had done as they promised. Mags dashed past his Companion into his room. He'd laid his good Grays out this morning. By his own mental reckoning, he was right on time. He shed his trews and tunic, washed himself down with tepid water from the basin on the stand, and pulled on the trews. Yes. He was going to be right on time.

Right on time—until he heard an ominous rumble in the distance.

He was only half-clothed, but he stuck his head out the window anyway—to see storm clouds the color of crows' wings *boiling* up out of the West. And the next moment, a blast of cold, damp air gushed across the stableyard, dropping the temperature from "oven" to "wine cellar" in next to no time.

Even as he watched, feeling a bit stunned, an enormous lightning bolt slammed into the ground in the distance, and thunder rolled and rumbled and shook the building.

Oh . . . hell.

::*We are not going to beat that, not even if we left this moment,*:: Dallen observed.

::*Beat it? We'd be bare lucky not t'drown.*::

The clouds raced toward them as he pulled his head in and the shutters closed, then finished dressing, taking his time, making sure that every tie was tied and every hem was neat, while more thunder shook the stable and grew louder as the storm grew nearer. Because there was absolutely no point in rushing now.

I'm a-gonna look like I don' care other folks gotta wait fer me. Or wuss, like I was a-waitin till ev'body was there so's I could make some kinda grand entrance. Dammit.

Then again . . . the gathering was supposed to be in the garden. Outside. And everyone at that party, if they had not noticed the clouds boiling up, had certainly heard the thunder and felt that blast of cold air. Right now people in expensive clothing that they did not want ruined would be making a headlong dash for shelter. Things would be utterly confused for a good long time . . . probably wouldn't be sorted out until he got there. With luck, he might even be able to slip in without a fuss.

Wind rattled the shutters and the first gush of rain hit them as he dug out his voluminous raincape and wrapped it around himself. It had flaps that he could tie around his legs to keep them more-or-less dry, and he did so. The oiled canvas was stiff, but he wasn't going to have to perform any acrobatic maneuvers in it, just get himself up into Dallen's saddle.

Dallen laid his ears back when he saw Mags. *::I wish there were one of those for me.::*

::Oh, hush. Do that thing ye did when ye shed alla thet dirt.::

::You weren't supposed to notice that.:: One of the grooms pulled a door open. Rain poured in, and Dallen, still with his ears flat, cantered out into it.

::Aye, well, there's a lotta thet goin' 'round.::

It was like standing under a waterfall. Or—well, Mags had never actually done that, so it was what he imagined standing under a waterfall would be like. He was glad that the cape had a hood and he had tied said hood up, because otherwise the rain would have just poured in through the neckhole of this thing. Lightning lashed overhead, and the thunder was almost continuous. He couldn't hear *anything*.

::*Mebbe I should git ye a cane t'feel yer way.*::

::*Just remind me how much better this is than the oven we had this morning,*:: Dallen replied, keeping up the pace.

::*Oh . . . gods. This is so much better nor th' oven we 'ad this morn,*:: he replied, with deep feeling. Cold. He was actually *cold*. It was *glorious*. And his headache had completely vanished with the first chill blast of wind.

They passed the gate and the Gate Guards, who huddled in their own raincapes, with warm light showing at the open door. They waved at Mags, grinning. They must have felt the same—maybe more so. Guard uniforms were dark blue, not the best color in the heat, and they hadn't been given leave to wear as little as they could.

Mags kept his head down to avoid being blinded by a sudden flash of lightning. ::*Is there any odds we'll git hit?*:: he asked a little nervously.

::*I'll see that we don't,*:: Dallen replied.

::*You'll—*:: Mags was at a loss for words for a moment. ::*Is thet somethin' all on ye kin do?*::

::*Aye. Why do you think, with all the terrible storms they ride through, Heralds never get struck by lightning?*:: Dallen seemed amused; his ears were up again. ::*However, I am not moving out of a walk. The streets are too uncertain.*::

A walk seemed more than fast enough to Mags. The rain was coming down so fast that it wasn't able to flow into the drainage ditches on either side of the road, and Dallen was splashing through an ankle-deep, swiftly moving stream where the road had been. ::*This's crazy. Ain't never seen rain come down like this.*::

::*Once in a very great while. Rather like the blizzard we got the year you arrived.*:: He felt Dallen's amusement. ::*Did you bring extreme weather with you?*::

::*Not thet I know of . . .*:: He peered gingerly under the rim of his hood, but he couldn't make out where they were. ::*'Ow far are we, anyroad?*::

::*At this rate? About four times as long as it would have taken in good weather.*::

::*Bah.*:: He wished he had a way to contact their host and apologize. Which was a little silly, since their host was, without a doubt, very much aware of how bad the storm was and would surely not be annoyed at Mags for being delayed.

::*He's more likely to thank you for coming at all,*:: Dallen pointed out.

Still. He wondered if he could somehow tell Amily what was going on. After all, he was able to make those who could not Mindspeak hear him on the Kirball team—he should be able to make her hear him.

Well, if he could contact her at all. The members of his Kirball team were always nearby and were aware that he was going to do this. They practiced it long before they did it on the field, and Mags was very familiar with how their minds "felt." He'd deliberately avoided Amily's mind, shielding himself tightly around her, so he wouldn't pick up any of her thoughts even by accident. This was not just because that was the ethical way to do things, but because he would have felt very uneasy invading her privacy like that, even if it was inadvertent. He hadn't even warned her by Mindspeech when they'd been attacked—though he hadn't needed to, since it was pretty obvious.

But *if* he could contact her at a distance at all, this was certainly the time to do so.

All right. Lessee if I kin . . .

He closed his eyes and let his shields down, just enough to send out a tentative thread of thought, looking for her—or rather, for something that "felt" like her. She couldn't be *too* far away now . . . he and Dallen were forced to stay on the road, but thought could go in a straight line.

Lots of thoughts, most of them along the lines of *Oh, my dear gods, we are all going to wash down the side of the Hill!* None of them at all familiar. He quested a little farther.

Finally he thought he sensed someone familiar. ::*Amily?*:: he sent, tentatively.

::*MAGS!*::

It was a mind-*scream*, full of fear and panic. ::*Mags! Mags! Help me! Hel*—::

He felt the blow to her head that knocked her unconscious as if he were the one who had been hit.

Dallen felt it too, and without prompting lurched into a frantic, splashing gallop, heading for their host's manor, utterly heedless of his own safety.

Mags pulled the hood off his head and peered through the rain, knowing that with two foreward-facing eyes his vision was better right now than Dallen's was. His heart raced, and he was afire with anger and fear, but somehow cold with it too. It had to be Ice and Stone; who else would have taken her? He had been wrong, *everyone* had been wrong. They had been clever enough to realize that *now* was the time to try to snatch her, precisely because everyone would think they would retreat and regroup after their failure—

As Dallen charged through the rain, he thought he saw something ahead of them—

::*There!*:: he shouted. A carriage! A carriage pulled by two horses that were galloping at breakneck speed.

Dallen didn't bother to reply, he just stretched his neck out and redoubled his efforts. And Mags locked his grip on the saddle horn, closed his eyes, and projected what had just happened to every Herald he could reach, straining until a bolt of pain lanced across his head and interrupted him. Now they knew.

Not that any of them would be able to get here . . .

He opened his eyes and saw that Dallen was gaining on the carriage. He couldn't make out who it was that was lashing the horses so savagely, and he couldn't sense *anything* human from it. Which could only mean those strange shields had locked down tight, and Ice and Stone were, for all intents and purposes, invisible.

Lightning hammered down and hit something just ahead and to the right of the carriage. The horses shied sideways, sending the carriage careening on two wheels before it dropped back down again. The figure on the driver's box looked back; he must have spotted them, because he sawed at the reins, and the horses— now in a blind panic—plunged to the other side of the road and skidded around a corner Mag hadn't even seen.

He and Dallen overshot; Dallen executed a muscle-pulling reverse and resumed the chase.

Another lightning bolt hammered down, and the horses shied. This time the carriage skidded back and forth wildly, and Dallen had to drop back a little.

Mags braced himself in the saddle. He could see in Dallen's mind what he wanted to do: come alongside so that Mags could jump into the open carriage. They could do it if Dallen could get close enough. Then Dallen, without Mags' weight on him, could surge ahead and shoulder the horses off the road while Mags protected Amily, who must be lying on the floor of the carriage.

The driver looked back again, saw them still on his tail, and viciously heeled the horses over again. The carriage slewed from side to side, and again, Dallen had to drop back.

But the horses weren't going to be able to keep this up for very long. They didn't have the stamina that Dallen did. Not even the fact that they were going downhill was going to help.

Every hair on his body suddenly rose up, and he smelled something sharp and—

Dallen swerved violently sideways, and another bolt of lightning struck where they had been. The heat of it scorched his cheek, it was so close, and it seemed to suck all the breath out of his body and blind him, all at once—and the thunder nearly flattened him into the saddle.

For a moment, he fought for air, mind utterly blank.

When his mind came back, the carriage was lengths ahead of them, and Dallen was standing like a horse made of stone, and both of them were *steaming*. His whole body tingled painfully, his skin felt burned, and for a moment he had trouble thinking of what they were supposed to be doing.

Suddenly Dallen shook himself all over, and lurched into a gallop again. Mags tried to make his mind work, but it was moving slowly, thoughts blundering around like blind beetles. Dallen closed the distance between themselves and the carriage, and Mags *finally* felt his mind staggering back to normal. The driver wasn't looking back. Did he think they'd been struck?

Had *he* somehow been the one that caused the strike?

It didn't matter. All that mattered was the carriage and making the jump.

Dallen closed the gap. His nose was practically at the rear wheel. Now his head was alongside the rear wheel. Mags tensed and raised up in the stirrups. This would take incredible timing. Rain torrented down, making it even harder. He would have to land right *in* the carriage, because in this rain, the chance of catching the side and saving himself was—not good.

A little more . . . just a little . . .

Neither he nor Dallen saw the object that hurtled out of the carriage into them—but they both felt it. It was big and solid enough to slam into Dallen's neck and flank with terrible force, and neither of them were ready for it.

Dallen lost his footing; started to go over, fought for it, hurtling sideways on the sluice that was the street, as Mags clung desperately to the saddle, breath completely rammed out of him.

They both knew at the same moment when Dallen was not going to be able to keep his feet.

Mags flung up his arms to shield his head; Dallen fell with as much control as he could muster. The pavement slammed into both of them, and everything went black.

"Mags! *Mags!*"

Mags hurtled up out of unconsciousness like a panicked starling shooting into the sky. His eyes flew open; his body registered *rain*, his mind recognized *Heralds*, and his memory shouted *Amily!* He tried to lurch to his feet.

Someone held him down.

He flailed at them. "Lemme go! Lemme go! They got Amily! They're gittin' away! *Lemme go!*"

A stranger in Herald's Whites grabbed his head in both hands and forced him to stop struggling. "Mags. It's too late. They're long gone. We got here to find you and Dallen lying in the street and no sign of them."

He stared at the man without comprehension for a long, long moment. "No—" he croaked. "No—they cain't—"

"Yes," said the man, with compassion, but without any attempt to soften the blow. "They can, and they did."

A million things raced through his mind. He wanted to burst into tears. He wanted to shove this fellow off him and go running down the street. He wanted to scream, or pull lightning down out of the sky himself, or—

He did none of these things, for none of them would

get Amily back. Instead, he looked up into the stranger's face. "What—what do I do?" he asked. "What do *we* do?"

The stranger gave him a long, searching look, then nodded. "They won't kill her; they won't even hurt her for now," he said. "If they'd wanted to do that, they wouldn't have gone to all this trouble. So for now, we go back where we have resources, and you tell us everything you can. Think you can stand?" He took his hand off Mags and his knee off Mags' chest.

Mags lurched to his feet, stumbled in the rain, and looked around. To his great relief, he saw Dallen also on his feet, even if the Companion's head was hanging so low his nose touched the street.

::*Dallen?*::

::*I'm all right. Bruised. Nothing broken. And furious.*:: The Companion raised his head and looked into Mags' face. Pure rage blazed at Mags from the blue eyes.

"Anything broken?" asked the stranger.

"Dallen says no—"

"I meant you," the stranger interrupted.

Mags took a deep breath—or tried to. Every muscle in his chest suddenly constricted painfully. But there weren't any stabbing sensations, and he answered, "Don' thin' so."

"Blessed Cernos, I have no idea how that happened. Do you see that?" The stranger pointed to a rectangular shape lying off to the side of the road. Mags guessed it was about at long as he was tall. "That was a seat in the carriage. At a guess there was one of them driving and one on the floor, making sure the girl didn't bounce out or come to and jump out. He ripped out that seat and flung it at you when you came alongside. It probably weighs about as much as you do."

"Oh." Well, that explained what had hurtled into them.

"You can thank all that game practice for keeping you both from breaking your necks." The stranger, who had an oddly familiar look to him, raised his head, rain streaming over him as he closed his eyes for a moment. "There. Everyone knows you're all intact. Friends are bringing Nikolas up from Haven."

He whistled shrilly, and a moment later, an extremely tall Companion came trotting in through the rain curtains.

"Any sign?" the stranger asked his Companion.

The Companion blew out a disgusted snort and shook his head vigorously.

"Well, it was worth trying. If anything could track them in this muck, it would be you." The stranger sighed and turned back to Mags. "All right, let's get you into the saddle. I'd rather you didn't walk too far until a Healer has a chance to look at you."

Obediently, Mags turned toward Dallen, but the stranger's Companion shouldered in between them. The blue eyes bored into his. ::*Not Dallen, he's in no better shape than you are,*:: said a crisp, clear Mindvoice with the sound of bells in it. ::*My saddle.*::

"Uh . . . oh . . . aight," he replied, blinking, and with every muscle in his body screaming in protest, he reached up to the saddle horn.

He managed that, but he couldn't get his foot high enough to go into the stirrup—

Before he could think, he felt the stranger boost him,

so he did manage to scramble into place. The strange Herald started trudging up the street, plowing with determination through the downpour. His Companion followed, and Dallen moved painfully alongside.

::*Who is that?*:: he asked Dallen, half of his mind trying to figure out why the stranger looked so familiar, the other half trying to think of some way, *any* way, he could find Amily and get her back.

::*Sedric,*:: Dallen replied, shortly.

That name was . . . familiar.

"You're lucky I was close, and I'm a strong Mindspeaker," said Sedric. "I have literally *just* gotten back from my first circuit. I was waiting out the rain at Master Soren's when I heard you shouting."

"You know Master Soren?" Mags asked, still thinking furiously, but fruitlessly.

"I should, I just proposed to Lydia." There was a sort of grim amusement in his voice. "It's a damn good thing she doesn't believe in evil portents, I suppose."

"Evil . . . Lydia?" With his mind racing in a hundred directions, he tried to make sense of that. "You—you're going to marry Lydia?"

"She seems to think so. I'm glad she knows what she's getting into, or this would likely have sent her screaming away from me." Sedric waited for a moment for the two Companions to catch up with him, and he put a steadying hand on Dallen's shoulder when he stumbled a little.

"If you're—why didn't I know about this?" Mags asked, staring down at the young man.

"Because, my dear naïve Trainee, it's generally *not* a good idea for the Heir to the Throne to broadcast his choice of wife when he's about to be away from the Palace for two years," Sedric said dryly. "Father tentatively approved when I left, provided Lydia felt the same when I got back. Reasonable—well, my *head* knew it was reasonable, even though my heart was sobbing worse than a mooncalf lover in one of Marchand's treacly ballads, and we will not mention in polite company how other parts of me took the edict."

Finally, the words penetrated the fog of anger and grief and guilt that swirled around inside him. Sedric. *Prince* Sedric. *Herald* Prince Sedric. The son of King Kiril's first marriage—made when the King himself was still a very young Prince—a marriage of state, in which the poor bride, very, very much older than the Prince, had not survived the birth of her son.

A son who had been raised by the very young second wife, the love match, a situation that in ballads, at least, was not inclined to end well.

"Mother was incensed on my behalf," he said fondly, then sighed. "Dammitall, these bastards have a wretched sense of timing. She'd be beside herself with joy except that right now she's beside herself with worry over Amily."

"It's—it's all my—" Mags began, the grief starting to overpower everything else.

"You can just stop that foolishness right now, Trainee," Sedric said fiercely, looking up at him through the rain, his eyes blazing as Dallen's had. "I know that you are thinking that if you had been with her, she wouldn't be in their hands now. It is not your fault. It cannot possibly be your fault. Did you call this damned storm?"

His relentless logic startled Mags. "Uh . . . no . . ."

"There you are. Now listen to someone who *knows*. From experience. If you wallow in guilt, you are wasting time you could be using to help figure out a way to get her back. You have only so much time and so much thinking power, so concentrate it *all* on her." When Mags nodded slowly, he appeared satisfied and hunched his head down against the rain again. "Now. All I know is what I've been getting from Father's letters and in bits and pieces from everyone mindshouting right now. Begin at the beginning. What in hell has been going on while I was gone?"

19

For all of Sedric's grim determination, no solutions presented themselves, and Mags felt himself teetering on the very brink of utter despair. Nikolas had already plunged headlong into that state, and for once it was the King and Queen who were trying to comfort the King's Own, not the other way around.

Lena blamed herself. She was the one, after all, who had persuaded Mags and Amily to leave the safety of the Palace to go to Marchand's concert. Mags, of course, knew that this was his fault—he *should* have said no. He *could* have asked to get off from that last class and gone with her. He had done neither, and this was the result.

Marchand, who had made all the arrangements, babbled about them to anyone who would listen and had not thought anything amiss when a strange carriage and driver appeared instead of the one he had hired. He blamed everyone but himself.

The Karsite agents had made no contact nor any demands, but that was only a matter of time.

. . . or Amily's lifeless body would turn up.

That was something no one wanted to think about, but it hovered in the back of everyone's thoughts like a specter. If the Karsite agents wanted to destroy the King's Own now, it would be heartbreakingly simple to do so. They had to know that.

If that happened . . . .

Well, Mags would find them and kill them, or die trying.

If Amily's kidnapping had affected only those who loved her, it would have been hideous, but the situation was being made even worse by the fact that it was getting political, with one faction demanding that Nikolas resign his position (as if he could!), another faction spinning hysterical suppositions about what demands the kidnappers were going to make, and a third faction quite ready, willing, and able to declare war on Karse and take the Army across the Border.

"And we all know how well *that* works," Sedric had said, dryly. "Always supposing that the goal is to get an innocent girl slaughtered and send her father and probably a good portion of the Heraldic Circle insane."

By the time the third day of Amily's captivity dawned, every possible wild scheme had been floated, from sending an army of bloodhounds (which they didn't have) to quarter Haven, to turning out and searching every single building within the boundary.

Mags was nursing a cup of tea—which was just about all he could manage—when Bear finally turned up and sat down beside him.

"Talk to me," Bear demanded. "Seriously. Talk to me."

Mags shook his head; Bear grabbed him by the

shoulder. "*Look*," he said sharply. "I'm not asking you to talk to me because I want to go all softy oozy-woozy-oo on you and pat you on the shoulder and go 'there there.' I want you to talk to me because you haven't offered up any ideas, but I *know* you, Mags, and I *know* there are ideas in there."

"Half-ideers, mebbe," he muttered, staring down at the tea.

"That's the point. They're half ideas because they're still in *there*." Bear tapped Mags' forehead. "If you talk about them, you'll move them outside into the light, you'll be able to get a good look at them, and then you can turn them into whole ideas. But you can't do that till you get them out."

"Right," Mags replied, dispiritedly. "'Cause I'm so good at thet."

Bear smacked him in the shoulder. Hard. More than hard enough to make all those bruises shout in protest. "Stop it," Bear said angrily. "Or I swear by every god there is, I will beat you senseless."

The mere idea of Bear even *trying* to beat him senseless, much less succeeding, finally roused Mags out of his lethargy. He sighed. "Aight. Look. Prollem is, we don' know where they got 'er. We know they ain't left Haven, 'cause a flea couldn' leave Haven right now. The whole edge of city locked down when I yelled. So they gotter be *in* Haven, on'y nobody kin find 'er, an nobody kin find *them*. It's them shields. I ain't niver seen anythin' like 'em. They—like—clamped down, like a river clam, when I got too near 'em, an' thet's made them Karsite bastards so's nobody kin find 'em. It's like they don' exist."

Bear's brow furrowed as he was joined by a dispirited Lena. "But they don't have a shield on Amily, do they?"

Mags shrugged. "I cain't find 'er, an neither kin 'er pa. Iffen they drugged 'er th' way they drugged you, there ain't much there t'find anyroad."

Bear nodded earnestly. "Well . . . I don't know . . . if you can't find her and you can't find them, can you find someone who's *thinking* about her or them?" Then he shook his head. "No, forget I said that. Practically everyone is thinking about her. That won't help."

If only there were a way to find those shields . . .

A vague memory crossed his mind. Something to do with . . . he sat up straight.

Bear looked at him with speculation, but he said nothing.

::*Dallen. What's thet stone?*:: he demanded.

He sensed Dallen wincing. ::*It's . . . easier to say what it isn't. It's not alive, and it's not dead. It can't think, but it stores memories. And the reason it's all those things is because . . . .if all of the Heralds and Companions are like a giant spiderweb, the stone is the hub. In a sense, it's all of us, all of us that are, and all of us that ever were.*::

::*So if anybody'd ever seen anythin' like them shields, then how t'find 'em'd be i' th' stone?*:: he demanded.

::*Yes, but . . .*:: Dallen's tone grew desperate. ::*It was never intended to be used that way. All of the connections and the memories, that's an accident.*::

::*Am I gonna hurt it iffen I go pokin' ' round i' there?*::

::*No . . . but it can hurt you.*::

Mags took a long, deep breath. ::*An' iffen I don't? How many people git hurt then?*::

There was a long, long silence.

::*Go to the stone. Take Bear and Lena. Tell Bear to bring his emergency kit. I'm getting some people who will meet you there.*::

————————

Waiting for them was Sedric, and Mags nearly backed out of the idea right then and there. Because . . . if using the stone to find out something could hurt him, that was acceptable. But hurting the Heir to the Throne?

Sedric raised an eyebrow at the look on Mags' face. "Did I grow a second head without noticing?"

Mags clenched his teeth. "Puttin' me i' danger's one thing. Puttin' you i'—"

"Stop right there. Nobody is putting me in danger. This is what we are going to do—" Sedric stopped and snorted. "We don't need to stand here in the open corridor and blabber about this. First, we are going to go in there and sit down. *Then* I will tell you what we are going to do."

Reluctantly, Mags opened the door to the little room and bowed the Heir inside. He and Bear and Lena followed.

They all took seats around the table, and Sedric closed the door. "Now, everyone get comfortable. Bear, you are here precisely because you are a Healer with no Gift, which means that no matter what happens, *you* won't be affected. I have to tell you, son, your father has no clue how valuable that is; I've been running the Pelagir border, and a Healer you know isn't going to get sucked into a bad situation because he has a powerful Gift is worth his weight in gold. Same on the Karsite Border; the Karsite demons go straight for the Gifted Healers, as if *you* were the ones with targets painted on you."

Bear looked at him in amazement. "They do?"

Sedric nodded. "Now, since you aren't Gifted, I don't need to worry that if Mags gets sucked into the stone, you'll follow. You'll be making sure Mags doesn't get into any trouble. If he starts to, it will be up to you to break him out of the state he's in. I assume you know a number of ways to do that."

Bear nodded soberly; he pulled off the shoulder bag that contained his emergency remedies and put it on the table, open and ready.

"Lena, you are here to help Bear extract Mags. As a Bard with projective powers, you can jar Mags loose by hitting him with emotion, even a projective vision if you can manage it. Meanwhile, I want you to look only at Bear, never at Mags, and doubly never at the stone."

Lena actually brightened at that; Mags got the feeling that she had not only been feeling guilty, she had been feeling useless.

"I am here because I am a Mindspeaker, and I will actually be the one making notes on what Mags finds out. Mags, you do *not* have to remember anything. You only have to extract the information. I'll be the one making sure it gets out of this wretched rock." Sedric looked around the table, then pursed his lips. "We are waiting for one more Mindspeaker to join us. I don't know you at all, and as you deduced, Father had a litter of kittens until I explained there would be someone who knows you well acting as a buffer between us."

Now who—before Mags could finish that thought, there was a tap at the door, and Gennie stepped shyly inside.

Mags blinked, then heaved an enormous sigh of relief. If there was a single person in whose hands he trusted a mindlink, other than Dallen, it was Gennie. She smiled at him and took a seat beside Bear.

Mags looked at the stone; it didn't change at all. For a moment he doubted, not the wisdom but the logic of this. But then he rolled his shoulders, wincing a little at the aches, and began his relaxation exercises, all the while keeping his gaze fixed on the stone.

His eyes unfocused a moment; when they focused again, they seemed to be looking deep into the stone, not the surface. He felt Gennie as a steady bulwark of a presence, trustworthy and reliable; felt Sedric as a watchful overseer, like a referee. He felt an held breath leave him as a long sigh . . . then felt as if he were sinking into sleep. But it wasn't sleep. It was a sort of communion . . .

Ah, it's you again.

Aye. Need to know something.

How to find those irritations.

That caught his attention. Why would the stone think of them as irritations?

Because they are. They are in the Web, not of the Web, and they cannot be dislodged.

An image passed through his mind of a useless bit of flotsam in a spiderweb. Every time the wind blew, it vibrated the web, irritating the spider. But the spider could not get it out, it was too big for her strength, and she could not cut it free without destroying her creation.

He passed the image to Gennie, who passed it in turn to Sedric.

That's interesting, but it doesn't help me find them in the real world.

What do you really want?

I need to find them, he repeated after a moment.

Need. Not want.

Dammit. The thing was being all obtuse and mystical again. Need, want, weren't they the same thing?

No.

He reined in his temper, as he felt his control and his ability to communicate with the thing eroding.

Need and want are sometimes incompatible.

Now he groaned inwardly, felt exasperation, felt despair, and again felt his connection with the stone slipping.

He clawed his way back and felt it regarding him dispassionately.

You are out of balance.

I'm . . . those bastards have someone I—

Trivial, in the long run.

Now anger filled him, and the stone started to thrust him away, until he throttled it down.

You are out of balance.

He went through his relaxation exercises again, keeping the front of his mind calm while the back of his mind raced, trying to figure out how to pry want he needed out of this thing. Obviously you couldn't force it. It would just kick you out if you tried. And you couldn't trick it—it knew all the tricks. You had to ask the right question—exactly the right question.

Every time he felt emotion, it tried to shake him out, too. What had it said?

I am balance, it repeated, in answer to his question.

All right, take that at face value. That this stone was a balance point. And Dallen had said that it was at the center of the Web of Heralds and Companions. So if he jiggled it with emotion—that jiggled the whole Web. The Web was supposed to stay stable, and being linked into it and feeling powerful emotion perturbed the whole thing. No wonder it kept trying to kick him out!

Yes.

Maybe that was why other people weren't able to get as deep into it as he was. Because as long as he had a problem, he tended to think, rather than feel; he saved feeling for when he had the leisure to indulge in it.

Yes.

He needed to know how to find the Karsite agents. And that was for everyone, for all of Valdemar.

Trivial. Valdemar will persist. It may weaken for a time, but it will return, so long as balance persists. And I am balance.

Miserable—*I won't get mad. I won't get mad. Stupid damn thing! Doesn't it know if the Karsites get their way—*

If the Karsites get their way!

This . . . thing . . . only knew what was and what had been. It couldn't imagine, or plan, or do anything that required speculation. It wasn't really alive, so all it could do was repeat what it already knew.

If there aren't any Heralds or Companions, there won't be a Web. There won't be a Valdemar.

There was a long, long pause.

Impossible.

That's what these irritations want. And they'll get it, too. Now he drew on every unlikely, hysterical, ridiculous scenario that Amily had used to frighten herself with and exaggerated them a hundred times over. He flung the whole house of cards at the stone and showed it Nikolas going to pieces, the King himself falling apart, the Monarchy in ruins, the factions in the Court taking advantage of the situation and bringing out every petty quarrel they'd ever had—

Then the Karsite army crossing the border with hordes of demons that sought out Heralds and Companions and killed them, until there weren't enough to sustain the Web, and the Web itself collapsed.

When he was done, he felt more exhausted than he ever had been in his life. If he'd had to crawl two paces to reach safety, he would never have been able to. He felt Gennie's alarm and her immediate instinct to get him to come out or pull him out herself.

::Mags—::

::Not yet.:: he replied instantly.

::Bear says—::

::Not yet,:: he repeated.

He waited. This thing might not feel emotion, and it might not exactly be alive, but it didn't want to die, either.

Suddenly he was engulfed in a flood of information.

It overwhelmed him, rolled over him, then scooped him up and tossed him about like a cork on a raging river.

Finally it tossed him out again, leaving him so drained he could barely breathe.

What do you want?

I want . . . to find Amily.

He sagged back, not expecting an answer.

Which one is Amily?

It seemed to think she was a Herald. *She ain't in the Web.*

A long, long, long pause.

Give me your mind.

He was too weary to object. Too weary, and too desperate, to do anything but obey. He completely opened his mind to the thing, half expecting to be swallowed up in something immensely bigger than he was, maybe to never come out again.

But that wasn't what happened.

Although he did lose all but a germ of his "self," as he was stretched thin as gossamer on the wind, that germ was held tight and cradled safely. And finally, he sensed Amily, wisps and hints and glimpses of drug-induced nightmare.

And that was when the thing that held him magnified everything *around* that tenuous presence in a way he could never have managed alone. There was someone with her.

Not Ice or Stone, someone else.

Like smacking the Kirball as hard as he could, he flung what he got at Gennie, who caught it and relayed it on.

Such a fragile connection could not be held for long, not when he was as exhausted as he was. It faded. His hold on the stone faded.

You have what you need. You have what you want. Hold the balance.

Then he found himself lying on the table, gasping like a fish out of water.

They'd been given a little room on the same lower-level hallway as the one with the stone in it, furnished with chairs, an ordinary table, and pens and paper. It was cool here—but not nearly as cool as the room with the stone. Bear read over Sedric's notes on Amily a second time, and then a third. Sedric had taken the originals with him, but he'd left them a copy. Lena then divided up the pages, and each of them made four copies of the pages they had. Bear had the ones at the end, describing the impressions Mags had gotten of Amily's captor, and the more he read, the deeper his frown grew.

"This doesn't make any sense!" he blurted.

"I know," Mags sighed. " 'Tis all like babblin'. I thin' mebbe I was so tired by then I was seein' things all cockeyed."

"No, that's not what I mean!" Bear exclaimed. "This doesn't make any sense because it *does* make sense, to me at least!"

"Now *you're* the one not making sense, Bear," Lena chided.

"You mean you don't see it?" He looked from face to face around the table; they all shook their heads. "Amily's been drugged, like I was. And there's a person with her all the time. And that person is a *Healer!* Look—here—" he pointed at a passage—"that's something someone who is Gifted does with someone who is drugged to make sure they don't burn through the drug too fast. But that doesn't make any sense! Why would a Healer *do* this?"

"Because he's a Karsite religious fanatic?" Gennie suggested. "Fanatics can justify practically any atrocity to themselves. The more untenable their position becomes, the harder they hold to it, and the worse the things they are willing to do to support it." She leaned over the table and put one hand seriously on top of Bear's. "Bear . . . not every Healer thinks the way we do. The way *you* do. If they did, there wouldn't *be* any Karsite Healers."

Mags was still trying to put the pieces together. Whoever was minding Amily was a Healer . . . "Would a Healer hurt some'un, or kill 'em, e'en iffen 'e was a Karsite religious fanatic?" he asked, slowly.

"I . . . I don't *think* so," Bear replied, after a very long moment. "He might stand by and *let* her be hurt or killed, but I don't think he'd be able to do it himself. I mean, he could, but he would have to be seriously crazy, right insane. You know, sort of an antiHealer, as seriously insane as that crazy person who kidnapped me, and there's nothing in these hints that looks that crazy to me." He paused, thoughtfully. "Actually, someone that crazy would be the wrong person to leave in charge of someone you wanted to keep in good shape. They just plain wouldn't be able to do that. They kind of feed on other peoples' pain; sometimes they feed on their own, too. If you left someone like that alone with Amily, he'd definitely hurt her."

Mags nodded. "Aight. Could it mebbe be some'un thet's jest . . . greedy?"

Bear looked at him oddly. "I suppose it's possible." He scratched his head. "I . . . never actually met a greedy Healer; even my father isn't *greedy*, just . . ."

"As bloody arrogant as Marchand," Gennie said crisply.

Bear flushed. "Aye. That. But I know they have to exist. There're plenty of rich people that want a Healer all to themselves, or want one who . . . who won't take just anyone. And I know there're Healers that will do that." He blinked and regarded Mags curiously from behind his thick lenses. "You think someone could be greedy enough to—to take the money of kidnappers to keep their captive healthy?"

Mags shrugged. "I seen a lotta good people since I come t'Haven. But . . . there was plenty'a priests what came by th' mine an took Cole Pieters love-gifts an' looked t'other way at starvin' kiddies. Iffen there's priests what'll do thet, why not Healers?"

"Last possibility . . ." Gennie said slowly. "Someone who got in over his head."

"Eh?" It was Mags' turn to stare curiously.

"Someone who . . . oh, I don't know, was like Marchand, didn't see any harm in blabbing everything he knew to someone who offered plenty of money—and, yes, by the way, under threat of Truth Spell, Marchand *finally* admitted that was what he's been doing. I thought Master Bard Lita was going to die of a brainstorm right then and there." Gennie smirked, then sobered. "But, what about someone who was taking bribes without thinking twice about it because he thought what was being asked seemed harmless enough. Then when the Karsites grabbed Amily, they needed a Healer, so they lured him to a meeting and grabbed him as well. Now he knows what's going on, he knows he's in over his head, and all he can do is try to keep Amily safe and pray we manage to figure out where they have her. Honestly? I think that's the most likely."

They all looked at each other. "In that case, Marchand is our Bardic informant, and this Healer is the other plant they said they had," Bear said. "We've filled in all the blank spaces. So . . . if that's true, then who's missing from the Hill, Healer-side?"

"I'll go interrupt the King and his emergency council," Gennie said, standing up. "You lot see if you can figure out a way to find where Amily is, if they haven't already."

Mags nodded, and they set aside the notes about Amily and her captor and picked up the ones about "the irritations."

Mags closed his eyes for a moment as the letters began to swim in front of them. Webs and vibrations and . . . it was all so complicated . . . he wanted to sleep, but no, he couldn't, he needed to . . .

The images that the stone had put in his mind swirled there again. Vibrations. Irritations. Vibrations. Interference. Irrita—

His eyes flew open just before he nodded off. ::*What if thet stone was bein' literal again?*::

::*That's more likely than not,*:: Dallen said after a moment.

::*Then—all that fightin' and squabblin'—thet wasn't jest 'cause of th' heat. It was 'cause them shields really are irritations!*::

He turned his mind to Gennie and gently "poked" her.

::*Still talking. What?*::

::*Marchand there?*::

He sensed her bitter amusement. ::*Being grilled like a fish. Why?*::

::*I need t' know iffen them rats he was talkin' to was meetin' him real close t' Palace.*:: He remembered now something that the stone had said—or that he thought it had said—when he had fallen asleep in its room. That Ice and Stone were "irritations" because they were "near."

He waited impatiently for the answer, but he didn't push things. It was one thing to be impatient, quite another to impose that impatience on someone else who was doing you a favor.

::*He says he met with them almost every day. Lord Lascal and his family close up their manor in the summer and move to their estate. There's only a skeleton staff and everyone around here knows their gardens are pretty free to roam in. That's where they met.*:: There was a pause. ::*He says he thinks they were actually living in a guest-house on the grounds. Why?*::

Well . . . that figgers.

Quickly, he explained what the stone had told him and his idea that whatever the stone did worked against the shields that the Karsite agents wore to act as an irritant to everyone's temper.

::*So we look for places where the worst fights are happening, and that's probably where they are?*:: she said. ::*Right, I'll pass that on. Good job, Mags. They just sent out pages to find out if there are any Healers missing from up here.*::

Ah, now there was another reason to be impatient. He got up to pace. "Iffen they thin' we got a chance at findin' Amily . . . might could be they kill this Healer an' 'er t'gether," he muttered, choking down his anguish at the mere thought. "So we gotta find 'em. Then we gotta get 'em away from 'er afore they figger out we ac'tually know they're there. There's gotta be somethin' that'll lure 'em out . . ."

"Hell," said Bear, looking extremely disgruntled. "There goes my plan. Well, it wasn't a very *good* plan . . ."

Mags looked over at him. "So? Mebbe we kin use part'f it."

::*Mags. Tell Bear that there is a Healer missing. Cuburn.*::

::*Oh thet'll sit well.*:: But after Bear got mad, this bit of information would probably give him some satisfaction. He told his friends what Gennie had said.

Bear blistered the air with oaths for a good long time. When he finally calmed down, Mags gave him a level look.

"Ye done?" he asked. "Cause iffen ye ain't—"

"I'm done," Bear told him in utter disgust. "I should have guessed it would be him. There never was a more venal—"

"Aye," Mags interrupted. "Ye said thet. A couple'a times. What I wanter know is, what was yer plan?"

Bear blinked at him, as the question took him by surprise, then shrugged.

"Oh . . . it's stupid. And if we did it, there'd be more carnage . . ." Bear sighed. "You know, how when a little one goes missing, you go around to all the neighbors and ask if they've seen her and could they help look? I was thinking if we sent out some of the Guard and all the Trainees with drawings of these bastards, or of Amily, or both, maybe somebody might have seen . . ."

Mags stared at him as a plan, fully formed, exploded in his head.

". . . Why are you looking at me like that?"

"'Cause Lena'd get mad at me if I kissed ye. Lissen—"

He explained the whole thing. Lena and Bear listened, skeptically at first, then their eyes got bigger and bigger until he finished.

"Now," he demanded. "Poke holes in't. Tell me what ain't gonna work."

The two of them looked at each other. "I . . . can't think of anything," Bear said, finally. "Well, other than the fact you might get killed . . . that's certainly a drawback."

"I'm countin' on thet they seem t' want me kickin'," he pointed out. "So 'less they figger out what I'm doin'—or they change their minds—"

"Or you misread them entirely," Lena put in, her eyes round and a little tearful. "And they'll just kill you!"

He shrugged, with an indifference he didn't feel. "They had a chance and didn'—"

"That was once," Lena pointed out. "The second time, they threw a huge great piece of wood at you when you were going at a full gallop! If you hadn't been a Heraldic Trainee, *and* on Dallen, *and* had all that training, the weapons work and the Kirball stuff—"

"Gotta chance it." That pretty much summed it up.

Bear took a long, deep breath. "All right then, do we

split up, go gather all the Trainees, find that cousin, explain this to everyone, and—"

Mags snorted. " 'Ell we do. I may be crazy, but I ain't thet crazy." He squared his shoulders. "No. Now I go talk t'King an' Nikolas an' th' Heir an who-the-'ell else is there an let *them* poke holes innit. Then iffen they like it, it'll hev more'n a ghost of a chance."

::*Gennie, tell 'em I'm comin',*:: he said, gesturing to Lena and Bear and pulling open the door to the little Palace room where they'd been left to think. ::*I gotta ideer.*::

T hey'd narrowed the spot where the Karsite agents had to be hiding down to a block—and it was pretty clear that there was something drastically wrong the closer they got. It was a middling sort of area, with a mix of cheap shops and houses on the outskirts of Haven. Not the sort of bad neighborhood like the one where Nikolas kept his shop, but shabby and populated by common laborers, the sort of place where you could have a pig or some chickens or even a cow in the yard and the neighbors wouldn't complain because they had the same. You wouldn't notice noise here, not even screaming, because the children were shrieking and babies crying all the time. But there were signs of trouble all the way there: broken shutters, a cart with a wheel off and people fighting over putting the wheel on, arguments everywhere you looked. And the closer you got to that designated block, the more often the arguments had escalated into fistfights. Even the children weren't playing; they were chasing each other with mayhem in mind or rolling in the street, squalling and tearing each other's hair. Mags got a wide berth, though, because he was wearing Whites. Whites, and not Grays, for two reasons. The first, that the full Heraldic uniform gave him a little more protection from the altercations around him, and would give him a little more respect as he worked his way around the block. The second—

Whites made him stand out here and would make him a very visible moving target.

He worked his way from door to door, shop to home, exerting himself to form every word correctly, so he didn't sound like someone easily dismissed. There was no trace of his accent in his speech, and he held himself as tall and straight as he could, copying, as well as he could, the Captain of the King's Guard. Everyone answered him; the uniform got him that. They might snarl, or eye him belligerently, or look as if they would *like* to insult or even hit him, but they answered when he showed them Ice and Stone's portraits and asked, "Have you seen these men hereabouts?"

They were good likenesses. The same Herald who was going to help Bear with his bone model had made it, taking Mags' memories and turning them into a double portrait. She was the one who worked for the City Guard and Constables, taking the images of criminals out of victims' minds and drawing them. And Mags figured that the two men would probably have someone other than themselves answering the door—that Healer, provided they had the man sufficiently cowed to be trusted to do so, or someone they'd hired to run their errands, so they didn't have to leave Amily. Every time he showed the picture, he was watching for the flash of recognition before a blanket denial; when he got it, then, following the plan, he would walk away and wait for them to go for the bait. Their door watcher would certainly go tell them that here was a Herald looking for them, and they would come out to deal with him. There would be a few moments before Ice and Stone realized who he was and went for a pursuit rather than just murdering him where he stood; those moments, he reckoned, were going to be the ones of highest risk. He had steeled himself for them. He was going to have to be . . . well . . . very, very good at dodging for what he hoped would be a very short period of time . . . .

So when he knocked on another nondescript door and started to go into his speech, then looked up into the face of Stone himself, there was a single moment of mutual paralysis.

The word he was going to say came out in a squeak, and he was certain that he was going to die, right then, right there.

But he broke the spell first. And now, the long hours he had spent mentally rehearsing this plan, over, and over, and over, gave him the reactions of a ferret and put wings on his heels. He ducked, whirled, and ran.

Stone's grasping hands met on air. Mags was already gone. But not running down the street, oh, no. He'd already scouted his path: a dash to the opposite side of the street, up a rainbarrel, swarm up the drainpipe, and up onto the roof.

Pause. Look back . . .

Stone was just about to the barrel. Ice was three paces behind him.

Holy . . . They were *fast!*

Now it was fear putting wings on his heels. He couldn't yet judge how quick they would be over the rooftops, where he had the advantage of being light. He *had* to keep them engaged in the chase and not thinking of anything else. No matter what happened, he had to keep them running after him long enough for Nikolas, Sedric, and a group of hand-picked Heralds and Guards to storm the house, take down any opposition, and get Amily out of there.

That meant he had to stay *just* frustratingly out of reach. And he had to do it without being able to read their level of frustration.

He scrambled over the rooftree, took a couple running steps down the other side, and leaped for the next house. He kept his breathing and his pace even— timing his breaths with his acrobatics. He could not afford to get winded. This one had a bit of flat roof, enough to make a good landing platform; his landing was solid, and he scrambled up the next roof using hands and feet. He didn't have to look back now, he could hear them, hear their feet on the thatch, since most of the buildings here had thatched roofs.

His heart was absolutely pounding—and if he hadn't been able to hear them, he would never have known that they were there at all; they were completely "invisible" to his mind.

A tiny sound behind him was all the warning he had that one of them was about to try something.

He took a gamble and leaped sideways, hit the thatch on his shoulder, rolled down to the very edge of the roof, timing the roll so that his feet were under him when he got there and made a *huge* leap out into thin air—

But he knew where he was, and his hands closed on a bar that had once supported a sign. He swung on it twice, then kicked for the balcony farther along the wall. Nothing fancy, and he barely made the catch, but make it he did, and he was off again, using a stanchion to get back up to the roof.

There were still behind him, but he'd gotten a little breathing room.

Then movement in the corner of his eye warned him something was going on. He risked a glance. Ice was on the next roof over, a flat one that was easier to run on, using that fact to get ahead of him.

Aight. Two can play thet.

He swerved toward the other roof, the very one that Ice was about to leave; Ice was so intent on getting ahead of him that he didn't notice what Mags was doing. He made a leap for the next roof to intercept Mags—

—except that Mags was leaping for the roof *he* had just vacated, landing and sprinting back in the direction he had just come from. Doubling back threw both of the men off; by the time they recovered, Mags was two roofs ahead.

Now he took just a moment to get a good look at them, and guage their intentions.

Without stopping, of course.

He leaped for the next roof, landed and rolled. Looked over his shoulder as he sprinted for the next.

Still comin'—

This one would be a two-footed landing and an

upslope scramble. He got a second look as he crested the ridgeline before he slid down the other side.

No weapons. No obvious ones, anyway. Probably knives somewhere on them, but they weren't going to throw knives at him on a run like this, even if they *did* want him dead. Odds were he'd dodge it under circumstances like this one, no matter how good they were, and no one with any sense throws his weapon away, even if he has a second or a third.

Well . . . thet's—

::*Mags!*:: Dallen called. ::*They have her! She's safe!*::

That was possibly the best thing he had heard in a year.

And that meant he was free now to go to the next—and far more risky—part of his plan.

He angled his flight so that Stone got a chance to cut him off; he skidded to a halt on the edge of his roof, stared for a heartbeat, then dashed *between* them and hurtled over the side.

There were balconies there; he caught the railing of the highest, got his feet on it, bounced off, and let go. Caught the railing of the second, bounced off. Let go. Dropped down to the street, rolled to break his fall, and ran like a scorched stoat back in the direction he had come from.

This was a big risk. He *knew* they could run faster than he could on a flat and level surface. He just had to hope that they would take enough time getting down from the roof that they wouldn't be able to catch him.

He *had* to be street level for this. So did they. He could not risk them getting even a glimpse of what waited for them.

Just before he reached the square in front of the house they had taken, Dallen dashed out of a side street, decked out in his Kirball gear. Mags grabbed the saddle on the run, jumped, and bounced into it. And as the two of them turned on a penny-bit to face the two Karsite agents, he was in fantastic position to see their faces as they skidded to a halt and saw what was waiting for them.

All of the members of the four Kirball teams. All wearing Whites.

All wearing *his* face.

Now pick a target t'kill, ye bastards.

Corwin's cousin, the illusion-making Herald, was out here somewhere. When Mags had asked, "If we're dressed alike, kin ye make some'un look like me?" the cousin had snorted and asked "How many?"

Because there would have been the chance that, when they realized they were trapped, Ice and Stone *would* go for a kill. But not if they couldn't tell which of their captors was the one they'd been told to capture.

The shock froze them long enough for the Heralds and Guards who had rescued Amily—all but Nikolas and Sedric—to close their escape route behind them.

Their street-level escape-route—

Mags saw what was coming in the tensing of their muscles and the sudden flick of their eyes to the right.

Then they moved impossibly fast. They had dashed across the square and were halfway up a building before anyone had a chance to move.

But Gennie screamed out the signal. "Mags! Pip!"

Because he'd planned for this too. These men were no good to them dead, and since those shields prevented

Mind-magic from striking them unconscious, there was only one nonlethal way to take them down. His hand was already on the Kirball stick as the Fetcher-boosted-and guided ball came screaming at him from the side.

Now he let out every bit of his fury at these bastards and stood up in the stirrups and smacked the ball with every bit of strength he had.

Pip's ball wasn't going quite as fast, so Mag's ball—still being guided by one of the Fetchers from the other teams—hit Stone in the back hard enough to momentarily paralyze him. He dropped off the building like the stone Mags had named him for, with Ice falling a moment later.

They hit the ground and were swarmed by Heralds and Guardsmen.

Mags jumped off Dallen's back and ran for them. By the time he got there, they were trussed hand and foot with so many separate bindings that you could scarcely see their clothing.

It was over. It was finally over. Now he would have his answers. Now they would all have their answers.

He pushed his way in to stand next to Stone, who glared up at him, the black eyes still opaque, still unreadable.

"We know who sent ye," he said, with quiet menace in his voice. "An' we know why. What we don't know—what I don't know—is why *me?* Why'd ye come after *me?* I ain't anythin' but good at a *game.*"

Stone stared at him, face impassive. And then, suddenly, his expression changed—from impassive to resigned.

What?

Mags sensed the shields stir; sensed them—poise to strike! Dallen threw his strength between the shields and Mags, but Mags *knew* that he wasn't the target—

He had no time to do anything but fling himself on Stone, frantically tearing at the man's garments in a futile effort to find that talisman before—

—Stone's eyes rolled up into his head as the shield contracted suddenly, viciously, around his mind, like a hand crushing a grape—

—it was too late.

Stone just . . . snuffed out, heart and breathing stopping immediately as his mind vanished. Ice followed a heartbeat later.

—And they were left with two rapidly cooling bodies, far too many questions, and no answers for any of them.

EPILOGUE

"**H**eyla," Mags said softly, as Amily's eyelids fluttered, and she finally woke up.

She smiled up at him. "Heyla," she said. "Is it good news or not so good news?"

" 'Tis all good," he said, sitting down at her bedside and taking her hand in his. "Ever'thin' went jest like Bear wanted. 'E says not t'worry thet ye cain't feel nothin'. One'a th' others figgered out how t'shut some pain stuff off fer a liddle so's ye kin git some sleep. He says 'tis better nor givin' ye Bear's nasty drinks."

She just smiled sleepily, then her eyelids drifted shut.

Mags continued to hold her hand, savoring the momentary peace. Nikolas had already looked in on his daughter, and been satisfied, and everyone else seemed to have agreed to leave Mags alone with her for a while.

And Mags was not particularly eager to leave.

Outside this room, there was more activity going on than the Palace had seen in quite some time. Mags knew about only part of it, and not a huge part, either.

Marchand was already on his way to a permanent assignment as the Bard and Chronicler for a Guard Headquarters at the Iftel Border. He was never to be allowed to leave—under house arrest for the rest of his life. Lita had wanted to burn his Gift out and send him to *real* imprisonment, but Truth Spell wielded ruthlessly could not prove him to be anything worse than foolish and greedy. Cuburn was on his way to a similar fate, as the permanent Healer-in-residence to prisoners at Greyscarp Prison. He was never to be allowed to leave either, and the only difference between him and the prisoners he cared for would be that there were no bars on his windows.

Security at the Palace and Collegia—well, it was not going to be anything like the same. Someone had sent down to the Ambassador to the Shin'a'in to try to find out if they had ever heard of anyone who was at all like Ice and Stone. If the little hints that Mags had picked up were even remotely true, there were sleeper-agents of their own on the Karsite side who were going to be activated with the sole purpose of discovering how the Karsites had found these men, and perhaps where they came from.

The bodies had been carefully preserved and were going to be delivered to a Karsite border post—a very unsubtle message that the best that Karse could send was no match for the people of Valdemar.

Sedric had been assigned to study the stone, because no one had ever guessed it was semialive. That was fine with Mags; if he never had to "talk" to it again, it would be too soon.

Working on the assumption that it was only a matter

of time before more of these mysterious assassins turned up in Haven, pretty much everyone had decided that getting Amily ambulatory and trained to defend herself should be a priority right along with reinforcing Palace security. So Bear and his team had gone into intense and detailed practice—so much so that the actual work on her leg turned out to be anticlimactic. Everything had gone well; the result was everything anyone could have wanted.

Outside this room, the Hill buzzed with so much activity that it looked like a hive preparing for winter.

In here . . . in here was momentary peace.

It would not last past the moment he crossed the threshold, but for now, at least, peace held Mags and his love in the shelter of its hands.

And for right now, this moment, that was enough.

MERCEDES LACKEY
The Novels of Valdemar

To Order Call: 1-800-788-6262
www.dawbooks.com

Mercedes Lackey
& Larry Dixon

The Novels of Valdemar

DARIAN'S TALE

OWLFLIGHT
978-0-88677-804-2

OWLSIGHT
978-0-88677-803-4

OWLKNIGHT
978-0-88677-916-2

THE MAGE WARS

THE BLACK GRYPHON
978-0-88677-804-2

THE WHITE GRYPHON
978-0-88677-682-1

THE SILVER GRYPHON
978-0-88677-685-6

To Order Call: 1-800-788-6262
www.dawbooks.com

MERCEDES LACKEY

THE BLACK SWAN

After his wife's untimely death, a powerful sorcerer dedicates his life to seeking revenge against all womankind. Scouring his lands for women who inspire his rage for vengeance, he turns them to swans that only regain their human forms by the transitory light of the moon. Only Odette, noblest of the enchanted flock has the courage to confront her captor. Can she gain the allies she needs to free herself and the other swan-maidens from their magical slavery?

0-88677-890-5

"Complex characters, rich detail, and a great sense of suspense"—*Dance Magazine*

To Order Call: 1-800-788-6262
www.dawbooks.com

DAW 49

MERCEDES LACKEY

The Elemental Masters Series

"Her characteristic carefulness, narrative gifts, and attention to detail shape into an altogether superior fantasy." —*Booklist*

"It's not lighthearted fluff, but rather a dark tale full of the pain and devastation of war, the growing class struggle, and changing sex roles, and a couple of wounded protagonists worth rooting for." —*Locus*

"Putting a fresh face to a well-loved fairytale is not an easy task, but it is one that seems effortless to the prolific Lackey. Beautiful phrasing and a thorough grounding in the dress, mannerisms and history of the period help move the story along gracefully. This is a wonderful example of a new look at an old theme." —*Publishers Weekly*

"Richly detailed historic backgrounds add flavor and richness to an already strong series that belongs in most fantasy collections. Highly recommended." —*Library Journal*

To Order Call: 1-800-788-6262
www.dawbooks.com

MERCEDES LACKEY

The Dragon Jousters

JOUST
978-0-7564-0153-4

ALTA
978-0-7564-0257-3

SANCTUARY
978-0-7564-0341-3

AERIE
978-0-7564-0426-0

"A must-read for dragon lovers in particular and for fantasy fans in general." —*Publishers Weekly*

"It's fun to see a different spin on dragons...and as usual Lackey makes it all compelling."—*Locus*

To Order Call: 1-800-788-6262
www.dawbooks.com